OUR COMEBACK TOUR IS SLAYING MONSTERS

BOY BANDS & DRAGONS
BOOK 1

by Kim Smuga-Otto

Riverfolk Books

According to the press, boy bands are made up of mediocre performers who get by on the strength of their non-threatening good looks. As if all it takes to have a platinum album is a record studio's marketing department. Bullshit.

The bands who make it put in more hours training than Olympic athletes, and once they're on tour, there's no downtime. But all that hard work is pointless if the band members—all the band members, boy bands don't have headliners—don't have that something special, that something extraordinary you can't help but be impressed by.

Bring five teenagers like that together, as I did with Never Boy Land, and you have the most popular touring band in the world in 2019. It should have been 2020 too, except Covid, fucking Covid.

Still, what goes around, comes around, and 2027 was going to be the year of the great NBL comeback. I had everything lined up, and then… the band vanished, literally.

Interview with Marjorie Banks, Never Boy Land manager
From the documentary *Straight on Till Morning – the Unexplained Disappearance of Never Boy Land*

CHAPTER 1

Kyle

Their text says, "Show up at the back door, before business hours. Be discreet." Never a good sign.

It means higher-ups had a moment of clarity when they realized just how south this collab could turn. So now they're freaking out and forgetting that heady excitement they felt when our manager sold them on the project. Can't say I'm surprised by their lack of faith; tech bros and our kind don't mix.

So here I am at seven thirty in the fricking morning, standing in the employee parking lot where the driverless ride share service dropped me off, and facing a nondescript security door with a sign dissuading me from unauthorized entry. There's probably a metaphor in all this. But I'm not going to go there. Instead, I text them that I've arrived.

The door opens. "Welcome to Sky Coyote Studios," says a young woman with glossy black hair and doe eyes. "I'm Mina Chawla."

Judging from her affordable business-casual blazer and nervous professionalism, I'm guessing she's an assistant, maybe an intern.

"Kyle Moretti." I extend my hand and get an awkward handshake. Mina's got a super serious expression, like she's filing away every detail of this interaction for later analysis. I flash her a half smile and watch as, yes, she blushes. I'd be flattered if this was due to my charming and engaging looks, or even the name recognition, but—let's be real—it's because I'm with the band.

In confirmation of my theory, she sneaks a glance behind me. "Is anyone else with you?"

"No, we decided to arrive separately."

"Oh, of course." Mina gives the parking lot one last look, just in case, before letting me in. "Sorry, they told me not to use the elevator."

It's unreal, all this enforced privacy and sneaking around. It's like we're on a secret mission when it's just PR freaking out that something might leak before their carefully managed official announcements.

And it's pathetic how much I missed it.

We climb three flights of emergency staircases and Mina uses her badge to access a nondescript hallway. I wasn't expecting the bronze dragon and faux stone walls of Sky Coyote's much-Instagrammed lobby. Still, beige? Then we turn a corner and a landscape mural four feet high and the length of a tour bus stretches out along the wall.

This is more like it.

Scraggly snow-capped mountains tower over a forest that starts out shadowy and ominous then transitions to fairytale cheery. Beyond the woods is a bucolic meadow with a winding dirt road that leads to a bridge. Finally, there's a castle sporting sixteen spires, which is somehow perched over a waterfall. Stamped at the end is the familiar logo for *Heroes Summoning*.

"Have you ever played?" asks Mina. Her tone is careful in case she's crossed some line between normal people and celebrities. What she doesn't realize is that—until the band's relaunch next week—I'm still officially a has-been.

"Absolutely, all the time."

"Wow," she gasps. And then in a relaxed, more natural voice, she says, "I just didn't think someone like you would play a video RPG."

I shrug. "I'm a geek."

Mina laughs. "I play a level nine rogue assassin. You?"

It feels good to connect as normal humans. "I'm currently a level four—"

An insistent chirping erupts from her pocket. Mina glances at her phone and any jovial nerding-out evaporates.

"Oh, he's here." The awe in her voice leaves no question who's arrived, and it brings me back to just how extra I am to this reboot. "They said not to keep him waiting. But I need to drop you off." She quick-walks us down the hall to a set of double doors and buzzes it open. "The studio's in here. I'm sorry, but I was told—"

"It's okay. Thanks for getting me here."

That gets me a grateful look before she dashes down the hall in order to welcome the genuine celebrity.

A poster stuck to one of the doors reads "Time to Live the Game" with the familiar tan parchment Mythreal map. In the corner, someone's written "Here Be Digital Dragons." Past the doors is a large room, all white and clean—pristine, that's the word. It's wider than it is deep. No windows, save for a wall of smoky glass at one end. I'm guessing from the blinking pinpoints of lights (as well as the ambient hum of the room) that that's where they keep the server farm. Six regularly spaced large flat screens, all currently black, line the wall. In front of each, there's a circular depression, like an inverted platform. They're four feet in diameter and probably a foot deep.

A lanky, bronze-skinned man immersed in his phone stands in one of circles. For once we're the same height so I get a good look at the top of his thick mop of midnight hair; he always cuts the sides close and trim. There's a hunched strain to shoulders that wasn't there when I saw him yesterday.

"Oscar," I call out.

He startles as if he's been caught out. His full lips pull at his features, giving him a solemn, even mournful expression. But with recognition, his familiar smile emerges.

"Kyle, my man!" His face comes alive with attractive creases, and even a dimple. "Gold star for most punctual band member."

"Last I checked the Wikipedia page, you were also a listed member of Never Boy Land." Before me, in fact, because they do it alphabetically and Jones comes before Moretti. And yes, I am that annoyingly detail oriented.

"Okay, so I'll give you the award for most logical." Before I can get in a snarky reply, he follows it up with, "Or should we just stick with band smartass?"

"You might want to hold off on bestowing that one till the others arrive."

"Okay, but I got a feeling today will be one of those 'Kyle Moretti explains it all' days."

It's crazy how easily we slip back into our roles. The five of us hadn't all been in the same room since 2023, but when I showed up for rehearsal a few weeks ago, it felt like we'd never been apart—at least on an emotional/social level; physically I'm pathetically out of shape. Not that Oscar would ever point that out. He'll always be the encouraging older brother to the rest of us greenhorn brats. He's only two years older than me, but back in 2015 when Marjorie Banks signed us on as a band, I was a fourteen-year-old with a YouTube channel looking up to this sixteen-year-old (practically an adult to us) who'd already been in two, albeit failed, boy bands. He wasn't just an upperclassman showing us the ropes; we trusted him to look out for us in the glamorous scary world of showbiz.

Now I'm twenty-five with three and a half years of college experience, while Oscar stuck it out in the music industry. Most of it's been background singing and dancing for established artists or cameos on his siblings' reality tv show, but making a living in this business proves he has both the talent and the passion. I respect that.

A note of seriousness slips into Oscar's voice. "You know, Kyle, I've been meaning to tell you. I'm glad you signed up for our comeback tour."

"So we can keep all the old choreography, right?"

"More than that. It's good to have the band back together." His eyes start to go dark and soulful; it's a technique they teach us in boy band school. "It wouldn't be the same without you."

He doesn't rush in with defending my musical contributions (nothing about my voice or dancing or stage presence). I decide that means he's being honest. "Thanks, man."

"Tristan—" Oscar's words are cut off by a buzz and click of the security lock.

"Speak of the devil." But I'm mistaken, it's someone else.

The guy who enters is sprouting facial hair that's three days past needing a shave but at least a week away from being recognizably a beard. He's also wearing a sagging hoodie with another internet company's branding. In other words, he's a techy hipster.

I pick up on the signaling because two months (and another lifetime ago), it was a look I was slipping into, save that I wore my belt two notches tighter. When I first showed up for rehearsal, our stylist went tight-lipped and scheduled me for bootcamp at a spa. I emerged with a lot less hair. What remains looks like I just rolled out of bed, but—improbably—every disheveled lock of highlighted brown hair manages to fall into just the right place.

"This is Dave. Dave, Kyle." Oscar's phone convulses with an angry buzz. He scans the screen and his features tense up. It's a look he reserves for when his siblings are getting themselves into trouble. I don't envy Oscar's celebrity family drama; it makes me glad to be an only child. Still reading his phone's screen, he says in a flat distracted voice, "Dave will get you fitted for the VR face-screen-thing."

"Headset," Dave corrects him, curt-like. You don't diss a nerd's tech.

Normally Oscar would be falling over himself to apologize, but each phone alert pulls his smile down. I step towards Dave to give Oscar the space to deal with whatever is blowing up. Marjorie Banks' 10th Law of Boy Bands: *The first thing anyone should recall of you is, "He was so nice."* I'm not the first choice for a Never Boy Land charm offensive. But like I told Mina, I'm a geek.

"Did you guys manage to get your hands on any of the new Opthallus MX360s?" I had one on my Christmas wish list, but supply issues made the manufacturer push back the release till April.

Dave perks up. "They wish we'd use their gear. But we've got something custom that blows those guys away." Yeah, I got this.

He takes me over to a cupboard and opens it with a flourish. What's inside elicits a spontaneous gasp of envy out of me. They're the size of ski goggles with a comfortable wrap-around that covers the ears. Dave hands me one and—damn—it's light. I'd had reservations that we'd be able to perform any of our dance moves for the virtual performance, but this could just work.

"Bluetooth?" I ask.

"It's got its own CPU and battery."

"What? It hardly weighs anything."

"Well, the charge is only good for ninety minutes. We'll need to arrange for an intermission to swap them out." He pulls out a digital caliper (because why would a computer engineer use a tape measure?). "I'm going to measure your head, unless you happen to know your head dimension."

"Metric or imperial?"

"Um, metric."

"Fifty-nine point seven centimeters. And it's sixty-two millimeters between my pupils."

"Wow, most people don't know that."

I shrug. "It's so our clothes fit just right." Which is true, although I doubt Oscar or the others could recite those measurements. I'm blessed/cursed with a good memory (which I'd trade in a heartbeat for perfect pitch).

"Yeah, I remember the way you guys used to dress." Dave gives me a different headset and inputs something on his phone.

I pull it on, marveling again at the lightness. The initial black screen switches to a color version of the room that's so clear I'd swear I was looking through glass and not viewing a real-time computed projection.

"Like those matching, embroidered tuxedos you wore to the Grammys." I'm not sure if Dave's laugh is ironic or sarcastic. The screen's momentary lag means I may just be misinterpreting the vibe, but I feel like we're done talking tech. I take off the headset to make sure we can both read each other's expressions.

"Yeah, those were pretty ridiculous. And hot. We sweated like pigs."

"Or those kilts with suspenders from the 'Can't Be U' video?"

I laugh. Maybe Dave did a recent internet image search, but he sounds more informed. Obsessed stalker? Unlikely. As a rule, boy bands don't have fanboys, much less crazed ones. Never Boy Land officially broke up in 2023, and Dave doesn't look much older than me. Most likely scenario: he was dating—or wanted to be dating—some girl who was way into us and this is just him blowing off years of suppressed inferiority. Or worse, she may have forced him to attend one of our shows.

"You know, my younger sister was obsessed with you guys," says Dave. Girlfriend, sister—close enough. "It was during the pandemic. She was twelve. I was eighteen. I should have been heading off to college; instead I was stuck at home taking classes online. And every day it seemed your band released a dance, or zoom chat, or some impromptu video on your TikTok channel. And she'd demand that I watch them too, to increase your view count."

Yeah, I remember those. I've heard people claim that 2020 was our big year and that we owed our popularity to the lockdowns. Like the best thing to happen to us was promoting our songs and brand religiously over social media. They forget all about us having to cancel our sold-out world tour, delay our third album, and basically put our careers on hold.

"And then there was your music. Stacy claimed headphones gave her migraines, so she played your albums out loud, nonstop."

"You must have hated us," I sympathize. I've spent plenty of time hating on NBL, and its members. That includes Kyle Moretti.

"There were times I fantasized about punching you in the face—not you personally—the main guys," Dave admits. "But you kept Stacy sane. She was stuck even more than me. She couldn't go to school, couldn't hang out with friends. The social media stuff Never Boy Land released helped her get through it. And… your music doesn't actually suck."

I hope he's not expecting me to say thank you.

Dave grins. "I know all your lyrics. I've got an NBL playlist I pull out when I need some ear-sugar. I even begged my manager to be part of the VCPT. That's Virtual Concert Performance Team."

"Wow," I say, and mean it.

"I was wondering, could I get a photo with all of you?"

"Of course. We can even record a hello for Stacy."

He laughs. "Oh, she's not that into you anymore. She's told me her music tastes have evolved."

I calculate; his sister would be nineteen or twenty now. "Emo girls with guitars?" I hazard.

"Metalcore. I know, right?"

And that—in a nutshell—is why we crashed and burned as a band. It's true; most boy bands' initial run of stardom doesn't last more than five years, but no one predicted our 2023 implosion. We'd built up so much goodwill during lockdowns, and venues were desperate to rebook our tour. But further Covid outbreaks kept causing show cancellations, and the stress brought out the worst in us. Then there was what Marjorie calls the "Comfy Pajamas Effect." That warm, fuzzy piece of clothing you wore every day during lockdown just loses its appeal afterwards. You want to put on real clothes and go out into the world. It's not like you hate those pajamas, but they're carrying a lot of baggage. You don't want to see them—much less wear them—ever again. Never Boy Land was the metaphorical equivalent of a hoodie-footie-onesie.

Makes me wonder why we're attempting the comeback tour. Of course, Marjorie has a rationale for that too. It's 2027. As a band, we've been out of the spotlight long enough for our old fans to be nostalgic. But we're still young enough—Oscar just turned twenty-seven—to radiate that non-threatening boyish charm. Plus there are opportunities, like performing the first virtual concert in an online video game. I wouldn't have thought that a massively multiplayer online swords and sorcery game like *Heroes Summoning* would attract our twelve-to-eighteen-year-old female target demographic, but according to the PowerPoint presentation the Sky Coyote marketing guy did, girls like slaying monsters and defeating demon lords— provided they get to wear cute outfits and the demon lords are hot (his words, not mine). Sky Coyote wants to lure their audience over to their newly-launched virtual-world platform and Never Boy Land has enough name recognition to build up a buzz without the demands and constraints of a current stadium-filling performer.

The door to the VR studio buzzes, and in walks the real reason we're getting a second chance: NBL's one successful breakout star, Tristan Ives.

8

CHAPTER 2

Kyle

Tristan walks in sporting a translucent white shirt. And just in case you missed the point, the top two buttons are undone with a pendant resting just above the third. No excuse not to appreciate his sculpted chest. He's come a long way since we started that YouTube channel together. From tween idol to A-list celebrity; there's no denying he's a superstar. Even here—without his entourage and cameras and fans—Tristan shines brightly, and I feel myself slipping further into the background.

He pauses to let us bask in his presence, or maybe he's looking for something. I can't tell, he's wearing sunglasses.

Behind him is Marjorie, our producer/manager/den mother. There's more silver in her brown curls these days, but—thanks to her plastic surgeon—fewer wrinkles. Don't tell her I said it, but the stretched-skin predatory look suits her. A single stride brings her fully into the studio; she's dressed to kick executive ass in her rust-red pantsuit and chunky-heeled boots.

Marjorie Banks is everything an artist could dream of in a supporter and protector (in the tough-love sort of way). I'd tell any singer Marjorie's offered a contract to that she'll encourage them at every stage, fight like hell for their career, and make an awesome godmother to any future children. But if anyone (especially a young woman), asked me about interning under her, I'd tell them to walk away. Quickly. Because part of what makes Marjorie so good at her job is how ruthless she's willing to get.

I see a slice of Mina peeking through the door before Marjorie shuts it on her.

"Kyle!" Tristan waves. "Oscar, and…"

"Dave," says Dave.

"Dave!" Tristan's enthusiasm is—as always—cranked up to eleven. Dave's smiling ear to ear. Whatever thoughts he might still be nursing about KO-ing the heartthrob of Never Boy Land melt into the ether. Tristan looks around the room, perhaps to see if there's anyone else he should warmly greet. Instead, he asks, "Is this where we're performing?"

"Yes," says Dave. "It's all brand new. Just finished the remodel upgrade last week." That explains the fresh paint and new-car-interior smells of the studio. "Besides the state-of-the-art headsets, you'll each get one of these motion-capture spaces. Plenty of room to do your dance." Dave jumps in and does a meme-worthy recreation of one of our signature hand, kick, hip-swivel moves. "See how we've graded the incline? It will give a gentle reminder when you're at the edge of the perimeter space. And these flat screens will show both what you're seeing and your overall location, so your assigned spotter will keep you in the right location in the game space."

Tristan frowns. "I know you guys worked really hard on setting all of this up, but I'm worried about visibility."

"Bro, we'll be wearing headsets. We won't be seeing any of this," says Oscar.

"But it's so dark."

Dave looks stricken by Tristan's pronouncement. Marjorie's brow furrows. Oscar gives me a confused, concerned look; silently asking me to step in as the Tristan Whisperer. Fine.

"Tristan," I say, "take off your sunglasses."

He does and looks around with unabashed wonder. "My bad. This place is awesome."

Dave leans in and sotto voce asks, "Is he on something?"

"Nope," I assure him. I've known Tris since we were six. He's always been this way.

Dave takes Tristan over to get him fitted with a headset. He's got the digital caliper out but seems unnerved by Tristan's perfect flowing golden locks (as if he might be breaking some contract by touching them).

Marjorie sidles up to me. "Good to see you here, Kyle. All chipper and on top of things?"

"Yeah, why wouldn't I be?"

"Because of what happened yesterday at rehearsal." She's referring to me learning the steps for the wrong dance and Oscar having to take me aside to help me put together the combos. It was embarrassing, but I thought I'd handled it okay.

"Sorry about that. I'll be more prepared next time."

"No, no. You've only been back a month. I'm impressed by how much you've retained," Marjorie reassures me. "And you've kept in shape, better than most college graduates." I notice the microsecond eye-twitch in the direction of Dave's stomach.

Option one, take the compliment and keep struggling to read the tea leaves. Option two, honesty. I go with two.

"I'm a work in progress. Oscar's been reviewing dance steps and choreography with me, and Tristan's letting me use his gym and personal trainer. I'm still slow with my timing, but I'll have it down by showtime next week." As supporting evidence for my commitment, I throw in some science. "I've been re-watching our old performances. I read in an article that doing so activates mirror neurons that can help with muscle memory."

"That's my Kyle, smart as paint."

"Beats being the quiet one."

I get a knowing smile from that. Back at the start of our careers when we were finalizing the band lineup, Marjorie had cornered me and confided that she wasn't sure where I fit.

"I'm fine with being a backup singer," I remember responding. It was the natural position for me; the others could out-sing and out-dance me. Well, maybe not Tristan. But with his face and charisma, the obvious strategy was to put him front and center.

"I'm talking about offstage." Marjorie was big into "offstage." Half of rehearsals were her lecturing about what was expected of us. It's where the Marjorie Banks' Laws of Boy Bands came from. "It's not like you couldn't handle the role of the cute one, or the responsible one, or even the bad boy, you've got the snark for it. But Micah, Oscar, and Cole all fit those better. Diego tells me we should make you the quiet one."

"Seems like a leftover can't-think-of-anything-else role. Doesn't Diego know any other one-dimensional stereotypes?"

"See? Snarky." Marjorie laughed. She liked it when we cleverly dissed her ex-husband business partner. "You kids are so smart these days."

She was acting all casual. It didn't stop my mind from racing. Five members was standard for a boy band. But what if they didn't need me, or maybe they were looking for someone with genuine talent?

"How about you make me the nerd? All teen tv shows have a nerd in the cast."

How much did that desperate tween impulse cement my identity and set me on my life trajectory? I used to study on the bus, and I kept enrolling in high school classes when the others just took proficiency exams. And then there was majoring in physics. If Tris hadn't called me about getting the band back together, I'd likely be picking out grad schools now.

Still, there are worse tropes to be saddled with.

The studio door buzzes and Mina walks in with two of them: Micah Cardigan—the baby all grown up—and Cole Silva—fresh from rehab.

"Sorry for being a bit late," says Micah. He got his growth spurt after the band broke up—so now I'm the shortest—but he's still rocking the cute china doll look: delicate features, alabaster skin, and gentle red curls. And boyish freckles, can't ignore those freckles.

"Funny how your 'a bit late' is always fifteen minutes past any meeting time," says Cole. His hoodie, which covers his buzz cut and tattoos, also shadows his dark skin and trimmed facial hair. All that pops are his piercing ice blue eyes.

They're opposites in more than just looks. Micah grew up affluent and overscheduled; his entire childhood was optimized to nurture his budding musical talents. Cole bounced around relatives' apartments and foster homes in New Jersey and made use of the benign neglect to develop his hip-hop and beatboxing skills. I'm not sure if it's their different backgrounds (or just their personalities) but they've never really gotten along. And time apart has not improved their interactions.

"Better fashionably late than being erratic and unreliable," Micah snipes.

"Fashionable? I don't think that shirt could get any more basic," says Cole.

They're each their own brand of snowflake. Micah is a musical genius, but he's also temperamental and (because he's the youngest) kind of bratty. Meanwhile, we're all concerned that Cole could fall off the wagon—again—but his tough guy exterior makes it hard to gauge what's really going on with him.

"You're both here now," Marjorie says before the sniping erupts into a full argument. "Mina and Dave will get you set up." They walk over to Dave who looks awkwardly between them trying to figure out who's got priority.

I say to Marjorie, "If you're worrying about someone not taking the comeback seriously, how about those two?"

"Micah and Cole are good. They need this chance for their careers and livelihood. But most of all, they need it for their identities." Before I can chime in that I, too, am a nobody without Never Boy Land, Marjorie continues, "If this doesn't work, you've got a degree from an Ivy League university. With good grades too, according to Tristan."

So, she thinks I'm slumming it in a boy band. I'm tempted to tell her that I could have gotten easy hookups and plenty of recreational drugs with a lot less work backpacking across Europe this summer, but no one wins a fight with Marjorie Banks. Instead I point out, "Tristan doesn't have anything to gain from the comeback tour either."

"I've given this talk to him. He says he wants to be back with you guys."

"I want that too." I look across the room to where Micah and Cole are now wearing the headsets. Oscar's taking a photo of them. Tristan's behind, photobombing them with bunny ears. "I want to be a part of Never Boy Land."

Even if I'm standing off to the side and watching.

"Okay then." Marjorie pats me on the back. "We'll make it happen." She clears her throat loudly and the entire room quiets down to pay attention. "It looks like we're all set here. I've got a meeting to straighten out Sky Coyote's lawyers on a few details." She looks around purposely and her eyes settle hard on Mina. "You'll remember to handle the lunch orders, right." It's not a question. "Perfect. Text me if there are any issues. We don't want to fuck this up." And she's gone. I sometimes imagine Marjorie as Superman, except if he were an asshole.

Dave and Mina exchange looks but don't say anything.

"Give her ten seconds," Cole advises. "If she's not back by then, she'll be gone for the rest of the day. Probably."

These don't seem to be the soothing words they need, so I suggest, "Hey, before we get started with the VR, should we take those photos?" It has the desired effect of cheering the Sky Coyote employees up, and this also guarantees Marjorie won't whisk us away before I can make good on my promise to Dave.

"Now you absolutely cannot show these to anyone until the official announcement next week," says Micah as we all line up.

"Dude, they already signed the NDAs," says Cole. "They know the drill." He's right. Tech companies take PR embargos even more seriously than the entertainment industry. Micah should know that given that his mom is a vice president at one of them.

Dave takes the photo with all of us and Mina; Mina makes sure to stand next to Tristan. Then Mina takes a photo of all of us with Dave; Dave makes sure to stand next to Tristan.

Of course they would. In the last four years, Tristan has put out two solo albums that have gone platinum, starred in a major Hollywood movie, and made *People*'s "Sexiest Man Alive" list three times.

And the rest of us? Micah's released one moderately successful record, and one flop. Cole appeared in a lot of tabloids (not in a good way) before taking a break to spend some quality time in rehab. None of the hip-hop or R&B groups Oscar's worked with have resulted in a full-time offer. And me? I've got that physics degree from Cornell.

Photos are taken, the good mood is restored. Mina hands us our equipment and leads us to our assigned spots. Dave pulls out a massive laptop.

"First session is just to get you guys familiar with the space and moving around," he says. We put on the headsets and make sure we're holding the controllers in the correct hands. "Later we'll get you into the body sensor suits for the dance routines. For now, let's do something fun, like slay a dragon."

I turn on my headset and see nothing. I wait patiently because techie things take time. Still nothing, not even a startup logo.

"Are any of you guys connected?" I hear Micah ask.

"I'm not seeing anything," admits Oscar.

"Maybe this is some sort of pregame meditation?" says Tristan. "Namaste."

"Yeah, something's not working. Hang on," says Dave.

"Wasn't there a problem last week with a non-registered company device?" asks Mina.

"That could be it."

Mina collects my watch and phone. I'm still in the dark, but I hear her moving amongst the group.

"Oh, this isn't a smart watch," says Tristan. "Check out the face."

"It says it's 1:45 a.m."

"Yeah, I got to get it fixed. But, like they say, it's still right twice a day."

An image of Tris's blue-faced Omega pops into my mind and I roll my eyes. Only Tristan Ives would wear a broken watch that still costs a semester's worth of tuition. I make a note to give him a piece of my mind about it later.

There's a beep as Dave restarts the system. More darkness. After another minute he sends Mina out of the room to track down someone called Todd. Next, he says he's going to check on something in the server room. I hear a security buzz and a door closing.

No one's saying anything. With the noise-canceling headphones doing their thing, I could squeeze in an impromptu mindfulness session. I'm starting to zone out when white text appears on the display.

The Realm of Mythreal is in Peril.

Dark Forces are Amassing to

Disrupt the Balance and Throw the World into Chaos.

Only You, Brave Heroes, can Avert Catastrophe.

Prepare for Transport.

I reread the words. Did they change the opening text for the virtual reality version of the game? And Papyrus font, really? The words fade as a bright light fills my vision and I experience some serious vertigo.

Drevo Woods
Goblin fort
Nothing here
Saitanna
Rozny Las
Gradskydd encampment
Stump house
Laska Bay
Bydlo
Northern Ozema

CHAPTER 3

Souffy

Souffy Ravenus presses her hand against the stones that frame the tower window and angles herself out. Thirty feet below her lies unforgiving cobblestone, but Souffy's gaze stretches further: beyond the fortress's courtyard, past the battlements of its protective walls, and out to the ocean, gray in the early morning light. It's that flat expanse of water, even more than the impenetrable mountains to the south or the oppressive forests that crowd the northern bay, that reminds Souffy just how cut off from civilization—from any place of importance—the town of Bydlo is. Since her banishment to this town three years ago, she has fervently wished for something—for anything—exciting to happen.

And now, maybe, it has.

Souffy had awoken before sunrise, her limbs prickled by a thousand invisible needles. It was as if she'd managed to sleep funny on every part of her body. She knows this physical reaction means that a powerful spell beyond anything a mortal magic user could harness has been cast. Souffy can still feel the hairs—quite literally—standing up on the back of her neck (it's a curious side effect when she casts or finds herself in the presence of magic). Not that her hair ever lays flat. She's blessed—or cursed—with a thick black halo of tight curls. But this morning's extra volume is unarguably due to magical residue.

The overhang of the tower's slate roof blocks much of the sky, but the section Souffy's striving to see lies just out to sea. It's not so much a beam as a ribbon of light twisting downward with its edges flashing silver. She can't discern where it starts, only that it comes from somewhere so up high that it muddles her thoughts when she thinks about it. Souffy can make out where the light ribbon ends, though, on a lifeless outcropping of rocks jutting out from the briny waters. From this vantage, she can't see the sand embankment that connects the islet to Bydlo's harbor; she can only make out a corner of gray roof tile. Maybe if she could just lean out a bit further out…

She climbs up on the sill, scooching forward until she's kneeling at the edge. From there she reaches out the window and grasps the outer tower wall. Gritty chunks of mortar from between the stones dig into her knee as she tips herself forward. Souffy hugs the wall and presses her cheek so close that she inhales the centuries-old mildew that permeates the fort. From here, she can make out most of the squat, salt-encrusted stone Hero Shrine and the ribbon of light terminating at its roof.

As a child, Souffy used to stare at the enormous tapestry in her grandmama's villa that recounted the exploits and great deeds of the Heroes of the Realm. The picture story it told began with a line of silver thread connected to the roof of the Hero Shrine in the city of Talenberg. That shrine had been depicted as much grander with massive stained glass windows and flying buttresses, but the ribbon of light means the same thing.

"The portal's been activated," Souffy squeals.

Just then, her right hand slips an inch, eliciting a gasp from Souffy as the precariousness of her position demands her full attention. Slowly, she lets out her breath, willing her body and thoughts still. This wouldn't be an issue if she'd been able to master the Soft Landing spell. But she hasn't. A sad pile of shattered bricks on the ground beneath her bedroom window attests to her many failed attempts.

Souffy knows you're not supposed to look down in these situations, but she does anyway. This close to imminent death, her vision achieves a remarkable level of clarity. She takes in the cobblestones' geometric patterns, notices the lighter gray of the recently replaced stones, and marvels at the tenacity of the weeds sprouting from the cracks. They're green now but destined to wither in the cold autumn nights and die a slow death.

Not instantaneous, like Souffy's demise would be if she were to lose her grip.

She's all but digging her fingers into the masonry. It's wet, either from the sea mist or her own cold sweat. Despite her vice grip, she slips what feels like another inch. Bit by bit, Souffy's body tips forward. If she does nothing, she will absolutely fall to her death. So why not try the idea forming in her mind? Souffy vaguely recalls a gravity diagram with arrows from her Non-Magical Sciences course that proved the impossibility of what she's attempting. Just as well she hadn't paid attention back then.

Souffy takes a deep breath and—with all her might—pushes backward. Her hands no longer hold the tower wall, and she totters on her knees. A tip forward means death. Thankfully, she tumbles backward. Her hip slams into the edge of the windowsill as she falls—head first—to the safety of the tower floor. At the last moment, she manages to twist so that her shoulder takes the brunt of the impact. She rolls onto her back and lies still for a while; her shoulder and hip throb painfully.

She's alive.

She's alive!

And, even more miraculously: otherworld heroes are coming to Bydlo!

It's the most monumental thing that has ever happened anywhere near her, and it sets her imagination aflame. Maybe she could arrange to be in the Hero Shrine when they come through. Maybe Souffy could be the one to let them in.

Souffy brushes the worst of the dirt off her official wizard-school smock. It hardly matters. There's no way that Souffy will be teaching basic spellcasting today, and she won't be wearing this frumpy old thing when she meets the otherworlders. She's grinning as she heads to the narrow spiral staircase carved into the tower's massive walls. Her dizziness as she bounds down the steps—two at a time—comes from the thoughts and possibilities spinning in her head.

Opening the portal won't be a problem. The magic required is just a variant of the Restore cantrip. She teaches Restore to all her beginning magic students, although not much beyond that. By the time she's got them comfortable casting cantrips and an elementary spell or two, they're apprenticed out to a trade-mage (usually in the logging industry or employed by the Laska Bay Trading Company). She's trained only one student in the past three years who showed any real promise. And he was sent away to a larger town to the south—over two days' journey by ship—that has an accredited magic school with Certified Wizard instructors.

Not that Souffy wants to teach. If she passes her wizard exams, she's determined to do something more exciting. When—not if—she passes her exams, she corrects herself.

But for once Souffy finds herself pleased with Bydlo's provincial attitudes towards higher magical education. It means that, with Uncle Ferimus away on one of his herbalistic expeditions, she's the only wizard with a formal education (or most of a formal education) in town. While a cleric or really any magic user could technically open the portal, everyone knows that wizards are the first choice when dealing with the Divine Wisdom's will.

It really could happen! All she needs to do is to convince the magistrate or the mayor of the rightness of her claim. Souffy decides to try the magistrate. Her offices are closer, within the fortress itself.

Souffy bursts into the courtyard, racing past moss-covered walls, stables with sagging roofs, and barracks in need of whitewashing. A century ago, when skirmishes and land disputes were common between Ozema and its neighboring countries, Queen Ella, the current King's grandmother, maintained two regiments in Fort Bydlo to protect its shipyards and sea trading routes. But then the Heroes of the Realm brought peace and goodwill between the nations and now the fort houses only a small garrison, made up mainly of locals. There's enough extra room for Magistrate Nevus and her staff, as well as Ferimus's magic school. Souffy hopes the new heroes will not be as bitterly disappointed in this meager outpost as she was upon her own arrival.

At least the Commandant's House, where Magistrate Nevus keeps her offices, is well maintained. Even impressive, with its red and white brick pattern exterior and the wide staircase leading up to the great hall. "Fit for the King," the mayor is proud of saying. It has been the mayor's lifelong dream to have the King (or, more realistically, any member of the royal family) visit Bydlo. Souffy doesn't see that happening any time soon, and she doesn't see why they can't hold a dance or something fun in there in the meantime. All she's ever seen the great hall used for is town meetings or the occasional trial.

Souffy doesn't slow her stride as she passes the stairs. The double doors at the top are always locked. Instead, she ducks into a side door and runs along narrow servants' passages past rooms with dust-covered floors and outmoded furniture covered in drop cloths. Eventually, she pops out into a larger hallway leading directly to the magistrate's offices.

"Hey Orley," Souffy greets the guard stationed outside the door to the offices. In the capital, Sernik, where Souffy grew up, active duty soldiers do not guard government offices, or police the town, or serve as protection on commercial ships. But here in Bydlo, the duties of militia conscripts cover any job that requires a sword.

"Souffy." Orley's relaxed posture snaps into alertness. "Is there a problem?"

Orley lives in the barracks, and a few months ago, her younger brother enrolled in the school to become one of Souffy's pupils. Given those connections and their similar ages—Orley is twenty-one, a year older than Souffy—it would make sense for them to be friends. But for various reasons (not all of them her fault) Souffy has had a difficult time finding companions in Bydlo.

"No." Souffy tries—and fails—to not sound defensive. "I just need to talk to the magistrate."

"About?"

"Something good, alright?"

Orley is the first to break eye contact. "Magistrate Nevus is having breakfast in the foyer." She stands aside but doesn't open the door.

You're a Ravenus wizard, Souffy reminds herself. She holds her head high as she lets herself in.

Souffy finds the magistrate seated at the head of a large table, a plate of pastries to her right, a stack of papers to her left. A few feet down the table, a messenger bird perches, pecking at a bowl of seeds.

Magistrate Lenora Nevus is a small woman with a formidable presence. Souffy has heard that when Lenora's gray-streaked black hair is combed out, it hangs almost to her ankles, but she has never seen the woman without it braided into tight coils.

When Souffy enters, Lenora looks up in alarm. "Is anything on fire? I mean metaphorically? Or literally?"

"No!" Why do people always make that assumption? It was only that one building and they were planning on tearing it down anyway.

"Glad to hear that. Now if you'll just let me get through these." Lenora returns to her paperwork.

"Actually, there's something amazing I need to tell you."

"Can it wait, dear?" The way Lenora stresses the term of endearment gives it an edge. "I need to finish approving the tax deferral requests. The deadline is next week and if the forms aren't filled in correctly, I want the applicants to have time to resubmit."

"But—"

"Souffy." There is iron in her voice, just enough to remind Souffy that Magistrate Nevus is more than a parchment-pushing bureaucrat. She is the appointed representative of the King. Her voice carries his authority. "Sit down and have a pastry."

Souffy chooses a sticky bun covered in crunchy sugar and munches as loudly as possible. Lenora pays her no mind. She proceeds through her stack, taking the same amount of time to check each line before stamping Accept or Reject at the bottom of the parchment. About the time Souffy is considering a second pastry, Lenora finishes with the last form.

"Well? What is this amazing thing?" She folds her hands and gives Souffy her full attention.

Souffy has been rehearsing phrases in her head. She wants to imbue the announcement with the gravitas it deserves. "Some very auspicious individuals are about to arrive in Bydlo." She pauses for effect. "At the Hero Shrine."

Lenora blinks, twice. "Oh, someone has petitioned you to request a hero for a quest? I can see how you'd be excited, but remember dear, the Divine Wisdom only grants a small fraction of all petitions. I don't think we've had heroes in Bydlo in five, maybe seven years."

"No, it's not a petition for a hero." Does Lenora think Souffy would be this excited about some professional adventurer or magic user called in to resolve a local problem? "They're here now, in the portal, in the Hero Shrine!"

"But, that's not how these things work, Souffy. There's a petition and a requesting ritual and a waiting period while the hero prepares for the quest. And only then, when everything is in place, does the hero actually travel between hero shrines."

"That's for regular heroes from other parts of Mythreal. These heroes are from another world. They've been sent because there's some great imbalance that only they can make right."

"So, no paperwork?"

Souffy shakes her head. She can see the import of her news finally dawning on Lenora. "You mean there are otherworlders down in the Hero Shrine right now?"

"Yes! They're still in the portal. Someone needs to release them."

"Is that safe?" Lenora sounds confused. Well, it has been almost seventy years since the last otherworld heroes came to Mythreal. And (Souffy reminds herself) this is Bydlo.

"For them? Oh, yes. They're in a state of suspension. They probably aren't even aware that time is passing." At least that's what Souffy vaguely remembers from her Introduction to Divine Wisdom Theology class. She waits for Lenora to question or challenge her. Instead, the magistrate nods silently, encouragingly. It isn't often that people treat Souffy as an authority. She decides to make the most of the situation. "We should open the portal as soon as possible. It's customary for a senior wizard to welcome the heroes but with my uncle away, I could cast the spell to unlock the gate, and then Father Aldonus could perform the Pathfinding Ceremony. It would be—"

A loud squawk interrupts Souffy's exposition. Both women turn to see the bird at the other end of the table twitching and ruffling its feathers. A moment later, a small, green-speckled egg drops into a padded bowl.

"Sorry, I need to take this," says Lenora.

She removes the egg, gives it a gentle tap, and cracks it open a couple of feet above the table. A gob of albumin spills out of the broken egg. It shimmers as it falls, becoming lighter, airier. By the time it makes contact with the table it's no longer a liquid but a mist, swirling and reflowing into the form of the head and shoulders of a man. The man is quite attractive, with smooth black hair and intelligent eyes. Daydreaming about that face has disrupted Souffy's study times on a few occasions. More than a few, unfortunately.

"Greetings Magistrate," says the man-shaped mist. There is just the slightest curl to his lips, a hint of a smile for those who know to look for it.

"Likewise, Captain. I assume your passage to Rozny Las went well?"

"Yes. The winds were favorable, and we made the journey in under two days. I think I should sail with priests more often. I had some wonderful conversations with Aldonus. He sends you well wishes."

"Wait, Arek," Souffy jumps in, "Father Aldonus is with you?"

"Oh, hello Souffy." Arek's noncorporeal form turns towards her. "Yes, Aldonus, Priestess Jasper, Cleric Malissa, pretty much all of the clergy are here. They're consecrating the grounds for the new church. You know about the new church in Rozny Las?"

Souffy didn't. She made it a point to pay as little attention as possible to the goings-on in Rozny Las, the outpost on the far side of the bay that makes Bydlo look positively cosmopolitan.

"But we need him back here!" Souffy tries not to sound desperate as all her careful plans fall apart.

"What? Did something happen?" The swirly mist that comprises Arek's eyes somehow seems to focus even more intently on Souffy.

"No, nothing like that, Arek," Lenora cuts in before Souffy can defend herself. "We'll need him back to perform a ceremony. Apparently, we're about to be visited by otherworlders. Fortunately, Souffy says we can wait."

"I didn't say that," Souffy cries. She's feeling hot, flustered.

"You said the heroes don't experience the flow of time while they're in the portal."

"Are you saying otherworld heroes are coming to Bydlo?" asks Arek.

"Yes, exciting isn't it? Imagine, otherworlders visiting our town."

Souffy doesn't know what frustrates her more: her words being used against her or the fact that Lenora is conversing with the swirling mist-Arek as if he is real. Messenger bird eggs are like an animated letter, capturing the knowledge and mental state of the sender at the exact moment they feed the bird the enchanted seed. Since Messenger birds' other magical ability is next-day arrival, regardless of distance, Arek must have made that magical connection with the bird when he arrived in Rozny Las yesterday. Nothing Lenora says to this magical copy of Arek will be communicated back to the original. Arek will know nothing of the heroes or the need to return as soon as possible until the bird is rested and ready to be sent back in two or three days.

"Have no fear, Souffy. I'll deliver the priest home as soon as possible, I promise." The not-real Arek smiles again at Souffy, and she finds herself nodding in overeager agreement. Drat, now she's doing it too! If only he didn't look so damn gallant.

"And speaking of our return trip," he continues, "I'm happy to report we've already unloaded the supplies and will start loading the export timber in the morning. It appears they've had a fruitful harvest this summer, top-quality trees and the infusion spells have held well. I was talking to one of the master trade-mages and they've developed a ritual to permeate freshly cut timber with magical termite repellent. Can you imagine how popular that will be in the south?" Lenora makes a noise of agreement as Arek launches into even more tree talk.

Souffy picks up another sticky pastry, forcing herself to listen. Hearing Arek drone on does wonders to settle Souffy's butterflies. It's a pity that behind that handsome face resides such a provincial mind. Arek might be a ship's captain and look absolutely dashing in his crisp white coat and cap, but both the uniform and ship belong to Arek's employer, the Laska Bay Trading Company. And more to the point, any happily-ever-after daydream that Souffy might conjure involving Arek would be dominated by unending monologues on trees, lumber, and sawmills.

Souffy finishes her second pastry. Lenora and Arek have finished discussing a lumber delay from a camp in the far north and have moved onto treaty complaints lodged by the Laska Bay Trading Company against the Trädskydd Druids, and treaty complaints lodged by the Trädskydd Druids against the Laska Bay Trading Company. Souffy supposes she could wait around for egg-Arek to fade but it's clear that Lenora does not consider freeing the heroes to be a priority. And when Lenora makes up her mind, you'd need a dragon attacking the town to change it. Souffy needs a different plan. She waves her goodbye to Lenora and slips out of the room.

"Did you say heroes are coming to Bydlo?" Orley asks her as she leaves.

"Ask the magistrate," says Souffy as she runs off.

Souffy's feet feel heavier and heavier with each step as she leaves the Commandant's House. She could still go see the mayor. But her earlier enthusiasm has evaporated, leaving behind only the thin gruel of reality.

It's common knowledge that Souffy's family sent her to Bydlo because she failed her wizard certification exams and needed a place to study free from distractions and "bad influences." And maybe, since her arrival here, she had acted impulsively on some occasions, like that time with Nugget three months ago. Not that she's sorry about her actions. It was inhumane for that man to keep a dancing bear and force her to perform at the town market. None of her teachers ever told her the Charm spell worked differently on ursines, and it only took a week to repair the market stalls. The town gossips who keep comparing the events to the Pandemonium are exaggerating and Souffy does her best to pay them no mind. She's glad that thanks to her decisive actions, Nugget is now freely roaming the forest.

But people listen to gossip, and no respectable citizen would think someone like Souffy should be the one to open the portal. Soon, everybody who is anybody in Bydlo will know about the heroes, and they'll all have their own justifications for why they should be the ones present in the Hero Shrine to meet the otherworlders. It isn't that large a shrine; Souffy probably wouldn't even be allowed inside for the ceremony.

Souffy is so lost in misery that she doesn't pay attention to where her feet are taking her. She's surprised to find herself at the base of the tower from which she earlier viewed the light connected to the shrine. She looks up at the window that she almost fell from and thinks: *This is where I would have gone splat.* Funny that makes her smile.

She could have called for help back then, but she didn't. She acted on her own. And it worked out. Some of the excitement Souffy felt earlier in the tower flows back into her. She wonders why she always feels her best when she's about to do something crazy.

Souffy has been told by family members she's a bit like her grandmama, the sorceress Zorianna, who in her youth fought alongside the Heroes of the Realm. The comparison is usually made when Souffy has been caught doing something she shouldn't, and it's not meant as a compliment. But once or twice, Grandmama had said it herself, and not in her usual sharp, sarcastic tone. Wouldn't it be something if Souffy could live up to Zorianna's deeds after all?

Souffy makes up her mind. She's going to free the heroes. But first, she needs an accomplice.

CHAPTER 4

Souffy

Souffy stands straight, head held high (or as high as she can in the low-ceilinged cavern) and extends her arms like she's a priest calling upon the gods, or a necromancer raising the dead. She pitches her voice low and intones, "I bid you welcome, brave heroes." She flicks her wrists and is pleased with the scratchy jingle her bangle bracelets make as they slide down her forearms. Her pleasure with her performance lasts until the crystalline tinkle fades, and then uncertainty rushes in. "Or should it be: 'Brave heroes, I bid you welcome?'"

Across from her, sitting on a large stone, her friend Havelin Hoglason purses his lips while he considers. She's called him to their secret meeting place to strategize. It's a fabulous hideout that Souffy found in her early explorations around the fortress: a hollow not-quite cave under a tiny rock outcropping nestled just below the massive wall, undetectable unless you're willing to scramble along a cliff edge forty feet above crashing ocean waves. During her first summer in Bydlo, seventeen-year-old Souffy had several partners-in-adventure, and they'd had to squeeze close to fit in the chamber. But by winter, most of those relationships fell away as her companions spent more of their time pursuing their chosen professions. Fortunately, Havelin being a ranger meant that he could always make time for Souffy.

"You said these otherworlders are being transported from their own world with no idea about where they are or what's happening to them, correct?" asks Havelin. It's taken some time for Souffy to explain to him how the portal works. Havelin was a child the last time the Hero Shrine was utilized. That time it was to summon some local heroes from a neighboring county to help clear out a band of goblins who'd been harassing farmers.

"That's what I wrote down in my class notes." Souffy drops her arms and knits her fingers together.

"Then starting with 'I bid you welcome' sounds a bit more…" Havelin scratches his nose. "Welcoming."

"Okay, that's what I'll say." She tries to sound confident. The monumentality of the decision to free the heroes is weighing more and more on her with each preparation. This situation is so unlike her grandmama's recollections. In those, the otherworlders were summoned in response to a monk's augury and were welcomed by esteemed wizards, high-ranking priests, and members of the royal court.

"And you'll be able to open the portal, right Souffy?"

Is that doubt Souffy hears in Havelin's voice or only a projection of her own fears? "Of course, I studied this in wizard school. And the Pathfinder spell to determine their hero classes is just a ritual. It's like reading a recipe. I couldn't find the Pathfinder wand in my uncle's workshop, but I can manage, probably. Maybe. I think?" Souffy's bangles jingle nervously as she wrings her hands. "This is a horrible idea, isn't it?"

"No!" Havelin says. He must sense her disbelief because he stands, takes hold of her arms, and repeats, "No." Havelin's head only comes up to Souffy's chin (his mother's father was a dwarf) so she must look down to meet his determined gaze. "Souffy, no matter what the magistrate says, no one in Bydlo has the knowledge or experience that you have. Most people in this town have never spoken to a person from outside of Ozema, much less another world. You said one of the Heroes of the Realm visits your grandmother all the time. Although I still think you're tugging my leg about getting to ride his griffin. You're absolutely the best person to greet the heroes."

"You know, you're right," Souffy says, this time feeling it. She's a Ravenus wizard after all, not certified, true, but the heroes won't mind. If they come from a non-magical world, they won't even know there's a difference. "Thanks so much for helping me out with this, Havelin. I'm lucky to have a friend like you."

Havelin blushes and steps back. "Are you kidding? I never thought I'd get the opportunity to meet an otherworlder. You make life interesting, Souffy. Like last month when you tried to start that business selling magic dancing shoes."

"That one didn't turn out so well."

"Maybe, but everyone got plenty of exercise."

Havelin has the most positive way of looking at things. Which makes Souffy want to ask him about the other thing that's been concerning her.

"Do I look okay? To meet the otherworlders, I mean?"

She's chosen one of the outfits she brought with her from the capital, a yellow-trimmed green tunic with puffy sleeves over a lace-edged chemise and tight black hose. It used to be her favorite until, one day early in her time in Bydlo, Souffy wore it to the market and a pinched-faced woman called her a strumpet.

"Absolutely, yes," says Havelin. "You look like an elf."

Souffy smiles. Havelin has a thing for elves.

"Okay," she says, "let's free ourselves some otherworlders."

They emerge from the cavern and pick their way along the cliffside, scaling the final ledge to reach the fortress's northeast corner. Normally, they'd take the hidden passage into an unused storeroom in the old tower and from there cut through the courtyard. But today it seemed wisest to avoid Lenora and the guards' attentions. So they scramble through the drained moat with its overgrown foliage and make their way to the dirt road that leads inland around the fort and into Bydlo. From the road, they're visible to anyone strolling along the fortress walls, but no guards are stationed to keep watch from this vantage.

The Heroes of the Realm brought peace to the various kingdoms, or enough peace that no one would bother attacking a place as remote as Bydlo. In fact, Bydlo has been boringly safe for over three centuries, ever since another set of otherworld heroes, the Triad of Valor, traveled to the isolated fortress and defeated the ice giants who had terrorized the land for thousands of years. At least, that's the local legend. Souffy hadn't even heard of the Triad before coming to Bydlo.

Guards or no guards, she's still in a rush to get out of sight of the fortress. As they start down the road that leads into Bydlo, Havelin stops so abruptly that Souffy almost crashes into him. He's looking back at the battlements and towers still peeking over the hill. His expression seems halfway between bemused and contemplative.

"You're good at bringing about change, Souffy." He nods with this pronouncement. "The results aren't always what you think they're going to be, but sometimes they're even better. I'd still be stuck in the fort as a militia soldier if you hadn't convinced me two years ago to follow my desire to protect nature. What I'm saying is, I'm glad you've decided to free the otherworlders. And I think the people of Bydlo will appreciate you for it, eventually."

Havelin takes off before Souffy can respond. They soon enter what townsfolk call the genteel part of Bydlo. Here, opulent houses are set back from the well-maintained cobblestone streets by trim lawns and ornate iron-wrought fences. But even with its ocean views, it doesn't measure up to the finer districts in Sernik. At least Souffy thinks it doesn't; after several years away from the capital the details are no longer sharp in her mind.

As they navigate narrow twisty side streets to avoid the town square, houses turn to shop-houses turn to artisan workshops, most of which are devoted to some sort of woodcraft for export. The freshly cut lumber smell gives way to the briny seaweed odor of Bydlo's harbor. Souffy and Havelin turn east, away from the docks, and head along a sandy beach past the Church of the Twelve. The church, perched a few feet above the high tide mark, is easily the largest, grandest building in town.

Only after they round the church corner can they at last see their destination at the end of the open sea wall: the Hero Shrine. It's plain and boxy, with plaster walls and a gray tile roof. Souffy's been told the stained glass windows are a recent addition, but otherwise, it's unchanged since it was built all those years ago to send the Triad of Valor back to their own world.

Today, its humble appearance is bathed in the light of the Divine Wisdom's magic tendril which snakes down from the sky and pierces the roof. It's radiating so much mana that Souffy's hairs aren't just tingling; they're positively humming from all the latent magic in the air.

Standing by the shrine is their first real obstacle. Acolyte Boryk Tuba has planted his considerable bulk in front of the building's doors.

"What—" Souffy starts to say.

Havelin holds up a finger to silence her and then points to his ear. She nods, approving of his quick thinking; Boryk's sharp hearing borders on the uncanny, and it's only become more acute since he took his vow of silence four months ago. Good thing she has a magical workaround. Souffy raises one hand to rub her dangling copper earring while she points her little finger towards Havelin. A click of tongue establishes the connection for the Magic Missive cantrip.

"Do you think Lenora sent him to guard the shrine?" She thinks the question. "What should we do?"

"I've got an idea," Havelin thinks back at her. "Could that Pathfinder wand be stored in the Church of the Twelve?"

"It's possible." Likely even, because who would trust Uncle Ferimus's memory with something so important?

There's just enough charge left in the Magic Missive for Havelin to add, "Okay, then follow my lead."

Boryk notices them when they're halfway down the causeway. He puffs up his chest and squares his shoulders. His face has always put Souffy in mind of a potato. She doesn't mean it as an insult—potatoes aren't unattractive vegetables—it's just what she thinks whenever she sees him. When Boryk was in the militia with Havelin, he was a potato in a helmet. When he shaved his head upon entering the church, he was a bald potato. Now, giving her a hard stare with squinty eyes, he's an angry potato.

"Hi Boryk, what brings you here?" Havelin fails at trying to sound casual.

Boryk points at the sky. Havelin looks up and gasps.

"The portal beam's gotten brighter," says Souffy. "I bet even the apprentice trade-mages can see it now."

Boryk rolls his eyes in a way to imply that Souffy isn't the first magically inclined individual to wander by the shrine today.

"So, you're here to keep people from barging in?" Havelin asks.

Boryk nods.

"That's great," says Havelin. "We're helping out too." He grins, or tries to. Souffy knows how much her friend hates to lie. Still, he soldiers on. "Souffy says there's an item called a Pathfinder wand that's important for the welcoming ceremony. But she couldn't find it in the magic school. Do you think it could be in the church's relic collection?"

Boryk shrugs, conveying both his lack of knowledge and caring.

"This is really important, Boryk. The magistrate asked us to find it," says Souffy, who (unlike Havelin) has no qualms about telling white lies. Or other lies, when circumstances demand it. "Maybe you and Havelin could go look for it?"

Boryk's eyes narrow like he's seeing right through her. Souffy knows Boryk has been studying magic as part of his clerical training. She hopes his god hasn't blessed him with any spells to detect deception.

"That's fine. I'll call Cornelius to go take a look." Havelin gives three sharp whistles.

Boryk's neck snaps up and his eyes bulge out at the name of Havelin's beast companion. A moment later, there's scampering and skittering on the shrine's slate roof and a small, masked face peers down at them. Cornelius the raccoon is rarely far from Havelin these days. On more than one occasion, he's gotten into Souffy's bedroom—once, she caught him paw-deep in her jewelry box. Maybe, in addition to being a distraction, Cornelius might actually find the wand.

"Hi Cornelius," says Souffy. "We're looking for a silver stick. It's a bit over a foot long with a ruby at one end. It might be in the reliquary in the church. You should be able to get in there through the bell tower."

Cornelius leans in towards Souffy; his eyes fixate on her gold pendant. Havelin snaps his fingers to get the raccoon's attention and repeats Souffy's request but more slowly, with hand signals and plenty of pointing toward the church. This time, Cornelius cocks his head and twitches his ears. "He's got it," says Havelin as the raccoon takes off running toward the church. "He's great at finding shiny objects."

Boryk's scowl deepens. He glances from Souffy to the rapidly receding backside of the raccoon, then back to Souffy, as if gauging which might pose the greater threat. Cornelius wins. Boryk gives Souffy one last menacing glower before turning and sprinting after the animal.

When Havelin chose to train as a beastmeister, Souffy was a bit disappointed that he picked a raccoon. A wolf or panther would have been more impressive. She'll have to tell him later that he was right. Raccoons are the best.

"I probably should go to keep him from getting into too much trouble," Havelin tells Souffy.

"Don't worry, I'll guard the gate," says Souffy loudly. Since Boryk is already halfway down the causeway, she risks whispering, "Thanks, I couldn't do this without you." With a wink, Havelin runs after Boryk.

When Souffy can no longer see either Havelin or Boryk, she pulls a metal ring the size of a bracelet, packed with keys, from her pouch. Uncle Ferimus claims he keeps his keys all together so he can't afford to lose them. In practice, it means he's constantly asking Souffy to help him find where he'd last put them. Today, his forgetfulness works in her favor. She jangles the keys in front of the lock, searching for the one that glows blue. After a quick glance back to make sure no one is watching, Souffy unlocks the door and slips inside.

The shrine is rustic, even by Bydlo standards. The rough-hewn walls are decorated with simple line art illustrating the exploits of the Triad of Valor. The Triad had traveled all over northern Mythreal and spent extensive time with the elves and dwarves before their Final Quest in Bydlo.

According to the stories, the three heroes arrived at the Bydlo fortress with a band of druid refugees, fought an epic battle to defeat the King of the Ice Giants, and planted some magic trees in the Drevo Woods in the far north. Because in Bydlo, even the otherworld heroes somehow have their fate tied to the forestry industry.

But more important than old legends is what's waiting for Souffy behind the thick tapestries that obscure the arched entrance to the shrine's apse. She walks between the wooden pews of the main chamber and pauses at the stone altar whose surface is buried under decades of melted wax. *Such a momentous occasion*, thinks Souffy, *warrants a bit of ceremony*. She dashes back to the entrance, drops a coin in the offering box, and grabs four candles— the same number as the Heroes of the Realm. Back at the altar, she wedges them in a row on the votive rack. There's a flint sparker on a chain, but Souffy ignores it. Instead, she brings her palms together and interlaces all but her forefingers. The motion brings the shape of the cantrip to the front of her mind. She aims at the candles and carefully whispers *"Ignatius."*

A spark flies from her pointed finger, evaporating the first candle and fusing the next two together, but succeeds in lighting the last one. Strange, she usually has no problems with Flame Bolt. It must be all that excessive mana in the air. The hairs on Souffy's head vibrate in harmony with the force emanating from behind the tapestries. *That's enough ceremony*, she decides.

Souffy pushes away the fabric barrier and has to avert her eyes. A ball of searing white light floats in the center of the summoning circle. It leaves ghostly afterimages on her retinas. She looks instead at the painted blue circle that takes up most of the floor. Spaced evenly along its perimeter are symbols for each of the gods and goddesses who contributed their powers to create the Divine Wisdom.

The light pulses and sends tremors through the floor strong enough to tickle Souffy's feet. This close, she can sense the life forces of these suspended heroes. There are four of them—no wait… five. Souffy forces herself to probe again. Can this be right? Otherworld heroes usually come in groups of three or—on rare occasions, if the intended quest is exceptionally epic—four. She's never heard of five heroes being summoned at once. A manic grin spreads unchecked over her face as she confirms her initial estimate. Whatever quest the heroes have been called for, it's going to be more than Epic. It could be Legendary or even Mythic.

Time to crack open that ball of light and release the heroes. The words of her Intro to Divine Wisdom professor come to mind:

"Such ingenuity, for the Divine Wisdom to utilize the meager, commonplace cantrip Restore to unlock the nearly limitless potential of the hero-to-quest match, a fantastical pairing that's blind to national and even racial differences, that supplies the best-suited adventurers and mages to right the injustices detailed in the petition." Professor Tippius had paused there to wag her finger wisely at the class. "That's ineffability for you." She had then gone irritatingly vague in describing how to actually release such perfectly-matched heroes from their stasis. What Souffy remembers is that it basically amounts to casting a Restore cantrip but incorrectly. And Souffy has plenty of experience messing up spells.

The neodymium stones she had stashed in her pouch have attached to the key ring. She peels them off the metal and holds them out in front of her. Their magnetism attunes her senses to the physical qualities of the now violently glowing orb. It feels like a giant plug, with spurts of mana leaking out from an immense reservoir. "*Restitutio!*" she cries out, as she imagines pushing that giant leaky spigot. At the critical moment, she intentionally— for once—lets her attention wander and feels the spell slip out of her mind.

Nothing happens. Of course, "nothing" is what usually happens when magic is mis-spelled—although Souffy has experienced some rather explosive exceptions—but this nothing is supposed to open a hole in the orb, or something.

Nothing.

She's somehow flubbed flubbing a spell. And now she'll get caught and punished and still not get to free the heroes. It's so frustrating! With an angry grunt, Souffy stomps her foot.

And then the cosmos seems to burp. The orb disintegrates, flooding the chamber with a syrupy translucence for what feels both like forever and no time at all. The brightness fades, leaving Souffy blinking tears until her eyes adjust to the now-dim light filtering down from the clerestory windows. Five figures stand within the circle: three in front, two in the back.

Souffy raises her arms and begins, "I bid you welcome, brave heroes—" Her brain seizes up as she catches her first real look at the otherworlders.

She has read that newly arrived heroes often emanate an unearthly quality, some residual magic from the transportation spell that could make them seem especially noble or courageous. But now that the spell is complete, Souffy doesn't sense any magic. The indescribable beauty emanating from these men can't be natural, can it?

She blinks, swallows, and blinks again as her mind tries to process the experience. It's like clouds glowing pink before sunrise, the wind rushing through a field of wheat, concentric ripples spreading out in a crystal-clear pond, the soft coo of a dove, the smell of a newly opened rose, and all those poetic things that Souffy never really understood.

Until now. Now she gets it.

Like a punch to the gut.

Souffy actually staggers. She catches herself on the railing separating the summoning circle from the rest of the room and hangs, head down, until her lungs remember how to draw breath. Still feeling a bit lightheaded, she forces herself to look up.

The otherworlder closest to her could be a young god: tall with flowing golden locks, perfectly-symmetrical soulful eyes, full shapely lips, and a chiseled jaw. His magnificence is too much. Souffy turns her gaze to the figure on his right.

This young man is of smaller stature—yet still sublimely proportioned—with delicate cheekbones, copper hair, and green eyes framed by gorgeous, long eyelashes. If the first was a god, then this one must be an angel. His purity and refinement make Souffy feel awkward and gawky.

The man on the left is almost as tall as the first, with dark skin like her own and a tumble of thick, midnight hair. While still striking, there's a warmth to his honey-brown eyes, a benevolence in the way he holds himself. Souffy feels like she might just be able to talk to this one without her tongue tying itself up in knots.

Perhaps she's building up a tolerance to their auras because when she looks at the fourth otherworlder in the back, she merely finds him handsome. He still far outshines Arek and every other man in Bydlo, but his spiky brown hair and shorter stature make him approachable. Then his blue eyes find Souffy's. His brow furrows as he scrutinizes her, and his calculating intelligence pierces her like an arrow. Souffy blushes, and she turns to the last hero.

No, this one is not a hero. He's a demon. But no ordinary demon either. He's a Prince of Darkness, resplendent in all his shadowy glory. It isn't just his close-shorn hair, rakish beard, ice-cold eyes, or even the elaborate tattoos just visible on his neck. His dark aura emanates from his whole being; his disdain for ordinary mortals is conveyed by the cruel, downward twist of his lips.

But he must be a hero, she reminds herself. They all are. The Divine Wisdom has called these men from across the void because they are moral and righteous. By noble deeds and selfless actions, they will surely save the realm.

Souffy tries to recall the scattered bits of the speech she'd prepared and barrels through what she can remember before she loses her nerve. "You have been summoned in our hour of need to fulfill a great quest. Your task will not be easy, but… but for the sake of justice and virtue, I beseech you to accept the mantle of heroes." Surely men so beautiful on the outside must be equally glorious on the inside.

The god-like one in the center takes a step towards her.

"Unbelievable." His voice is deep and melodious, as if he's serenading her. Souffy's body seizes like a deer frozen by a flash of lightning. The otherworlder reaches out his hand. "This VR scene is just so life-like!" The tips of his fingers gently brush her cheek. They're as soft as a flower petal. Souffy's eyes meet his. He smiles a smile so powerful it could end wars and so gentle that it feels like a caress.

Her body feels like it's floating. Her ears fill with buzzing bees. Her vision clouds with white sparkles. And Souffy faints dead away.

CHAPTER 5

Kyle

I'll admit, Tristan's catch-the-fainting-fangirl-before-her-head-hits-the-pavement maneuver is hella impressive—the first five times you see it. But after that, it's just another convenient skill he's acquired to make it back from the concert venue to the hotel without having to call for an ambulance. Marjorie Banks' 8th Law of Boy Bands: *Thou shalt not leave a fangirl collapsed or bleeding on the pavement.* Still, kudos to Tris for springing over the railing and catching the priestess while the rest of us were still in shock.

"Check it, she doesn't even feel like a hologram," says Tristan.

Nope, I take my kudos back. He still thinks we're testing out the headsets.

We're not, obviously!

I want to snap at him to stop being such a moron, that this isn't how virtual reality works. Those headsets were light, but you still knew when you were wearing them. And we're not now. Even if we were, I wouldn't be able to feel the chill of this stone-wall room or smell the incense-laden air. Every one of my senses is affirming that we're no longer in the studio.

But that would mean we've defied the laws of space and time to get here. I'm not ready to reconcile that logical inconsistency just yet. So, my mouth stays shut.

Tristan—oblivious oaf that he is—keeps talking. "Hey, I can even smell her!"

I want to scream "You can't smell in VR, Tris!" But I don't.

He leans in for a deeper sniff. "She's kind of ripe." Somehow, he manages to come off as not creepy.

"I don't think this is a video game, bro," says Oscar. He runs his hand through his short, curly black hair as he takes in our surroundings.

"Where?" asks Micah. He's gone pale, making his freckles stand out. "Where are we?" Points for uttering the required line from every portal fantasy ever.

Judging by the décor—stone walls muraled with flat, mis-proportioned human figures, stained glass windows alternating with hanging tapestries—we appear to be in some sort of church or temple. There's also a briny note to the fragrance of incense and varnish. Which, along with the sound of crashing waves, makes me think there's probably a sea or an ocean outside. And we all just heard the generic "please save my world" line from the rather attractive cosplay girl currently passed out in Tristan's arms. Church, ocean, priestess—all generic fantasy world tropes. What's specific is the summoning circle we're standing in. It's the one Sky Coyote plasters on half its merch, and it's literally the first thing you see when you log into the game. All it's missing is a trademark symbol. We're either in Mythreal or a fake Mythreal created by some talented and well-funded imagineers.

But if this is some elaborate prank, how did we get here? How could we be wearing headsets in a climate-controlled studio one moment and then be here—really here—the next? It's just not scientifically possible. And if we're throwing out science, then we're left with the *M-word*. Not that my bandmates are there yet.

"Maybe this is some sort of optical overstimulation and we're all unconscious or dreaming?" Oscar proposes.

"Can't be," says Tristan, "I don't dream in color." Not true. He must have seen this on one of those viral "10 Things You Didn't Know about Tristan Ives" listicles. I'd call him out on it, but then we'd both have to come clean about reading fangirl posts.

"Maybe we were drugged?" Micah automatically glances towards Cole who's pulled up his hoodie.

He's got his resting bitch face firmly in place but dials it up to a full sneer in response to Micah's insinuation. "I'm sober."

"What then?" Micah snaps back. "We're dead and this is the afterlife?"

Coma, dreams, drugs, handwavy science, death and reincarnation. It looks like we've covered all rationalizations except—you know—"this is really happening." Maybe I'm just being contrarian, but with every passing moment, I'm more certain the magical explanation is the correct one. Still, I take a moment to consider the other hypotheses. While it's technically possible that I could be dreaming or in a coma, none of what's happening matches what my subconscious usually cooks up. Getting on the wrong tour bus and being forced to perform K-pop choreography with twelve hot Asian guys was the one I had this morning.

There's nothing weird with my senses, so I'm nixing being drugged. I refuse to believe that a video game company would have the resources to secretly develop teleportation technology. Death is enough of a singularity point that I guess I can't rule it out, but if this is some sort of afterlife, then isn't that just another reality?

My thoughts are interrupted by Tristan yelling at the ceiling.

"Hey Marjorie! Something's wrong. There's not enough room in here for our dance routine! Also, there's only one fangirl! And she's fainted!"

"Look, we're not in *Heroes Summoning*, ok?" snaps Cole.

"Actually…" Since I've waited this long to speak, everyone swivels to give me their full attention. "I think we might be. Only it's not the game, it's the real thing."

"What are you saying, Kyle?" asks Oscar.

"I'm saying"—I can't believe I'm speaking these words, but here we are—"we've been magically teleported to a fantasy dimension that appears to work like the *Heroes Summoning* video game. As the girl said, we've been summoned here to complete a quest." The stunned shock on their faces is genuine, none of us are that good as actors. I could lead them through my chain of reasoning, but it's faster just to appeal to their egos. "I mean, if you could have your pick of any five guys in the world to save your kingdom, wouldn't we be your first choice?"

Contemplative looks all around. Heads start to nod in agreement. I know my bandmates.

Micah says, "Marjorie Banks' Third Law: *A Boy Band with dedication, devotion, a bit of luck, and great hair can accomplish anything.* Guess that includes saving the world?"

"We've always had a problem with the luck part," Cole points out. "That's why we were hoping, begging for a comeback tour."

"What do you mean?" counters Tristan. "Marjorie's got the press release ready to go. In two days' time, it'll be all over the news. This tour is going to be epic!"

"We're. Not. On. Tour. Tris," I hiss. "We're in a magical world where we'll have to, I don't know, battle a demon lord or something." I'm feeling peevish, so I twist the knife. "Nobody here even knows our songs."

"Naw," Tristan scoffs, a silly grin plastered on his face. "This is just a high-tech simulated virtual reality publicity thingie that Marjorie and that company, Sky Wolf, cooked up. I bet you they're recording us even now and they'll use the outtakes as promotional material for the concert."

"It's Sky Coyote. And no, they're not!" The others look back and forth between Tristan and me.

Marjorie's parting words come back to me: "They need this, for their identities." Naturally, they'd cling to the flimsiest of narratives if it somehow leads to a comeback, even if it's coming out of the mouth of Tristan Ives. Hell, *especially* if it's coming out of the mouth of Tristan Ives. I can't compete with that.

I give Tris a "you win" look. He responds with a confused, vaguely apologetic expression, like maybe on some level he knows his theory doesn't hold up.

"But it doesn't matter, right?" Tristan says. "Either way, we need to do this quest thing and look good while doing it. Amirite?" He flashes me the same smile that took down the priestess. As if it had a prayer of working on me.

"Okay," says Oscar, "but does anyone know how this works? I know they made accounts for us to play the game, but I didn't have the time to check it out."

"Yeah, me neither," says Micah, all sweet innocence.

"I forgot my login," says Tristan. Based on my temp password, it was likely Tives_1234.

"I'm not playing some online nerd game," says Cole, folding his arms across his chest.

Looks like it's time for me to come clean and lose any remaining shred of coolness in my bandmates' eyes. "I've been playing *Heroes Summoning* for the past year or two"—five actually—"on and off"—on, mostly. Online gaming's been my chicken soup for the soul since the band broke up. I usually go by my middle name, Dylan, and use cartoon icons as avatars that look nothing like me IRL. It's nice not being constantly bombarded with questions about Cole or Micah. Or Tristan.

"That's awesome, Kyle," says Tristan. "Tell us how it works!"

I play a lot of games, but *Heroes Summoning* is by far my favorite. There's no player-versus-player fighting and not too much grinding or repetitive monster slaying needed to level up. But what I really like is the earnestness of the quests, like the one where the NPC barkeep asks you to track down his missing son. His dialog was so heartfelt, and animation so expressive, that I could almost believe he was real. Or that time my team took down a band of orc raiders who'd been trashing some peasants' farms, and it felt so deeply right and virtuous to get rid of those jerks. Not that I'm intending to geek out about any of that now. Best to start slow.

"It's a mostly straightforward massive multiplayer online role-playing game, set in a fairly standard but well-fleshed-out fantasy world. You start out by choosing your race and class, and then level up based on the monsters you slay and the quests you complete."

I get nothing but blank stares in response. What are the statistical odds of four American males in their mid-twenties knowing zilch about online video gaming?

Thankfully, the priestess girl picks this moment to stir in Tristan's arms and opens her large, pretty eyes. She's a native here, so I'm sure she can explain all the basics to our crew of fantasy quest noobs. Maybe she'll even tell us what happens next.

CHAPTER 6

Souffy

Held in arms strong as a horse, soft as a lamb, Souffy feels completely safe and protected. She curls into the warmth and relaxes into the rhythm of the beating heart, the rise and fall of breath, the heady fragrance of flowering jasmine layered over cloves and vanilla. Her eyes flutter open. From above, something… no, someone, golden and heavenly, shines down upon her.

"Are you alright?" His full lips pull back as he speaks to reveal perfect teeth of polished marble. When he smiles, a disarmingly charming dimple forms on his otherwise baby-smooth cheeks.

"Never better," she manages.

"Give her some space, Tristan," another voice says.

Tristan. Souffy repeats the name in her mind, playing with the length and stress on each syllable: Trissss-tan, Tri-stan.

Ever so gently, Tristan—Tri-st-an, Triiis-stan—shifts her into a sitting position against the wall; the smooth cotton of his shirt glides across her forehead. As he steps back, she puzzles at his white-as-fresh-snow shirt, his silk-smooth pants. The others wear similarly simple but elegant apparel, differing only in their color schemes. Except for the menacing one who wears what appears to be a sweater with a hood sewn on. They're staring as hard at her as she is at them. Souffy awkwardly reaches up to smooth out her hair.

She fainted, how embarrassing is that? At least they're all giving her kind, concerned looks, even the Prince of Darkness. Souffy worked so hard on her welcome speech; she'd thought up so many eloquent ways to assuage their confusion, to inspire and guide them into their new lives as heroes. She opens her mouth. "I'm… Souffy." It's all she can manage. A fierce heat spreads across her cheeks. She's profoundly grateful not to have Havelin's fair skin, otherwise she'd have turned pink as a piglet.

What's with all these farm animal comparisons? Her stay in Bydlo is turning her into a country bumpkin. *Focus*, Souffy reprimands herself, *focus*.

"Oh, yeah," says the angelic one, "we should introduce ourselves."

"Official-like. In case Marjorie is live-streaming this," says Tristan. The others nod.

Tristan offers Souffy his hand and pulls her up. Once she's on her feet, he steps back over the railing to rejoin the others inside the summoning circle.

Such odd words, thinks Souffy. Grandmama told her that otherworlders speak in strange ways. But Grandmama also claimed that otherworlders arrived confused and incredulous, with an unending stream of questions about where they were and what had happened. Not so with these heroes. Instead, in a graceful, confident manner (as if they do this all the time) the men form a line with Tristan at the far left.

"Hey there, I'm Tristan." He's looking at her as if she's the only person in the world. Souffy gulps. He breaks the tension with a wink. "But then you already knew that."

"I'm Oscar," says the tall, dark-skinned man. "Nice to be here." He gives a little wave.

"Cole," the Prince of Darkness intones. He smiles a genuine smile, and his eyes squint playfully, erasing any negative impression Souffy may have had.

Next comes the scruffy one with the spiky hair. "Hi, I'm Kyle." His voice is the softest of them all. "We're going to put on a great, um, quest for you!"

"Hello," says the right-most hero in a sing-song voice, "it's Micah!" He raises both hands, palms up, fingers splayed, and vibrates them at her. Souffy, not knowing what else to do, returns the strange greeting. Micah's smile gets even bigger. "And together, we are—"

"Never Boy Land!" they speak as one. They shift into a pose and hold it, perfectly still. It's as if they'd been hit by a Suspend Animation spell. Souffy's younger brother was fond of casting that one on unsuspecting people—usually while they were eating or yawning—and the results were never flattering. Not so with the frozen tableau before her. Exquisite is the word that comes to mind. The heroes' shoulders are relaxed, their hips twisted, their heads tilted, their eyes directed only at her. They make her feel strange things in the pit of her stomach (and lower down).

"Never. Boy. Land," Souffy whispers. If she could, she'd spell the world to stop and replay this moment again and again and—

"Maybe we should knock?" a voice comes from outside.

As Souffy turns to look, the door to the shrine flies open. Reality comes crashing down in the stocky form of Boryk stomping his way through the pews.

"Or, we could just barge in," finishes Havelin. He's tugging helplessly on the folds of Boryk's habit as he's dragged into the apse.

Boryk halts at the sight of the otherworlders. His mouth drops open and his hands fall limp to his sides. He blinks slowly—deliberately—several times. When that fails to clear the heroes from his eyes, he turns to Souffy and doubles the intensity of his scowl. He speaks in a dry, creaky voice, not unlike a hinge rusted after years of disuse, "What. The. F—"

"Vow of silence!" Havelin coughs. Boryk's mouth snaps shut. Getting caught breaking the vow of silence means that you have to start over again. "Oh, look." Havelin's voice is syrupy with fake surprise. "It seems like some otherworld heroes have arrived."

"Yes." Souffy matches his tone. During Boryk's theatrics she's recovered her bearings. "Here they are. May I present to you Tristan, Oscar, Cole, Kyle, and Micah." The heroes relax from their group pose and wave as she speaks their names. "They traveled here from the land of Neverboy to aid us in our hour of need." She turns and gestures. "And this is Havelin and Boryk. Did you bring the Pathfinder wand, Havelin?"

"Yes, it's right…" Havelin looks down at his belt, then vaguely pats his leather pouch. He turns to Boryk who shrugs and shakes his head, visibly disgusted with the proceedings.

Something nearby chitters. Oscar and Cole jump back. Balanced on the railing to their left, sits Cornelius the raccoon. A wand, with a glowing ruby on one end, is clenched between his teeth.

"Cornelius," says Havelin, "that doesn't belong to you." He holds out his hand and advances on the raccoon. In response, Cornelius pivots and scurries along the guardrail. He takes a running leap onto a hanging silk banner and leaves snags in the fabric as he climbs. "Come down this minute! I'm counting to three. One. Two." Cornelius jumps down but away from Havelin, landing in front of Tristan.

"Oooh, is this a talking raccoon?" Tristan coos and leans in dangerously close. "Like in that movie?" Souffy has a nightmare vision of

Tristan's flawless skin being shredded by those claws. Oblivious to the potential carnage, Tristan beckons with his fingers. "Hey there, little guy."

To Souffy's ears, there's something to the tone and timbre of Tristan's voice that causes all other sounds to fall away. Cornelius must be likewise affected because he drops the wand and madly dashes straight into Havelin's open arms.

A miraculously unscathed Tristan kneels to pick up the discarded wand. He stands, as radiant as ever. No, Souffy realizes, more than ever.

"Tristan, you're glowing," says Kyle.

The air around the otherworlder is hazy, burning like a sunset. It softens his already perfect features, backlights his hair with a spun silver sheen, and brings out flecks of gold in his hazel eyes.

"Goodness. He's sparkling!" says Havelin.

"Yes." Souffy sighs dreamily. "Yes he is."

CHAPTER 7

Kyle

So, our band's lead singer is sparkling like an angel or a vampire from a YA romance—take your pick.

"Is this, like, part of the video game, Kyle?" asks Oscar.

"No," I admit. I was hoping for the girl to rattle out a convenient info dump so I could compare this reality to what I know from playing the game. Instead, Souffy and her friends are apparently working through their own drama and are of no help. If I don't give my bandmates something to chew on, they'll be back to assuming we're filming a reality tv show. I pull together what I can. "This circle we're standing in is the summoning circle. That's how new players enter the game, or fantasy world, or whatever this is."

"I vote for whatever-this-is," says Micah.

"Hashtag whatever-this-is," Cole adds, and cracks a smile. Then he realizes he's just agreed with Micah and they both go awkward.

Micah recovers first. "How very last decade."

Cole snorts derisively and turns away.

I attempt to refocus the group. "Anyway, you show up here and are greeted by the…" I stop, realizing that "non player character" might come off as derogatory. Souffy, Havelin, and even that silent, brooding Boryk obviously have their own lives beyond their interactions with us. "…inhabitants and are presented with a starter quest. You can either sign on with an established adventure party, or the system puts together a new group based on everyone's classes."

"Classes?" asks Oscar. "Like, socioeconomic?"

"Yes, classes!" Souffy jumps in. "When the Divine Wisdom blessed the Realm of Mythreal with heroes from other worlds, It saw fit to bestow on them several distinct collections of abilities and talents, to assist them with the challenges and trials they would encounter. Each such collection comprises a class." She evidently recited this speech from memory, but I'm glad not to have to do it in her stead. Plus, she's cute. "The Divine Wisdom has already determined the roles that best fit your dispositions and backgrounds. The Pathfinder wand simply illuminates which class you align with. With my extensive training as a wizard, I know how to decipher it." At this, Havelin gives Souffy a measured look. The silent monk looks like he's swallowed a lemon.

"So, it's like a career aptitude test," says Micah. "This stick will tell you if we're the magical equivalent of a computer programmer or therapist?"

"Or forest ranger?" Cole deadpans, making Tristan, Oscar and me chuckle.

"Oh, I'm a ranger," says Havelin, all serious-like, "and I live in the forest. What's a therapist?"

My bandmates are taking all this surprisingly well. Perhaps they're still in denial? Or maybe they're just chalking it up to one of those things that happens when you're a member of a world-famous boy band, like the time we were performing for a prince in Qatar and a freaking tiger jumped up on stage.

And how am I taking it? I look around and take stock: pagan medieval temple, Souffy and her friends, sapient raccoon, Tris magically lit up like a holiday yard decoration. The geek part of me badly wants this to be real, wants this fantasy-magic world to actually exist behind my favorite "online nerd game." Meanwhile, the logical voice in my head is humming loudly in order not to consider the consequences of such an outcome—little things like the existence of deadly monsters and how unlikely it is that this Divine Wisdom grants respawns.

"So, how does this work?" asks Tristan. He's still fingering the wand. "Do I just point it at myself and ask 'what class am I?'"

"Not exactly," says Souffy even as Tristan points the wand at himself. A floating, glowing screen with text in an ornate font pops up over his head. Is this evidence that we *are* in a video game?

"Dude, it says you're a level one fighter," says Oscar.

Souffy squints, confused, at us all looking up. I'm guessing she can't see the display stats. I wonder if it would be a faux pas to discuss this hack/bug/hashtag whatever-this-is to the world's inhabitants?

The contents of the screen then scroll to list his skills (athletics, performance, and persuasion), inventory (empty, save for his clothes, watch, and sunglasses), and attributes (surprise, surprise, Tristan's charisma is at eighteen).

"May I?" Souffy holds out her hand for the wand. When Tristan passes it to her, the display screen over his head winks out of existence, and he—thankfully—stops doing the lightbulb thing. I decide the stat screen is a level of weirdness that I'm not dealing with right now.

Souffy pulls out a scrap of paper and reads it silently, lips moving. She takes a step back, mutters some nonsense syllables, and traces an elegant series of circles and crosses with her hand, punctuating her gestures with crisp flicks of the wrist that make her bracelet bangles clink pleasantly.

After a few moments of nothing whatsoever happening, she says, "Oh, drat, wrong direction." She repeats her previous actions but clockwise this time. The wand in her hand finally flickers blue. "Fighter," she proclaims, then frowns. "How did you know?"

"My aunt runs a kendo dojo," Tristan volunteers. "She placed a bamboo shinai in my hand when I was four. I made Yondan two years ago." Which doesn't even come close to answering Souffy's question, but everyone nods in agreement, because… because Tristan.

Breathe in, Kyle. Breathe out. Let it go.

From what I've observed so far—the circle we're standing in, Souffy's spiel, and Tris's stats sheet—it's likely that the rules of this world are similar to the *Heroes Summoning* game mechanics. Killing monsters and completing quests will reward us with experience points and allow us to level up, hopefully on an accelerated schedule because I doubt we'll be saving the world as level ones. Tristan's class assignment as fighter is grounded in his real-world experience, and—let's face it—because it's always the guy with the big sword who's the front and center of any hero party. If the Divine Wisdom wants to give us a fighting chance of success, It will bestow on us different classes to maximize our combat potential. I look over the remainder of my non-gaming bandmates and wonder who will score the choicest class.

"Okay, who's next?" asks Tristan.

Oscar volunteers. He's such a good human being that I wouldn't be surprised if he ended up being a paladin. Only I hope not because I don't think he could pull a sword out of its sheath, much less swing it. I don't have to wait long. Souffy gets the incantation correct this time, and a golden flame envelopes the wand. "Oh, you're a cleric," she says.

That makes sense; Oscar's the only one of us who's religious. Souffy's shoulders visibly slump. she's obviously disappointed with this outcome. Meanwhile, a grin breaks through Boryk's perma-scowl.

"What's a cleric?" asks Oscar.

"It's like a priest," I explain, "with your prayers working like magic spells, miracles I suppose. They're mostly for protection and healing, but you can cast some spells that cause actual damage. It depends on which of the gods you pick to be in the service of." Or maybe in this Mythreal the gods do the choosing. They're gods after all.

"Gods. Plural?" Oscar's eyebrow shoots up.

"Twelve gods. They're like the Greek Pantheon," I reply, but Boryk shakes his head and flashes me five fingers twice followed by three. "Thirteen. Thirteen gods," I correct myself. I glance down at the twelve symbols in the circle and decide that sorting out Mythreals theology isn't critical at this juncture.

"My Gram is *not* going to be happy about this," says Oscar, frowning.

"I'll go next," says Micah.

Mumble, mumble, flick, jingle, flick, jingle. The wand tip glows green. "Ranger," Souffy pronounces. On hearing this, Havelin stands taller—he may be up on the balls of his feet. I wasn't expecting Micah to become a defender of nature and warrior of the wilderness. He grew up in San Francisco, never left the comforts of the city, and is known for always staying out of direct sunlight to protect his complexion.

Cole snickers. "Forest Ranger."

"Probably better than what you'll get," Micah snipes back.

Cole advances towards Souffy and she instinctively takes a step back. She hasn't yet discovered that Cole's habitual scowl masks a sensitive soul. Souffy recovers and does the wand thing again. Jingle, jingle. She's got it down. But for some reason, the tip stays dark this time.

"Guess you don't get to play," says Micah. His dulcet voice drips with saccharine. A bit of Cole's I-don't-care swagger slips away.

"No, no, it's working," says Souffy. "It's just glowing black." She pauses, puzzled. "But that means… Cole's a rogue." She looks positively perplexed now. "I've never heard of an otherworlder becoming a rogue."

Cole turns to me. "What's a rogue?"

"It's like a thief," I begin but realize that might not sound very appealing. "Or an assassin." That sounds even worse.

"Figures."

"It's a popular class. You get to do a lot of cool stuff, like pick locks, sneak around, and wear all black," I say.

"So, I'm the bad guy?"

"Yeah, but you're OUR bad guy," says Oscar.

"Thief with a heart of gold," adds Tristan.

And now it's my turn. I've been holding myself back on purpose, like when you leave the most promising Christmas gift under the tree for last, because there's no way it will be what you really wanted. So long as it sits unopened, you can pretend. I force myself to march forward. Souffy waves her hands around once again, and the whole wand turns red.

"You're a wizard, like me! That's great, every party needs a wizard." She's right. We'd be screwed without a wizard. I feel something colossal yet immaterial shift inside me, and the air suddenly feels different. I sense the latent magic all around us, just waiting for me to unlock it. The secrets of the universe are calling. Who wouldn't want this?

"Way to go, Kyle!" Tristan gives me a brotherly slap on the back. "You'll be an awesome wizard."

"Yeah," I say. My smile is firmly glued back in place. I knew all along that I wasn't going to get what I really wanted. Still sucks.

"Alright, on with our quest then." Tristan turns questioningly to Souffy.

"Yes…" Oh man, Souffy's poker face sucks. "Your quest."

A rising sequence of chimes (that my brain immediately identifies as C–E–G–C) saves Souffy from having to deliver the bad news. The sound appears to come at us from every direction at once.

The chimes are then replaced by a voice. "Apologies for the intrusion, citizens." The crisp, distinct words likewise seem to emanate from the shrine's ceiling and painted walls. "Magistrate Nevus requests the immediate presence of Souffy Ravenus in her chambers."

At this, Souffy positively cringes.

The magical PA system continues, "Magistrate Nevus also wishes to convey that she knows Miss Ravenus is currently in the Hero Shrine and that the city guards have been dispatched to assist with her timely arrival."

CHAPTER 8

Dryden

"Magistrate Nevus also wishes to convey that she knows Miss Ravenus is currently in the Hero Shrine and that the city guards have been dispatched to assist with her timely arrival." The voice of the town's proclamation annunciation system booms from the walls of the Church of the Twelve and nearby buildings.

Dryden Larkus wishes he could sneak into the shrine and catch Souffy magic-handed. But at least this way everyone in the town will know that Souffy is up to something she shouldn't be doing. Again. Also, the last time the guards attempted to apprehend Souffy mid-casting, it was in a bakery, and it got messy. Dryden still hasn't managed to clean out all the dried frosting from the crevices in his plate armor.

"Let's go." He motions to Orley and two other guards Lenora assigned to him when she charged him with retrieving Souffy. They leave the cover of the church and head out onto the seawall.

Somehow, Dryden always gets assigned to Souffy problems. It's been just over three years since he enlisted in the regiment, so he doesn't expect to be busting up smuggling rings or even reporting on druid activities in the north, but he likes to think that his training and talents could be put to better use than damage control for a wizard school dropout. Although infiltrating the Hero Shrine when the Divine Wisdom has sent heroes to Bydlo is a step up from her usual mischief. He almost finds himself admiring her gutsiness but stops himself in time. Souffy is trouble, Dryden reminds himself. Trouble.

He sees her leaving the shrine wearing what Havelin calls her "elf outfit." Dryden is unsurprised to see the ranger with her, but Boryk's here too. Did she invite everyone but him?

"Dryden!" Souffy shouts as she rushes up to him. Dryden, oddly pleased that she recognized him in full armor, stands a little taller. He's just being professional.

"Uncertified Wizard Souffy Ravenus, we are here to escort you to Magistrate Nevus."

"Yes, but—" She's trying to talk her way out of it, like she always does.

"You got caught. You know what happens next." A slap on the wrist and some community service hours, unfortunately. Just once, Dryden wishes the magistrate or the mayor would lock Souffy away in the dungeon. The fort has one after all. But then Bydlo would be without its one decent magic instructor.

"I know, Dryden." She tugs at his arm. "But look!" Over by the shrine, five more individuals have emerged.

"Just how many people did you rope into this scheme?" Dryden's plan is only to collect Souffy—no need to get Havelin or Boryk in trouble—but matters have evidently gone out of hand. He turns to Orley, "Go tell Magistrate Nevus we've got too many trespassers to fit in her office."

"They're not trespassers, Dryden. These are the heroes!"

"Heroes?" Dryden considers the young men standing in front of the shrine. Their clothing doesn't match any style he's seen on visitors from other parts of Ozema. Maybe they're from the southern continent? Still, something isn't right. These heroes don't have the rugged, disheveled look of seasoned adventurers. "Them? Where are their weapons? And what are they wearing?" It doesn't look like armor or anything practical.

"They're otherworlders!" Now Souffy is acting exasperated, as if Dryden is the one being slow.

"Like the Triad of Valor?" Dryden grew up hearing stories and ballads of the greatest heroes ever to set foot in Bydlo. But he's pretty sure they brought weapons with them.

"Yes, they were sent here by the Divine Wisdom! Something very bad is coming, and they'll be the ones to save us. That's why I released them from the portal."

"You released them? You mean, you used magic?" Dryden scans the shrine. It appears to be in one piece and none of the windows have been blown out.

"Who else? And I did a good job. I even found out what classes they belong to. Tristan's a fighter and Oscar…"

Souffy's words wash over Dryden as he considers this new information. Somehow, Souffy managed not to mangle the spell that brought these otherworld heroes into Bydlo. That the spell hadn't caused any collateral damage is almost more unbelievable than the presence of the heroes.

Meanwhile, the otherworlders are walking towards him. The tall blond one has the musculature of an adventurer; the others have less meat on their bones. Dryden recalls that the members of the Triad were all siblings. These otherworlders don't look related, although there is a unifying quality to them. Dryden frowns as he figures out what it is. They're all uncannily handsome. Of course, Souffy would prioritize good-looking otherworlders.

"You opened the portal when you weren't supposed to, Souffy. You're in big trouble." Shock and confusion spreads across the otherworlders' oh-so-attractive faces. Dryden smirks as he shouts, "You all, you're coming with us."

CHAPTER 9

Kyle

Well this is a first, we've never been arrested before. Protective custody doesn't count.

"We're all going up to the fortress now for your official welcome," Souffy lies. I like her chutzpah. She'd do great in the entertainment industry. Souffy takes the lead, arguing with the obviously pissed-off guard (I think his name is Dryden) as we walk along the narrow land bridge. I gaze inland to see the Germanic town rising up the hill. To my left, the land flattens out into a harbor; to the right it's hemmed in by a cliff. It reminds me of a West Coast beach town, without the tourists or the mansions dotting the hills. I do see a gray stone something further up the cliff that I'd bet money is the fortress that is our destination. Boryk and the other two guards trail behind, which leaves us with the ranger, Havelin.

"So, is this your first time traveling to a different world?" he asks.

"Yes, how could you tell?"

"I just, well, I mean," he sputters.

"It's okay, I'm joking." I grin and he relaxes. "This is a brand-new experience for us."

As if to prove my point, Tristan lets out a low whistle. "This place... Wow."

We're falling behind Souffy and Dryden, but my bandmates are looking everywhere except down. They'd probably trip and land in the surf if I try to rush them. Also, I suspect this is the point where it's sinking in that we really are in a different world. I wonder how they'll take it. Part of being famous—of living a celebrity lifestyle—is acting natural and not losing your head regardless of the circumstances. We've had to gently extricate ourselves from potentially deranged fans, humor batshit crazy "visions" from "genius" video directors, and in every interview, every meet & greet, smile and laugh like we're totally stoked to be there. Still, Mythreal is on another level on the freakout scale.

"I can feel a breeze!" says Oscar.

"And that briny ocean smell, totally legit," says Cole.

"There's no distortion; everything's in perfect focus," says Micah.

They turn to each other, eyes wide, mouths hanging open. I hold my breath.

"Can you believe they constructed all this for us?" asks Tristan. He hasn't gotten it.

But the rest of them have.

"I don't think anyone constructed this, Tristan," says Oscar while Micah nods.

"Kyle's right," says Cole. "This is fucking real!"

Then they all start talking over each other. I should really interject myself into the conversation to reassure and talk them through the paradigm shift. But I'm feeling selfish. I mean, we just arrived in a magical fantasy world. I kind of want to play tourist and savor the experience.

We're passing a stone church with writing carved above the door. Some part of my brain is telling me it's not English, although I have no problem reading it: The Church of the Twelve Gods. So how did Boryk get thirteen, maybe he's counting the Divine Wisdom? I'm starting to recall bits of Mythreal's mythology. Back in the world's prehistory, there was an epic Ragnarok-level god-war, and when the dust settled, the remaining gods created the Divine Wisdom to be an all-powerful judge to keep them and the rest of creation in line. If your gods are real, that's not a bad theological setup.

Beside me, Havelin is glancing uncomfortably at my bandmates and their confusion. We're now about half a block behind Souffy and Dryden.

"I'm sure they'll explain everything when we get to the fortress," I tell the others. "Let's keep moving so we don't get left behind." To Havelin I say, "They need a moment to process."

He nods, grateful that we're walking faster.

"So, where exactly are we?" I ask.

"Oh, this is Bydlo."

I've never been on a *Heroes Summoning* quest set in Bydlo.

"What country is it in?"

"Ozema."

"Okay." I have heard of Ozema. It was one of the countries in the original online version back in the early 2000s. By the time I started playing, there had been a massive story overhaul and the new release shifted the action to the southern continent. According to the older gamers on the server, those Ozema adventures (basic by modern standards) had been bleeding edge at the time.

We've entered into Bydlo proper now. It's a quintessential medieval town, with half-timbered houses and shops built to the edge of narrow cobblestone streets and everything crammed together in ways that would never pass modern building codes. Townsfolk dressed in petticoats and jerkins cluster on corners and lean out of windows. They stare openly at us, making no attempt to hide their curiosity. The whole thing reminds me of the time I visited Tristan on his movie set—when they were filming the fourteenth-century scenes, not the future time travel ones—and the extras were all milling about between takes.

The differences, besides the staff running around and peasants consuming soft drinks, are in the smells. On the soundstage, the AC blasted stale air tinged with fresh paint and WD-40 for greasing the camera-track scaffolding, while the actors, despite the makeup and costumes that implied they hadn't bathed in a week, actually smelled of floral haircare products and Axe Body Spray. Bydlo's olfactory palate is reminiscent of the final day of an August outdoor music festival—sour sweat, rotting trash, and porta potties in need of emptying—mixed with barn animal odor, hay, and burnt wood. That last one stings my eyes and I hear Micah cough. Fortunately the air clears out as we climb the hill towards the fortress.

"Is the magistrate like your mayor?" I ask Havelin. Government isn't really a thing in *Heroes Summoning,* unless you're taking down an evil overlord.

"Oh no, the magistrate is appointed by the King. Our mayor is elected by the city council."

"So you have both?" Oscar joins in.

Oscar asking questions hopefully means he's passed the shock and awe stage and is on board with hashtag whatever-this-is. In which case, Cole and Micah will follow his lead. That leaves Tristan. He's smiling the same eager horse grin he had plastered on throughout his movie—Tristan's idea of acting—and I catch him winking at a gaggle of shopgirls who have been not-so-discreetly following us. Guess he's found his coping mechanism.

I turn back to Oscar's point and ask, "Yeah, how does that work?"

Havelin's face darkens. "Not so well."

We leave the town and our followers behind and crest the hill for our first unobstructed view of our destination. Calling it a fortress doesn't do it justice; it's a full-blown medieval castle. My brain keeps upping its size estimate the closer we get. It's easily as big as a sports stadium with massive stone walls, imposing towers, and a moat, although there's no water. The gate has a portcullis and as we pass through the arch I see the holes in the ceiling for pouring boiling oil on invaders. Despite its military design, inside the walls things look more civilian. There's a vegetable garden and several chickens running about.

Havelin points out the various buildings. "These are the barracks. You can see the stables behind them. The tower in the back is where Souffy teaches classes." The tower is square with a high-peaked roof, and it looms over the rest of the fortress. The other structures Havelin points out are similar in their style to the buildings we passed in Bydlo, but the tower is constructed from the same ancient gray stone of the walls. As we proceed deeper into the fortress, I realize it's actually part of the wall.

"The whole tower's a school?" asks Micah.

"No," Havelin says, "just the top two stories. The rest is used for storage. And this is what we call the Commandant's House."

In the center of the courtyard is a grand house—a mansion really—with a red brick facade and arched windows. Souffy and Dryden stand at the top of an imposing staircase. Behind them the double doors have been propped open. They beckon us to follow them inside. My eyes take a moment to adjust to the dim lantern light. We're in a large, grandly appointed room with dark wood paneling, parquet floor, and several crystal chandeliers. Along with the female guard from earlier, there are two other women in the room. One is older with her hair done up in complicated braids and she sits in a high back chair on the raised dais; the other is relegated to a desk. I'm guessing the one on the almost-a-throne is Magistrate Nevus and the other is probably her clerk or secretary.

"So the magistrate's a woman," says Cole. "Progressive."

"Yes, that's Lenora Nevus," whispers Havelin. His healthy tan has turned pale and his eyes dart between Lenora and Souffy. How much trouble has Souffy gotten herself—and possibly us—into? The magistrate is giving us a long hard stare.

"Who are these people?" She turns to Souffy but Dryden rushes in to speak first.

"They are otherworlders, Magistrate. When I apprehended Souffy she admitted to letting them out of the portal."

"What an asshat." Micah's barely audible insult echoes my thoughts.

"Souffy, is this true?" Lenora asks.

Souffy fidgets for a moment before answering "Yes."

"Even after I explicitly instructed you to wait?"

Another pause. "Yes."

Lenora sighs loudly enough for everyone in the chamber to hear. "I wish I could say I was surprised." She rubs her eyes and turns to her clerk. "Please enter into the record that Souffy Ravenus admits to unauthorized spellcasting in a restricted magic zone." She turns back. "That's not just a civic misdemeanor. There will be consequences, Souffy. And for you two as well." Her gaze drills into Havelin and Boryk.

"What will our punishment be?" Havelin asks. He looks resigned but not stricken. With each of Lenora's pronouncements, I'm less and less worried that anyone's going to be subjected to cruel or unusual punishment.

"There are many tasks around town that would benefit from community service." Lenora looks to her clerk who gives an enthusiastic nod. "Many, many tasks."

That doesn't sound too bad, as long as it's not cleaning out latrines or something. Still, if it weren't for Souffy, we'd still be stuck between worlds. I'm trying to think of something we can do for her when I see Oscar take a step forward.

"Um, excuse me ma'am." He gives a slight bow followed by a toothy white smile. "It sounds like Souffy should have waited. But as I understand it, your Divine Wisdom transported us here for a quest and the sooner we complete it, the better off everyone will be, correct?"

Lenora's disapproving look softens. Tristan may be the one to make the ladies swoon, but Oscar's the one to charm them senseless. "Pray tell me your name, hero."

"Oscar, Oscar Jones, Your Magistrate. And these are my band—uh, my quest-mates." He takes a step back and gracefully motions to each of us. "Our ranger, Micah Cardigan. Our wizard, Kyle Moretti. Cole Silva is our rogue, and this is our fighter, Tristan Ives. Oh, and I'm the cleric." He flashes another dazzling smile.

"Fitting." Lenora looks to her scribe who nods in acknowledgment that she'd written it all down. "Well, Oscar," the magistrate continues, "you make a valid point. And, had someone petitioned me with a wrong that required the summoning of heroes, then you'd be correct. Time would indeed be of the essence. Or, were there an obvious danger threatening the town or surrounding areas, then of course I would have had you released immediately."

She turns to her scribe. "Have there been any formal petitions? Either sent to my office, or submitted on parchment at the Hero Shrine?"

"No, Magistrate."

"And, in my most recent report to the King's Council, did I report any disturbances or potential issues?"

"You mentioned a rat infestation in the granary but also that Wizard Ferimus had the problem under control with his magical mouse traps."

"Thank you." Lenora looks back at us. "So, you see, Oscar"—then she turns to Souffy—"Bydlo has no need for heroic services."

I won't deny that I'm relieved that the village isn't under the imminent threat of an orc invasion or anything, but Bydlo not needing heroes is something of a letdown.

"You mean your Divine Wisdom messed up?" Cole says. He's not smiling.

Lenora's response is steely. "The Divine Wisdom does not 'mess up,' although Its will, under these circumstances, is on the ineffable end of the scale. Sorting it out is outside my appointed duties. I expect that somebody from the King's Council or the Ravenus College of Wizards will be able to figure it out. There's a ship leaving within the week that can take you to the capital."

"You're sending them away?" Souffy wails. I think we may have scored our first Mythreal fangirl.

"I'm sending them to where they can do the most good," counters the magistrate.

"No," booms a new voice, "where they can do the most good is right here in Bydlo!"

In strides a well-fed, middle-aged man. His clothing is a step above what I saw on the townsfolk, both in terms of tailoring and flamboyance— yellow hose and a starched neck ruff. A quick glance at our resident fashionista, Micah, confirms that the newcomer is pulling off the look. With an easy confidence, he makes his way into the middle of the chamber.

"Mr. Mayor, I believe this is a matter of importance to the kingdom, not the local administration." Lenora gives him a tight smile.

"Stuff and nonsense, Madam Magistrate. They weren't sent to the capital." He flings his hand dramatically in our direction. "They were sent right here!" He points emphatically at the ground. "The Divine Wisdom saw a need for them in Bydlo."

"And what need is that? Please enlighten us, Galam."

"Why, we have all manner of urgent needs. Once the news gets out that the heroes have arrived, we'll have petitioners up to our ears!"

"Asking for what, precisely?" Lenora stands. She isn't much taller than Havelin, but like the small powerful women I've met in our world, she doesn't need height to assert herself. "Collecting rare herbs in the forest? Finding lost treasure? Running messages between fishing villages?"

"Indeed! What you mention are all useful ways to gain experience and become familiar with our world. And think of all those people in need, coming into town, raising our prestige, spending their money, here, in Bydlo."

"You want to display these heroes like a sideshow attraction?"

"Display? What an innovative idea, Lenora." Galam snaps his fingers, "I hadn't even considered that, but your womanly instincts are onto something there."

"My womanly what?"

Galam spins towards us and frames us with his fingers. "These otherworlders are astoundingly attractive. Perchance the beneficiaries of their quest would like to purchase a likeness of the heroes on a painting—or maybe etched into a plate—to remember them by. Why, I'd buy one even without a quest. Don't you think it might look good over the fireplace?"

"Next you'll be wanting them to perform songs and dances for profit."

"That's even better!" Galam turns to Tristan. "Do you know how to sing or dance?"

Tristan grins. "Oh, do we ever."

"You don't need to humor him." Lenora wedges herself between Tristan and Galam.

"Oh, it's alright," says Micah. "Marjorie Banks' Second Law of Boy Bands: *Never say no to an opportunity for self-promotion.*"

"So long as you follow Law Number One: *Always have legal read the contract first,*" adds Cole.

The mayor and magistrate aren't listening. Lenora grabs a handful of Galam's elaborate neck ruff and yanks him down to her eye level. "This is lunacy, even for someone as addled as you, Galam Nevus. I will not have such shame brought on my town!"

"Last time I checked, my dearest, I was the one elected mayor."

Wait a sec. "Galam Nevus? Are they…"

"Married?" Havelin sighs. "Yes."

CHAPTER 10

Souffy

The argument between magistrate and mayor continues to devolve with references to past slights, broken promises, and poorly chosen anniversary gifts. Souffy casually twirls her copper earring and flicks her little finger in Havelin's direction across the room. "I have to agree with Lenora," she mentally speaks, using the Missive cantrip. "A wheelbarrow, even a monogrammed one, is in poor taste."

She waits for Havelin to crack a smile. Instead, the Neverboylander, Kyle, turns and regards her curiously. "Souffy, is that you in my head?" His words are clear in her mind.

She gulps and thinks, "Oops, sorry. That was meant for Havelin."

"Is this telepathy? Are you reading my mind? And what does—" the spell cuts out mid-phrase.

Souffy twirls her finger and points again, not bothering to conceal her casting this time. "No, it's just a cantrip for sending short messages."

"Ahh, that's useful." He winks at her.

Accusations between the mayor and magistrate continue to fly, but all Souffy can hear is her own hammering heart. She Missives, "Maybe I could teach you later on?"

Kyle doesn't respond, and Souffy is at a loss to decipher his expression. Is he composing a reply, or did he lose interest? The moment stretches on and on, and then she hears in her ear, "Thumbs-up emoji."

Perplexing, but he's smiling, so his response probably means yes. She is about to ask for clarification when Lenora's voice—pitched so low it's almost a growl—cuts through Souffy's distracted thoughts.

"Enough!"

Instinctively, Souffy drops her hands and stands straighter. Thankfully, the magistrate's focus is still on Galam.

"In four days' time, Galam, the Seolia will return from Rozney Las. She will be loaded up and ready to sail south a day or two later. And by Lyr's flame, the heroes will be on that ship!" Lenora folds her arms, waiting. Quiet descends upon the hall as Bydlo's power couple squares off.

Galam meets Lenora's glare with a smile. "So, you're saying that I can have them for almost a week? Unless, that is, you were planning to keep them for yourself."

One week. Souffy looks at Kyle and the others. It isn't much, but it's something. She gives a quick prayer to whatever god might be listening that Galam will let her help out with his plans for the otherworlders.

Lenora throws up her hands. "Fine. Take them. Dress them up, parade them around, give them the keys to the town. I wash my hands of this insanity." She stalks over to her clerk.

"Did you hear that, lads? Time to get you looking like true heroes!" Galam says. "Lenora, may I borrow Dryden for some acquisitions from the armory?"

"That's crown property." Dryden looks beseechingly towards Lenora. Souffy also expects her to voice an objection, but the fight has gone out of her.

"The heroes are here as guests of our nation. We will, of course, make sure they are properly attired. Just make sure you draw up an itemized list." A bit of liveliness returns to her face. "Oh, and Souffy, please stay. You and I have things to discuss."

Souffy watches as the heroes follow the mayor and Dryden—Dryden of all people—out of the room. Kyle gives her a long backward glance, but she doesn't risk sending him a message now. She wouldn't even know what to say. Magistrate Nevus is in conversation with her clerk, whom she then sends out with Boryk and Havelin. Now it's just Souffy and Lenora in the chamber.

"Let's go to my office, Souffy." Lenora's tone is soft. Souffy follows. Each step feels like she's being led to the gallows.

Up in her office, Lenora motions for Souffy to sit in the high-backed chair closest to her desk, and she busies herself as if Souffy isn't there. She shuts the heavy wooden door, opens the shuttered window, and examines a stack of papers before finally seating herself behind her desk. Still not looking at Souffy, Lenora opens the ink pot, dips her quill, and begins to write on a fresh sheet of parchment.

Scritch, scritch, scritch goes the quill until Souffy can be quiet no longer.

"You said you wanted to discuss something?"

"Yes, your punishment." Lenora doesn't look up. "Community service. I'm writing up the order so you can start right away." Scritch, scritch.

"Wait. What, now?" This was the absolute worst! Lenora clearly planned to saddle her with some drudgery that would take days and days, and by the time Souffy finished, the heroes would be gone.

"Yes, now. It's an urgent need that can't be put off."

Souffy feels tears welling up. It's too unfair.

Lenora sighs. "Souffy, actions have consequences. You're old enough to know that."

"Yes," Souffy replies. She's a Ravenus wizard, she won't cry.

Lenora carefully blots the parchment and hands it to Souffy, who braces herself for a week of sorting paperwork in a windowless closet.

"By order of Magistrate Nevus," the parchment text starts. It's followed by the usual official proclamation flourishes. Souffy skims until she sees her name. "Unaccredited Wizard Souffy Ravenus is hereby assigned to serve as Liaison Officer to the Heroes of Neverboyland for the entirety of their stay in Bydlo. Her duties shall include, but not necessarily be limited to, caring for their well-being, educating them in the ways and history of Ozema, and preparing them for their duties as the successors to the Heroes of the Realm."

Souffy wipes her eyes. She re-reads the entire document, carefully this time. "But I thought the mayor would—"

"Cart them around like show ponies? Yes, that's his plan." Lenora presses her hand to her forehead. "Galam means well, but using the otherworlders purely as economic stimulus is shortsighted. At best, they'll look the part and make fools of themselves. At worst, it might hinder their ability to fulfill the Divine Wisdom's intended quest, one that almost certainly won't take place in Bydlo."

Souffy knows that. Nothing ever happens in Bydlo. It wouldn't be fair to the heroes to force them to stay and perform for the locals. "So, you want me to make sure he doesn't keep them here, that they're on that ship when it leaves?"

"No, I can get them on the Seolia. What I need is for you to make sure that by the time they leave, they're proper heroes, and not just otherworlders playing dress-up."

Souffy's imagination is momentarily hijacked by the image of a dolled-up Tristan heroically wielding a sword, and then, for some reason, his shirt buttons fall off. She manages to stop those thoughts before they veer off into improper territory and focuses back on what Lenora is saying.

"Weapon training for the fighter and ranger should be straightforward. As for the rogue? Honestly, it would probably be best if he does just play dress-up. But the magic users need to know how to cast spells. I need your experience."

"My experience casting spells that don't work?"

"Oh, for the love of Verhalty! Souffy, your grandmother was a sorceress who campaigned with the Heroes of the Realm. Your uncle told me you were captivated by her stories, that she even took you to meet the paladin, Martin Wu. According to your transcripts"—Lenora shuffles through the papers on her desk—"you took a class in otherworld meta-magic and apparently scored top marks. That's more experience right there than the rest of this town combined."

It's too good to be true. It has to be a trap.

"But what if I…" She tries to remember the quaint term the otherworlders used. "Mess up?"

"Is that what you're worried about?" asks Lenora.

If she's being honest with herself, Souffy hasn't thought enough about what she'd be doing after she freed the otherworlders to worry about doing it poorly. But with Lenora's offer—order really—it's possible that Souffy could do real damage, and not just to herself, but to the heroes.

Lenora sighs. "Souffy, why do you think you ended up in Bydlo?"

"I had to be kept away from bad influences and give my full attention to studying for my wizard exams." These were her grandfather's words. Souffy has heard them so often they roll off her tongue.

"Is that what you really think?"

Souffy's head shoots up at the tone. Lenora is looking straight at her. Snippets of overheard comments coalesce into a horrible truth that Souffy has long known, but never dared to speak aloud. "It was because they were ashamed of me, of a Ravenus wizard who couldn't even manage a simple Charm spell, who would probably flunk out of the school of magic her great-grandfather had founded, and who would just be an embarrassment to the family name if she stayed around."

She'd grown up knowing that she would never match her older sister for studiousness, or her younger brother for talent. The only thing that made her stand out was being a failure. She looks down, embarrassed.

"From what I've heard Ferimus say about his family, you're probably correct. But Souffy, you're an adult now. That means it's up to you to choose your path in this world." Lenora somehow looks both earnest and exasperated as she continues, "Or you can let someone else write the story of your life. It's your choice. So, tell me, why do you really think you ended up in Bydlo?"

Souffy is flooded with the same feeling as earlier this morning in the tower, that certainty she felt as she unlocked the portal. "Maybe, the Divine Wisdom wanted it to be me to free the heroes?" she whispers, amazed that she has the audacity to speak such a thing aloud. She squeezes her eyes shut and tenses, expecting a lightning bolt to smite her for hubris. Theologically, lightning and thunder fall under the domain of Kalimos, but the Divine Wisdom holds power over all the gods. After a moment in which no smiting occurs, she takes courage and repeats in a louder voice, "Maybe the Divine Wisdom wanted me to free the heroes. To guide them and assist them in this world and help them complete their quest."

"Well said."

Souffy shivers. She often imagined herself doing great things, but it was always in her head. Saying it aloud to Lenora makes it real.

The magistrate continues, "What's important is that you believe it. And believe it for yourself, not just in this room in front of me. You understand?"

"Yes, I will." Souffy walked into this room expecting Lenora to be her executioner, but instead, the magistrate has turned into a fairy godmother. "Thank you."

"Well, this has to be the most unexpected thing to happen today: Souffy Ravenus thanking me. Now, get out there and guide those heroes."

Souffy nods and heads to the door. She pauses before leaving. "Wait, just so I'm clear on this, my punishment for disobeying you is to help and guide the heroes?"

"Yes, and if you do a bad job, there will be a punishment for your punishment." This is the Magistrate Nevus Souffy is familiar with.

"Then I'll do a great job!"

Then I'll do a great job, she repeats to herself as she heads for the stairs. When she leaves the Commandant's House, she spots Havelin across the yard. Not bothering with being sneaky, she openly twirls her copper earring and points at her friend.

"Havelin," she sends, "you're never going to believe this!"

Before she can say more, Havelin waves and shouts. "Souffy, come quick! You've got to see the heroes!"

Souffy runs to where Havelin is standing in front of the stables with Dryden and Boryk. She's never seen Dryden look so sour. He's making Boryk—pursed-lipped, squinty-eyed Boryk—appear as a cheerful potato in comparison.

Havelin speaks rapidly, "So, Dryden wanted to provision them in this boring armor—"

"Practical armor," Dryden interjects.

"—But then, do you remember last year when that troupe of actors tried to sneak out of town when they couldn't cover their debts, and how the magistrate confiscated the wagon with all their props? Well, Cole found these trunks full of costumes."

"They look idiotic," says Dryden.

"Pshah! They look fabulous!" says Galam, emerging from the barracks across the courtyard. "You're just in time for their, uh… they're calling it a 'fashion show.' I assume you're familiar with this otherworlder ritual?" he asks Souffy.

I'm the expert, Souffy reminds herself, *the Divine Wisdom's chosen one.* "There are many strange and wondrous customs in the other worlds," she pronounces, trying to sound wise and learned.

"Marvelous. They asked me to read this," says Galam. He unfolds a sheet of paper. "Shall I begin?"

"Please do!" comes Micah's voice from the barracks.

"We now present," Galam reads solemnly, "the latest Never Boy Land fashion collection: 'New Heroes of the Realm.' First off, ready to charge into battle against mythical monsters and dastardly dragons, Tristan Ives!"

Out comes Tristan. Souffy gasps. It's now clear what has put Dryden in such a foul mood. Tristan is wearing parts of a standard-issue soldier's plate mail, but not in any configuration Souffy is familiar with. He's somehow fitted the breastplate beneath his cropped jacket while the shoulder pauldrons and other bits of armor protecting various joints are somehow strapped to the outside of his clothing. He wears multiple belts, one of which holds an impressive longsword with an ornate hilt and scabbard. The remaining armor plate typically worn by soldiers is nowhere to be seen, allowing Souffy to appreciate Tristan's well-defined body.

"Don't worry, he's wearing chainmail underneath most of it," says Havelin.

"So that he'll look pretty the first time somebody slashes him through the middle," says Dryden, unimpressed.

"He does look good!" Oops, Souffy realizes she spoke her thoughts out loud.

Tristan smiles and starts toward them. He doesn't move in that awkward, jerky manner of a newly recruited soldier. Rather his strides are long, confident, bounding with energy. He comes to an abrupt stop a few feet from them and, shifting his stance, strikes several attractive poses.

He flashes the inside lining of his indigo jacket. "Check it out, Souffy. Blue, just like the Pathfinder wand!" Then he pivots gracefully on one foot and strolls away. Souffy watches him leave, telling herself she's simply appreciating the aesthetics of his new look from the backside.

Galam frowns and squints at the sheet he's holding. "Someone's written something in the margin…" He mouths some words. "Okay, I've got it. Next, straight from patrolling the forest with his friend Smokey the Bear—"

"Hey! That's not funny, Cole!" Souffy hears a voice that sounds like Micah's, but less sweet than usual.

Disregarding the muted angry voices that might be an argument, Galam continues, "We present Ranger Micah Cardigan."

Micah strolls out, remnants of thin-lipped tension melting into an expression of angelic sweetness. His gait is similar to Tristan's, but a bit brisker, with an exaggerated precision to the way he swings his arms.

Souffy recognizes Micah's leather armor. It's the one she had donned for an archery contest the previous spring. Her condition for agreeing to compete was that her uncle spell the boring guard uniform into something trimmer and more stylish. Souffy thought—and Havelin agreed—that she cut quite the fine figure in the engraved leather top and tasset. But Micah wears it better. He too has multiple belts (Souffy supposes it's the standard in their world) and is armed with a quiver and elegant bow. A flowing green cape with gold embroidery completes his outfit. Micah executes his turn in the same spot Tristan had, his cloak billowing around him despite the lack of any detectable breeze.

"And here comes Cleric Oscar Jones!" continues Galam.

Oscar's step is positively bouncy, despite his heavy plate mail. Even with the armor, he wouldn't be mistaken for a common fighter. The untarnished gleam of the metal, the immaculate condition of the fabrics, not to mention the gold trim, mark him as a holy warrior. He stops, strikes a pose, and turns back.

"He said he wanted as much protection as he could bear to carry. The cape was for something called 'flair,'" says Havelin.

"The gods will be duking it out to recruit him as their follower," remarks Galam. "Next up, this rogue is going to steal your heart! Presenting Cole Silva."

A shadow slips out of the barracks and (after a confused moment) Souffy identifies it as a man. The midnight black of the armor, boots, cloak, and cowl blend to obscure any sense of depth. The illusion persists even as Cole strides forward.

"Wouldn't want to meet that one in a dark alley!"

The mayor's tone is jovial, but Souffy sees Cole twitch. He pulls back the cowl and softens his stern expression with a shy smile. With her own smile, Souffy tries to communicate that she has no fear of him.

"And finally, Wizard Kyle Moretti."

Unlike the other four, Kyle wears no armor. He's dressed in a simple red vest, jaunty cravat, and tight black pants with—strangely—a single belt under a long flowing brown coat. Individually the pieces making up the ensemble are ordinary, like something a respectable merchant or well-to-do townsman might don. Together they almost convey an adventurer, but not quite a wizard. Something—Souffy's not quite sure what—is missing.

As Kyle strikes his pose, he catches Souffy's eye and jerks his head just a bit sideways. He does it again, and it dawns on her what he wants.

"You look great," she Magic Missives him.

"How come I'm the only one who didn't get any armor? I'm even wearing a frickin' red shirt!"

"It gets in the way of casting spells," she sends. "The armor, not the red shirt."

"They better be ranged spells. I'm leaving all the close combat to Tristan. You'll teach me the spells, right?" His question is less bitter, more hopeful.

Souffy feels her cheeks heat up as she nods.

"Let's bring them all back onstage," Galam finishes reading.

The otherworlders join Kyle and arrange themselves in the same ordered line as they had earlier for Souffy in the shrine. Back then, they were handsome; now they're downright heroic—at least in appearance. She remembers the magistrate's words: "At best they'll look the part and make fools out of themselves."

Souffy feels the full weight of her new responsibilities. She supposes she could teach Kyle some spells, but what about the others? Maybe this is all some plan of Lenora's to shift blame for poorly trained heroes onto her. No, Souffy pushes that thought away; she's done doubting herself. She regards the heroes, forcing herself to see past their stylish but impractical attire and dashing good looks. The Divine Wisdom must have had good reasons for choosing these five, for sending them here to Bydlo.

She looks around at Havelin, and Boryk, and even Dryden, and feels the beginnings of a plan forming. Maybe not a good plan, but at least it's something.

CHAPTER 11

Dryden

This day has gone topsy-turvy, upside-down crazy, and Dryden has no idea how that happened. He'd caught Souffy at the shrine. She'd admitted to casting the spell to let the heroes out of the portal. Her confession is part of the official record, for Mu's sake! So why is she the one now giving orders?

"We have less than a week to get the heroes some proper training," she announces and gestures to the otherworlders.

Dryden glances at the lot of them, loafing around in their colorful "armor"—perfect target practice for any aspiring archers. Given how they're handling their new weapons, he figures it will take at least a month to keep them from accidentally gouging their own eyes out.

Souffy continues, "But if we all work together, I think… I mean, I know we can do it."

"It's convenient how your classes match up," says the mayor. Even the mayor is agreeing with Souffy's plan? What in the underworld is going on?

"Boryk, you'll help Oscar. Havelin, I'll have you work with Micah, and Cole also. I'll take"—Souffy's eyes flick towards the otherworld fighter before settling on the wizard—"Kyle. And Tristan, you'll go with Dryden."

The blond-haired man steps forward. "Awesome," he says. He turns to the shortest of the otherworlders, their wizard. "Which one is Dryden?"

"The soldier with the beard."

Souffy motions Tristan over to Dryden. "This shouldn't be too difficult. Back in his world, Tristan trained in the martial arts." Around them, the other heroes are pairing up with Dryden's friends. With a sinking, sour feeling in his stomach, Dryden realizes he's been roped into another one of Souffy's schemes. Again.

The one called Tristan continues speaking, "I also received personal instruction on stage combat with rapiers from Harvey Gormansky; he's a legend in Hollywood. He was the stunt coordinator for that movie with Genghis Khan and the yetis, and—"

"Tristan, focus!" hisses the wizard. His name is Kyle. Dryden realizes he's going to have to learn their names, great.

"Oh, sorry. Pleasure to meet you, Dryden." Tristan extends his hand to Dryden. The otherworlder's fingernails are smooth and shiny, without a speck of dirt underneath them. And his skin is soft, dough-like. Dryden has seen hands like that on a party of dukes' sons who came to Bydlo to hunt dire wolves a few years back. They hadn't lasted two nights in the forest. It wasn't even the monsters. No, apparently the ground was too hard and cold to sleep on and they didn't like how the bushes snagged their fine clothing and boulders scratched up their ceremonial armor. It would serve Souffy right, Dryden thinks, if he exposes this "hero" as nothing better than those cockscombs.

Dryden squeezes Tristan's hand hard, hoping to make the man flinch, or at least grimace. But Tristan squeezes back, just as hard. "Strong one, aren't you?" He grins at Dryden, then at Souffy. She giggles.

"Practice area is this way," says Dryden dryly and leads him away. "We have some wooden sparring sticks, or I suppose you could use that sword of yours."

Dryden steals a quick glance at the ornate scabbard inlaid with blue stones that hangs from Tristan's belt. Dryden had initially given Tristan one of the standard-issue longswords. Sure, it had a few nicks in the blade, but it was far nicer than the one Dryden had been allotted when he first signed up for the town's militia three years ago. Except then the mayor had insisted they unlock the cupboard where they kept the old regimental weapons, the ones that only came out during ceremonies. Dryden had dug for one at the back, expecting—hoping—it to be dull and rusty. But when Tristan pulled it out, the sword practically hummed as the blade's edge caught the light. Tristan had been less graceful re-sheathing the sword; it took him three tries. He didn't manage to slice any fingers off, unfortunately.

As they walk through the courtyard, Dryden tries to see what Souffy finds so special about this otherworlder. He is clean, and moves well— Havelin might have been correct about the modifications to Tristan's armor allowing for more graceful movement. But the way the fighter is currently gawking at the fortress's walls and towers is less than heroic, making him appear more like a country bumpkin.

Tristan's eyes keep darting everywhere. "The attention to detail in this place, it's unreal! I don't know if you're part of the production team, but good work to whoever was responsible."

"This fortress was built over thirty generations ago." Dryden speaks slowly, as if to a dim-witted child.

"Oh, we're staying in character. My bad." Tristan stage-whispers as he runs a hand through his hair. It passes through effortlessly, and the golden locks shimmer down like the fine hairs on a sun-ripened cob of corn. The family farm Dryden came from grew a lot of corn, and he hates it with a passion. Tristan stretches out to his full height which is a couple—maybe a few—inches taller than Dryden. "I thank you good sir, and look forward to crossing blades with you." His voice is now deeper, with an unplaceable accent.

"Let's start by seeing your form and fighting stance." Dryden pivots so he doesn't have to look at Tristan and his foppish face. Why couldn't Souffy have summoned normal heroes?

He stomps the rest of the way to the militia's practice grounds. It's an open space tucked into the side of the barracks and shaded by the fort's walls. The ground is hard-packed dirt, and a circle of white stones large enough to hold a horse and carriage mark off the fighting ring. On one side is a large post that someone has conveniently left Goliath leaning against. The towering straw man is one reason it's good to have a wizard around. Souffy's uncle had embedded an Animate spell within the fighting dummy along with a Restore spell so the trainers didn't have to keep reattaching its arms.

"Just step into the circle," Dryden tells Tristan, "and draw your sword."

The sound of steel sliding against its scabbard brings Goliath from languid repose to towering hulk. Its straw innards crunch as it lumbers forward. Tristan jumps a good foot in surprise, but he doesn't back away. He points his sword—one-handed, his wrist raised, the blade edge vertical—at the dummy.

"Oh, don't be scared of old Golly. Show us what you can do." Dryden pitches his voice loud enough to draw a crowd. He has a good idea of the scrimmage's outcome and he wants witnesses to Tristan's inevitable and shameful defeat.

"Uh, okay." Tristan straightens his stance while Goliath takes another two steps into the middle of the circle where it waits patiently. "I'm not really warmed up." Tristan swoops and his arm left and right, drawing a sideways figure eight with the blade. "Wow, this thing's heavy!"

"You can use two hands."

"Oh, right!" Tristan grasps the hilt with both hands. His swings accelerate and are accompanied by an impressive swooshing sound as the sword cuts through the air. Several militia men and women gather around the circle.

"Enough with the theatrics, let's see what you've got, hero," Dryden says.

Tristan steadies his sword and runs at Goliath. Just before the blade connects, the dummy takes a small step back. The sword still finds its target, but at an unexpected angle. Tristan stumbles. As he rights himself, he pulls the straw man towards him, onto him. The resulting scene looks like a drunk lover smothering Tristan with kisses. Short bursts of laughter come from the crowd. Tristan smiles obliviously, he even waves. Undaunted, he attacks Goliath again and again, to no better results.

"It's strange. It's just human enough that I feel bad hitting it, especially since it's not wielding any weapon," says Tristan after another failed swing.

"If that's your problem, why don't you fight me instead?" Dryden enjoys the horrified look on Tristan's face.

"With real swords?"

"Naw, with these." Someone throws Dryden two wooden rods. They are simple: made of oak, about waist-high, and infused with anti-splintering and anti-cracking magic because Bydlo prides itself on the quality of its wood.

"Okay." Tristan sheaths his sword. The action deactivates Goliath, and the straw man collapses. A burly sergeant pulls its still form out of the circle. Tristan removes his scabbard and takes up one of the wooden practice rods, testing its weight with greater familiarity than he'd shown with the longsword. Dryden doesn't pay his opponent much attention. He's seen enough of Tristan's technique, or lack thereof. He'll easily take him.

They stand facing each other. Tristan's wooden sword is an extension of his straight arms. Dryden's is pulled back, ready to swing.

"Fight!" someone shouts.

"Kote!" Tristan yells—barks really. This explosive intensity startles Dryden so much that he barely registers the arcing swoop of Tristan's stick until it thwacks painfully against his wrist.

"Did you see how fast that guy moved?" says someone. The crowd has gone dead silent.

"What?" Dryden manages to work his mouth. Somehow the foppish pretty boy has transformed into a nostrils-flared, cheeks-flushed, piercing-eyed warrior. "What was that?"

"Kote? It means wrist. Because I hit you on the wrist."

"I know where you hit me," Dryden snaps. "I'm asking about…" He waves his hand in Tristan's direction, looking like he's shooing away flies. "That."

Tristan's eyes light up, not in berserker fury, but in delight. "Oh, that's Kendo. It means the Way of the Sword." His grin grows as he speaks. "It's a traditional Japanese style of fencing derived from the fighting styles of the ancient samurai, but it can also be a means for cultivating discipline, patience, and spirituality. In the—"

"Enough. Let's just fight."

This time Dryden makes sure to be ready. His wooden sword catches Tristan's before it can touch him. But then Tristan bounces like someone has cast an explosion spell under his feet.

"Do!" he shouts as his weapon strikes Dryden's chest. The crowd applauds.

If this were a real fight, there wouldn't be enough power behind Tristan's blow to do more than knock the wind out of him. But then, thinks Dryden, if this were a real fight, the sword could be enchanted to slice through him like butter.

"Again," he says before Tristan can start talking.

Tristan swings and Dryden steps back, just out of range but close enough to make use of the gap when Tristan will be open and defenseless. That's where he'll strike the otherworlder with his full force. Dryden focuses on Tristan's stick, so he sees the instant it reverses itself. It happens faster than anyone not magicked up on a Haste spell could respond to.

"Men!" cries Tristan as his sword cracks down on Dryden's helmet. Dryden loses his balance and falls backwards as the crowd goes wild.

Tristan Ives

Class: Fighter
Level: 1

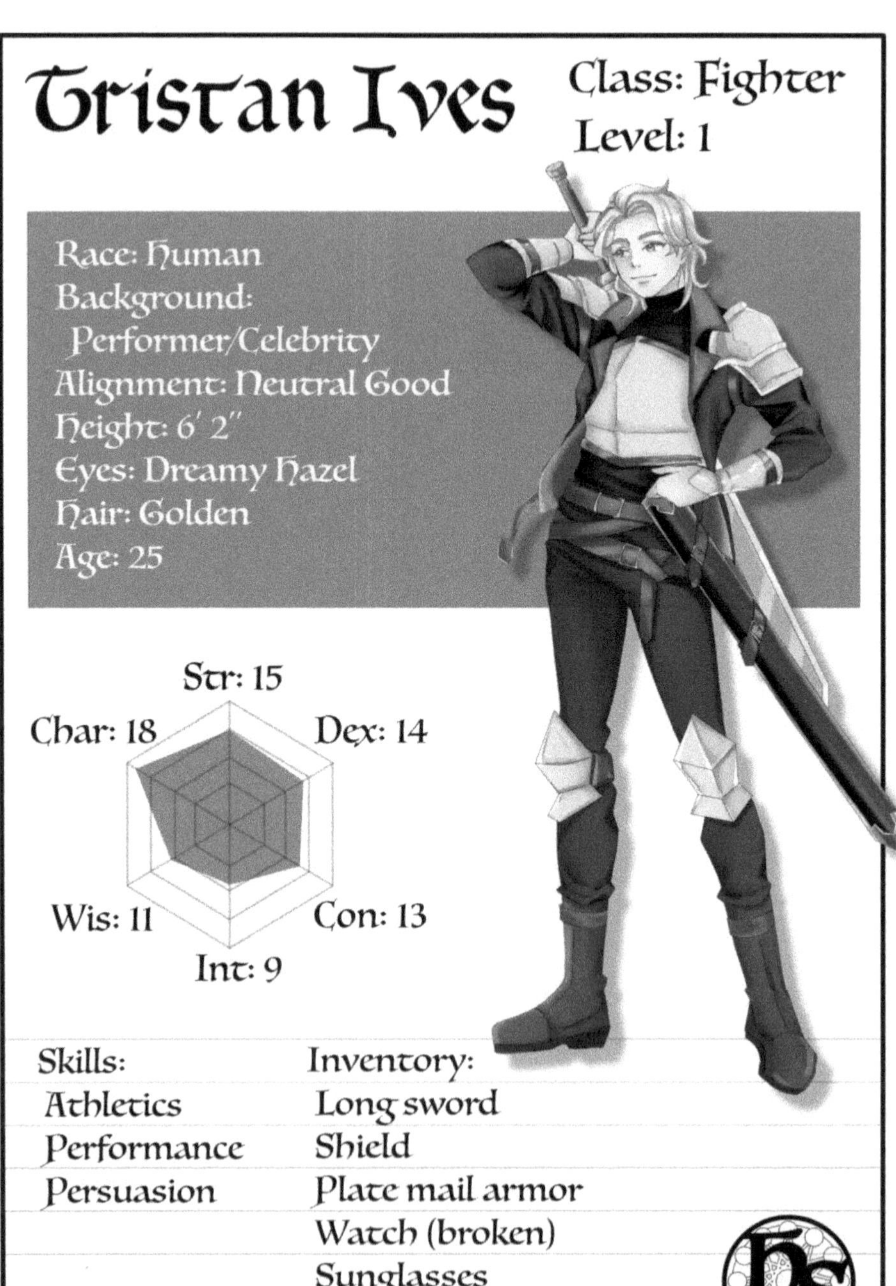

Race: Human
Background:
 Performer/Celebrity
Alignment: Neutral Good
Height: 6' 2"
Eyes: Dreamy Hazel
Hair: Golden
Age: 25

Str: 15
Dex: 14
Char: 18
Con: 13
Wis: 11
Int: 9

Skills:
Athletics
Performance
Persuasion

Inventory:
Long sword
Shield
Plate mail armor
Watch (broken)
Sunglasses

CHAPTER 12

Havelin

"You think I'm copying you?" challenges Cole. He dips his canteen into a bucket of water drawn from the fortress well.

"I'm just saying, I added a cloak to my outfit first," says Micah. He grabs for the bucket with a bit more force than necessary.

"Hardly original. You're dressed up like Robin Hood," says Cole.

Havelin stands behind the two heroes, considering Micah's cloak. It's green, not red like a robin. Overall, the cloaks are as un-alike as their owners. Micah's is woven from the softest wool; it's the kind of garment one could derive comfort from on a cold winter's night. In contrast, Cole's cloak is the essence of night. The silky fabric falls almost to his ankles, transforming his steps into gliding strides. It seems odd to Havelin for them to bicker over their cloaks. After all, everyone owns at least one.

The heroes continue their puzzling disagreement as they walk out of the fortress.

"Rogues are supposed to be sneaky, hiding in shadows and all that shit. Obviously, I need a cloak."

"Ninjas don't," says Micah.

"Ninjas don't what? Hide in the shadows?"

"Wear cloaks. And when did you become an expert on rogues? You didn't even know what they were until the glowy stick said you were one."

"Like you're an expert on nature. You get nervous whenever we're out of cell service. The only one of us who knows anything about this sword and sorcery stuff is Kyle. You're just as clueless as me."

"Probably more," says Micah. "You did get arrested for shoplifting."

Cole stops abruptly; his angry gaze drills holes into Micah. Havelin, standing between them, is relieved to be well below Cole's line of sight.

Micah doesn't flinch. Havelin holds his breath. And then Cole breaks the tension, shaking his head and snorting.

"Whatever. Havelin's here to teach us, so why don't we let him."

"Fine by me," agrees Micah.

It relieves Havelin to see the argument resolved, but now the heroes' focus shifts to him. This would all be much easier if the Divine Wisdom had provided a handbook, he muses. Souffy has entrusted him with two otherworlders. The others have just been assigned a single one each. He appreciates her confidence in him, but the responsibility is also daunting.

Staccato chirps interrupt his worries. It's Cornelius. He's perched on the wooden railing on the bridge leading up to the fort gatehouse. The raccoon had wisely made himself scarce when the guards showed up at the Hero Shrine, but he must have known where they'd be taken. Or perhaps he just came by to check out the barracks' kitchens. As they pass underneath the gatehouse, the raccoon jumps on Havelin's shoulder and shoves his cold nose in Havelin's ear.

"All right. I suppose it's both of us looking after the heroes," says Havelin.

"I was wondering, is that raccoon magical, like a telepath?" asks Cole.

"No, he doesn't have any special powers." At this Cornelius makes a sound that could be a snort, or perhaps he's hacking up a hairball. "Well, other than being super sweet and adorable." *And he's an excellent thief*, Havelin doesn't say. It's a skill he is trying—and failing—to train Cornelius out of. "I'm told that sealing a companionship bond with an animal enables them to comprehend simple words and commands, but I suspect that Cornelius understands a lot more than that." Havelin affectionately strokes his raccoon behind the ears and the happy rumble this action elicits instantly makes him feel better.

"Do all rangers need companions?" asks Micah. "Because I'm allergic to most kinds of fur."

"No, not all rangers are beastmeisters. And you could choose an animal without fur, like a reptile." At this Micah shudders. "Or a bird, birds are very popular."

Havelin imagines how striking a bird of prey on Micah's shoulder would look. He could teach the otherworlder bird calls, even the Talk to the Animals spell along with so much ranger lore. Havelin doesn't have the same confidence regarding Cole's training. He supposes a rogue could be considered a sort of… urban ranger. If he thinks of cities as forests, houses as trees, the townsfolk as fauna with the nastier thugs and scoundrels as predators, then maybe he could adapt certain principles of ranger-hood. He'll need to channel that feeling of connection and peace he feels in nature—the inviting call that draws him deeper into the woods—and find its Bydlo equivalent.

They pass through the gatehouse and Havelin inhales an unpleasant tang of rotten cabbage and dank smoke which causes his stomach to flip. Maybe he should just focus on weapons training for now. There's an archery range nestled up against the side of the fortress walls. Havelin leads the heroes there and positions them about ten paces from the straw bale targets.

"I see you picked the crossbow," Havelin says to Cole. "Do you have any experience with it?"

The rogue glances at the lightweight weapon strapped to his waist. "I told that soldier guy, Dryden, that I'd been to a shooting range. He didn't know what a gun was, so he gave me this instead."

"This is a medieval world. They didn't have guns in the Middle Ages," says Micah.

Cole shrugs. "Not like they had magic either. Besides, the way these people talk, they seem pretty modern to me. I don't think they handed out 'community service' as a form of punishment in the Middle Ages." Havelin makes a mental note to ask Souffy more about the world these heroes came from.

He approves of Dryden's choice of crossbow. It's a straightforward mechanism; once it's loaded, you simply point it and take your shot. Novice militia recruits pick up the technique quickly. Now a full longbow (like the one Micah has chosen) will require serious training.

Cole follows Havelin's gaze. "I suppose you know how to use that thing?"

Micah braces the end of his bow against his foot—it's almost as tall as Micah himself—and applies pressure to arch the stave. Then with quick, nimble fingers, he loops the string to brace the weapon. "I had some experience back home," he says.

"When? You never even went to summer camp," says Cole.

"After the band broke up."

"After you quit, you mean? To devote your 'full creative talents in the pursuit of your eclectic and unique musical vision.' Did I get the press release right?" There's venom in his words, and Havelin tenses as their sniping turns once again into an argument.

"Not much to quit from, with you in and out of rehab."

"And whose fault was that?"

"We staged an intervention!" Micah's cool voice takes on a desperate edge. "You were spiraling out of control. We couldn't just watch." Quietly, he adds, "We only wanted what was best for you."

Cole isn't listening. "And what was convenient for you. You get to record your own music, Kyle gets to go to college, Tristan gets to be a movie star."

"You had just as much chance to do something with your life," snaps Micah. "Instead you kept hitting the clubs and making a fool of yourself in front of the paparazzi."

"You don't know what I went through." Cole's hands ball into fists.

"Right, because you're the only one saddled with a public persona that they're expected to embody for the rest of their lives. Guess what? Except for Tristan, post-boy-band life hasn't been easy on any of us."

"Yeah, must've been quite the blow to your ego when Tristan's solo album went platinum and yours bombed and the label dropped you."

They're face to face, close enough for one to headbutt the other; both look angry enough to do so. Souffy would be crushed if Havelin were to bring them back damaged. Or worse—they do both have weapons.

"Should we maybe get on to practicing?" Havelin indicates the targets some ten yards distant. "Who wants to go first?"

"Age before beauty," says Micah as he steps back.

"Fine."

Havelin takes Cole's crossbow and demonstrates how to engage the stirrup at the front to pull back the string. He places a small dart into the chamber and hands it to Cole.

"Just squeeze this?" Cole indicates the long trigger. Havelin nods.

Cole rests the crossbow on one arm and bends his head down to take aim. He presses the trigger and the tension releases with a thwump. The weapon shudders, sending the bolt flying high over the target. Cole glares at the weapon. "How do you aim this thing?"

Havelin examines Cole's crossbow. It isn't the finest workmanship, and the balance is a bit off, but the weapon feels solid enough. He reloads it and this time demonstrates the technique. There's a moment of concern as he squeezes the trigger that he'll make a fool of himself, but the bolt goes straight, thwacking into the middle-third circle of the target. Quite respectable.

"Okay, let me try again." Cole loads the crossbow himself and hefts it with renewed determination. He brings the shaft to just below his chin. His eyes become slits, and his posture projects an entirely different vibe than before. Havelin holds his breath. He glances at Micah, who is staring intently at Cole.

Click. Woosh.

Havelin turns to the target, certain he'll at least see the bolt sticking out of the straw frame. But no, it's gone wide again.

"How many of those bolts are you allowed to lose?" asks Micah.

"Don't worry, I've trained Cornelius to retrieve them," says Havelin.

Cole just grunts. Silently he loads, fires again, and misses. But the next time he hits the corner of the board, and the one after lands closer to the center than Havelin's.

"That's quite good for a beginner," says Havelin.

"Your turn." Cole turns to Micah, a sly smile on his face.

"Would you like a lesson?" asks Havelin.

"I think I'll try it on my own first, thanks."

Micah tilts his head and considers the target. In a single, practiced motion he plucks an arrow from his quiver and notches it. He draws the bow and the air around them seems to still. Micah holds this pose, motionless save for the single finger smoothly releasing the string. They all hear the thwack as the arrow pierces the target. Havelin unglues his eyes from Micah and turns to look: bullseye. The arrow may be a bit to the right of center, but it's still a bullseye.

Cole stands open-mouthed. "When did you learn to do that?"

"We all had our coping strategies when we became has-beens. Judging from what I saw of your escapades in the tabloids, you were spiraling out of control. After I cut ties with my record label, I joined a live-off-the-land commune. They put me in charge of securing the meat for dinner." He speaks the words flatly; only the slight curl on one side of his mouth betrays his smugness.

Cole's body tenses along with the bowstring. The moment stretches out. It breaks when Cole snorts and stalks off.

Micah Cardigan

Class: Ranger
Level: 1

Race: Human
Background: Performer
Alignment: Chaotic Neutral
Height: 5' 10"
Eyes: Verdant green
Hair: Red
Age: 24

Str: 13
Dex: 17
Con: 9
Int: 11
Wis: 14
Char: 15

Skills:	Inventory:
Music	Long bow
Performance	Leather armor
Languages	Cloak (forest-green)

CHAPTER 13

Boryk

Boryk is pleasantly surprised when Souffy assigns one of the heroes to him (she has a habit of forgetting he's around). But this shows that she recognizes and values his dedication to his sacred calling.

"Oscar," Souffy says, "Boryk will take you down to the Church of the Twelve and find someone to help you select a god to pledge yourself to." Or, she just needs someone to make sure Oscar doesn't get lost. Boryk wants to utter a curse at his bad luck for taking a vow of silence now of all times—except he's taken a vow of silence.

"Couldn't I just pledge to the Divine Wisdom? It's the one that called us here after all," asks Oscar.

Souffy frowns thoughtfully, like she's familiar with the tenets of the faith. Boryk could count on one hand the number of times he'd seen her show up for devotional services. "The Divine Wisdom is a hands-off deity. The others are more personable. Plus, they adore heroes!"

"Okay, if you say so. Lead the way, Boryk."

Even if Oscar hadn't been revealed as the party's cleric, Boryk would have liked him best. He's brave—standing up to Lenora for Souffy's sake—and Boryk sees how he looks out for his fellow otherworlders. But he wonders who is looking out for Oscar. He's putting up a good front, but Boryk can spot a crisis of faith. Oscar has a big one in the making.

Boryk doesn't have to wait long. The otherworlder's fears spill out as they leave the fortress. "I know the rules of this world are different, but not worshiping other gods is one of the major commandments where I'm from. It's one of the two I haven't broken. It's not like I'm a bad person. It's just… being in the entertainment industry makes it hard, you know?"

Boryk doesn't, but he knows to give a sympathetic nod. He slows his pace until they're walking side by side.

"I'm not what you'd call religious, but my Gram is. She's this amazing woman, raised my dad and uncle by herself. She's the one who's always been there for me. And her love is unconditional, not like the rest my family…" His voice trails off. "With my siblings… and my parents… we love each other, but things are complicated."

Since taking his vow of silence, Boryk has learned to listen to what is said and—more importantly—to what isn't. And there's a dragon's hoard worth of unsaid behind Oscar's words. Boryk pats Oscar's back, and some of the otherworlder's good cheer returns.

"But I suppose if I pick a kind and generous god, or goddess, and if by serving them, I become a better person, that would be a good thing, right?"

Boryk nods vigorously in assent, especially to the part about picking a morally upstanding god. As a member of the clergy of the Church of the Twelve, Boryk assists with feasts and observances for all twelve gods, but that doesn't mean he has to approve of the ones who are right bastards. Just because he's religious, doesn't mean he's naïve.

"I bet you serve a good god, Boryk."

Feeling a bit self-conscious, Boryk pulls up the sleeve of his tunic to reveal a tattoo of a stylized cornucopia overflowing with fruits, vegetables, and grains.

"Sweet ink. So, harvest goddess?" Oscar looks at Boryk, reading his expression, "Or harvest god?" Boryk confirms with a nod and smile.

Boryk wishes he could tell the hero the story of how he chose his god. It happened when he was three and was separated from his family during a harvest festival. Boryk remembers crying alone and seeing strange shapes in the darkness. Suddenly, the moon—full and bright—broke free of the clouds, and a tall man with a mantle of woven wheat stalks stood before him. He offered his hand and Boryk took it. That hand had been dry and calloused, but warm, like sunlight on his face. Boryk awoke the next morning surrounded by the food and other offerings for Temisoto, God of the Harvest. And ever since then, he'd felt Temisoto's comforting presence—like a good friend in another room—hard at work making the world a better place.

For the longest time he'd served Temisoto privately and that was enough. Then, two years ago, he'd decided to leave the militia for the clergy and to pledge himself officially to Temisoto. It had brought new meaning to his life and he's been grateful every day since. Had he been able to speak,

Boryk would have finished his story with a heartfelt endorsement of Temisoto over the other—more flashy—gods.

Stupid, stupid vow of silence.

By now they've arrived at the church.

"Oh, I know where we are. That's the Hero Shrine out there. And this is your church?" Oscar points at the stone building that dominates the corner of the harbor. "Impressive."

It is indeed a picturesque setting—if one chooses to disregard the occasional high tides that necessitate the deployment of sandbags and bucket brigades to keep out the seawater. The entrance is lined with life-sized sculptures of the gods. Souffy had complained about these being crudely carved out of local wood, as opposed to the more realistic marble replicas common in the capital. Boryk doesn't mind. He's grown up with these effigies, and it doesn't bother him that the real Temisoto doesn't look anything like the gaunt, hollow-cheeked statue they're now passing.

They step out of the bright sun and wait for their eyes to adjust.

"Welcome, gracious hero!" The voice is one Boryk recognizes, and he grimaces. A large man emerges from the darkness. His white robes are smooth and immaculate, and there's not a hair out of place on his head. "I'm Jefry Haricolt." The man bows to Oscar; he doesn't spare a glance for Boryk.

"Hi, I'm Oscar Jones from Never Boy Land." Boryk notices the stiffness is back in Oscar's voice and posture.

"Yes, I heard, and a cleric too." Jefry has never taken a vow of silence, nor embarked on a religious quest, or renounced even one worldly possession to better serve his god. Instead, he cultivates a talent for always being around when a new responsibility or position in the church becomes available. He might not be able to call on the powers of the gods, but he's adept at wheedling plum assignments and climbing the church hierarchy.

"I am according to the Pathfinder wand. I don't know much about being a cleric," says Oscar.

Jefry gives Boryk a pointed look, as if Oscar's lack of certainty was somehow his fault. "Not to worry. I'll give you the condensed catechism and once you've pledged yourself, your god can fill in the details."

"About that pledge and the god I select, can we make sure they're—"

"Of appropriate stature for a Hero of the Realm," Jefry cuts in. "I understand, you want the right kind of god after all."

Oscar tenses. "Aren't all gods created equal?" he asks.

"Of course, of course." Jefry brings his fingers together in front of his face and closes his eyes before quoting from the *Book of the Gods*. "And then, putting aside past grievances and animosities, the gods joined hands in a symbol of their new-found unity. And lo, by this gesture was born the Divine Wisdom who was of them, but also not of them. And the Divine Wisdom let its will be known: 'You beings who hold immeasurable power, shall each be awarded a domain suitable to your nature. And with each domain shall come control and responsibility, which you shall execute as you and your fellow gods see fit for the continuation and benefit of the Realm of Mythreal.' And thus was the covenant made and the Twelve granted their dominions." Jefry switches back to his normal voice. "So, of course, equal, but..." he gives Oscar a meaningful look.

"But some are more equal than others?" Oscar's voice has gone strangely cold.

Jefry claps his hands. "Yes, so well put! You are a clever one, and the gods appreciate clever! Let me give you the basics."

He takes them to the front of the church where twelve wooden figures stand in a semicircle. A ribbon of gold thread winds around and between them, symbolizing the covenant. They were carved by another local artist, and the faces are all nearly identical. They differ mainly in the items each holds.

"Right here in the center, we have the original gods: Mu for earth, Lyr for fire, and Sher for the oceans. Obviously as an ocean town, the folks of Bydlo have a sweet spot for Sher. But no one would fault you for pledging yourself to Lyr, after all she created the first humans. Those three are undeniably powerful, but perhaps a bit old-fashioned. Many people feel the new gods are a better fit for the modern hero. Take Ethei, Goddess of Law and Learning, or, if you want to maximize your offensive spells, you can't do better than Niau, Goddess of War." He points out a statue holding an open book and another with a sword strapped to her back.

"Which one is the God of the Harvest?" asks Oscar.

"Temisoto? Oh yes, he's fairly popular with farmers around here. Along with Orthorus for blacksmiths, and Beryl for the artisans." Jefry indicates a trio of gods at one end of the circle. "They're the gods you sacrifice to when you need to plow a field, pound out a horseshoe, or weave a decorative basket, but—take my word—not much help in slaying monsters. Now, I admit that I'm biased because he's my chosen deity, but I think you should consider Kalimos, God of Lightning and Storms. He's in the very center, right next to Lyr on account of his role as leader of the Pantheon. I have some sacred texts on him I could fetch. They're very illuminating."

Oscar looks back and forth at the statues. After a moment he says, "Yes, why don't you get them." As Jefry scurries down the aisle, Oscar leans towards Boryk and whispers, "I need some air. Can we get out of here?"

Silently (because how else could he do it) Boryk motions for Oscar to follow him through the vestry and out a small door that leads into a walled orchard.

Oscar stretches out his arms. "Not a heroic exit, but I needed a break before I said something I'd regret. This place is charming. Thanks, Boryk."

It is charming. A lawn of green spreads beneath apple trees and dense bushes grow along the edges. The tall stone walls block the sounds of the harbor and the incessant crashing of the waves. Instead, Boryk hears the rustling of birds and small animals and the humming of bees. The apples are still green. Boryk picks one and covers it with his hand as he casts the Ripen cantrip. As he does so, he feels the grace of Temisoto flow through him like a summer breeze. He passes the now-red apple to Oscar who takes a bite, then another, until he's eaten it, core and all, leaving only the stem.

"Thanks, that was so good. We missed lunch, back in our world." He looks up at the sky. "I wonder what's happening there."

Boryk spots another suitable apple—this one already red. When he turns back, Oscar is examining a modest shrine. It's the width of his forearm with a peaked roof. A wreath of woven wheat stalks decorates the opening and inside is an offering of two ears of corn.

"Is this a shrine to Temisoto?" asks Oscar.

Boryk nods. While the shrine hasn't been officially consecrated to Temisoto, its location in an orchard means that most offerings placed in and around it are intended for the harvest god. Boryk sometimes sees wildflowers meant for Minstay, Goddess of Nature, but today's corn means that it was most recently connected to Temisoto.

Boryk considers the shrine, then considers Oscar. He has (as instructed) taken the hero to the Church of the Twelve where someone explained the gods to him. If Oscar had wanted to pledge himself to Kalimos, he'd be inside with Jefry by this point. Oscar said he wanted a kind and generous god. Boryk hands Oscar the apple and looks meaningfully at the shrine.

Oscar catches his intent. "Yeah, why not." He kneels before the shrine. "Not sure if I'm doing this right, but here goes. I'm Oscar Jones, I'm yours, if you'll have me."

Oscar then reverently places the apple inside the humble shrine and as he does so, Boryk notices the web spun across the top of the enclosure with an orb weaver spider perched in the center. He realizes belatedly—with dawning horror—that Oscar hasn't named a god.

Boryk reaches out to signal a warning, but it's too late. Two doves alight upon the shrine with a rustle of feathers and a chorus of coos. They immediately begin to nuzzle.

Reality shifts. The air warms and the ocean breeze loses its harsh sting. Colors intensify, their hues skew red and orange, and daylight shimmers like liquid amber. A woman appears before them. She speaks:

"Well, hello there. Did I just hear someone asking for a god?"

Her appearance is striking; she's easily eight feet tall but ideally proportioned. Her skin is brown with rose pink and apricot tones. These concrete impressions muddle in Boryk's mind the longer he tries to behold her. Simple observations of how she's well-endowed with wide hips are soon addled with adjectives like voluptuous and sultry and metaphors about ripe peaches and spicy peppers.

Boryk lets out a strangled wail as emotion overcomes him.

"What, did a pixie steal your tongue?" She speaks with a voice that flows like honey. Eyes gleaming, she runs her own tongue over her lips, slowly, very slowly. Even if he'd had leave to speak, Boryk would be at a loss for words.

"Boryk took a vow of silence. I'm Oscar Jones, pleased to make your acquaintance," says Oscar. He gives the goddess his easy smile and holds out his hand.

She takes his hand like it's a novel experience. "Well met, Oscar Jones. I am Verhalty, Goddess of Love."

"Wow, I guess I should have realized. Am I doing this right? Should I genuflect?"

"Oh, you're doing just fine." She winks at Boryk, and his cheeks warm like they've been sunburned. "You'll find I'm not one of those stuffy deities all hung up on ceremony." The parts of Boryk's brain that are still functioning recall several legends directly contradicting her statement. "All I want from my followers is good intentions and a pure heart. Are you pure of heart, boy?"

Oscar's smooth manner slips, and something hard enters his eyes. "I'd prefer it if you don't call me that."

Verhalty blinks twice. Contradicting a god could lead straight to smiting territory. But Verhalty regains her smile and corrects herself. "Polite but direct, I'm liking you more and more, young man." The timbre of her voice turns sultry, "That alright by you?"

"Yeah, that works."

"Excellent. You, Oscar Jones, are something special. You are going places, that's my instinct talking—I don't heed prophecy. We should talk, don't you think?"

Oscar turns to Boryk. "Is it okay if I go with her?"

If Boryk hadn't taken a vow of silence, he might have said something foolish, embarrassing, and pointless. He glances at Verhalty and observes her cat-got-the-mouse expression. The goddess has already made her choice. He shrugs (what else can he do?).

He watches Oscar take Verhalty's proffered arm and walk away. The orchard explodes with yet more life: the buzzing of bees and raucous chirping of birds. The fecundity of spring fills the air.

It's true, thinks Boryk, romance and fertility are good things, but Verhalty is also the goddess of jealousy and heartbreak, and has several nasty wars to her credit. Boryk comforts himself with the thought that there are worse gods to be claimed by. It could have been Niau, or Wirell, God of Death. Oh, and Jørge, the Trickster God. Jørge would've been a complete disaster.

Oscar Jones

Class: Cleric
Level: 1

Race: Human
Background: Performer
Alignment: Lawful Good
Height: 6.1"
Eyes: Soulful brown
Hair: Black
Age: 27

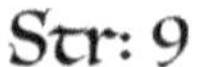

Str: 9
Char: 15
Dex: 13
Wis: 17
Con: 14
Int: 11

Skills:
Insight
Medicine
Performance
Persuasion

Inventory:
Mace
Plate mail armor
Signet of Love Goddess

CHAPTER 14

Cornelius

The strange human in black slows his pace. When the rogue dashed away from Havelin, he was at a near run. Now his steps are deliberate and careful as he makes his way down Bydlo's backstreets. A reasonable approach, Cornelius supposes as he watches from his perch on a roof. It was in this very alley that he'd lost several tufts of fur in a scuffle with a one-eared cat that rumor held was once a wizard's familiar.

It's a pity that this strange human didn't stay to train with Havelin, but Cornelius understands why. Havelin and the other strange human both smell of green and dappled sunlight, whereas this one smells of shadow and unexpected pointy bits sticking into your flesh. One needs sticky fingers to understand and teach his sort, and Cornelius's paws are still tacky from the blackberries he'd swiped earlier from a fruit seller's stall. Being a raccoon, that is enough justification to offer assistance to this strange human.

But first, Cornelius sniffs at the dried berry juice on his paws. It smells of tasty things. He puts his tongue out. Yes, definitely tasty. Three more licks and all he tastes is paw. He should find more blackberries, or really any fruit, he isn't a picky raccoon. Oh bother, the human has disappeared.

Cornelius scampers up to the peak of the nearest roof and soon locates the hooded black figure. He's heading towards an intersection. And coming around the other corner, Cornelius spots two city guards. That meeting could turn more disastrous than the raccoon's own earlier alley cat encounter.

As fast as if he's being chased by a pack of stray dogs, Cornelius races over the intervening rooftops and drops down to the ground in front of the rogue just in time.

The man jumps back but recovers and bends closer. "Hey, aren't you Havelin's raccoon?"

But Cornelius doesn't have time for talk-words, he's better with action-words anyway. His eyes catch a flash from the golden disc on a chain hanging around the strange human's neck. It's a Shiny! Corneilus leaps, grabs the Shiny, and scampers down a back alley away from the guards. He hears some unfamiliar curses and the sound of feet pounding after him.

Zig, zag, stop. He's chosen a deserted alley; now he can put the Shiny down on a cobblestone. Hopefully the human will understand that Cornelius was only borrowing-stealing, not keeping-stealing. And, just in case the subtlety is lost on the scary human, Cornelius retreats deeper into the shadows.

"What the?" The human catches up; his cowl has fallen back to reveal his sheep-shorn head, the markings that cover half his neck, and his water-blue eyes. His gloved hand snatches his Shiny up from the ground and turns it from side to side. "Did Havelin send you?" The human looks up and down the street. "Micah? Is this a joke? Is this whole world a fucking joke?" His focus returns to the Shiny in his hands; his fingers trace its edge.

Cornelius emerges from the shadow and makes soft squeaking sounds until the rogue comes over and squats in front of him. "I don't speak raccoon." His voice is flat, his face hard.

Cornelius stretches his eyes wide and twitches his whiskers.

"Really, you're pulling the cute critter card?" The human scowls.

Cornelius drops his ears, tilts his head, and scrunches up his nose. The human sighs. Almost there. Cornelius puts his two front paws together.

"Okay, that's pretty good," the human admits with something resembling a smile on his face. "You're Cornelius, right? I'm Cole."

Coal, like the black rocks with fire trapped in them that Havelin uses to heat their hut in the winter. Cornelius rarely bothers learning human names, but this one fits. He can smell the hidden heat radiating off of Coal.

Coal reminds Cornelius of that elf from long ago, the one with snow hair, night skin, and clever fingers that slipped easily in and out of people's pockets. She had been his companion before Havelin. They had spent their nights together in Bydlo's hiding-and-watching-and-jumping-out spots. She had shown Cornelius how to see the strings that connect the shadow people and taught him just where to tug to make things happen. These are skills that a Coal-human would need.

Cornelius chirps in happy anticipation; this is going to be more fun than sticking one's paw into the box with the honeycombs.

He starts down the street, turning to see if Coal is following him. Coal stands up and after a measured pause, crosses over to Cornelius. Not looking at him, just walking in the same direction. "Okay, I'll follow you. But, just so we're clear, no one—not even Havelin—can know that I'm getting help from a raccoon."

Of course, that's what humans always say.

Cole Silva

Class: Rogue
Level: 1

Race: Human
Background: Performer
Alignment: True Neutral
Height: 6'0"
Eyes: Ice blue
Hair: Black
Age: 26

Str: 13
Char: 15
Dex: 17
Wis: 9
Con: 11
Int: 14

Skills:	Inventory:
Acrobatics	Crossbow
Intimidation	Studded leather armor
Performance	Cloak (midnight-black)
Stealth	Sobriety medallion

CHAPTER 15

Kyle

"*Dexterarious.*" I try to say it dignified-like, and not as if I'm cosplaying.

The setting helps. This is the oldest building in the fortress and it feels as if it was built for giants. The walls are made of this rough, gray-white stone that is literally a yard deep, and the ceilings are so high they're hidden in shadows. The place is lit by massive candelabras that I don't feel comfortable standing under. It's cold in here, not AC-cold, rather this is a damp-that-never-got-warm cold. It's easier to concentrate on the human-sized stuff: the bookshelves full of magic tomes, the desks where Souffy teaches basic spells to local kids, a couple of worn, comfy chairs with bits of stuffing showing.

"Okay, now wiggle your fingers," instructs Souffy.

"Random, like this? Or more like this?" I pretend I'm playing the piano.

"Either is fine. Phantom Hand cantrip doesn't require precise movements. The motion is more to establish whether you're conjuring a mystical right or left hand. Also, some wizards like to control the phantom hand's actions by moving their own hand. But you don't have to, if you don't want to."

I nod, trying to look like I'm taking careful note of all this practical advice. But inside I'm a mix of anticipation and skepticism. What I'm attempting is impossible according to every principle from every science test I've ever aced. And—not to brag—but I graduated from Cornell with a 3.8 GPA. Okay, that's bragging.

Deep breath. Focus. "*Dexterarious.*" Wiggle hand. Nothing.

"No one ever gets it right on the first try," says Souffy. I notice she's chewing on her lower lip, and I feel like she's got more riding on this than I do.

"*Dexterarious!*" I synchronize the hand movements to the incantation to give it a little pop. Still nothing. "Should I be feeling something?" I think back to Souffy's mental texting spell and try to remember if there had been any sensory sensations.

"Magic feels"—Souffy rolls her eyes up as she thinks—"magicky."

This is why I went for a math-based major.

"Oh, I know. You need a hat!" She walks over to a large wardrobe.

"You don't have a hat," I point out as she rummages inside.

"With this hair?" Souffy points and shakes her head. Her made-for-a-shampoo-advertisement afro floats like a fluffy cloud. "How about this?"

Souffy presents me with a large—almost two feet tall—pointy witch hat. This is not a cheap Halloween accessory; it's fashioned out of a lustrous red leather, with a gold brim and straps and buckles. Okay, maybe it's outright ridiculous, but nowhere near as embarrassing as some of the outfits I've donned for music videos and award shows—I will forever regret allowing our stylist to dress me in that hot pink silk tux for the Grammys.

I don the hat. Despite its size, it fits. Souffy lets out a happy squeal and points at a mirror. It's on the cute side—something that wardrobe would more likely have put Micah in—but I kind of like it.

"Now you look like a wizard," says Souffy. Okay, but I'm still not feeling the magic.

"Given that I'm the one who doesn't get any armor, do I really want to call more attention to myself on the battlefield?"

"Oh, don't worry about that," says Souffy. "I can teach you how to cast Mystic Armor and I think there's a Shield spell in one of the textbooks." That sounds promising.

But first, "*Dexterarious.*" Nope, still doesn't work. "Maybe I should try my other hand?" I'm ambidextrous, which is a fun fact known only to the most ardent Never Boy Land stans.

Souffy frowns. "Maybe? This isn't one of my cantrips."

According to Souffy, beginning wizards can choose three cantrips to burn into their minds. Once they take root, they become akin to superpowers, and they are always available no matter how low on mana—magic fuel—one may get. Cantrips are the freebies. Full spells require work. Each spell takes extensive study, needs to be written down with personalized annotations in my spellbook, and must be reviewed regularly so I can call on it in battle. Plus, there's a limit on how many spells I can keep in my head based on how experienced I am. Wizard builds in *Heroes*

Summoning always seemed unnecessarily complicated. That's a big reason why I never bothered playing one—oh, the irony.

"But I've taught Phantom Hand to plenty of children." Souffy's hand covers her mouth and there's a blush to her cheeks. "Not that I'm comparing you to a child."

"It's fine. I am completely new to this. How do you teach your students?"

"This sounds silly, but I make them jump off a cliff. Into water. It's perfectly safe."

"How does that work?"

Her mouth moves as she tries to find the words. She's got amazingly expressive lips. "It helps make the connection between your physical self and the magic. You need to be able to reach out to the magic to use it. It's easier to experience than explain. There's a two-hour hike to the north of Bydlo that leads to a swimming hole with a rock ledge that's about fifteen feet above the water. I tell the kids to run and jump off, and that's what it feels like to do magic."

"Okay." I try—and fail—to imagine it.

Souffy screws up her face; it makes her look twelve and adorable. "It's like just before you leap, you don't actually believe you're going to do it. It's not something you can think yourself into. You just need to let your legs take control, and off you step. And in that moment, when your feet have left the ground, but before the earth starts pulling at you, it's possible to believe you won't fall. That's the feeling you need to connect with magic. Once you succeed, then the laws of the universe cease to apply."

"And the kids start flying?" That would be cool.

"Oh, no. Fly is an advanced-intermediate spell, plus you need a feather. There's something about the physical act of jumping and falling that loosens the mind. Most kids can cast their first cantrip after the second jump."

"Is that how you learned?"

"I wish. My first cantrip was Simple Illusion. I was supposed to make the sound of a bell. I remember my teacher ringing this little silver bell for me to mimic. She did it again, and again, and again, for two weeks before I got angry enough to just cast it. The sound of a bell still puts my teeth on edge." When Souffy described teaching her students, there was an animated glee. All that drained away as she recalled her own experience. I can't help it, I want to get her out of her funk.

"So, shall we go swimming?"

She blinks and her eyes travel down my body only to look away when she sees me noticing. She's definitely not thinking about that bell now. I'd be lying if I said I didn't like the attention.

"I don't think we have time. But maybe if you visualized it?"

"I have a better idea. Step back." I remove my hat and jacket and shake my arms to loosen up. Even if this doesn't unlock my magic, it is a chance to show off. Better not mess it up.

I take a moment to focus. Then, like Souffy said, I let my body commit. I swing my hands up as I jump and concentrate on pulling up my knees so their momentum tips me backwards while my arms fly over my head. That's the in-between moment, all right. I feel an uncomfortable lightness in my stomach, and then it's over. Gravity slams my soles into the hard stone floor and I'm waving my arms to keep my balance. Not too bad. It's been a while since I did a backflip.

Souffy's clapping and laughing. Micah and I learned backflips for the choreography for "You Got It Going (On)." The tour company's lawyers tried to nix it but—as demonstrated by Souffy's reaction—the fans loved it.

Before I lose the feeling of the in-between moment, I cry "*Dexterarious!*" Hand. Wiggle. It clicks!

A ghostly white hand appears before my own. I make a fist; it makes a fist. I rotate my wrist; it twists and keeps twisting (no tendons to hold it back).

"You did it!" says Souffy. "Now, try to pick up a book from the top shelf."

It feels a bit like a VR game. I extend my arm, and the ghost hand floats across the room. I tense, and it slows down before it runs into the shelf. I pinch my fingers. The pantomimed gesture is mimicked by the magic hand and it grabs the book, which is Oxford English Dictionary-sized but there's no feeling of weight or need to adjust position. My phantom hand holds it steadily, effortlessly.

"Now bring it down to the table," directs Souffy.

I'm still using my own hand, but it's more suggestive, just a gentle tilt downwards. The book alights easily on the table and opens up, the pages fluttering. Flipping pages utilizes a thumb motion similar to how I'd navigate my smart phone. I flip my hand and the book slams shut. Pretty fucking sweet.

Souffy hops over and grabs my real hand. "Fantastic! I knew you'd get it. You're a natural!"

That's a compliment I don't usually receive. Mostly our choreographer and voice coaches tell me I'm a hard worker, or that I'm a deep thinker, or as Cole says, a perfectionist—that's his way of saying that I'm not going to nail the dance step or hit the high note and to just move on already.

"I have a good teacher." I try to make it sound offhanded, but it comes out earnest. Souffy blushes and lets go of my hand. "No really, Souffy. According to Mayor Galam, the instruction at the magic school's improved since you arrived."

"That's only because my uncle is a classic absentminded wizard."

"Just take the compliment, Souffy."

I'm rewarded with a smile. "Okay. And you, of all the otherworlders… you seem the most…"

I'm bracing for "smartest." It's the remaining adjective for the journalist who's already used "drop-dead gorgeous," "sweet," "talented," and "edgy" to describe my bandmates.

"The most aware of how this world works," she says. "You're special." There's a rising blush in her cheeks, a flare to her nostrils, a light in her eyes.

I've been here before. Well, not with a magic pixie dream girl, but I've had way-too-pretty girls gaze up at me like I'm the second coming: Heidi, who interned for Marjorie one summer, Deedee, the podcaster, Maria, the columnist for *Jezebel*, and countless proactive fangirls who managed to get past security.

At the start of NBL fame, I was stupid enough to believe the adoration was for me personally. Even after I wised up (and should have known better) I still took advantage of my celebrity status. It never ended well; relationships built on idolized versions of real people never do. Either I broke their heart, or—more often—they broke mine. Remembering those painful experiences isn't helping now, not when Souffy's looking at me with her big, amber eyes. So, I fall back on Kyle's Rules of Relationships. Number Two: *Looks aren't enough, she's got to be amazing-cool.* Cool, like doing her dissertation on coral reef restoration, or spearheading a nonprofit that helps homeless kids finish high school, or writing and drawing her own comic book. Something to wow me and make me feel like an idiot, but in a good way.

That's where I get the strength to shrug, half laugh and divert her with honesty.

"I have a bit of a cheat. I heard about Mythreal in my world."

Souffy's twitterpation is replaced by curiosity. "Oh, like a story, or legend? That does sometimes happen."

"Sort of like a story, but also like a game. See, where I come from we have these machines, kind of like clocks." The middle ages had clocks, right? I miss Wikipedia. "But with millions of tiny, tiny gears, so we can use them for calculations and to store libraries full of information."

She's nodding, meaning she totally doesn't understand.

"Oh, you mean computers?"

Or, maybe she does.

"You know about computers? How?"

"I took a class about otherworlders and where they come from. There are many other worlds besides Mythreal and your world, did you know?" Nope, news to me. "I had to learn an equation to calculate the number of them. It was fifteen million and thirty-one. I nailed that test. Some worlds are similar to ours, with slightly different kinds of magic, but others, like yours, rely on technology. Learning about the technology was one of my favorite units. Like televisions and washing machines and cell phones, oh and flying cars."

"Flying cars?"

"They must be so amazing to ride in, right?"

I feel like an idiot. In a good way.

Kyle Moretti

Class: Wizard
Level: 1

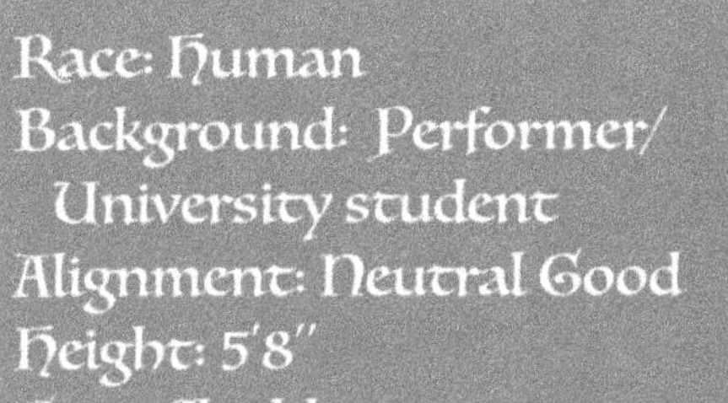

Race: Human
Background: Performer/
  University student
Alignment: Neutral Good
Height: 5'8"
Eyes: Sky blue
Hair: Brown
Age: 25

Str: 11
Char: 14
Dex: 15
Wis: 13
Con: 9
Int: 17

Skills:
Arcana
Investigation
Performance
Mathematics

Inventory:
Red shirt
(no armor)
Spell book
Wizard hat

CHAPTER 16

Souffy

Kyle isn't nearly as unapproachable and scary as Souffy first imagined. They'd only just met, but she feels as comfortable around him as she does with Havelin. And they have so much in common! Kyle is as interested in the otherworlds' histories and sciences as she is. He asks her questions, listens to her answers, and makes connections, saying odd things like "Oh of course, because Archduke Ferdinand wasn't assassinated."

He has a way of being smart without making her feel dumb. Maybe that's why, once they're back to practicing magic, she does something she's never done with another wizard. She lets Kyle see her spellbook.

Wizards jealously guard their spellbooks. It's where they hide the tricks and secrets that actually make the spells work. Not that Souffy had ever been able to make sense of her older sister's spellbook those times she'd snuck a peek. It was just pages and pages of Mallynda's cramped handwriting, listing off every possible detail and condition related to a given spell. Trying to decipher her sister's notes confused Souffy even more.

Souffy's own reason for never showing her spellbook to anyone is because it's an embarrassing mess of misspellings, crossed-out words, and ink blots. Plus, she sketches and doodles in the margins. But Kyle doesn't seem to mind.

"It's your notes, Souffy. You should include whatever helps you cast the spell. My friend Kelly's notes look a bit like this, but with even more colors and arrows. She always got better grades than me. Now let me see if I can write in this language." He dips his quill and brings it to the first page of the spellbook Souffy gave him. "It's so weird, so long as I don't think about what I'm doing, my hand just forms the words."

Kyle's own handwriting, as he copies out the Mystic Armor spell, is careful and orderly and includes occasional equations and graphs. He successfully casts it on his second try.

"I think I could get used to this wizard business," he says.

"I'm glad. You seemed disappointed when the Pathfinder wand glowed red." She'd seen his shoulders slump before he rallied with a smile, and it had been bothering her.

"Oh, about that." Kyle sighs and shakes his head.

"You don't have to tell me."

For a moment, it seems like he won't. Then Kyle takes a deep breath and says, "You remember how I said there is this computer game about Mythreal in my world? Well, I play it. A lot. And the character class I usually play is Bard."

Souffy bites her lips to keep from laughing. It's ridiculous to imagine someone as serious and intelligent as Kyle singing at a tavern with a lute. But then she recalls some of the things he's told her about his world. "You said you and the others were troubadours in the Never Boy Band. I guess it would make sense for you to pick a class that was related to music."

"Never Boy Land," Kyle corrects her. "And I got into *Heroes Summoning* after the band broke up. I missed playing music in a group. Choosing a bard was a bit of vicarious living. But now that I'm here, now that I'm learning real magic, I'm seriously glad to be the party's wizard. I think it suits me." Kyle smiles at her.

It's hard to believe how just this morning Souffy had thought of Arek as the handsomest man in the entire district. But Arek's looks pale before Kyle's: that soft-spiky hair, lips that keep breaking into a half grin, and cornflower-blue eyes that Souffy could get lost in. And unlike with Arek, she genuinely enjoys spending time with him. Plus he's a wizard!

"Absolutely," Souffy agrees. Maybe she can get to know the other heroes this well too. Oscar, Micah, Cole, and maybe even—her heart skips a beat—Tristan.

CHAPTER 17

Souffy

Swish, thump. Tristan's sword leaves a gash in Goliath's side and sends it spiraling towards the white stones that mark the edge of the practice ground's fighting circle. The magical barrier stops the animated manikin from crashing into a trio of young women seated on a wood bench. They flinch and jump to their feet, but their squeals are of delight, not distress.

"Tristan, Tristan, Tristan!" they chant in unison as Goliath rights itself and lumbers back into the center of the ring.

Souffy claps and cheers from her spot next to a corner of the barracks. She has some time before her morning meeting with Lenora to discuss the heroes' training progress. How things have changed in just four short days since their arrival. For one, the mayor had installed benches for all the spectators that had started coming to watch Tristan practice. She glances at the girls now sitting back down. One of them waves in her direction. Souffy reflexively looks over her shoulder but there's no one else around.

"Souffy, come sit with us!" calls another of the three. It takes Souffy a moment to recognize Orley. The soldier has let her hair down and is wearing a daisy-embroidered dress. Souffy does her best to appear casual as she walks over.

"Tristan's footwork has gotten rather good, don't you think, Souffy?" says the one who waved earlier, a plump girl with brown curls. Souffy thinks she might be one of the barmaids at The Chicken or the Egg, the tavern where the Neverboylanders have been staying. The girl moves over to give Souffy some space to sit. "I'm Dinnah, I don't think we've met."

Metal clangs in the background as Tristan resumes blocking the swings of the manikin's sword.

"We're debating which hero is the most impressive," says Orley. "My vote is for Cole. Did you see him yesterday when he scaled the fortress walls? I was lucky to be on guard duty right then."

"How about Micah's archery skills?" says Dinnah. "I saw him hit four bullseyes in a row. And I fancy his green cape, Cole wears too much black."

"Fighting's important, but there are other qualities that make a hero. Oscar's devotion to his deity is so impressive. I see him praying and making offerings every morning," says the third girl, a trade-mage named Tasha who performs metalworking spells for the fort's blacksmith.

"Every morning?" asks Dinnah.

"You know me," Tasha giggles. "I'm so religious."

"I bet you're partial to the wizard, right Souffy?" Orley gives her a knowing wink. "You spend a lot of time with him up in the tower."

"Oh, well, there are a lot of magic spells to cover." Although Souffy isn't certain how much use she is to Kyle. He's absorbing spells at a prodigious rate and even studying from Souffy's textbooks.

"I love his hat," says Tasha. "I want one just like it."

On the field, the manikin attempts another swing that Tristan blocks, their swords clanging inches from Tristan's face. The straw man leans forward, pressing its weight down on its opponent. Souffy sees Tristan's body tense and his foot slip backward. Somehow he manages to shift his weight forward, his right leg hooking the straw man in the process. The manikin goes over backwards, and Tristan puts his sword to its neck. A bell clangs, awarding the match to Tristan. Souffy can't help smiling.

"Or maybe you prefer swords to wands?" asks Orley. Souffy blushes.

"That wouldn't work in a real fight," says a male voice behind them. Souffy turns around to see a peeved-looking Dryden. He always looks like he's eaten a raw lemon these days, especially whenever Tristan is around.

"It looked dashing," says Orley.

Dryden snorts. "Golly doesn't have a real mind, it's nothing more than reflexes and techniques Ferimus wrote down and stuck in its head. That Tristan Ives is all show. You're a trained soldier, Orley, you should see that."

Orley doesn't respond, probably since Dryden is her superior officer. Dinnah and Tasha quietly exchange looks.

"He beat you in combat," says Souffy. *And you haven't dared to face off against him since*, she wants to add, but Dryden has already turned tomato-red and she doesn't actually want to be cruel. Even if he deserves it.

"That was just fooling around with sticks. Real combat is when your opponent means to kill you, when it's no longer a game. It separates warriors from… from whatever these otherworlders are."

Dryden never refers to the Neverboylanders as heroes; it's another thing Souffy's noticed. Meanwhile, on the field, Tristan is attempting to help Goliath up. Because he's put down his sword, the magical safety system has turned off the manikin's animating force, so it keeps flopping over.

"Maybe you could take Tristan out to a swamp and find him a froggywog to fight against?" suggests Dinnah, turning to Souffy.

It's not a bad idea. As it happens, Kyle and Souffy have already discussed finding a small quest for the Neverboylanders, but there just hasn't been time.

This elicits another snort from Dryden. "Souffy wouldn't want to risk her otherworlders getting dirty or injured. Got to keep them looking pretty for that… that singing thing they're putting on tonight. That's her idea of training adventurers."

"Souffy's doing the best she can," says Tasha. "They'll get plenty of that kind of training in the capital."

Souffy appreciates Tasha defending her, but the heroes' impending departure is something she's trying hard not to think about. The Seolia is already a day late in returning, and Souffy's bracing for the proclamation announcement system to broadcast its arrival at any moment.

"Can't happen soon enough for me," says Dryden, his dismissive tone bordering on cruel.

Souffy's had enough. She stands and gives Dryden her best Ravenus sneer. They're the same height, but Souffy's hair gives her an extra inch on Dryden.

"You're just jealous! And you're wrong about the heroes. The progress they've made in the last four days is incredible. They could take down a whole glob of froggywogs, or worse. And instead of making snide comments and hurling insults, you should be grateful for even the chance to have met them. The Divine Wisdom chose those five because there is some grave threat looming over Mythreal, and Never Boy Land will be the ones to save us all!"

"Wow, Souffy," Tristan calls out from the ring, "that was amazing! You've got to write that last part down. Don't tell him this, but you're better than our publicist back home."

The other girls clap in delight and pat her on the back. Dryden opens his mouth, snaps it shut, and then stalks away.

CHAPTER 18

Kyle

Oscar and I are discussing magic spells at a table at The Chicken or the Egg while we wait for breakfast to be served. The inn, despite not having electricity or running water, is better than several of the hotels Marjorie put us up in during our early tour days. I'm trying to fit in as much hero stuff this morning because we'll need all afternoon to rehearse for the concert tonight.

Yep, we're putting on a show.

The mayor's question about us singing and dancing was probably just to irritate his wife, but my bandmates have grabbed hold of a chance to perform like it's an oar and they're drowning. I shouldn't be surprised. Finding one's self living in a magical medieval society, albeit a highly anachronistic one, would be culture shock enough without Souffy and the others asking them to learn weapon combat and magic. They need some hip-hopping and harmonizing time in their comfort zone.

Which isn't to say that rehearsals are going well. Back home we always had a full support team to assist with music arrangements, choreography, and tech issues, plus conflict resolution and ego massaging. Without them, our practices have felt very amateur hour. Not high-school-talent-show bad, more like community-theater mediocre. Our unspoken fear is: What if the problem is us? What if, in the past five years, we've lost those unique qualities that when combined formed the superstar act that was Never Boy Land? And if we can't come together to win hearts and minds, what does that say about fighting monsters?

It's too early in the morning to deal with this. I return my focus to Oscar's quixotic spell choices.

"Preparing Holy Shield is a good idea. It will be useful in a fight, but why was your other choice Purify Victuals?" I ask. Unlike the wizard-class spells I've spent the last three days deciphering, Oscar's cleric spells get zapped directly into his brain by his Love Goddess. Ask, and thou shalt receive. The downside is there's no text, or crib sheet, of exactly what's available. Oscar doesn't seem to have a clue about what to ask for and I get the impression that Verhalty hasn't had much experience with adventuring cleric disciples. Still, who picks Purify Victuals?

"It's a darn useful spell," Oscar insists. "They don't have refrigerators or food inspectors here. You remember what happened in Philadelphia?"

"You mean when we played Lincoln Stadium? The time Tris misplaced his cell phone and locked himself out of his room and we were all freaking out because we couldn't find him?" He was hiding all afternoon from fangirls in a VFW hall shooting pool with Iraq War veterans.

"No, I meant way back, when we were still doing mall performances. We all got salmonella poisoning from the salad bar at the food court and our single bathroom tour bus was stuck in a four-hour traffic jam on the way to Baltimore."

"Oh, yeah." I'd been suppressing that one. "That was bad."

"That's why I requested the food purification spell."

I'm about to remark that an orc charging at you in battle is a more urgent issue than an upset stomach, but at that moment the waitress (I'm not calling her a tavern wench because that's rude) comes over with our breakfast. Today it's porridge with honey and sliced apples, along with fresh-baked bread, some sort of preserved fish, and a pitcher of water. Having lived as a college student for the past four years, I'm not a picky eater. But even I can see there's-wormholes in the apples, a slimy film on the porridge, and a green tint to the fish. I turn to Oscar.

"Okay, you were right, I was wrong."

Oscar grins. He stands up and raises his arms like he's at the Last Supper. "*Verhalty, I implore you, bless this meal. May it give us healthy sustenance to face whatever challenges we encounter today.*" His hands glow, and—despite our meal being nowhere near a window—a gentle sunbeam cuts through the dusty air, alighting on the food. A moment later it's like somebody's applied a Food Network filter on our breakfast, and I'm salivating like Pavlov's dog.

"We still need you to get a healing spell, but I'll talk to Souffy about getting hold of some healing potions as backup," I say as I serve myself up.

Cole creeps over to the table while we're eating. He's wearing the same outfit as yesterday. Back in our world this would have meant he'd been out all night. Oscar's scoping Cole out too; he's probably running through his "Is Cole backsliding?" checklist. I don't smell any alcohol, and Cole's eyes aren't dilated. They say the most dangerous places for recovering addicts are the locations and circumstances where they used to get high. In that case, Cole's in his best place. But it's not like he can order sodas here.

"How's it going?" asks Oscar.

Cole gives us a smile like a kid who's discovered where his parents keep the Christmas presents. Oh boy.

"That good?" I try to sound casual.

"Check it." He slides down his arm gauntlet and twists his wrist. Halfway to his elbow is a brand-new tattoo. It's not fancy like the airbrushed oni demon taking up skin real estate on his bicep, just a simple bluish-black lined mandala. Cole clenches his hand and the ink turns sparkly, like the Milky Way in a sky without light pollution. There are streaks of purple and maroon and as they shift, they create the illusion that the whole tattoo is rotating. He lets his palm open. The pattern settles back to its previous form, and then the whole tattoo fades until there's only a shiny quality to the skin.

"Where did you get that?" asks Oscar.

"Thieves' Guild, can't say more than that."

I roll my eyes. "Good thing I taught you how to pick locks, isn't it?"

"You taught him to pick locks? That's crossing the line!" Oscar is referring to Marjorie's line between okay activities that are edgy and cool to tweens and those verboten ones that would draw parental disapproval or require a social media apology. Given Cole's post-band-break-up escapades, I think he's long past any lines.

"Worshiping a pagan deity isn't any better," says Cole, then he adds, "Don't worry. What happens in Mythreal stays in Mythreal."

"I just don't want you getting hurt. I don't want any of us getting hurt."

Cole and I share a glance.

If you'd asked me which band member would be most likely to crack when isekaied into a fantasy world, my first choice would be Micah because of his fastidiousness and hours-a-day social media habit. But no, he's leaning into his role as Legolas. Instead it seems our usually most dependable member is having coping issues.

As kindly as possible, I say, "Oscar, it's likely that we'll all get hurt at some point. That's how these stories work. Our best shot at getting through this alive is to maximize the skills and abilities available to our classes. We'll need Cole's sneakiness and underworld contacts, just like we'll need your protection magic."

Oscar nods. "Just promise me that you won't kill anyone." Cole does that thing where he raises one eyebrow without moving any other part of his face. "Okay, promise me you won't kill anyone who's not evil," amends Oscar.

"Or actively trying to kill us," I add.

Cole shrugs. "Sure."

"And you, Oscar, see if you can get an actual healing spell out of Verhalty, okay?"

"I see your point, Kyle. I've planned a special offering for her this morning. I expect she'll be in an agreeable mood afterwards."

"Special offering?" asks Cole.

"Micah helped me write her a song. There's crooning in it."

Yeah, that should do it. Oscar has an innate ability to charm women over forty. Being immortal puts Verhalty squarely in that demographic.

I wait until Oscar leaves for his morning prayers. "You are being careful, right Cole?"

"Yes, unlike the rest of you guys, I didn't spend my childhood pampered and helicopter parented. I have real world experience."

He gives me a calm, even look that I'd totally buy if he hadn't used that same expression four hours before the time he overdosed in my hotel room.

"This isn't our world, Cole. It's fantasyland, and things aren't always what they seem. Even here in boring Bydlo, there are tensions in the north between the Laska Company and these Trädskydd Druids. And we're heroes, not entertainers. We don't get to party with bad guys anymore. We need to be careful about who we trust." I'm not trying to nerdsplain. Cole still takes it the wrong way.

"Thank goodness we have someone as smart and magical as you to take care of us, Kyle."

He grabs a plate. We eat in silence. Micah shows up, yawning.

"I need an americano, triple shot," he says.

I pour him a mug of Oscar's purified water and, with a snap that's more stylish than necessary, say, "*Alakazam, Beans of Java, Encaffeinate.*" The Prestidigitation cantrip is more state of mind than specific phrasing. I'm visualizing a Starbucks coffee: the brown bubbles that cling to the edge of the cardboard cup, the roasty, caramelized smell, the way the first sip always burns my tongue. Transmutation spells—illusions too—are all about envisioning the exact shape you want the magic to take, down to the last detail. Specificity counts more than desire, which is why Souffy has such problems with these kinds of spells. That, and her undiagnosed dyslexia.

The liquid in the mug darkens and steam rises up. Micah raises it to his nostrils and breathes in the aroma. He takes a sip and makes a satisfied sound. "Roast is still too dark, but you're getting closer."

"Is it really coffee?" asks Cole.

"For the next hour at least." I'm not sure if I transubstantiated the water molecules into caffeine or if the placebo effect is just that strong. Either way, Micah's perking up.

"Where are Tristan and Oscar? I need to go over the song arrangements with them before we start rehearsing."

"We're just doing covers, right?" I ask. We'd brainstormed a list of Americana songs we could sing acapella for the show tonight. Otherworlders were expected to be different, but we didn't think Bydlo would be up for Billboard Top 40, much less Cole's rapping.

"Actually, I think I can get a lot of our stuff to work by simplifying the chord progressions and dropping the tempos," says Micah. "And Souffy's found a ritual spell that can generate sounds. I'll ask her if she could simulate some instrumental backgrounds."

"You can try, but fine control isn't Souffy's strong suit." The bigger and louder the better. After she demonstrated her Alarm spell, my ears rang for ten minutes.

"I can make it work. I just need everyone's time this morning for a few hours." It's never just a few hours. Experience tells me Micah will be messing with arrangements and harmonies until just before the show.

"Tristan is still working out at the fortress; he'll probably need a rest first. And I sent Oscar to see if he could score a healing spell from his deity," I say. "I don't want to interrupt him."

"You make it sound like a drug deal," says Cole.

I laugh at the suggestion, but Micah doesn't join in.

"How are we going to prepare with everyone doing their own thing?" He diva sighs.

"We're performing for a bunch of middle-aged shopkeepers and farmers on the same platform they use to auction off cattle," says Cole. "We don't really need to bring our A-game."

"Some of us have pride as artists." Micah sniffs. It's 9 a.m., time for the first Cole-Micah spat of the day.

"Some of us have pride in staying alive," Cole shoots back. "Right, Kyle?"

He's correct, but if I side with either of them, things will escalate. "I'm just a backup singer."

"I am too, under these circumstances. I don't think any of your arrangements leave room for a rap solo, do they Micah?"

"Please, I'm not cutting your parts. I've been researching the local music traditions and I think I've found a way to work in some spoken word segments. You'll see when I show you the arrangements." He pulls out a stack of parchments. A very tall stack of parchments.

"Wait," I say. "How much time have you spent researching? You have been training with Havelin every day, right?"

"Sure, we do some archery each morning." Micah waves a hand dismissively.

"But you're practicing other ranger stuff as well? Like learning about plants and um…" What exactly do rangers do?

"Orienteering, tracking?" supplies Cole.

"It's a forest with trees. What's important is that I hit targets with my arrows. Speaking of which, how's the crossbow training going, Cole?"

I stand and pound the table before Cole can respond. "Micah, please tell me that you haven't been wasting all your time learning period music?" Micah looks down at his coffee. "Fantastic." I pick up my hat and walk away.

I honestly don't care, I honestly don't care, I honestly don't care, I repeat over and over as I leave the tavern.

I'm hot and cold at the same time, and I keep swallowing down saliva. Having had to perform in front of stadiums full of screaming fans, I'm familiar with the symptoms of a panic attack. I dealt with those by charging on stage, counting on countless hours of training and muscle memory to get me through. And trusting my bandmates. I knew that Oscar would be dedicated, Micah a perfectionist, Cole would rise to the occasion, and Tristan would smile like it was the best night of his life. Everything always turned out fine.

But stagecraft doesn't take down goblins, and missteps in a real battle could get one of us killed. I read in one of Souffy's history books that some of the otherworld heroes chosen by the Divine Wisdom ended up dead. Not like they took one too many hits and magically disappeared to who knew where, but dead as in dismembered bodies on the ground, usually left to decompose under a cairn of stones for a grave marker. No respawns, no save points, no AFK.

I've walked about two blocks from our inn, all the way to the main square that's still hosting the morning market. Closing my eyes, I lean against an alley wall and force myself to take deep calming breaths. In and out, in and out. Bydlo air lacks the stale tang of car exhaust; it's just that honest warm grassy-gassy smell you get from horses. I hear a subdued clank of armor and turn my head to see Tristan standing next to me, smiling like it's the best day of his life.

"It's weird," he says. "This place is like something out of a theme park, but without the shops and tourists." Tris exudes only the faintest smell of sweat. His hair is windswept, his cheeks flushed, and there's a smudge of dirt on his chin. The look comes together like something from central casting. It's not natural for us to continue looking this good without dedicated stylists and an arsenal of personal grooming products. I suspect Oscar's Love Goddess must be bestowing beauty sleep on us, which is a perk we wouldn't be getting if Oscar had gone with a more practical god.

"Good workout?" I ask.

"I took down Golly four times."

I don't remember that guard's name—I'm memorizing everyone we meet in case they're important later on. "Golly?"

"The magic fighting scarecrow."

"Congrats." Not that I should be surprised; I've been to Tristan's kendo matches.

"Yeah, this fighter class suits me great. Just go out swinging, and…" he looks at me to see if I remember the punchline.

"No need for thinking," we say together. It was from his movie, which I may have rewatched a few times.

"What, no smile? I'm losing my touch." He squeezes my shoulder and gives me puppy dog eyes. He's trying to make me feel better.

"It's great that you're getting good at wielding that sword, Tris. But I just, I feel…"

"What?"

"That we're not cut out for heroing. We're nowhere close to combat-ready. You know what Micah's been doing instead of learning ranger lore? Music arrangements."

"Yeah, for the performance tonight. It'll be great!"

"We didn't get called here to do shows." I push away from the wall and start pacing. "We're here to fight monsters, or evil wizards, or stop a demon army. Maybe all three. And at this rate we're totally unprepared. It's not only Micah. Oscar doesn't know any healing spells. Cole spent last night getting a new tattoo. I've mastered Magic Mortar, but my mana levels are still too low to cast more than two spells in a fight."

"Hey, Kyle. It's not so bad as all that. They'll train us in the capital. And Souffy says it's common for other adventurers and magic users to join our party. By the time we need to fight, we'll be ready."

"I'm the only one of us taking this seriously." I feel silly even saying this, but it's true.

"Kyle." He catches my hand, holds me in place. "Kyle, it's going to be okay."

Tristan looks directly into my eyes. I should be immune to this, should remember that this is the same dork who gets the minute and hour hands on his watch confused so we'd always arrive an hour early. Back in grade school his favorite snack was peanut butter and American cheese sandwiches skewered with pretzels to give them crunch. Still, his certainty calms my nerves.

"Marjorie would never let anything bad happen to us. Whatever, however, she's doing this, we'll come out of this fine. And afterwards, we'll finally do our world tour."

The rational half of my brain bitch-slaps the emotional half for being an idiot. Of course Tristan's taking this in stride. He still thinks this is an elaborate PR stunt to generate buzz. And why wouldn't it be? Everything has gone perfectly for him ever since our YouTube channel blew up. He's never had music training, but he gets scouted for a studio-backed band, whose first album goes double-platinum. The band falls apart and the next month he launches a solo career. He's in a movie that's universally panned by critics for being an incomprehensible hot mess, but it still makes enough money to green-light a sequel. He doesn't even know that it's possible to fail.

I yank my hand out of his, turn to stalk away, and immediately collide with a young woman. She squeaks as she reels backwards. I catch her hand just before her butt hits the street.

"I am so sorry," I apologize. The woman—teenager actually—is wearing a fluffy petticoat with grass stains and burrs along the hem. As I pull her back to standing, I note that she smells strongly of lanolin and wet dog.

"Are you"—she's not letting go of my hand—"the otherworld heroes I've been searching for?"

CHAPTER 19

Dryden

Souffy's unreasonable outburst plays over and over in Dryden's mind. And she had to say it in front of her friends, and Tristan. He isn't jealous of Tristan. The very idea of it! Sure the otherworlder looks good swinging his sword. But that's all it is, looks. Damn that Souffy.

Dryden needs something to comfort his soul. He finds himself wandering into The Chicken or the Egg because they bake the best custard tarts. The barkeep passes him the last two. But angry voices interrupt him before he can take his first bite.

"What's wrong with the first one?" The voice is male, but pitched high.

"If you didn't want my opinion, why even ask?" comes a menacing reply.

Dryden isn't on duty, but that's no reason to let a fight break out in his presence. Plate of untouched tarts in hand, he gets up and makes his way towards the source of the commotion, where he finds two of the otherworlders staring daggers at each other. Dryden curses at himself; how could he have forgotten that this is the tavern where the Neverboylanders are staying? He should just walk away. They're Souffy's heroes, her responsibility. Before he can make himself scarce, Micah, the ranger, waves at him.

"Dryden, come over here! We need you to settle something for us." When Dryden reluctantly makes his way past the intervening tables, Micah shoves a couple of pieces of parchment in his face. Each is covered in lines and squiggles. Cole deftly takes Dryden's plate and sets it on the table, thereby freeing up the guard's hands.

"This is for the opening number. Should we have Tristan come out alone and perform the first verse solo, or do all of us come on stage at once and go straight to the chorus?"

Dryden isn't sure which is more unintelligible, the bizarre glyphs on the parchment or the odd words coming out of Micah's mouth.

"We always start with all of us on stage." Cole directs this at Micah. "Always. And why are you even asking him?"

"Because I want to get a feel for the music scene and he's a local under thirty. I need his opinion."

It's never a bad thing to be needed, but all Dryden desires at this moment is for Cole and Micah to go back to arguing with each other and let him be. He darts a longing glance at his tarts. Any distraction would be fine.

Cole looks over Dryden's shoulder. "Hey Tristan, you're back!"

Or, any distraction except for that.

"Great news guys, Kyle found us a quest! Oh, hey there Dryden."

Dryden turns and nods the barest acceptable amount of acknowledgment. He finds himself surrounded: Tristan is accompanied by their wizard, Kyle, and a youngish woman who looks vaguely familiar— something about her sandy-brown ringlets or watery blue eyes. Dryden squeezes himself into a spot between Cole and Kyle, just out of reach of his pastries.

"This is Malza Stennish. She's asked for our help," says Kyle.

Dryden recognizes the name. The Stennishes own a farm a couple of hours outside of town and sell honey, beeswax candles, and various dyed yarns at the market.

"Please, I've lost my sheep, I don't know what I'll do without them," says Malza on cue. She looks imploringly at the Neverboylanders with her hands clasped together, her fingers intertwined, her eyes swimming with barely held-back tears.

A memory snaps into Dryden's mind.

"Please, I've lost my puppy, I don't know what I'll do without her." That's what Malza said, what is it, almost four years ago? Dryden had been a recruit for no more than a week when his superior officer charged him, Havelin, and Boryk to help find the dog the twelve-year-old girl had managed to lose in the market. They spent the better part of the day cornering the mutt only to have her miraculously slip away from their grasp every time.

"Looking for sheep, Kyle? That's a quest? Really?" asks Cole.

Dryden slips into a brief reverie imagining the otherworlders wandering around the forest for hours: burrs catching on their clothes, insects biting every exposed inch of skin, one of them might even fall into a patch of stinging ivy!

"It's a starter quest," explains Kyle. "It builds experience. Gives us a chance to test our abilities and try out our newly acquired skills." He looks to Dryden for support.

"Yes, it's just the experience you need!" Dryden—suddenly inspired—takes a page out of Souffy's book and improvises. "Why, I believe the Heroes of the Realm's very first quest was finding a cow." A lovely image forms in Dryden's mind of these "heroes" showing up for their performance tonight, muddy, disheveled, and stinking of sheep.

"And exactly what kind of skills does one hone by finding sheep?" asks Micah.

"Tracking, orienteering, other forest ranger stuff," enumerates Cole. Micah glares at him.

"We have a concert tonight. We don't have time for this," says Micah flatly.

"Don't have time for what?" Now the cleric, Oscar, joins the group. He slips in between Kyle and Dryden. Dryden moves back to make room and marvels at how anyone can keep their white clothing that pristine.

"You heroes have to help me find my sheep. They're lost," states Malza. She seems oblivious to the debate raging amongst the otherworlders. As things stand, Dryden counts two against, and two for, making Oscar the deciding vote.

"That shouldn't take much time," Oscar says. "Where did you lose them and how many did you lose?"

"In the forest behind our farm. I lost all seven, but now there's only five left… that we know of."

"What happened to the other"—Tristan pauses, a look of concentration passing over his features—"two?"

"Basil found them this morning, mauled to death."

"Who's Basil?" Tristan asks.

"More importantly," Kyle cuts in, "mauled to death? Like, by wolves?"

"Could be, but the gouges are larger than wolf fangs," says Malza.

"How large is 'large?'" asks Oscar.

Malza holds her hands apart about six inches. Kyle and Oscar exchange worried glances.

"That's the size of a dagger," says Cole. "Could it be bandits?"

"Why would bandits maul a sheep?" asks Micah.

"It might be goblins," suggests Malza.

Goblins. Dryden tries not to roll his eyes.

Farmers blame everything on goblins. Bloodthirsty screams in the middle of the night, must be goblins. Horses stolen from the barn, definitely goblins. Chickens spooked and not laying eggs, yep, goblins. Weird circle patterns cut into the fields, goblins, goblins, goblins. Six years back, there actually had been a camp of goblins in the woods west of town in the general vicinity of the Stennish farm. But the militia and several summoned heroes—regular Mythreal ones, not some fancy otherworlders—launched a coordinated offensive against the encampment and the vicious creatures were driven into the far north, never to be heard from since. Still, it's fun to see the discomfort this revelation has caused in Souffy's heroes. But if Dryden wants the otherworlders to go on Malza's mutton quest, he realizes that they'll need some additional nudging.

"Oh, you fellows can handle a couple of goblins. Take down one or two and the rest scatter in fear. So long as you have adequate armor to protect you from the arrows, you should be fine," Dryden says.

"He's right," says Kyle. "Goblins make for ideal opponents to heroes just starting out. And we always have healing spells.... Oscar, please tell me you obtained a healing spell."

Oscar gives him a thumbs-up. "I told Verhalty that I was worried about scarring. She bestowed on me a spell to heal wounds right away. And you'll be with us, right Dryden?"

"Of course." Although as he says it, the idea of being stuck with Tristan while they look for some sheep starts to lose its sheen as a worthwhile prank. Maybe he'll claim a last-minute militia errand to excuse himself?

"I'm not sure about this," says Micah. "The show's tonight and we need more time for rehearsal. We could help her out tomorrow."

"We weren't sent to Mythreal to perform music, Micah," says Kyle, his voice tight and clipped.

"Guys, guys," Tristan intervenes, "we can do both. Picture this: moments before we hit the stage, the mayor uses the magic PA system to announce that we're just back from slaying goblins and rescuing this lovely girl's sheep. The crowd will go wild. Then we run onstage and perform our best songs. They're going to love us! And if we miss a dance step or two, they can fix it in edits." Tristan's voice drops conspiratorially at the end of his little speech.

Beside him, Dryden hears Oscar say to Kyle: "He still thinks we're on some sort of virtual reality TV, doesn't he?"

"Yep."

"So, you'll help me find my sheep?" Malza asks.

Micah sighs. "How long does it take to get to this forest? We need to be back by mid-afternoon at the latest."

"Oh, it won't take any time at all. I've got Basil, she's a blink dog."

"What's a blink dog?" asks Oscar.

"It's a fairy-dog," explains Kyle. "It can teleport over short distances, along with anything attached to it."

It surprises Dryden how knowledgeable the wizard is, and not just in contrast to his ignorant comrades. Dryden sincerely wishes he had known about a blink dog's abilities before he'd wasted a full day chasing Basil in the market that day back when he was a novice. Still, something about what Malza is saying feels off.

"I know Basil's a grown dog, Malza, but she can only transport one person at a time. Do you think she'd be able to make that many trips in a row?"

"Don't worry about Basil," says Malza. "She's a big dog now."

"Big dog" turns out to be an understatement. As they leave the tavern, Malza jams two fingers in her mouth and lets out a piercing whistle that rivals Souffy's Alarm spell. Thunder cracks—even though the day is sunny and clear—and a dog larger than a full-grown bull suddenly materializes in front of them, along with the smell of rotten eggs.

"So, that's a blink dog," says Kyle. "Kind of like if someone crossed a pug with a rhinoceros."

"She's not a purebred," says Malza. "Okay everyone, grab the collar and hold on tight!"

Hold on tight. Dryden repeats the words in his head. He's just thought of a simple way to extricate himself from this pointless adventure.

Malza giggles as Basil bathes her owner's face with her giant, slobbering tongue, and takes hold of the dog's collar. Oscar follows suit, but manages to avoid the tongue washing. Cole and Micah take hold of the collar on Basil's other side, keeping as far from each other as possible.

Finally, Tristan, taking advantage of his height, grabs the top of the collar, which leaves no more collar to hold onto.

"I think we're out of space," says Kyle.

"If you hold hands with one of the others, it should still work," says Malza.

"This will be fun!" Tristan says. He holds out his hand to the wizard, but Kyle hangs back with a frown on his face.

"Is momentum conserved during teleportation?" he asks. When no one answers, he sighs. "I'm not slipping out of your grip and ending up halfway between Bydlo and wherever it is we're headed." Instead of taking the offered hand, Kyle takes a step closer to Tristan and, standing side to side, wraps his arm around the other's waist. Tristan puts his free hand across Kyle's back, gripping him under his armpit.

Dryden grabs Kyle's other hand.

"You sure?" Kyle asks him, looking dubiously at their connection.

Dryden squeezes Kyle's hand. "I'm ready."

"To the forest, Basil!" Malza shouts.

The air hums. The humming starts low and rises in pitch. Dryden counts in his head. *One. Two.* He loosens his grip. *Three.* There's a sharp crack and Kyle's hand—along with Kyle himself and the rest of the otherworlders—is whisked away, as if blown back by a massive wind. Dryden thinks he sees the human-dog cluster several streets down the way, then there's another crack and they're gone. Dryden finds himself all alone, still standing next to the tavern. There's an uncomfortable feeling in the pit of his stomach, like maybe this may have been a mistake.

But, no. The otherworlders will be fine, he reassures himself. Malza probably embellished the story and exaggerated the size of the gouges. By now the remaining sheep will be wanting to return, and Micah has been trained by Havelin, who can track a weasel blindfolded. The wizard likely has a locator spell on him. Everyone knows the woods are only dangerous after sunset. Souffy bragged in front of everyone that her heroes are more than capable of completing a quest. When they get back (probably only a little worse for wear) Dryden will buy them all, even Tristan, a round of ale and they'll all have a good laugh about it afterwards. Everything will be fine, just fine.

Having thus rationalized away his sense of misgiving, a mostly guilt-free Dryden walks back into the tavern, hoping to find his tarts still on the table.

CHAPTER 20

Kyle

As I'm repeatedly yanked sideways and then slammed into Tristan's hip, I find the answer to my question. Yes. Yes, momentum is conserved during magical teleportation.

At least magical teleportation via blink dog. I feel like an accordion as I'm tugged and squeezed through a series of locations, each one more rural than the next. Tristan's got a good grip on me so I'm not too worried about being thrown off. Not like Dryden, whose hand ripped out of mine during the first jump.

Or before… I remember his grip slackening before the first thunderclap.

But if it was intentional, then why? Was it a convenient way to get us out of his hair for a few hours? Or perhaps he means for us to miss our concert, or worse? We are in a fantasy world. This place should be crawling with villains. But then I picture Dryden: his bucket helmet, his river of facial hair, the way he's constantly throwing lame insults at Tristan. If Dryden was intending to betray us, wouldn't he first try to—I don't know—be nice to us?

We complete our final jump and Basil does the wet dog shake which knocks us all down into the grass. I disengage myself from Tristan and check to make sure I still have my hat. Yes! I'm way too attached to this piece of apparel.

"One, two, three, four, five, six…" Oscar counts out. He's always paranoid about leaving anyone behind. "Where's Dryden?"

"Our grip broke with the first jump," I say. I'm not throwing the guy under a bus. Marjorie Banks' 9th Law of Boy Bands: *Just smile at the haters.*

"I hope he's okay," says Oscar. "At least there'll be someone to let Souffy know where we are." Right, we forgot to mention to anyone about our impromptu quest adventure. While I don't see Dryden rushing out to tell anyone, we weren't exactly discrete in our leave-taking. Should something happen, I'm confident Souffy will extract the details from Dryden.

With that settled, I take a moment to look around. Basil has landed us on a meadow halfway up a hillside overlooking the bucolic countryside. No sign of Bydlo anywhere. Down the hill, I see several cultivated fields and, in the distance, a brown strip that could be a road. The meadow ends in a wall of green forest dappled with the yellow and orange of deciduous trees trying to get a jump on autumn. The vibe of this forest skews towards Hallmark greeting cards rather than a "beware these woods," and even with whatever was up with Dryden's machinations, I have a good feeling about us locating the missing sheep.

Then I spot the patch of white and red at the forest's edge.

I start towards it, my bandmates along with Malza and her dog following. As we approach, a low buzzing fills the air accompanied by a rank, musky smell. I hold my breath, and not just because of the smell. A moment later, we've found our first sheep, or what's left of it, bloodied and crawling with flies. Further evidence that this was not a natural death, the bones and hoof of one leg have been dragged into the woods and the remaining limbs sprawl outward, pushed aside to expose the sheep's stomach. The belly is torn open, and bits of intestine tumble out.

"I'm going to be sick." Micah's voice is scratchy and weak as he takes several steps backwards.

"I thought you said you were in charge of hunting down meat for your commune?" asks Cole. That's harsh. My stomach's not liking this either; I prefer my protein wrapped in plastic in the grocery cooler.

"Rabbits mostly. They were clean kills, and it was someone else's job to prep the meat. That face…"

The angle of the sheep's mouth and the way its gums are pulled back, you could imagine it dying mid-scream. Or maybe it's just rigor mortis. Only, there's something else off about it.

"Is it just me," says Oscar, "or is this sheep larger than the ones back home?"

He's right. It's cow-sized, maybe bigger. I think back to the pixelated livestock from the online version of this world. They hadn't seemed abnormally large. Horses were normal size for sure. It's not like everything from the video game Mythreal needs to match. Still, I glance at the bison-sized Basil and remember how Dryden had seemed taken aback upon seeing it.

"Say, Malza, has Basil always been this large of a dog?"

"No, she was the runt of the litter." Malza reaches up—way up—to rub her dog's muzzle. "All those people used to tease you. But now that you've gotten your growth spurt, no one's making fun of you anymore, are they Bazy?" A tongue the size of a salad plate laps her face.

"Exactly when did she get her growth spurt?"

"A couple of weeks ago, the same time the sheep got big. We had to cut a larger door just to get them in and out of the barn."

"Is that… normal around here?" asks Micah.

"No." The way Malza pauses makes me think that this may be the first time she's considered this angle. "At least, I haven't heard of it happening before."

"So, for some reason," I say slowly, "your animals all suddenly got big?"

"Yes."

Way to bury the lede, Malza!

"Lucky for me," she continues. "I'm going to get a bunch more wool this winter, once you find the sheep." She glances down at the carcass. "Once you find the rest."

I look at the size and depth of the cuts in the dead sheep and wonder if more than just Malza's livestock became supersized. And it could just be the sun hiding behind a cloud, but it's looking darker under those trees.

"We should find these other sheep," says Tristan. He's looking around, and not in a nervous way.

We cross the bushes up to the edge of the trees, but Basil holds back. Oscar is the closest and he reaches under Basil's collar and gives a little tug. Basil sits down and howls in a creditable impersonation of Scooby Doo.

"Come on boy," Oscar says.

"Girl," Malza corrects him. "And Basil doesn't go into the forest. She still thinks she's small."

So much for my backup plan of grabbing the dog and making a fast escape in case the goblins or whatever prove to be more than we can handle.

"I'd feel better with the teleporting dog close to us," Oscar says, clearly on the same wavelength.

"Let me try," says Tristan. "I'm good with animals." He gets close to Basil and holds her head, looking deep into her eyes. "Hey girl." He drops his voice. "We could really use your help. I know it's scary in there. I'm scared too. Together, we can do this. But not without you, okay?" At this, Basil gets up, pants loudly, and starts for the forest, proving Tristan's charm offensive is occasionally practical.

As a group, we make our way around the dead sheep and past the first line of trees. The temperature drops a degree or two under the forest canopy. We're stepping on a bunch of leafy plants that look pretty much like the ones back home (not that I've ever paid much attention). There are no informative signs exhorting the wonders of nature or directing us to stay on the trails. No trails either.

"Which way should we go?" I ask Micah.

He tilts his head, confused. "How should I know?"

"You're our ranger. Telling us which way to go in the forest is kind of your job."

This being Micah, he doesn't even bother to try to look apologetic. "What about you, Malza? You know the woods right?"

"No," she shakes her head, "I stay out of the woods. There are wild animals. And some folks say it's haunted."

"But only at night, right?" jokes Tristan.

Malza shrugs.

"The earth seems disturbed here." I point down. "What do you think Micah?"

Micah studies the ground. He's self-centered, not stupid, and it's in his best interest to find those sheep as quickly as possible. Oscar and I gained spellcasting abilities with our class assignments. Hopefully Micah will have gained some sort of tracking instinct.

"Hmm, that looks like a hoof print." He moves a bit further in. "And look!" There's a note of excitement in his voice as he plucks a bit of white fuzz off a nearby tree. "I think I've got this, come on." He's humming under his breath, and there's a lightness to his steps. A bit of the world-weary artist vibe he's been affecting drops away, and I'm reminded of the unabashedly enthusiastic kid he used to be.

Come to think of it, all of us—me included—are acting a little less jaded-2022-NBL and a little more upbeat-2019-NBL. Maybe this could lead to a bonding moment? Maybe me thinking that jinxes the possibility? I force myself back into sheep-finding mode.

After a bit of wrestling through bushes we come into a more open area. The trees here are coniferous and there's a layer of decaying needles.

It's got that sacred nature feel. The birds fall silent around us; I'm blaming Basil for that.

Micah pauses every few steps looking for traces of the sheep's passage. We work our way down a hill around giant ferns and boulders covered in moss. Eventually, we come to a stream with rocks conveniently placed to make for an easy crossing to what almost looks like a trail on the other side. We follow this path downstream until it ends at a massive and very spiky bush. The second stream crossing doesn't have any convenient rocks, but on the plus side, magic waterproofing is very effective, so my feet are dry as we wade across. Micah leads us up an embankment of loose soil and I'm glad for once that I'm not weighted down with armor.

"Are you sure the sheep went this way?" asks Cole. He's marching up front with Micah, because of course he's not letting Micah be the more athletic one.

"Yes. This just sounds, I mean, feels right." Micah replies curtly.

Next to me, Oscar slips back downslope, catching himself by digging his shield into the ground. The higher we trudge, the steeper it gets until it's only by grabbing tree roots that we can keep upright. Up at the top I see Cole pull himself over the lip like he's a swimmer exiting the pool. Showoff. It's not just the four inches he has on me, the guy's got crazy long arms. I'm clumsily trying to position my leg for leverage when I hear a sudden crackle and pop and a bark above me. I look around to see that there's no one but me and Oscar still climbing; Malza and Tristan must have caught a lift from the dog.

"Hey, that's cheating!" calls Oscar.

"Sorry," says Tristan. He crouches at the top and offers a hand. I take it and he pulls me up easily. Well, someone's gotten stronger.

"All that sword practice," he explains as if I'd just complimented him aloud. Which I explicitly hadn't. I don't reply because I'm taking in the scene that's unfolded before me.

It's brighter up here, owing to the lack of canopy, and the lack of canopy is because most of the trees have been knocked over. Some have had their trunks snapped like toothpicks, others are fully uprooted. Something massive went through here taking this part of the forest with it.

"What happened here?" asks Oscar after Tristan hauls him, and his plate mail armor, up.

"A fire?" guesses Cole.

"The trees still have their leaves," observes Micah.

"There's a burnt smell, but it's not like a campfire." Oscar wrinkles his nose. "It's more chemical-like, bleachy?"

A memory from Chem 121 lab hits me. "Ozone."

This isn't random destruction; the fallen trees lie in a blast pattern. We make our way towards the center, climbing over trunks, pushing through branches. We must be getting close because the ozone is making my eyes water. At last, we work our way around a final tree that looks like it was thrown and behold the source of the chaos.

It's a pockmarked rock—a bit larger than a bowling ball—in the center of a crater of charred and cracked earth. It's such a deep black that it makes the burnt earth look gray. When I stare at it, it's like looking into a spotlight, but inverted. A black circle imprints in my vision, darkening everything else, and when I blink and look around, the afterimage stays a few moments.

"Is that a meteorite?" asks Tristan.

"Wizard Ferimus called it a sky rock," says Malza in her infuriating matter-of-fact way. I recall that Ferimus is Souffy's uncle.

"But you said you'd never been in the forest," says Cole.

"I meant the one in our barn that put a hole through the roof. We found it one morning. Then Ferimus showed up. He said it fell off the huge shooting star that everyone saw pass through the sky the previous night. The rock in our barn was smaller than this, and Ferimus asked if he could keep it. Of course, we said yes."

"Malza," I say, slowly, "did the sky rock fall through your barn roof the same night that all your animals got bigger?"

"Um… yes. It was the same night."

I can't help myself, I bury my face in my hands and silently curse our luck. Malza, you are officially the most useless, least informative NPC, ever.

"Do you think there's a connection, Kyle?" says Tristan, faking naïve innocence. He winks because he knows I know he isn't that dense.

And that's when the silence is shattered by a bloodcurdling, inhuman scream. Which stops suddenly, even more unnerving.

"My sheep!" cries Malza.

"It came from over there," says Micah, pointing in the direction Basil is desperately backing away from.

This wasn't the sheep hunt we'd signed up for. I brace for our group to freak out and fall into chaos.

Instead, the strangest thing happens. We click. We take off as a team in the direction Micah's pointing. Once clear of the meteorite debris we break into a run. Our signature opening number, "Tonight's the Night," is playing in my head and my feet are pounding the ground with each drop beat. Not just me, we're synchronized in our running. There's a small gully we leap across, a pile of rocks we jump over, a copse of trees we round. It's like how it was before a performance when five cynical, whiny teenagers transformed into focused professionals whose only desire was to give their fans the show of their lives

Only this time, we've become heroes.

"Sheep!" cries Micah. He's in front of me with Cole; I think we've outrun the others.

The ground here is lower with trees around the edge. On the other side of the clearing, something big and fluffy tries—unsuccessfully—to hide itself behind a tree. It is indeed a sheep, the size of a cow. No, make that two, there's another one hiding behind the first. Nope, three. But this one's not hiding. It's sprawled flat on the ground, about ten yards from the others. It must be injured; I can see it twitching.

Except, that's not right. Twitching would involve its limbs or head; it wouldn't be coming from the chest and belly. That's not the sheep moving, there's something digging around inside it.

CHAPTER 21

Kyle

Whatever's burrowed inside the sheep cadaver emits sharp clicks and squishy gurgles. I see something rope-like slide out and whip against the ground. My brain jumps to "snake" but switches to "tail" when I see a scaled foot back out after it. The wool of the sheep's carcass shakes some more. The monster (I can say monster because normal lizards aren't wolf-sized, and they don't hunt livestock) is wriggling its way out. I take in the details: three toes per foot, each with an inch-long talon, two batlike wings. It's dragging out an organ, I think a heart, and once it's cleared the carcass it tosses its prize up and gobbles it down with its… beak?

Micah comes up alongside me. "Does that thing have a rooster head?" He whispers. The beast shakes its head. What I thought was sheep entrails is a red comb.

It's only Micah and me here. What happened to Cole? I glance behind to check and my movement alerts the creature to our presence. It hops around and considers us with its beady eyes.

"What is that thing, Kyle?" Micah presses.

"Some kind of chimera." Which just means any creature with body parts from multiple species of animals, not that Micah necessarily knows that. It's not a hippogriff, and definitely not a griffin. I'm running out of half-remembered mythological animals. It's sad how much of my encyclopedic knowledge comes from video games. Then it clicks. "Cockatrice." That fits. "It's a cockatrice."

"And it's a monster, right? An evil monster?"

"Yeeees?" And I'm sure they have some special attack. It's infuriatingly just out of reach of my memory.

"Got it." Micah takes a step forward. The cockatrice's head snaps back and forth between us, calculating our threat level, or maybe deciding who's tastier. Either way, it starts for us. It sways with each step, its tail acting as a counterweight. Like a rehearsed dance move, Micah raises his bow, positioning an arrow at the same time he draws it. Meanwhile, I reach for one of the small squares of leather I packed in my side pouch. Even as I'm sliding it out, I use my thumb to circle twice clockwise, once counterclockwise. "*Be my armor, be my protection, Armatus.*"

A warm, comforting weight descends on my shoulders, arms, legs, and head just as Micah lets loose his arrow. The shot hits the cockatrice squarely in the chest, and it falls backwards. Staring at the dead body, I feel foolish for panicking and casting my Mystic Armor spell. I remember to breathe.

Then, with an angry cluck and a flap of its wings, the cockatrice bounces back onto its feet. Micah's arrow skewered the creature, but its energetically swishing tail tells me this fight is not over. It looks between the two of us as if trying to determine who shot it. You'd think it would go for the larger target with the bow, but my bright red hat keeps drawing its eyes. I'm so glad I've got my Mystic Armor.

"How can it still be alive?" asks Micah.

"It is a magical beast." And suddenly I remember its superpower. "Careful," I say as the cockatrice drops low and lets out a threatening hiss, "I think it spits acid."

"Acid?" Micah fumbles the next arrow he's reaching for. It falls and bounces off the ground at the same time as the cockatrice charges. It's hobbled by Micah's first arrow, but even limping, there's a fire in its eyes. I'm just about to leap to the side when a figure steps out from behind the tree; I hear a woosh, catch a glint of steel, and the cockatrice freezes in its tracks. There's a hilt of a dagger sticking out of its neck as it falls over, thrashing briefly. Then it turns limp, dead for reals this time.

"Bragging rights go to whoever lands the finishing blow, right?" asks Cole from his lurking spot. I think even Micah is happy to see the smug look on his face.

"Careful. Kyle says the thing spits acid."

I startle at a movement behind me, but it's only Malza running towards her remaining live sheep. Tristan and Oscar have also now arrived at the grove. The fight with the cockatrice took less than a minute, although it felt like forever.

"There might be more of them," I say, and as if on cue, we hear a squawk from above.

A second cockatrice drops down from the branches of a nearby tree. Its ungainly flapping would be comical if only it weren't aiming right for Tristan's face. He fumbles for his sword. It's still in his scabbard. What was he thinking, not unsheathing his sword? And what am I thinking, gaping at the scene and not casting my attack spell?

In the precious seconds it takes for me to ready the incantation in my head, the cockatrice strikes. Tristan blocks the monster's beak with what I hope is the hilt of his sword. He cries out in pain, but I can't see where he's been hurt because now Oscar's on the offensive, swinging his mace like it's an extension of his limbs. I assume he's aiming for the creature's back, but he catches a wing instead. It's enough to knock the monster out of the air and ram it into the ground. The cockatrice in turn scrambles up and lunges at Oscar, who jumps back.

Oscar's attack creates just enough of a diversion for Tristan to grasp his sword in both hands and swing it like he's Conan the Barbarian at the cockatrice's neck. It's not a full decapitation, but close enough. The head falls limply forward, blood spurting from arteries in the opened neck. Like a giant chicken, the cockatrice's legs keep moving. Head dangling, it runs about five yards before colliding with a tree and collapsing.

Tristan stands in place, taking huge gulps of air, his skin glistening and eyes dilated. I've seen him in this state as we take in the crowd's wild applause at the end of an act, usually with a triumphant grin for his fans to bask in. This time his mouth just hangs open.

"Did we just kill some monsters?" asks Oscar.

"And rescued the sheep," deadpans Cole. "Quick, pics or it didn't happen."

Even Micah smiles at that one.

"Two sheep saved is pretty good for a first quest," observes Oscar. "Maybe we can call it a success and get back to town?" He's right, we could lose these two while looking around for the last one.

"But Sugarplum's my favorite," Malza wails.

"Fifth Law of Boy Bands." Micah sighs. *It only takes one disappointed fan girl to start a viral backlash campaign.*

"I hate that law," I say. Whenever Marjorie would quote that one, I'd think, *c'mon, you can't please everyone.* One time I even said it aloud.

Without missing a beat, she replied, "That doesn't excuse not trying." That woman. Half a decade later and a whole universe away, we're still conforming to her expectations. Were Tristan's delusions correct about this being a simulation, she'd be smiling right now.

"But it's not safe for these two surviving sheep to stay here," says Cole. "Or you, Malza. The woods are too dangerous."

Malza nods, but lets out a sniffle, her eyes welling up with fresh tears.

I eye the giant dog, who would clearly rather be getting the hell out of Dodge. "Maybe Basil could blink the sheep out of here?"

Oscar nods. "And Malza could go with them. She can come back with Basil afterwards."

Basil takes a step towards the sheep, only to have them take a step back.

"We'll have to tie them up," says Cole. "Anyone got some rope?"

"When we get back, I'm writing up a list of useful quest supplies," says Oscar.

Luckily Micah—of all people—happens to be carrying a length of cord. There's just enough of it to tie around both sheep's necks and pull the remainder through Basil's collar. At that point, Cole and Micah start arguing about the proper knot to use and how to tie it.

Tristan used to be a cub scout, so I look around to consult him. He's sitting down on a fallen tree, his skin paler than Micah's complexion. He's got his handkerchief wrapped around his hand, and it's red all the way through.

"You're bleeding!" I make him pull the cloth back, exposing a deep cut across his knuckles.

He wriggles his fingers experimentally; I'm surprised the beak didn't slice a tendon.

"It wasn't that bad, not at first. But after I swung, it just…"

I worry he might be going into shock. "Oscar!"

Our cleric runs over. "Dryden was right, Tristan. You're getting a pair of gauntlets, I don't care if they look unfashionable." He digs around in his bag. "I think I have a flask of alcohol, we need to sterilize the wound."

"Didn't you just get a healing spell from Verhalty?" I ask.

"Oh, you're right. I completely forgot." Oscar pushes the bag aside and covers Tristan's bloody hand with his own, placing the other on Tristan's forehead. He bows his head and says something in that soft, deep voice he uses to croon to fans. A warm glow like morning sunlight covers Tristan and as it does so, the blood, including the stain that's soaked into the cloth strip as well as Tristan's clothing, fades to nothing. The skin on Tristan's hand is so smooth, it could be featured in a moisturizer ad.

"Did I just hear you say 'Behold?'" I ask Oscar.

"Be. Whole. Like, no bits missing or out of their proper place." That explains where all the blood went. "That's why I need to touch the patient's head as well, so that their memory of themselves guides the healing process. That's how Verhalty explained it to me."

"Convenient." Wizards' spells are way more complicated. Each invocation requires extensive calculations, memorization, and applying contorted logic, not unlike studying for a physics exam. "Do you have enough mana to cast another one like that if we need it?"

Oscar grimaces. "No, I used the remainder of it up with the Purify Victuals casting this morning."

"I'm down to a single spell too. But I also have a cantrip for attacks."

"Me too," says Oscar. "Verhalty didn't think it was right that a Warrior of Love couldn't dole out some punishment." The more I hear about Verhalty, the more I feel like she might be this world's version of Marjorie.

"What is it?"

"It's called Dead Ringer."

"That sounds promising. Does it, like, call zombies to help you with an attack?"

"I hope not. Maybe I shouldn't—"

I stop him. "Oscar, next time we run into one of those cockatrices, I want you to use that cantrip."

Oscar looks confused. "Cockatrices? You mean those lizard chickens?"

"Yes, those. Promise?"

"Promise," he agrees.

Over by the sheep I hear Cole pronounce, "I think that's good." He gives the rope a sharp tug, eliciting angry baas from the sheep.

"Glad they still act like they're normal-sized sheep," says Micah.

"You're good to go, Malza. Come back to the sky rock crater, we'll meet you there with Sugarplum, okay?" says Cole.

"Alright." She grabs Basil's collar, and they disappear with a pop. Now it's just the five of us to find one sheep.

Micah's looking very ranger-like as he scans the forest. "It would probably be more efficient if we split up."

"No," I say firmly, preparing for an argument.

"Kyle's right," says Oscar. "It never ends well when the team splits up in movies."

The others, even Micah, nod in agreement.

It's like earlier when we heard the sheep scream and charged headlong into danger. I feel that sense of camaraderie and self confidence that kept us going in those first two years of boybandhood. Back then we thought we could do anything, and I've got six boxes in storage stuffed with awards saying we did.

The five of us struggled to take down two entry monsters, I remind myself. And my contribution was to cast Mystic Armor on myself.

I walk over to the sheep cadaver. Its gashes seem shallower and more closely spaced than those on the one we found earlier at the edge of the forest. There might be other, bigger, monsters around. I'm adding this to my worry list, along with a growing doubt that the cockatrice's magical attack is actually acid, and concern about how abnormally quiet Tristan has gotten.

We head deeper into the forest with Cole and Micah walking a bit ahead to scout out the best path. They're working together; I'm purposely not commenting on it so as not to jinx it. I drop back to where Tristan is lagging behind. He's still looking pale.

"You were right, Kyle." He's got a lost quality to his voice.

"I'm always right," I say as I match his pace.

No smile. "About all of this. You were right. It's not something cooked up by Marjorie and the video game people. It's real." He swallows. "This forest. These swords. That demon rooster snake that tried to kill me." He considers his magically healed hand. "I could be dead. For real dead."

He's not watching where he's heading and stumbles. My hand shoots out and he grabs it, stabilizing himself. I really hoped that Tristan would have this epiphany when we were somewhere safe, like at a tavern with easy access to alcohol. This isn't the type of conversation I'm good at. Snappy comebacks during an interview, impressing the studio execs by remembering their kids' names, keeping everyone's food orders straight, those are my boy band superpowers. Talking someone out of a nervous breakdown, not so much. Thank god—or goddess—for Oscar.

He hears our conversation says, "You can die in our world too, Tristan. Car crashes, cancer, accidents, Covid." I remember that Oscar's uncle died from Covid. "But here, if you die, you die helping someone. And through your actions back there, we just made this world a better place."

I'm not sure if saving Malza's sheep counts as making the world better, but I keep my mouth shut. Maybe Tris is thinking it anyway, he doesn't look like he's buying Oscar's pitch.

"If you hadn't finished off that cockatrice," Oscar continues, "it would have turned on me. Probably melted me with its hydrochloric acid saliva."

Hydrochloric acid saliva. I recall a gaming session where someone had used that phrase. But that had been in reference to a giant demon praying mantis. Cockatrices did something else. What was it?

Oscar's still talking, "And you would have bled out if I didn't use my magic."

Tristan's quiet for a moment. Eventually he speaks, "That fight. I've never been in a real fight before. It was crazy and scary, but also"—he thinks a bit—"pretty cool, right?" I can see the compartmentalization already happening in his head, standard celebrity coping mechanism.

"How's the hand?" asks Oscar.

Tristan makes a fist and then opens it halfway. "There's no pain, but I'm having some problems moving my fingers. Almost like they're getting stuck."

Stuck.

Petrification.

That's what cockatrices actually do.

Fuck.

But Tris is still moving, and it only seems to be his hand that's giving him problems. I recall *Heroes Summoning* featured a Hail Mary mechanism that could—if a player was lucky—negate major damage. The game developers included it because otherwise players died way too quickly, especially in earlier levels. Maybe something similar is at work here, and Tristan has evaded a full petrification. This could just be the residual damage.

"You should have that looked at when we get back, Tris," I say. No need to worry him further.

CHAPTER 22

Kyle

"Hey guys, check this out." Ahead of us, Micah points at a trampled bush. "I think the sheep went this way."

We scramble over a fallen tree to where he's standing. I see white fluff caught on a bush's spiky branches. We've entered a clearing: just small trees, scrub, and several large boulder outcroppings.

"Great job, Micah. We're all getting the hang of this hero stuff," says Tristan. He seems to be doing okay both physically and psychologically.

Micah pauses mid-stride, cocks his head and dashes behind a clump of rocks. A moment later he reappears, dragging a horse-sized ball of fluff that can only be Sugarplum.

"I found it!" calls Micah. "I tracked down a sheep!"

"Master tracker indeed," says Cole. "Maybe next time you can find us a cow."

"Future quest," says Oscar. "I say we call this a success. Let's get the sheep to Malza and head back to Bydlo. We've got a concert to—"

He's interrupted by weird ticking—no, clucking. You just had to say it, didn't you Oscar?

There's a scrabbling sound and over the top of the largest boulder emerges another cockatrice; its beady eyes hone in on Sugarplum.

This time I'm ready. I clap my hands and shout, *"Sagitta-inspira."* Three glowing cylinders with needle-sharp points rise up in front of me. Three matching target symbols floating mid-air appear in my field of vision. I pretend I've got a touch screen and drag the bullseyes over to the cockatrice's body. One for the head, another for the neck, the third for the chest. I snap my fingers, once for each missile, and they race out like bottle rockets. The cockatrice dives for the ground, but evasive maneuvers won't work. This spell has guidance tracking. The missiles find their mark and the cockatrice staggers back. I think I must have damaged its eyes and hearing because it doesn't even turn when Tristan runs at it, hollering a battle roar. He raises his sword high over his head and this time when he swings down, the stroke cuts clean through the neck. The giant chicken head assumes a confused expression as it bounces and rolls away.

"Way to go Kyle!" shouts Oscar.

"Those rockets were awesome," says Cole.

"Okay, I'm officially jealous," says Micah.

My cheeks heat up, but I'm also wearing a stupid-big grin. It's not like they never compliment me. I mean it whenever I say in interviews that my bandmates are super supportive. But usually this spontaneous outpouring of praise and appreciation comes from Tristan. And he's like that with everyone, so it doesn't count.

Speaking of Tristan… I turn to congratulate him on his first full beheading and see him hunched over, clutching the previously wounded hand. I can't see his face.

"Tristan," I shout while running over. Oscar's right behind me. Tris's eyes are squeezed shut; his usual smile a grimace.

"Hey, Oscar"—he gasps as he lowers himself to the ground—"you got another healing spell on you?"

Oscar seems stricken. "Sorry man, I should never have used that stupid Purify—"

"It wouldn't matter, not on this," I cut off his self-recrimination. "I'm so sorry, Tris. I got it wrong about cockatrices, they don't spit acid. They petrify." To his look of incomprehension, I explain, "They turn people to stone."

"Like Medusa?" asks Tristan.

"Yeah." It's not my fault. It still feels like it's my fault. "I was hoping you resisted it but…"

Ever since we arrived in Mythreal, I've been running scenarios in my head where one of us gets hurt, or worse: Oscar because he's too trusting, Cole falling in with the wrong crowd, Micah for being a diva. Or most likely me, for being too clever for my own good. But I never imagined Tristan in trouble. Tristan's lucky, Tristan always lands on his feet, with style because… because Tristan.

"But even if he turns to stone, it's not like he dies, right?" asks Cole. The others have come over and we're all crouching around Tristan.

"Yeah, all evil magic has a counter spell," pronounces Oscar with—I'm sure—no factual basis.

"Of course, it has to," says Micah and for once I'm grateful for his unwarranted confidence. "Don't worry Tristan, we've got this. We'll get you to a doctor, or a witch."

"Or a witch doctor," assures Cole.

Tristan's trying his best to smile.

"For reals?"

"Absolutely," I say with conviction I don't feel. "The priests and wizards will be arguing over who gets to cure you. And no matter how handsome a statue you make, we won't let anyone use you as a lawn ornament."

Tristan laughs. "I'd make a seriously good-looking statue."

"Pics or it didn't happen," says Cole.

I'm still not sure how this will play out. But with everyone working together, maybe… Under my breath I whisper Marjorie Banks' 3rd Law, "*A Boy Band with dedication, devotion, and a bit of luck can accomplish anything.*"

"You forgot the part about great hair," says Tris, unconsciously—or maybe consciously—running a hand through his golden locks.

While I'm giving him my best encouraging smile, I hear a heavy shuffling somewhere from the woods. Another cockatrice approaches.

"You protect Tristan," Cole says to Oscar and me. "Micah and I got this." They move away from us, triangulating on the source of the sound.

The steps are coming closer, each one louder, more ominous. Then (in a sure sign that things are going to go very bad) Sugarplum starts screaming. I never knew a sheep's vocal cords could pull off something so human and raw. As it goes on, I wish I never did know.

"Here it comes," calls out Micah.

The screaming stops, or maybe I'm cutting out the sound, because the cockatrice has emerged from behind a clump of spruce trees and it's big. Not dog-sized like the others. I'm looking at six feet of pissed-off snake chicken. It's not just the size, the bird features are more developed, more mature. Feathers run down its chest and up its wings. Its comb is deep red, its beak hooked with a sharp overhang at the tip. Full-grown, that's the word.

"Those others," whispers Oscar beside me, "those must have been its chicks."

"Micah, fire!" Cole shouts.

139

Micah's on one side and he lets loose an arrow that flies right into mama cockatrice's eye. From the other side, Cole fires his crossbow into the drumstick. The cockatrice staggers sideways as its leg collapses underneath it.

"Poison bolts, worth every copper," says Cole.

The beast now lies immobilized. We could make a break for it, leave the sheep, carry Tris back to the meeting spot, and hope that Malza shows up. Not the most heroic exit but between looking heroic or living to fight another day, I'd choose the latter.

The cockatrice screeches and I hear a heavy woosh as it flaps its wings. It's pulling itself up, first to standing, and then higher up until it's a good ten feet in the air. It's a labored ascent. Like all chickens, it wasn't designed to fly much less hover. But then, I realize its plan is not to fly away, but to drop itself on us.

Now would be a great time to fire off Magic Mortar, only I'm out of spell mana. All that's left is the offensive cantrip I told Oscar about. Casting a cantrip is the magic equivalent of bringing a knife to a gunfight. But when a knife is what you've got…

I raise up my hand and imagine dry ice, how it's so cold that it turns the air around it to white smoke and how it burns when you touch it. I also visualize the equation for calculating absolute zero, because it can't hurt. *Frigus Digitorum!* I vibrate my fingers in a perfect jazz hand. A glowing blue skeleton hand shoots out from my real one and buries itself in the feathers of the cockatrice's neck, pulling at its skin, sending out tendrils of death. It's a necromantic spell and the sensation of ripping out another creature's life force reverberates inside me—twisting up my stomach and leaving a foul aftertaste in my mouth. The cockatrice's body jerks as it tries to peck at the hand. I'm doing damage, but it's not enough.

"Oscar! Cast Dead Ringer!"

Oscar bows his head in a quick prayer, or maybe just a deep cleansing breath. When he looks up, his eyes are black pools. I feel the air changing. His lips move, full and expressive as when he's singing, but no sound comes out. Instead, I hear a bell, the giant church kind. Tristan's not reacting, so it's probably a magic thing. The bell rings in low sonorous clangs; the pitch drops until it makes my teeth hurt. The cockatrice's body pulsates in time to the beat. The cantrip is creepy AF, but even at my beginner magic user levels, I sense it's more show than power.

Thankfully, we don't need a killer spell at this point. The cockatrice has an arrow sticking out of its eye, one leg dangles limply, and it's whipping its head back and forth trying to dislodge my Frostbite hand. If it had a health bar, it would be way down in the red. Just a little more.

Come on.

Come on.

Come on.

The bell tolls its final gong. The chimera gives one last shudder. Its wings fold. Its head drops. It's dead before it hits the dirt.

The impact shakes the ground, knocking Oscar off balance. He comes to, blinking. No one speaks, maybe it's the spell's aftereffect, maybe we're in shock.

I look down at Tristan, he's positively beatific lying on the earth. Eyes closed, he takes shallow breaths.

"Did we win?" he manages to croak.

"Yeah, we won."

A small grin starts to form on his face. It never makes it to a full smile. It freezes—along with the rest of Tristan—as he turns to stone.

CHAPTER 23

Souffy

Souffy stands vigil in the dark courtyard. There is no moon and clouds obscure all but the brightest stars. The only light comes from candles that cast dancing shadows on Tristan's unmoving face. Somehow, the visage is both identical to, and nothing like the Tristan who laughed and complimented her this morning.

Living, breathing Tristan is almost too much for Souffy to handle. The intensity of his gaze coupled with the effortless way he'd raise a single eyebrow sends her stomach flopping like a fish in a net. Throw in his half-smile and the dimple to the right of his lips, and her reflex is to blush and look away.

Stone Tristan, on the other hand, can't wink or chuckle or do any of the things that cause Souffy's brain to seize up. The cockatrice curse has turned his beauty ethereal, like the marble sculptures of the demigods that stand outside the King's palace. Souffy can now gaze upon him as long as she likes. He's close enough to touch, yet forever out of reach.

Tristan isn't dead, Souffy reminds herself, no one ever died from being turned to stone. But if they don't find a cure for him before the Seolia arrives, and it almost certainly will by tomorrow, then he'll be shipped out in his current state for healers in the capital to handle. This might be her last memory of Tristan. That possibility—probability—is breaking her heart.

The day had started so well, filled with such promise and anticipation. Souffy, immersed in preparations for the concert, hadn't even realized that the heroes were missing until they failed to show up for their rehearsal. She spent the next hour searching for them while fighting down a rising panic. But none of the worst-case scenarios she imagined held a candle to the reality of Oscar teleporting into the center of town with a giant blink dog and announcing that Tristan had been petrified.

The carpenters who up till then had been reinforcing the performance stage stopped their hammering, and switched to sawing planks to construct a seven-foot-long box for transporting the petrified Tristan, which they then filled with wood shavings. Oscar insisted on carefully padding the box with shavings. He told Souffy the Neverboylanders have a sacred law forbidding damage to their faces. The rescue party, with Souffy at its head, then hitched two strong plough horses to a cart and set out. They arrived at the Stennish farm near sunset to find the heroes already waiting. Somehow, they had rigged Stoned-Tristan—Cole came up with the name—to Basil to teleport him out of the woods. The process had involved Kyle using his Phantom Hand cantrip to steady the body during the teleportation jumps, and the concentration required had left him utterly exhausted; he barely woke up as Souffy arrived. It was crowded in the cart—all the heroes insisted on staying close to Tristan's still form—but silent, as if Tristan wasn't the only one who'd been turned to stone.

The worst part of the journey came when they entered the town. Plastered along every street were concert playbills with the word POSTPONED scrawled over the heroes' likenesses. By then it was well past midnight, but the houses still had lit candles in their windows. No one was going to sleep, not until they heard news of the heroes.

To avoid prying eyes, the mayor suggested they place the crate containing Tristan in a secluded part of the fortress's courtyard behind the Commandant's House. Souffy remembers how Cole jumped to tear off the lid as soon as it had been unloaded.

"If he recovers on his own, we don't want him waking up in a casket," he had said. "Knowing him, he'd probably think he died."

He still might, thinks Souffy. The lit candles around the wooden box make it feel like a wake. All the more so because of Tristan's frozen pose: hands crossed over his chest, eyes closed, face serene.

Kyle had excused himself to look through Uncle Ferimus's library for a possible cure. The other Neverboylanders milled around until Souffy sent them off to get some sleep. She promised to stay by Tristan's body; she'd do anything to spend just a few more precious hours in his presence. She hadn't said that last part out loud.

Souffy doesn't dare to touch his face. His hands, though, she allows herself to stroke. Their texture is rough and porous, like sandstone.

"This isn't supposed to be how we spend our last night together," she says with a sniffle.

Tristan had promised, once the performance concluded, to take her to something called an after-party. Souffy fantasizes how wonderfully it could have gone.

There would be speeches and toasts and the mayor and magistrate thanking her for how well she'd organized the concert and trained the heroes. Then, while Souffy basked in their collective admiration, one of the heroes—probably Kyle, but maybe Tristan—would have said, "Souffy, you've been such a great help, you should come with us." And of course, she'd say yes, and everyone would immediately agree to this new plan. She'd pack her bags and it would be goodbye to Bydlo. Goodbye to old failure-Souffy. Hello to companion-to-heroes-Souffy.

Only none of that is going to happen. Not now. She's failed in training them. They were completely unprepared for their encounter with the cockatrices, they've been injured and turned to stone, and it's only right for the Neverboylanders to go to some other place, free of screwups like her. She knows this wallowing in self-pity is pathetic, but what else is there to do?

Souffy becomes aware of the soft fall of footsteps. Hoping it's Kyle—maybe with a magical cure—she turns her head to look. Souffy's smile vanishes as she sees that it's Dryden.

"What are you doing here?" She doesn't bother to soften the accusation in her tone. He doesn't deserve softening.

"I live in the barracks," Dryden shoots back. But his eyes shy away from hers. After a moment spent contemplating his boots, he asks, "How's he doing?"

"He's petrified!" Souffy says, furious. She turns her whole body to face him. "Want to come over and rap on his head to make sure?"

"I'm sorry, Souffy. I'm truly sorry."

"Are you? Really? Seems to me you got what you wanted." After years of being on the receiving end of her grandfather's dressing-downs, Souffy knows how to twist the knife. "You sent them off to fight monsters, hoping they'd get hurt or worse!"

"I didn't know there were real monsters. The quest was just to find some sheep. There's nothing dangerous about that. I thought it would be good to get them out of town, help them hone their skills in a real forest."

Souffy barks out a hollow laugh. "If you wanted to help them, why not go with them? Why purposely let go of Kyle's hand the instant before Basil teleported?" Dryden blanches, proving the hunch Kyle had told Souffy about to be true. Souffy stalks over to Dryden, daring him to break eye contact. "Well, I'm waiting."

Dryden takes a step back.

"I'll cast Case of the Giggles." She reaches into her pouch of spell components and pulls out the requisite feather and peppermint candy.

"All right, all right. I was hoping they'd have a hard time, but only a bit. Enough to show everyone they weren't the amazing, perfect heroes you keep bragging they are."

"What? This was all to embarrass me?" It's no secret that Dryden doesn't care for Souffy, but this has gone way beyond a simple dislike. "Do you hate me that much?"

Dryden crosses his arms and hunches over, not answering (but not denying it either). Souffy wishes he would say something nasty, so she could blast him with the spell. Only somehow her anger has already burned itself out, leaving her feeling empty and fragile. She should have outgrown these maudlin sentiments by now, but she hates it when people hate her.

"It's ironic," Souffy says, mostly to fill the lengthening silence. "You were the first friend I made when I came to Bydlo."

Those early days had been lonely ones. The townsfolk would stare at Souffy, speaking stiffly to her face while—she was certain—gossiping behind her back. When she complained to her sister's messenger bird projection, egg-version Mallynda told her to treat it as an opportunity to study.

Instead, Souffy had wandered over to watch the militia training exercises. Non-magical dueling was considered uncouth in the Ravenus household, and her mother would have had conniptions if she'd seen Souffy mingling with common soldiers. Or at least she tried mingling; it was as if she'd had a Barrier spell around her. Souffy had resigned herself to misery when Dryden, a new recruit back then, came over and asked her what she thought of the fight. He'd been happy to explain details of the combat techniques he'd been practicing, and somehow the afternoon had transformed into something pleasant.

"You introduced me to Havelin and Boryk," she recalls. "We had fun that summer."

They'd explored disused rooms in the tower looking for relics left behind by the Triad of Valor, discovered a maze of catacombs beneath the fortress, and even traveled up to Rozny Las and located one of the forest's sacred trees. That last escapade had earned them a thorough tongue-lashing from an angry druid.

"Yeah, we did. Until you blew us up."

"What?" Souffy had never—*oh, he's speaking metaphorically*, she realizes. But even that doesn't make sense. "How? When?" She'd always wondered what caused Dryden to stop talking to her.

"It was the night of the shooting star."

Souffy becomes even more confused. "You mean the one two weeks ago?" It had been huge, like a fire-breathing dragon drifting across the sky. Souffy had been captivated by that object's shimmering colors. She had stared at it for the entire five minutes it took to pass overhead. That hadn't been the smartest of ideas; everything else looked shades of gray for the next hour. She recalled Ferimus had been quite excited about the metaphysical implications of the celestial artifact, but the otherworlders' arrival had caused the star to completely slip her mind until this moment.

"No," says Dryden, "the shooting star two years ago, after the winter solstice, when we were up on the wall drinking. The one the four of us made wishes on. And you insisted that we all share what we'd wished for."

"I guess I remember that."

"Boryk wished he could be an acolyte to Temisoto, and Havelin wanted to spend more time in nature and then you—"

"Wanted to pass my wizard exams?"

Dryden ignores her. "—said Boryk and Havelin should follow their dreams, that they should make them happen. And they did. They both quit the militia the very next week. They gave up on OUR dream. Havelin and Boryk and me, we'd been planning to join up and protect Bydlo since we were kids. You broke us up." Dryden's face turns red and he sucks air through his nose.

"But wait." The night is coming back to her. "You made a wish too. You wanted to travel with the King's army, to see all of Ozema and beyond."

"Because you said you'd never accept being courted by any guy planning to spend the rest of his life in Bydlo."

Souffy blinks twice. "You wanted to court me?" she asks just to be sure.

"Not that it matters. A couple of days later, Arek showed up with his ship and suddenly it didn't matter if a guy was sticking around Bydlo, so long as he was handsome." Dryden pulls out a handkerchief and blows his nose. He's as red as radish, a hairy red radish. "It's the same with the heroes. Some idiot with golden curls and straight teeth shows up and that's all you can think of."

"What?" Souffy had been feeling sympathetic up to this point. Not anymore.

"That's all you know about the guy, how good looking he is." He points a finger at Stoned-Tristan.

"That's not true!"

"Then tell me, what do you like about him that isn't connected with his looks or that he's… decent with the sword."

Souffy opens her mouth to counter this, but her mind fills with how good Tristan looks, and how good he looks with a sword. Honestly, she doesn't know much about Tristan. He only arrived four days ago. But, in those four days…

"It's not just his appearance. It's his presence. Tristan makes any place—even Bydlo—feel magical and wondrous and full of possibilities!" Souffy turns away from Dryden, back to Tristan. "It's like I've spent my life locked in a dreary cell, and now Tristan's broken down the door. He's calling for me to join him in the sun." Even in his petrified state, she feels the pull. "I want to see the hero he becomes; I want to be by his side, helping him." Souffy reaches out, this time daring to stroke Tristan's cheek. Right then, Souffy makes up her mind. "And I will be by his side."

The magistrate might try to stop her from boarding the ship. Her grandfather will surely be livid when she shows up at the capital. They'll never agree to let her take wizard exams, and she'll be unaccredited forever. It doesn't matter. "I'm going with him. I'm going with the heroes." For the first time since the disaster this afternoon, she is at peace. Behind her, she hears Dryden stomping away.

CHAPTER 24

Another awesome reason to use Phantom Hand: no pain receptors. The angry rooster I'm holding at bay can peck away at the ghostly hand clamping his beak shut all he wants. I feel nothing. He's also inflicted several attacks on my non-magical hands gripping his wings, but my Mystic Armor is mitigating that damage. Magic is this world's technology: mind-blowingly amazing at first, but after a few castings you can't remember how you got by without it. And—like tech—it only feels cool to the person using it; to those watching, you're a pathetic nerd. If anyone were awake at this hour, watching me awkwardly holding the struggling fowl as far from my body as humanly possible while navigating the dark courtyard, I'd turn as red as my hat. Luckily no one showed up while I was raiding the chicken coop outside the mess hall, so I make my way back undetected to the corner of the fortress where we've stashed Tristan.

When I get there, I see that Souffy has pulled up a stool next to the box containing Tristan and fallen asleep. The top half of her body is laid out across Stoned-Tristan's chest. That can't be comfortable. She stirs awake as I walk over and looks up at me bleary-eyed. She rubs her eyes, blinks a few times, and rubs her eyes again.

"Yes," I respond to the question she hasn't yet asked, "I am holding a pissed-off rooster."

"Why?"

I'm actually grateful for a chance to explain myself. "Because, petrification by cockatrice is classified as a transient transformation, which means that there's a concentration of mana surrounding Tristan, keeping him in his stoned state. Mana ebbs and flows based on atmospheric phenomena, which include events like sunrises and sunsets. Just as people wake up if you turn on the light, Tristan might break the petrification curse and regain consciousness at sunrise. But the idiot froze with his eyes closed, so I figured an auditory signal could jar him awake." His wake-up phone alarm is even set to cock-a-doodle-do; it was seriously annoying when we were living together.

Souffy locks eyes with the rooster, who stares right back.

"Roosters do crow at sunrise in Mythreal, right?"

"Oh, yes," she assures me, "among other times. Sorry, you were sounding like one of my professors. I think I'm conditioned not to pay attention when someone is lecturing."

So much for impressing her with my brains.

The sky's lightened above the fortress walls. And as I look up, I'm confronted with a fundamental flaw in my idea: we can't see the horizon from our present position.

"Do you have a watch?" I ask. That's not anachronistic. I know the mayor has one tucked into his cummerbund. But Souffy doesn't have one. Not that it would be of much help, I realize, because I don't even know what time the sun rises at this time of year. *God, I miss my smartphone.* "Maybe you could run up to the top of the wall and signal when you see the sun pop up?"

"I don't think there's time. It will happen any moment now."

"How do you know that?"

"I've always been attuned to fire and strong elemental forces," Souffy explains. "Did you know the sun is actually this unbelievably enormous ball of, not fire, but this thing that's so hot it melts air together?"

Plasma, with nuclear fusion transforming hydrogen to helium, my brain substitutes. That knowledge is as useless here as it was back in my own world. "Um, yeah."

"Oh, of course you'd know that."

Great. Now I'm arrogant as well as dull. You're here to save the realm, Kyle, not pick up girls. And I'm striking out at both. After that quick mental chastisement, I catch up to the important thing Souffy said.

"Souffy, you can sense the movements of the sun?"

She nods.

"So, you could tell me the exact moment it rises, so that I can release the rooster and see if it wakes Tristan up?" It sounds stupid when I say it aloud, but Souffy claps her hands with delight.

"That's a great idea!"

She rewards my perceived brilliance with one of her beaming smiles, or—more likely—it's because we're talking about curing Tristan. I'll take what I can get. Souffy stands up and raises her arm. She strikes a similar pose to when she first opened the portal. Was that only a week ago? It feels like forever.

"Tell me when," I instruct her.

"Okay."

And now we just stand there: Souffy looking like a diva in front of an adoring crowd, and me holding a rooster. I wonder if I could make some offhanded but cool-sounding comment that would make her smile, perhaps giggle even, and I'd use that opening to thank her for everything she's done for us, for me, and maybe—

"Now!" Cries Souffy.

I toss the rooster gently into the air, to give him time to flutter his wings and prevent himself from slamming into the ground. He settles down on the edge of Tristan's box and gives me a hateful demented-chicken look—like he'll stay silent, just to spite me. But then, he flaps his wings and belts out a perfect cock-a-doodle-doo which echoes off the surrounding walls.

"Tristan!" Souffy dashes over to the box and looks in expectantly. The seconds tick by and I see her shoulders sag. I walk over and confirm that Tristan continues to rest in his silicon state.

"I'm sorry," I say.

"Don't be," Souffy insists. "It was a good idea, Kyle."

She doesn't look up when she compliments me. Her gaze stays firmly on Tristan. The moment stretches out, and the silence between us becomes uncomfortable. I should probably leave, use the excuse of needing to research petrification cures and make my exit. But as I'm working out how to phrase this, Souffy speaks.

"You're a good friend, Kyle. You care a lot about him."

Her compliment makes me feel a bit better. I may be working through some serious wizard imposter syndrome, but I'm solid on my desire to cure Tristan.

"Well, we've known each other since we were six."

"Really?" Souffy tears her eyes away from Stoned-Tristan. That's promising. "You must know a lot about him. What's he like?" Oh.

I want to tell her that he can't open his mouth in the presence of a pretty girl without flirting, and that he's never had a relationship last for more than five months, but I don't because A) Marjorie Banks' 11th Law of Boy Bands: "*Never speak ill of your bandmates.*" And B) I know from bitter experience that airing out Tristan's dating track record perversely makes him an even more enticing challenge. Not that it matters what I say. Whenever a girl asks me about Tristan, it grinds our getting-to-know-each-other conversation to a halt and torpedoes any chance of me asking her out. Which is why I usually just cut my losses and trot out the old anecdote about Tristan being the one to suggest adding lip synching and dancing to our yo-yo tricks channel on YouTube, which started us down the road to stardom.

Only, bringing up our cheerful-quirky origin story feels off, what with Tristan turned to stone. The locals keep assuring us it's only temporary. But he's a fricking chunk of rock. Every time I look at him, I get a tiny flashback to the moment he changed, and my guilt—along with my adrenaline—levels spike. I need to tell Souffy something more personal, more real.

"He wasn't always good looking."

I get the expected incredulous look from Souffy.

"Really. When he showed up on day one of first grade, he was a classic dork." I elaborate on the term for Souffy's benefit, and not because I want to fondly remember a time when Tristan didn't turn heads whenever he entered the room. "He was short and pudgy, missing his two front teeth." And one of his eyes was bandaged up because his optometrist was trying to correct his lazy eye, but I'll spare Tristan that indignity. "He had a speech impediment back then. He was the new kid in the school, who on the first day walked up to five different kids and asked them 'Wanna be beth fwends?' No one said yes, a couple of them flat out said no. He was all alone at snack time." I remember watching him hunched over in his red Elmo T-shirt and thinking, *What first grader still wears Sesame Street gear?* "I guess I was feeling sorry for him, so I walked over and offered him a trial best friendship for one week."

"That was sweet of you."

"That's what my moms said when I explained why I'd brought Tris home to play that day." We'd walked to my house after school without telling anyone and Tristan's mom called the police, but that's a different story. "But they also told me that it can be worse to end a friendship than to fail to start one. Luckily, Tris liked LEGO as much as I did, so he passed."

Souffy is looking perplexed and I'm wondering if she'll ask me about LEGO. Instead she says, "You call him Tris?"

"Childhood nickname. Only me and his family still use it."

"So you did become friends."

"Yep, best friends actually. But there's the unanticipated twist to the story. By the end of the month, Tristan had become the most popular kid in our class." By the end of the year, even the cool fifth graders greeted Tristan by name in the hallway. "He just…" I don't know what pheromone or brain chemical powers the Tristan-effect, I only know the results. "Even when he was little, and dorky, he instinctively said the right things to make people smile, make them laugh, make them happy to spend time with him. Befriending Tristan was the best impulse I ever acted on. Because I was his first friend, he—I don't know—feels obligated to include me in all the opportunities he's offered." When our yoyo-dancing-and-singing YouTube channel blew up, it was Tristan who was initially scouted. I only got an invite to the audition because Tristan refused to go without me. "He's loyal."

"So, he makes people happy and he's loyal," says Souffy. Yeah, I'm *so not* the topic of this conversation. "Anything else?" She's all attention and information gathering now. About Tristan. That's when I throw Law 11 out the window.

"He's got a lousy memory. We used to purposely address people by their name during conversation, to keep him from just calling everyone mister or missus. He's pathetic at managing his time, or pretty much any executive function skills. And don't get me started about his taste in movies."

"Moovees?" Souffy's confusion probably means most of my insults were lost in translation. I'll go with that being intentional. It sounds better than losing my temper and being petty.

"Um, they're like paintings that move to tell stories. Tristan likes the sappy ones with happily-ever-after endings. He's got a soft spot for fairy tales." His repertoire of Disney Princess songs is disturbing in its completeness, but that's because having three sisters meant that the videos were looping nonstop in his house.

"Huh, none of the tales I know involving fairies have happy endings," says Souffy.

"They're not usually about fairies, they're more likely to have witches or talking animals or flying carpets." I realize around here those could be realistic literary fiction. I reach for a more specific example. "Or, like an enchanted princess who's been asleep for one hundred years and is awoken by a kiss. Not that we have magic in our world."

Souffy looks thoughtful. "But we have magic here."

Our eyes turn to Tristan. He's a dead ringer for an enchanted prince in his current state.

"Do…" Souffy blushes. "Do you think that could work?"

No, it's ridiculous. In a world with a well-defined magical system there are immutable natural laws governing manaphysics—yes, that's a real word here. You don't just get to free-associate aspirational magic spells as an excuse to lock lips with your crush. The rooster clucks pointedly in my direction from its perch on the box as if to remind me of my own equally ridiculous plan. What we really need is an advanced magic user with expertise in transmutation. On the other hand, we're likely leaving in a day or so. Souffy may never see Tristan again, and I can't stand the pained look in her eyes.

"It can't hurt." Ah, the things I do for fangirls. I give her a you-go-girl smile with a thumbs-up. Regardless of the outcome, Tristan's ego is going to love this.

Souffy takes a deep breath, like she's jumping off the cliff at the magic-training swimming hole, and leans over Tristan. Her fluffy hair obscures the deed. But then she jumps back with such force that I know that something's happened. Sure enough, a moment later I hear the familiar monster yawn Tristan makes when he's waking up.

"Tristan!" Souffy squeals with joy.

"Souffy! How did you… How did I… Hey, are these wood shavings?"

"You were turned to stone but thankfully cockatrice petrification isn't permanent, and the curse wore off!" Souffy conveniently skips over a few key steps.

"So, everything's alright?" Tristan sits up, scattering wood chips and scaring off the rooster.

"Cockatrice!?" In one fluid motion, Tris jumps out of the crate, takes up his sword, and points it menacingly at the bird. I guess we don't have to worry about any residual petrification issues.

"Tris, it's just a rooster!" I shout before Tris swings at it. I'd feel guilty if the chicken died, regardless of its earlier behavior to me.

"Hey, Kyle!" He stops mid-swing. "You're here too?"

"Yeah, we were kind of worried about you."

"Man, I'm sorry about that."

"It happens." Look at us, all cool and seasoned adventurers. Fake it till you make it.

I'm about to say we should go find the others to let them know of Tristan's recovery when I'm startled by a splash of brown, a crash, and a thud. My brain reconstructs a feathered projectile hitting a closed window of the house we're standing next to. A small stunned bird lies twitching on the ground. Tristan, who's closest, leans over and gently scoops it up.

"Poor guy, hope he's alright." He cups the bird in his hands. It's about the size of a pigeon with a Dr. Suess-style dangly feather sticking out of its head. Souffy peers at it.

"That's a messenger bird," says Souffy. I take a step closer to get a better look at it. I'd been reading up about these.

"There, there," says Tristan. "I think it's—"

"Squack." The bird puffs up. Tristan jerks his hands in such a way as to send the still-confused bird airborne. It seems to have recovered enough to hover for a moment before making a landing on a nearby stool. The other object in Tristan's hand—a small green egg—doesn't fare so well. It sails upward, slowing in its parabolic arc as its initial momentum is countered by gravity, and it begins its downward journey that predictably ends as it shatters on the ground by Tristan's feet. At which point, the laws of science cease to have relevance.

CHAPTER 25

Kyle

Thanks to Tris's fumble, we need to get down on our knees to see the egg-borne mist congeal into the head and shoulders of some person, or at least attempt to do so. The mist rising from the yolk splatter looks like it's fighting gravity.

"It's a bad imprinting," explains Souffy. "I wonder if they didn't let the bird rest long enough between trips."

It's not so much the noisy signal disruption of Princess Leia's "Help me Obi-Wan" hologram scene; the effect here is more like a lava lamp with bits bulging out, sending the face it's trying to render into claymation territory. I think it's a man.

"Arek?" Souffy gasps in recognition.

"Souffy!" The man's voice comes in clear at least. "Is that you?"

"Yes, Arek are you okay? You look…"

Blobby, is my first thought. But when I look closer I see red patches on his skin and what appears to be a cut across his head. And there's a desperate, spent look in his eyes. It's not just the quality of the transmission; this Arek guy is in trouble.

"Thank Sher of the Waters the bird made it. Souffy, Rozny Las is under attack!"

Well, that's straight and to the point. Tristan looks to me and tilts his head just so. It's a signal we used to use back when we first entered the industry and Tristan found himself out of his depth. He stopped doing it when he realized that people found his ignorance charming. I suppose almost getting killed and turned to stone could make even Tristan feel he needed to be more knowledgeable.

"Rozny Las is the logging outpost on the north end of the bay," I tell him. "It's where the ship that's giving us a ride to the capital is coming from."

"Attacked? By what, Arek?" asks Souffy.

"The Trädskydd Druids."

"Nature magic users, they live in the forest by Rozney Las," I explain to Tristan.

"They've broken through the town defenses and their plant magic is running wild," Arek continues. "We're still in control of the western side of town and the harbor, but they've moved so quickly. I don't know how much longer we can hold our positions."

"But what about the townsfolk?"

"I sent as many as I could out on the Seolia. I pray she makes it to Bydlo safely. You'll want healers at the ready, the assault plants release toxic fumes." At this, he pointedly coughs.

"Oh, Arek." There's real concern in Souffy's voice.

The image is breaking apart and I'm not sure how much more information we can get.

"Why did the Trädskydders attack?" I ask. From what I'd been hearing there's a logging-industry-versus-environmentalist tension between the two groups, ongoing grumbles over the terms of some historic treaty, and snide comments from the villagers about sacred trees. I had pictured the druids as hippy tree huggers, not militant eco-terrorists.

"We don't know," says Arek. "They first attacked a logging camp to the north. Left no survivors. It escalated from there." He stops to peer intently at me, his eyes seeming to go squinty. "That hat, are you a wizard?"

"According to the Pathfinding Ceremony I am." I'll feel more wizardly when I can take out a giant chicken on my own or cast more than two spells a day.

"Yes, he's a wizard. He's Kyle, and I'm Tristan. We're heroes from another world."

"Otherworld heroes?" Arek's face lights up, or maybe he's becoming more transparent. "Ah, the magistrate's messenger bird mentioned you had arrived. Heroes, I beseech you, please help us."

"Of course, we'll totally save the day," Tris overpromises. Although it doesn't matter because the real Arek isn't hearing this. The real Arek sent this message twenty-four hours ago. The town could have fallen since then. Arek could be injured, or dead. This is on a whole other level from finding lost sheep, and look how that turned out for us. Not for the first time, I question the Divine Wisdom's grasp of game mechanics.

"Thank you, Hero Tristan. Please come quickly. And Souffy…" Arek's face is positively melting now, I'm guessing the egg is almost out of mana. "Tell my mother and father that I love—" the image distorts like a soap bubble, pops, and is gone.

Behind me I hear a little shriek. We turn to see the mayor and magistrate. Lenora is clutching at Galam's ruff, as if she's using it to stay on her feet. Galam is white as a sheet.

"Arek," he says in a wavery voice.

Souffy looks from the couple to the crushed eggshell on the ground, before looking up at Tristan and me. "Arek is their son."

CHAPTER 26

Souffy

Souffy knows she should be pleased—thrilled even—to be included in the Rozny Las Investigation and Response Committee, or "War Council" as most here are referring to it. With Uncle Ferimus still out on his herb-gathering expedition, the mayor had asked her to be their magic expert. Souffy has been given a spot at the front table with her name etched on a wooden block in front of her. They're holding the meeting in the council chambers. It's easily the fanciest public space in Bydlo; every inch of the wood beams and panels are carved and polished so they glow under the candelabra lights. Today, the room is packed with representatives from the various guilds and government divisions. It's all very respectable and grown up, not that Souffy feels she's being treated that way.

"Souffy," Lenora cuts her off mid-sentence. "I'm not asking for an explanation about the underlying magic. What I want to know is whether your uncle wrote any notes or instructions on how he animated artificial soldiers like Goliath." Her finger rapidly taps the table.

Souffy's eyes keep straying to this movement. "Uncle Ferimus's notes aren't that much use. If there are instructions, they'd probably be in his spellbook, and he took that with him. But it wouldn't matter. That's an advanced spell and we don't have anyone capable of casting it."

"Is that so?" Lenora's gaze shifts to Souffy's left. "Wizard Kyle?"

Kyle glances in Souffy's direction before replying. "What Souffy says. My spellcasting is more rudimentary than hers."

"Very well." Lenora turns her attention to Father Aldonus to ask if he's received any interpretable signs from Minstay, Goddess of Nature, that might give them some clues to the Trädskydd Druids' intentions. Aldonus, who's still recovering from the injuries he received escaping from Rozny Las, stammers his reply.

Without looking away from the proceedings, Souffy worries her copper earring between her thumb and forefinger and flicks her little finger in Kyle's direction. "Thanks for supporting me," she sends through Magic Missive.

"Of course," comes Kyle's voice in her head. "It's not just you she's snapping at. See?" Lenora has just shut down the priest's theological excuse for his lack of progress with a suggestion that perhaps he should pray harder. "The magistrate's in full momma-bear mode today."

"Momma bear?" Souffy asks. She's actively recharging the cantrip so that they can continue their conversation.

"In my world you don't want to find yourself between a mother bear and her cub. Lenora's son, Arek, is in danger and she'll take on anyone or anything that stands in her way."

"Is your mother like that?" Souffy messages.

"Oh yes, and I've got two of them. LOL."

Souffy turns and sees Kyle's face relax, like it had when he told her the story of Tristan as a child. When Kyle smiles—really smiles—his eyes and whole face soften. He looks almost as cute as Micah. Souffy likes seeing this side of him.

"How about your mother?" Kyle asks.

Souffy remembers the last time she saw her mother. It was when Souffy was walking up the plank of the ship bound for Bydlo. Penelope Ravenus waved without looking and left before the ship departed. "She's more of a cuckoo bird, laying her eggs and having the servants raise us."

This time Kyle is the one to turn to her. "I'm sorry, that sucks."

The warm feeling rising inside of Souffy counters the unpleasant memory. She grins and turns her attention back to the discussion. The master shipwright is giving an update on the state of repairs to the Seolia.

"After the last refugees disembarked, we found one of those magicked plants growing in the bilge. It had started working its roots into the hull. Fortunately, it couldn't grow very fast on seawater, so we were able to dig it out. She should be seaworthy in three days' time."

"Three days?" Lenora asks sharply.

"Maybe two," the master shipwright stammers and lowers her eyes. "We're working as fast as we can."

"And when they finish, the militia will be ready," adds Lieutenant Jorgsen. He's the militia's acting-commander. All of the senior officers were visiting Rozny Las and stayed to fight. "We've had several townsfolk and farmers sign up to fight as well. They're especially keen given that the Heroes of Bydlo will be leading the fight. You will be leading the fight, correct?" He addresses this question to Kyle.

"We'll help out in whatever capacity we can," says Kyle. Under the table, Souffy feels a tap on her foot; it's Kyle's signal for more conversation.

"Yes?" she Magic Missives.

"This is moving too fast. The guys are training seriously now, but we're not up for full combat, not against other humans. We're more—you know—lovers than fighters." Meanwhile, Jorgsen is enthusiastically detailing the punishments his forces will mete out on the enemy druids.

"It will be okay." Now it's Souffy's chance to reassure Kyle. "This is the quest the Divine Wisdom called you here for. You'll be ready."

"If the Divine Wisdom wanted heroes from our world to participate in military action, it should have picked a K-pop band, at least they have conscription," Kyle sends back.

Before Souffy can respond, a terse voice interrupts the proceedings. "As the council continues to discuss its plans for the Seolia, I'd like to remind everyone that she is not part of the navy fleet. The Seolia belongs to the Laska Bay Trading Company." It's the company's representative, Tianne Marr. She's a broad-shouldered woman who has the manners of someone used to getting her way. "Our company's charter and exclusive rights were granted under the terms stipulated by the Triad of Valor. That means we are an integrated but independent private entity."

Tianne's verbal gymnastics remind Souffy something her grandfather is fond of saying: "For some reason, lawyers seem to be under the impression that their words can work magic."

Tianne's still talking. "Unless or until Ozema formally declares war on the Trädskydd Druids, the Seolia can't be commandeered by the crown or any other governmental entity." She looks expectantly at Lenora.

"Given Laska's investment in Rozny Las, I'd assumed your company would be eager to launch a military counteroffensive." Lenora's tone is calm, but Souffy notices all four of her fingers are now rapidly tapping the table.

"It's true that we have invested a great deal in the town and its industry—"

"I was speaking about your people. My son, for instance, is one of your company's employees. He's currently defending those executive rights. Would you abandon him and the other men and women who stayed behind?" Lenora stops tapping and holds Tianne's gaze until the other looks away.

"The messenger birds from the company heads in the capital should be arriving by tomorrow," Tianne says. "I'll bring them over and you can talk to them."

"You're right," Souffy missives Kyle. "Momma-bear."

"What I still don't understand is how the Triad of Valor plays into all of this," he replies.

"Oh, that I can tell you." Souffy is grateful for something to focus on while the war council argues over how many fighters versus supplies can be transported, and at what cost, as well as the amount of time it would take for the Seolia to make it to Rozny Las. Every argument is couched in careful phrasing so as not to draw Lenora's ire. Souffy rubs her earring to recharge the cantrip as she thought-speaks the story.

"The Triad of Valor were otherworlders like you, except there were only three of them. Most of their adventures took place in the Kingdom of Latanza, so I hadn't heard much of them before I came to Bydlo. But around here, they're practically worshiped." Every Bydlo festival would feature some reenactment of the Triad's exploits, and there were several catchy songs immortalizing their accomplishments.

"When they showed up," she continues, "Bydlo was barely a fishing village and its inhabitants lived in fear of ice giants who controlled the land to the north. The Triad arrived and killed the ice giant king and his warlock, or maybe the king was also a warlock? There are different versions; it all happened over three centuries ago. Anyway, defeating evil monsters is a pretty standard otherworld hero adventure. What raised it to Final Quest level was that the Triad restored the forest."

"Final Quest?" asks Kyle.

"It's when the otherworlders right a great imbalance in Mythreal and the Divine Wisdom grants them a boon to return home." Souffy's pretty sure she'd already mentioned that part of questing.

"How did they restore the forest?" he asks. "Did they plant some trees?"

"Pretty much." Souffy shrugs. The Heroes of the Realm had stopped the Pandemonium as their Final Quest, which was the more impressive accomplishment in Souffy's opinion. "In ancient times, before any of this happened and Ozema wasn't even a country, these lands were populated by the elves. I think they may even have had a city deep in the Drevo Woods.

And of course, the forest was enchanted, filled with talking animals, magical beasts, fairies, witches, the usual. But according to legend, some humans—we don't know who—built this fortress and the elves departed." A classic case of elven flight, as Souffy's history professor would say. "Without the elves in the north, the ice giants moved in and started wreaking havoc, especially on the trees."

"Like burning them or clear-cutting?"

"Mostly just knocking them down. Giants don't like anything taller than they are. They're insecure that way," Souffy explains. "Eventually, their vandalism led to the collapse of the magical ecosystem and unbalanced the world. That's why the Divine Wisdom summoned the Triad. Apparently, their earlier questing earned them the respect of the Elves of Nordenweiss, who then presented the Triad with these magic seeds to plant in the forest once the giants were driven out. The Triad brought along some humans from Latanza—refugees I think—to care for the trees. Those were the ancestors of the Trädskydd Druids."

"I see," says Kyle. "So the treaty dividing the forest into druid-run areas and those accessible to the Laska Company's operations was to protect the magic trees?"

"The treaty is between the town of Bydlo and the Trädskydd Druids. The Laska Bay Trading Company only showed up a few decades ago when someone noticed that all the trees in the forest had high levels of mana and could be infused with useful spells, like fire resistance." This part of the story she knows from spending time with Arek. It's hard not to learn about lumber industry practices and forest management around him. "You need to preserve more than just the groves; there are these tree corridors that facilitate mana flow through the forest or something. And they're called sacred trees, not magic trees. My first summer here we went up north and found one. Havelin always wanted to see one."

"How was it?" asks Kyle.

"It was a big tree. Pretty, I guess." Havelin had been ecstatic. Boryk had tried to leave an offering. Dryden and Souffy had been setting up for a picnic when they were interrupted. "We didn't stay long, a caretaker druid chased us off. They may care a lot about nature, but they're not very nice people."

"Apparently," says Kyle.

After the first message, Arek's messenger bird had laid two more eggs. From those, Lenora and Galam were able to find out that the trouble started with a druid attack on a logging camp. The militia stationed in Rozny Las retaliated and afterward there were several skirmishes culminating with the sneak attack on Rozny Las. The next day the refugees arrived on the Seolia and told more tales about animated vines, walking trees and other druidic offensive magics.

And just like that, the provincial town of Bydlo began preparing for war. There was no more talk of shipping the otherworlders away to the capital. Public opinion settled on the narrative that the Divine Wisdom had foreseen this conflict and had sent the Heroes of Bydlo (Souffy prays to the gods that name doesn't stick) to defend Rozny Las—or what's left of it— against the druids. And everyone agreed that it was excellent thinking on Souffy's part to have released the heroes right away.

Souffy should be grateful. She is being recognized for her efforts and—after three stultifying years—exciting things are finally happening. But she can't help but notice how much less happy and content the people of Bydlo now are.

CHAPTER 27

Souffy

After what feels like forever to Souffy, but is probably closer to two hours, the council finishes addressing everything on the agenda (or people might just be worn out from arguing) and the meeting adjourns. Souffy and Kyle are seated furthest from the door, and the room is nearly empty by the time they stand up to leave. The only other person still at the table is Galam, who is just sitting and wringing his hands.

To Souffy, the mayor has always seemed larger than his physical body; it's strange to see him so shrunk in on himself. "I'm sure Arek will hold on until we get there." She feels silly as the words leave her mouth, but Galam smiles appreciatively.

"I'm sure Arek will be quite pleased to be rescued by otherworld heroes. He used to love it when I'd tell him bedtime stories of the Triad of Valor: Fighter Hannah, Cleric Isaac, and the Wizard Daniel. I think that's what sparked his interest in trees."

Souffy nods. Her intent is to keep walking, but some of Galam's animation has returned. He reaches out for Souffy's arm. "One of those stories was an odd one my grandmother told me. She said that just before Cleric Isaac stepped into the portal to return to his world, he had a prophetic vision that one day there would come a great threat to the forest and its people. But the evil would be stopped by the Wizard of the Fortress wielding a holy weapon. It was due to that prophecy that there's always been a wizard installed at Fort Bydlo. I don't suppose that your uncle ever mentioned a holy weapon?"

"No, sorry."

He turns to Kyle. "Perhaps you might find something in his workshop?"

Kyle looks to Souffy, who shrugs. "I could take a look," he says.

"Yes, yes." Galam beams. "I'm sure there are several useful magical devices there. Ferimus is such a creative wizard. He built the proclamation announcement system, you know, as well as those marvelous mouse traps."

After a few more assurances for Galam, Souffy and Kyle leave the town hall and walk through the town towards the fortress.

"I feel bad getting Galam's hopes up like that. Uncle Ferimus is a sweet person, but he's not much of a wizard."

"Well, no. That's because he's an artificer," says Kyle.

"What?" Souffy thinks she's heard wrong. "Artificer? No, he studied illusion." Not that he showed much talent for it; he could never get rid of his beard when he'd cast Disguise on himself.

"Have you seen his workroom? And the PA system? That's artificer work."

"No, no." The very idea is ridiculous to Souffy. "A member of my family would never study to be an artificer."

"What's wrong with being an artificer?" asks Kyle. "That would be like an engineer in my world. Those guys are in high demand."

"Ravenuses are wizards, or they aren't anything at all. That's what my grandfather always says. I mean, maybe a sorcerer, but an artificer? That's practically a trade-mage."

Kyle chuckles. "Your family is full of snobs." Before she can inquire about what this means, he adds, "They think they're better than everyone else, right?"

Souffy opens her mouth to argue, but the faces of her immediate and extended family flash through her mind, and each relative confirms Kyle's judgment. There's always Grandmama Zorianna, but she isn't a Ravenus. It was her son, Souffy's father, who'd married into the family and took the name. "Grandfather likes to say we have standards."

"He does, does he? He sounds like Micah's mom. So, what are these standards?"

"Well, wizards are obviously the pinnacle of magic users because they acquire their spells through academic study. Next are sorcerers who are exceedingly rare and born with their magic abilities. And then come the warlocks who get points for being brave, or crazy, enough to strike a pact with an otherworldly being to enhance their magical abilities. Artificers would come next, because their magic does require some study. After that, you have all the magic users who are gifted with spells because of their devotion, like clerics to their gods, or druids because they love nature. And then you have trade-mages. And then you have bards." Funny how she'd never doubted that philosophy back in the capital.

"And for your wizards, I'm guessing they need to go to the proper schools?"

"Right. And pass the wizard exams." Not that one needs certification to be an adventurer. It's an idea Souffy has given serious thought to since the night she'd announced to Dryden her desire to travel with the heroes. She wonders what Kyle would think about having her tag along. "Not like those wizards who attend classes just long enough to learn to lob fireballs and head out to be adventurers," she says to gauge his reaction.

"I thought lobbing fireballs was the whole point of learning magic," says Kyle. Souffy can't tell if he's being sarcastic.

"At the Ravenus College of Wizards, we called them explosion-mages." And worse. "They only taught us evocation magic in the first year, and it was largely for self-defense."

Kyle nods thoughtfully. "How did you do in that class?"

"I set fire to the building."

"On a quest, I'd rather have an evocation wizard over someone who specializes in divination or enchantments." He raises his eyebrows.

Is Kyle implying that he wants her to be an evocation wizard to join their party, to fight as an adventurer alongside them? No, he must be speaking hypothetically. Still, if any of the otherworld heroes would welcome her, it would be Kyle. Souffy wonders if she should ask him now, or would it be better to wait until she'd had a chance to prove herself? Maybe she should try again to learn that intermediate Fire Orb spell she'd once copied out in her spellbook.

Her mind floats with possibilities as they walk through the town and up to the fortress. The reality that meets her when they pass through the gate drives away her fantasies. The courtyard is overflowing with people, just like during Fort Bydlo Days, but there's no gaiety or festive mood to this crowd. Instead, people are sitting or wandering listlessly, and the air hangs heavy with uncertainty.

The Seolia had been spotted yesterday, just before dawn. It was surrounded by a flotilla of fishing boats, all of them crammed with exhausted and hungry refugees. Most escaped with only what they could carry. They were the elderly and families with children, and many of them were injured. With the exception of the few who had relatives in Bydlo, they all needed a place to stay.

The solution was to put them up in the fortress. The Commadant's House was fully opened for the first time in decades. The refugees filled the rooms, then the great hall. Empty barracks and even some unused corners in the old tower were converted for the refugees as well. But after several days inside the cramped ship quarters, most chose to spend their days outside.

Souffy notices a large group clustered by the crumbling wall of the unused chapel dedicated to the Water Goddess, Sher. Sher is also the goddess of healing, and Souffy wonders if the refugees might be praying. But then she hears singing.

> *Your smile brightened the room*
> *Your love hung the moon*
> *Now it's only yesterday, now it's memories*

It's unlike any melody she's ever heard: less poetic, more earnest. Beside her, Kyle rolls his eyes.

The voice, a rich baritone, warm and comforting despite the sadness of the words, is joined by a second; its tone is lighter but no less emotive.

> *Time goes by*
> *So much we've lost*
> *If I could only*
> *Go back, go back*
> *If I could only*

Souffy squeezes through the crowd of mostly women. Some are older and holding babies, others are closer to Souffy's age. Beyond them, she finds a circle of children. And in the center, Tristan and Oscar weaving the lyrics between them. Then Tristan steps forward, his voice ringing pure and clear.

> *Your spirit set my world alight*
> *You got me through my darkest night*
> *Now it's only yesterday, now it's memories*

It isn't just Souffy who's caught up in the music. The children and adults are all swaying, spellbound. Almost all are smiling, even the ones with tears flowing freely down their faces. Souffy never realized before how cathartic it could be to share sorrow with others. She turns to Kyle to say something, but he's gone.

CHAPTER 28

Kyle

I promised Galam I'd see if Ferimus had any magical weapons. That's the reason I skipped out on Tristan and Oscar's impromptu performance. Or excuse, I suppose.

Ferimus's workshop is located on the top floor of the old tower, up a tight spiral staircase set within the wall. The windows are spaced further and further apart the higher I go. Just at the point I've decided to go back for a candle, the staircase opens up into a large room illuminated from above. There's a skylight that, looking at the ironwork and latch system, probably opens up for moving large items in and out. All the light makes it easy to see what a mess the room is.

There are gears and pulleys and tools and piles of machine parts. Magically stuck to everything—Post-it style—are hundreds of bits of parchment. Each with numbers or equations or tiny sketches. I find one parchment note with what looks like a drawing of a trebuchet, but with a piece of cheese attached. Probably that better mouse trap everyone keeps raving about.

Souffy may have been right about her uncle not being a trained artificer. He's clearly a DIY maker. Or a crazy inventor. Either way, I have hopes of finding something useful.

I take off my hat to better poke through the room's many nooks and crannies and whistle while I search. It's the one musical ability I'm better at than any of my bandmates, even Micah. Still, I frown when I realize I'm whistling the chorus from "Only Yesterday," the song Tristan and Oscar were performing.

I remember Souffy's rapt expression. She wasn't the only one. Music hipsters may deride our songs, but they're catchy. And the guys know how to perform them. They might be getting into this whole LARPing business but—let's face it—they belong on tour. They belong back in our world. I consider Souffy's talk about Final Quests. Maybe if we somehow defeat the evil druids then the Divine Wisdom could send them back. Send us back, I amend. Or, maybe just send them back? Does it make me a bad person that I'm not missing friends and family and obsessing about returning to our world?

There's no point in dwelling on it.

First, I've got to see if there's anything useful in this place. An hour later I can definitively say that if there is a magical weapon around here, it's been disassembled into multiple pieces.

You know the thing I'm not seeing in here? Plants. No herbs drying, or even a work surface that might be used for cutting them up. I'm growing more and more suspicious of this "gathering herbs" explanation for Ferimus's absence.

Souffy assured me that it's not a euphemism for any unsavory activities. She says that he disappears fairly often, usually for two or three days. It's now been nine whole days since anyone's seen him. My gameplay senses are telling me the missing wizard is significant, although it could just be a side quest we missed because we went looking for those stupid sheep. Still, it wouldn't hurt to look for clues.

A careful examination reveals some green eggshells, a keychain loaded with what must be over fifty keys, and a prominent bookcase. I spend a few minutes pulling out books and poking at promising wood knots but the bookcase stays put. So, not a hidden doorway.

But I feel there must be something here. Why go to the trouble of having such a visually detailed room if it isn't hiding a clue? Okay, I admit, that's video game logic, but still.

Souffy said Ferimus is an illusionist. From what I've read, illusions are purely mental; they hijack your neural net to make you believe you're seeing, hearing, touching, smelling something that isn't there. The more complicated the required mental gymnastics, the more likely the suggestion will fail. What this usually means is that the illusion needs to be realistic: no polar bears on tropical beaches. But realistic can also apply to how light behaves around a real object. And if you can reverse and bend light (as a certain physicist-turned-wizard may have learned in his advanced lab course in optics and lasers) then you might push the illusion past believability.

Within the clutter I locate both a mirror and a magnifying glass. I call up my Phantom Hand to position the mirror and examine the reflections of various objects in the room through the magnifying lens. The images are blurry but discernible. There's nothing special about the bookcase, but in the area next to it I spot something that could be a door handle. I turn around to inspect the space directly. There's a mounted porcupine with a surprised expression and fully extended quills. I gently touch it—*ouch that's sharp!* Back to looking through my reflected distortion setup; again, I see the door handle. Keeping my eye on what I think is really there, I reach backwards while gritting my teeth and reminding myself that Oscar has gotten really good at the wound healing spell. This time, instead of porcupine quills, I feel… a door handle.

I grasp it and turn around. There's a door there now. A locked door, but it's progress. I instruct the Phantom Hand to bring me the key ring and rifle through it for one that's the right size. I try over a dozen keys, either too big or too small. Next, I methodically check each key, to no effect. There's simply no way anyone would need this many keys. So what are they, camouflage? An illusion? What if I search the other way, from lock to key? I look at the keyhole, imagine the size of the key's biting that would fit it, and only then do I turn to the key ring. I give it a shake, and one of the keys glows blue. It has an ornate head that I know I didn't see before. Of course, the whole ring is some sort of skeleton key system. Clever, clever Ferimus.

"Here goes nothing," I say as I turn the key and open the door.

CHAPTER 29

Souffy

"I found something," Kyle tells Souffy in a conspiratorial tone that has her grinning with anticipation. Then he adds, "Bring the others."

"Everyone? Like Dryden?"

"Oh, I was just thinking of the guys, the…" Kyle's lips move like he's trying out words, then he rolls his eyes and says, "Neverboylanders. We certainly don't need Dryden."

Souffy breathes a sigh of relief.

Kyle continues, "But including Havelin and Boryk would make sense. I'm not sure whose help we'll need to figure this one out. And have everyone bring their adventuring gear, just in case."

Souffy could probably have gotten him to tell her more, but the not-knowing makes it more exciting. On Souffy's invitation, they gather in Ferimus's workshop up in the tower. It's a cramped space for so many people. Souffy takes advantage of the lack of space to squeeze a bit closer to Tristan while they listen to Kyle recount his earlier discovery.

"And that's how I broke the illusion spell and found this," Kyle finishes with a flourish as he opens the previously concealed door.

Micah looks in. "You brought us all here to show… a fireplace?" But he still ducks through the newly revealed entrance with the rest of them.

It is an impressive fireplace. Its white marble is carved in an aggressively Elves-Nouveau style—geometrically intertwining vines with flower accents—and over the mantel stretches an ornate-to-the-point-of-unreadable inscription. But despite the builder's attempt at implying antiquity, the fireplace is obviously a recent addition to the ancient fortress.

"Can you read it?" asks Kyle, pointing to the engraved script.

Souffy had struggled with modern Elvish when she took the course four years ago. However, she doesn't want to waste mana on the Translate spell for just a few sentences so she squints and sounds the words out in her head. "It's addressed to the fortress wizard. About what to do in the magical forest's darkest hour. Um, something, something, insidious evil, something, magic weapon?" She shakes her head. "It's pretty generic."

Cole points to the solitary blue flame dancing within the man-sized hearth. "Natural gas?"

"Magic," says Kyle. "There's no heat coming from it, plus there's nothing there to burn. And come look at it up-close." He gestures to the flame. Tristan obliges by kneeling down and leaning in.

"It's like I can see another room in there!" Tristan exclaims.

One by one, they all line up to take a look. When it's Souffy's turn, she squints through the flame as if it were a keyhole. The scene on the other side is blurry but she can make out wood panels and warm light. Maybe it's some sort of a study?

"It's a mystic hearthstone!" She's always dreamed of finding one. As a child, she ruined several outfits crawling into other wizards' fireplaces. And all this time, there was one right here. She wondered why Ferimus hadn't told her about it, or maybe he didn't know it was here.

"I thought as much," says Kyle. Taking a look at the confused expressions of the other Neverboylanders he explains, "These are in the game. They're magically linked fireplaces so you can teleport from one to the other. Like in Harry Potter, but it's point-to-point single destination, not a network."

It's convenient, thinks Souffy, that Kyle can use real examples from his world to help the others understand.

"Did your uncle make this?" asks Cole.

"No." Of that Souffy is certain. "Ferimus only came to Bydlo twenty years ago. This is older than that, a century at least."

"Maybe three centuries," says Havelin. He looks to Boryk, who nods in turn. "In one of the Triad of Valor legends, Wizard Daniel used his magic to teleport them from the fortress to the Drevo Woods to fight the ice giants."

"Drevo Woods? That's where Rozny Las is, right?" asks Micah.

"So, we could use this to zap ourselves up north and rescue everyone?" asks Tristan in a manner that Souffy finds quite heroic.

Unfortunately, she knows it wouldn't be that easy. "Opening a hearthstone takes a tremendous amount of raw mana, more than any one of us has available. If we could find a way to pool our combined mana into a vessel and then feed it to the flame, then maybe—"

"You need mana? How about this?" asks Cole. He flicks a small black disk—rather like a coin—into the air.

As it spins, the mana it contains causes Souffy's hair to poof out. She recognizes what Cole's thrown. Every year in the wizard college, at least one student is caught smuggling a Vantacoyte in for their magic practicums. Before Souffy can say anything, there's a pop and a sucking sound as the bespelled token lands in the hearth and releases its compressed mana. A moment later, the flame erupts into a fire that fills the whole hearth with dancing pale light.

"How did—Where did you—" demands Oscar. When Cole merely smiles and shrugs, Oscar says, "Oh, of course, Thieves' Guild. Never mind." Although it's clear that he does.

"Neat! Let's see what's on the other side," says Tristan, even as he steps through.

"Wait, you're just going to waltz right in?" asks Kyle, as he follows Tristan and disappears into the flame. Cole shoots Micah a nonchalant look and strolls next into the fire. Micah snorts daintily and saunters through. The room is suddenly considerably less crowded. Havelin looks from the blaze to Souffy, who motions for him to follow the otherworlders. She's about to go next when Oscar grabs her sleeve.

"Not that it matters at this point, but is this safe?"

"Oh, the transportation spell? Yes, absolutely. And I expect there are protection wards around the portal at the other end. The only issue is how long the hearthstone will remain open." The blaze already seems less intense.

"And when it closes?" asks Oscar.

"Maybe Cole has another Vantacoyte?" Not likely. It was impressive he'd gotten someone to give him one in the first place.

"So, no one will know where we've gone," says Oscar.

Beside him, Boryk nods empathetically. The problem with thinking things through, thinks Souffy, is that it presents good reasons against doing the things you want to do.

"Maybe you could go out to town and tell people," says Oscar to Souffy. "And then gather enough mana to reopen the fireplace to come after us?" Souffy nods at this. That's a completely reasonable suggestion. By now Oscar has to duck to push his way through; the flames are receding quickly.

She's being responsible and mature, and (to use Kyle's phrase) it sucks. But what else can she do? The fire is only coming up to her waist now. If she can hold herself back for a few more moments, then this source of temptation will be gone. As Souffy watches the fire shrink, she feels a hand on her shoulder.

It's Boryk. He's more of a resigned potato at this moment than his usual sulky tuber. He tips his head towards the hearthstone. When she doesn't react, he gives her a shove in that direction.

"Wait, you want me to—"

Boryk interrupts her by throwing both hands up in exasperation and then points to the fire, now barely three feet high. It's now or never.

"Thanks," Souffy calls out as she dives into the rapidly vanishing flame.

CHAPTER 30

Souffy

As she passes through the flame, Souffy braces for heat. Instead, the hearthstone's fire sends a chill across her skin. Then the burn of the magic engulfs her, overwhelming her physical senses and leaving only her magical ones.

It's a strange spell. Not as powerful as the Divine Wisdom's portal, which is like being in a house on fire—not just metaphorically. But this spell lacks the intentionality of human-cast magic. Those (in Souffy's experience) range from a comforting warm blanket to painful hot pokers depending on the caster's motivations. Maybe the Triad's wizard had initially cast the spell, but it's been used by so many people since that the personality of the magic has been washed away. It starts as intense numbing prickling in her extremities before mellowing into a pleasant afterglow—the magical equivalent of soaking in a hot spring. Souffy can't help herself from relaxing into it.

And then she's out. Souffy finds herself sprawled across a hearthstone identical in size and proportions to the one she'd just entered through. But this one's caked in layers of dirt, especially in the crevices from which moss and climbing plants with tiny yellow flowers sprout. By her foot, a single blue flame flickers.

She hears voices and footsteps.

"We could be anywhere."

"Havelin is certain this is the Drevo Woods."

It's Oscar and Kyle.

"Okay, so we're somewhere in the Drevo Woods." Oscar's voice is tighter than usual. "That doesn't help us get to Rozny Las. I'm worried we may just have made the whole situation worse."

"It'll be alright. You told Souffy to tell the war council our situation and then… Oh, hi Souffy."

"Hi." Her elation and glee from catching the last of the hearthstone's transportation spell succumbs to guilt. "Boryk said, or motioned, that he'd tell Lenora and the others."

Kyle and Oscar give each other a look. They wouldn't scold her, would they?

"Okay, amend that. Boryk will tell the war council—he's literate, right?" Kyle asks Oscar, who nods. "And with Souffy here, we'll increase our spell-casting potential by fifty percent, no, wait, Havelin has some magic too, so…"

As Kyle calculates, Oscar comes over and offers Souffy a hand up. "Any of this look familiar?" He motions to their surroundings.

It looks like they're in the middle of the woods. A few tiles surround the fireplace, but beyond that, it's just earth and plants. The walls Souffy had thought she spied through the flame turn out to be tree trunks, and the reflected glow of the lantern, simply late afternoon light. Perhaps both mystic hearthstones had been spelled into place at the same time. In which case, why put one here, exposed like this to the elements? She understands Oscar's concerns.

"Hey, Micah thinks he found a trail!" Tristan's head pops out from behind a tree. "And Souffy's here?" His smile gets bigger. "Awesome. Come on, guys."

Oscar shrugs and follows Tristan.

"The transportation magic did something funny with time," Kyle explains. "We each came out ten to fifteen minutes apart. And I think it's later in the day now, or maybe we're just really far north."

Souffy nods. In her mind's eye, she's replaying Tristan's face lighting up when he saw her.

"And, um." Kyle turns to Souffy. "I'm glad you're here. And not just for your magic." Kyle's smile is less exuberant, shyer than Tristan's. Souffy likes it too.

The others are gathered in a clearing among the trees just out of sight of the hearthstone. To Souffy, all forests look similar: green and nature-y. But the heroes make everything better. They—Souffy included—are going on an adventure!

"Souffy." Havelin motions her over. "Do you think this might be your uncle's footprint?"

She considers the patch of disturbed dirt indicated by Havelin and tries to see a print in it. "He does have big feet," she offers. That seems enough of an endorsement for them to set off in the direction of the print.

Souffy considers her uncle as she trails after Micah and the others. Ferimus is always looking for some item he swore he had a moment ago, or just standing in a room trying to remember why he'd come in. Then there was the time she caught him walking around as an empty suit because he'd gotten distracted halfway through casting an invisibility spell. And he constantly oversleeps and shows up late for his classes. His usual apology for his tardiness is that he'd been up all night engrossed in his research. What if all those times he had instead been using the hearthstone to come here? No, Souffy shakes her head. That's just wishful thinking.

Havelin guides them around giant ferns and tree roots and towards a uniform line of trees with red, papery bark; each tree is large enough that it would take two Souffys to wrap their arms around it. As they approach, she realizes the trees are growing in a circle.

"It's like a fairy ring," she muses.

"Do you mean that literally? Or were you being poetic?" asks Kyle.

"Oh, poetic. Fairy rings are made of mushrooms. Although, dryads are a type of fairy, and they're all about trees." Souffy considers the possibility. "But they don't dance around naked in the moonlight. Which"— she makes sure to note—"is a perfectly fine cultural tradition to choose to follow."

"So noted," says Kyle.

And even if her uncle were sneaking out here all the time, what would be the purpose? Souffy has always assumed that Ferimus was exiled to Bydlo because he was the same kind of failed Ravenus wizard that she is. Souffy recalls Galam's words earlier that day: *There had always been a fortress wizard since the Triad left.*

"Tada!" sings Micah, interrupting Souffy's thoughts. He's found a gap between the trees and scrambles though. Cole and Havelin follow.

"Hey," comes Micah's voice. "I think this tree stump is a secret base. Or home. Or something."

"What gave it away?" Cole asks drolly. "The door or the potted plants?"

Souffy in turn pushes through the outer ring of trees to behold an enormous tree stump in the center of a small clearing. Its girth is equivalent to one of the fortress's smaller towers and is overgrown with ferns. Before its demise, the full tree must have dominated the canopy. Now it's only a ragged stump; probably a giant had torn it down back in the day. However, enough of the base of the stump remains to accommodate a round, four-foot-tall door in its side. It's flanked by two modest clay pots planted with blue and purple pansies—Uncle Ferimus's favorite flower. He likes to tuck them in the brim of his hat.

Havelin gives the door a knock. "Anyone home?" Everyone waits silently, but nothing happens.

Cole jiggles the handle. "It's locked. Want me to pick it?" He and the other otherworlders look at Oscar.

"If I said no, would it matter?" Oscar asks. Cole waits. "Just do it. I somehow doubt Verhalty has a problem with breaking and entering."

Oscar's blessing thus obtained, Cole gets to work. Souffy's eyes wander back to the flowers. She doesn't recall seeing any pansies around the fortress. That isn't proof of anything, she reminds herself. She just wants it to be.

She wants Uncle Ferimus to be up to something mysterious, something significant. Since the arrival of the refugees—no, before that— since Arek's messenger bird, life in Bydlo has turned serious and consequential. It makes everything before: the canceled concert, the quest for missing sheep, Souffy's resolution to defy her family edict and leave with the otherworlders, seem silly and childish in comparison. But if there had been something bigger going on all along—and if her family is somehow connected to that—then maybe, just maybe, she does have her own role to play.

Cole lets out an otherworldly curse Souffy hasn't heard before. The configuration it proposes is so impossible it's cute, but none of the others are laughing.

"Having problems?" asks Micah sweetly.

Cole just curses again. It probably isn't helping that they're crowding him.

"Why don't we try these?" Kyle steps up to the door and pulls out a familiar ring of keys. He gives them a shake; one begins to glow.

"That's Uncle Ferimus's key ring, he really did come here!" Souffy's heart is pounding. Since she'd arrived in Bydlo, she has been looking for an adventure, something wondrous to discover, some secret to expose. And it had been right under her nose all along.

"Not necessarily," says Kyle. "I think this is more of a magic skeleton key."

"Oh." She goes back to hoping. Magical skeleton keys, though. She recollects several scrapes she's found herself in that a magic skeleton key might have gotten her out of.

"Okay, who wants to go in first and set off all the traps?" Kyle asks as he opens the door.

"Are you serious?" asks Oscar. When Kyle shrugs, Oscar turns to Cole, who smiles.

"I got this."

Cole certainly has the swagger down, Souffy thinks as she watches him duck through the door.

"I think we need some new boy band laws for these kinds of situations," says Oscar.

"All clear," Cole calls out. "I think."

One by one, they follow Cole in through the door. Souffy awaits her turn. If her uncle had stayed here, there's sure to be something of his inside. It's universally agreed that Ferimus would forget his beard if it weren't attached to his face.

"Just one sign, please," she whispers, in case the Divine Wisdom is listening.

In front of her, Tristan ducks his head through the door.

"Will we all fit?" she asks. The tree stump is large, but there are already five people crowded in.

"Oh yeah," says Tristan as he disappears inside. "We've held parties in hotel rooms smaller than this."

Souffy takes a deep breath and steps through. There's a small landing and steps leading down into a space hollowed-out beneath and beyond the edges of the stump. The floors and walls are made of packed dirt with the occasional larger root twisting down. This space had been carved out with magic, Souffy is certain. Not only is there no dust, but it's illuminated by magic wall sconces. The overall effect is cozy, but not stuffy, and large enough to accommodate three beds, two desks, a large table surrounded by stools, and several cupboards embedded into the walls. It's spartan and orderly. Souffy's heart sinks; Ferimus was never this tidy.

It's still an adventure, she consoles herself as she starts down the stairs into the room following the otherworlders.

Two steps down, Oscar gives a shout. "What the—bird! Look out Souffy!"

A mess of brown, white, and yellow streaks across the room heading straight for her. She drops to her knees and hears it fluttering overhead.

"It's trying to get out, Kyle!" Cole shouts. "Shut the door."

"No, let it out!" counters Micah. "It must have gotten trapped here."

Souffy turns to see Kyle still up on the landing. His eyes are wide as he holds his hands up to shield his face. Unnecessary, as the bird is already settling down on the brim of his wide wizard hat. Souffy knows that bird.

"That's Uncle Ferimus's messenger bird!" Proof, she has proof! *Thank you, Divine Wisdom*, she silently adds.

Kyle carefully removes his hat. The bird remains tucked in next to the buckle, as if a milliner had sewn it in. "How can you be sure? They all look alike to me."

"See the yellow tailfeather?" Souffy raises a finger and holds it up; the bird ignores her. She presses her finger against the creature's belly and after a moment it ruffles its feathers and steps on. "Ravenus messenger birds are spelled with yellow tail feathers." She spies a perch on one of the desks and deposits the bird there.

"Well, that solves the problem of communicating with Bydlo," says Kyle. "Now we just need to gather enough useful information to send back. So, let's go all Sherlock Holmes and find us some clues!"

Cole is first to speak after a brief moment spent searching. "First point goes to me. I found a map." He's next to the second desk where a piece of parchment is held in place by a black rock the size of an apple. "It has a bunch of marks and writing on it."

"Any of those say, 'you are here,' perchance?" asks Kyle.

"Not in English or anything I can read." Cole goes to push the rock out of the way, and his hand flies back. "What the..." He reaches out more tentatively and gives the stone a poke. "It feels weird, electric."

"What?" Kyle comes over and touches it, frowning. Then he too reaches out and picks it up. "I don't feel anything. It's heavy and"—he gives it a sniff—"smells like... ozone."

"You said that about the meteorite bits we found in the forest," says Oscar. Souffy remembers Kyle using that word to describe the rock that fell from the shooting star. "Malza said Ferimus took the meteorite that crashed into their barn. This could be it."

"And we think it's what made the animals bigger, right?" says Tristan from across the room. "That means it's magic."

"It felt like magic when it was crossing the sky that night. Uncle Ferimus said it temporarily altered some properties of light," Souffy recalls.

"Properties?" Kyle twists the rock. "Like the wavelength? Or the amplitude?"

Strange otherworld terms, thinks Souffy. Although the others seem equally confused.

"I have a Sense Magic spell I could try," she offers. This is her chance to be useful. "Just so you know, it turns my eyes completely red."

"It's quite unnerving," Havelin adds, helpfully.

Souffy covers her face with her hands. "*Videre quod est magia*," she intones, letting herself feel the hum of the words in her teeth. Despite Havelin's warning, Kyle still gasps when she looks at him before turning her uncanny crimson eyes to the meteorite.

"Oh, it's definitely magic," she declares as she tries to blink away the searing white light she can now see radiating from it. The Sense Magic spell usually imparts colors to magical objects from which she can decipher the type of magic involved, at least for cast spells. Naturally occurring magic is trickier because the colors tend to shift. Pure white light means a divine origin, which is fitting if the rock had indeed fallen from the sky. But it isn't giving off a consistent glow. As Souffy leans in, squinting, she catches flashes of color darting across the surface, leaving trails of vivid hues that quickly fade back to white.

Souffy focuses the spell, trying to see deeper. It's surprisingly easy. Most magics have an innate self-preservation component bound to them which grants them resistance to other spells. But this rock's magic is almost welcoming; it's hungry for her discovery spell. The meteorite turns red, then blue, then octarine, and then it begins flashing through a rainbow of colors too quickly to identify. Faster and faster and faster they flash until they smear into a dull white. What does that mean? As she wonders what to try next, the light as well as her Sense Magic spell both blink out simultaneously. That's strange, Souffy's spells usually fail more percussively.

"It's not complete." She isn't sure how she knows, she just does. "It's more like a fragment of a larger, powerful spell, something cast by a celestial or demon or… something. We didn't cover this in any of my classes." Not any of the ones that she took notes in at least. It wasn't the dazzling, brilliant, insightful reveal she had been hoping to give. Souffy looks to Kyle to see if he's disappointed. Instead, his eyes are wide; his mouth hangs open.

"Tris! What the frick are you doing?" Kyle shouts.

Souffy jumps. She isn't the only one. Everyone turns to look at Tristan; he's standing with the messenger bird perched on his wrist. The bird is eagerly dipping its beak into his cupped hands.

"It was hungry," Tristan apologizes. He looks more shocked than upset. "I found some birdseed, so I thought…"

How sweet, Souffy feels with her heart.

Oh shit, Souffy thinks in her head.

Kyle slams the meteorite onto the table. "You idiot!"

Oscar starts to speak, "Kyle, he—" but stops when Kyle stalks past him.

"Stupid, moronic noob," Kyle mutters as he makes his way over to Tristan. "It's imprinting on you! Do you even know what that means?" The messenger bird startles at all the commotion and takes flight. Its wing nearly clips Kyle's cheek; the wizard doesn't flinch. "No, of course, you don't, you himbo! That bird has recorded a snapshot of you, right at this moment. It knows everything you know at this instant, and nothing that you don't know—like where we are or what our game plan is. You've just rendered it completely useless for sending future messages."

Realization creeps across Tristan's face. "Wait, you're saying this bird will lay egg-copies of me? And anyone who gets a hold of them could learn my deepest secrets?"

"Yeah, like the starlets you've kissed, and plot reveals for your movie's sequel. No one here cares about that stuff, Tris." Kyle's sarcasm seems more exhausted than mean. While he's rubbing his temple, the messenger bird re-settles itself on his hat.

"No, you don't have to worry about that," Souffy assures Tristan. "The impression is an accurate copy of you, it wouldn't say anything you wouldn't say. There's no magic or other means to force the projection to reveal anything you wouldn't want it to."

"Oh, that's a relief." Tristan looks back to Kyle. "Man, I'm really sorry."

Kyle just shakes his head. Souffy feels like she should do something, say something. She feels a hand on her arm, it's Oscar.

"It's best to just let them work it out themselves." His voice is just above a whisper. "They always do," he reassures her with a smile.

The room is quiet, save for the messenger bird's contented cooing.

Micah breaks the uncomfortable silence. "Hey. There's a bird egg here already."

The egg in question lies on a small pillow next to the perch. Souffy can tell from its nearly spotless white shell that it's at least a week old. "I'm not sure if that's still good anymore."

"It can't hurt to try," says Kyle. His mood appears to be somewhat restored. Micah passes the egg to Kyle and everyone gathers around the table. Kyle taps the egg twice and deftly cracks it with just one hand.

"Show-off," says Cole.

A hint of a smile graces Kyle's face. But now all eyes are on the egg's contents. A face Souffy has never seen before emerges from the swirling mist. At first, Souffy thinks there's a distortion, like in the egg version of Arek. But it soon becomes apparent that it's a tolerably accurate image of a very old and very wrinkled man.

The ancient visage's eyes open wide. "Hello." His voice is scratchy and thin. "Ferimus, are you there? It's so dark." It appears they've caught the egg just in time.

"Do you recognize him?" Havelin asks Souffy, who shakes her head, puzzled.

"Hello." The head spins lazily about, contemplating each person around the table. "Ferimus, are you there? It's so dark."

"Ferimus isn't here," says Souffy, causing the head to snap back to look at her. "Can you tell us who you are?"

The man contemplates her. Souffy holds her breath as he squints.

"Hello," he says. "Ferimus, is that you? It's so dark." Maybe the egg has gone bad after all.

"This is Ferimus's niece, Souffy," Kyle enunciates each syllable. "Can you give her the message? Ferimus isn't here now."

"Oh." The man's face lights up with something other than confusion as he turns to Kyle. "Ferimus, there you are. That's your niece, you said? I can barely see you, it's so dark."

"He thinks you're Ferimus," Cole supplies, unnecessarily. He pitches his voice so low Souffy can barely hear it. "Play along."

Kyle keeps the brim of his hat low and leans in. "Do you have a message for me?"

"Yes." The face smiles, gaining even more wrinkles in the process. "I wanted to tell you everything was done as you requested. I'm not sure why

Janassy isn't back yet, but I'm sure she's located your sky rock by now. Oh, and there are strange things in the forest."

"Strange things?" asks Kyle.

"Yes, there are strange things in the forest."

"What sort of strange things?" Souffy jumps in.

The man's face snaps back to Souffy, his open mouth is mostly gums. "Hello. Ferimus, are you there? It's so dark here."

"Well, this is getting us nowhere," says Kyle.

"Hey, you," Cole not-quite shouts. The head spins around at this. "Can you see this map? Do you know it?" He holds out the map.

"Why, yes, I know that map," says the figure. He looks flustered, but also more alert.

"Which dot corresponds to the house dug under the tree stump?"

"We-well…" the projection's voice wavers.

"The one with the pansies in front."

"Oh, the pansies," the old man croaks out. "Janassy planted those pansies."

"Where. On. The. Map?" Cole insists, his voice pitched menacingly. *Impressive intimidation skills*, thinks Souffy.

"That's the green one, in the corner, Ferimus…" His eyes become distant again. "Are you there? It's so dark in here."

CHAPTER 31

Kyle

We try Cole's trick of hitting the hologram with direct questions a few more times before the egg runs out of albumin or whatever and the old man fades away. He didn't manage to tell us much about the map, but did direct us to a cupboard with some vigor potions and a cleverly designed man-purse stuffed with miscellaneous spell components.

Still, vigor potions can be quite useful for an all-night hike. Yep, that's the plan. If we are indeed at the green dot in the far corner of the map, we can head east and intersect with an old logging road while it's still light. Then we follow that road to the coast south of Rozney Las and from there locate the fishing village where Arek and his troops were planning to regroup at. Comparing the scale to a map I saw at the war council, I'm estimating it's four miles through the woods, another five on the road, maybe one to the village. And that's totally doable.

Totally doable. I repeat the phrase in my head a few more times. I'd feel better if we could send the messenger bird to Lenora to let her know our plan. But thanks to Tristan, that's not happening.

I shouldn't have snapped at him.

We're all feeling the tension. I can tell, because no one says much as we eat the beef jerky and dried fruit rations that we found packed along with the vigor potions. I'm left thinking about what Ferimus might have used this place for, about how this might fit within the bigger story, the one we're not yet seeing.

I chew a leathery apricot and free-associate: three beds, three bears, three little pigs. Everything in fairytales comes in threes, what else? There's the Triad of Valor everyone keeps name-checking. I visualize them charging through the fireplace in the woods, kicking some giant ass, and chilling out here afterwards on those three beds. They traveled all over Mythreal, but it was here, in the Drevo Woods, where they completed their Final Quest. Meanwhile we're on our first real one in the same magical forest. What are the odds that this is a complete coincidence? Are they greater than the chance that I'm engaging in sloppy narrative thinking? Even worse, video-game-narrative thinking, where every plot has to be dumbed down so that the average thirteen-year-old boy who's multitasking watching YouTube shorts can follow the storyline while they're busy button mashing.

Still, narrative thinking seems to be working out for us so far.

What's the worst that could happen?

Death. Yeah, death could happen.

While we're eating, Souffy and I mentally prep our best offense and defense spells, which are mostly defense. For an attack spell, I've got my Magic Mortar; Souffy's got one that makes you laugh so hard you end up in a hospital.

"What about this one, Fire Orb?" I ask as I page through her spellbook.

"That's the one I burnt down the building with."

"Sounds promising. Just make sure it's aimed at the enemy and not us," I tell her.

After dinner, Oscar insists we suit up in the most protective versions of our adventure outfits—shields for himself and Tristan, leather gloves for everyone, plus extra bits of armor—for those allowed to wear armor. And with those careful and considered preparations, we head out.

Bushwhacking isn't so bad, at least not with Havelin and Micah up front doing most of the whacking. I'm in the rear with Cole and Tristan, who's unsheathed his sword and is clearing away the taller vines the others can't reach. Now would be a good time to apologize for reaming him out over the bird mishap, but he seems to be in good spirits so I think he's over it. Or maybe he's forgotten, in which case, why bother?

Besides, my attention is caught up in this forest we're traversing. The Drevo Woods is… the big time. If tree biomes were performance venues, the sheep-hunting, cockatrice-fighting forest would have been a restored downtown theater and Drevo would be a sports stadium. They both have plenty of trees and greenery. But the scale here changes everything. The Drevo Woods doesn't just have big trees, it has charismatic megaflora giants whose roots snake along the ground while their branches basket-weave together to form a cathedral ceiling canopy. And scaffolded to those trees is even more life: masses of mosses, crenulated lichens, cascading ferns, plate-sized tree mushrooms, and those never-need-water air plants so beloved by interior design influencers. Then there's the understory: bushes so bushy we're practically hacking tunnels through them, and every patch of dirt is busy supporting a complete flourishing ecosystem of its own. Is this the result of the magic everyone keeps mentioning? Or maybe this is just what nature is capable of when humans are taken out of the picture. Untouched natural majesty aside, I wouldn't mind a patch of clear-cutting, since the sooner we get to the logging road the better.

Two hours in the sun begins to set. I had been counting on more daylight. We decide to sample the vigor potions to give us a boost. And boy, do they deliver—they're like everything that the most outrageous Red Bull ads promise, and then some. Souffy says the potions are good for four to six hours, at which point we can take another swig from them without too much concern about adverse effects. But, she warns us, when the second re-up wears off we'll be crashing hard. Hopefully that won't happen until after we've safely reached our destination. I'm ambivalent about this better-living-through-alchemy—it's not like we kept our bodies as pure as temples back when we were on tour. Although at least then we had four-star hotels with memory foam mattresses and Egyptian cotton sheets to collapse in.

Dusk encroaches and the soft light filtering through the forest fades, greens turn to gray, and shadows muddle details. I stub my toe twice and almost trip over a tree root. I'd probably see better if I took my hat off, but it's keeping my head so comfortably warm. Who knew I was a hat person?

"Does anyone have a light spell?" I ask. You know, one of those practical, useful spells. I'm recognizing that my concerns over not getting hurt and/or killed have resulted in me maxing out on defense spells to the exclusion of anything else useful.

"Oh, I've got a cantrip that'll work, Will-O-Wisps," says Souffy. "I just need some phosphorus." I pass her a matchbox. "And I need to think of a simple song that I can easily keep in my thoughts so I don't have to keep recasting it."

From the back of the line, Cole starts singing—with feeling. He's doubling down on his smooth R&B delivery and nailing the high notes. The first "never gonna" hits my brain like the aural equivalent of an ice cream headache.

"Arrggg, I'm going to kill you, Cole!" shouts Micah.

Which only encourages Cole to belt the lyrics out louder, rattling through promises to never disappoint, cheat, abandon, cause tears, say goodbye, tell a lie, or otherwise hurt the subject of the song.

"That's perfect," says Souffy, without a trace of irony. I wonder if she'll still feel that way after an hour of it stuck in her head? She hums the melody to herself and nails it on the first try. I hear the strike of the match and catch a whiff of fireworks smell. The air shimmers and four glowing bulbs materialize in a line. Their hues gently cycle through the colors of a children's basic crayon box set and cast corresponding warm shadows on the tree trunks. The effect is charming and lovely and comforting. I open my mouth to express these thoughts to Souffy, but Tristan beats me to it.

"That's really pretty, Souffy," he says. Souffy giggles. I stay quiet.

Another hour passes like this without any sign of civilization. We take a break while our rangers, along with Souffy, scout out the best route down a ravine. The glowing balls depart with Souffy but the moon comes out so it's bright enough for us to see each other.

"How much longer until we get to that road, do you think?" asks Tristan.

I raise up my empty hand. "No cell phone GPS."

"I can't believe it's been a week since I last checked my phone," says Oscar. "I still find myself looking for it when I leave a room."

"I know, right?" says Tristan. "It feels weird not having it."

"What do you miss most about it?" I ask. With the exception of Micah, who's constantly bemoaning the lack of some modern convenience, we haven't talked much about our own world or even our absence from it.

"Checking social media," Tristan replies without hesitation. "I like to know what everyone's up to."

"I miss calling my Gram every night," says Oscar.

I remember that, he even did it on tour. "How's she doing?"

"Oh she's good. She's a spry seventy-eight-year-old." Oscar smiles a small, wistful smile. "But since my Uncle JJ died, she's all by herself. It cheers her up when I call and tell her about my day. She'd love hearing about all this."

"I miss Wordle," says Cole.

"People still play that?" asks Tristan.

He shrugs. "I don't do it to be social. I just like to do it every day at the same time. It's a ritual, gives me structure." I don't think he's aware that he's rubbing his AA medallion. "How about you, Kyle?"

My flippant answer would be to say that I miss looking up random facts to appear smart. But I don't, not really. Learning magic spells is way more self-validating.

"Kyle was never on his phone, remember? Too busy getting smarter reading books," says Tristan. He lightly elbows me. His gentle teasing reminds me that I still haven't apologized for earlier. I'm about to when Cole cuts in.

"Hey, what's with that tree?"

CHAPTER 32

Kyle

Cole points to a deciduous tree some ten yards away. Its lowest branch is swaying, rocking back and forth really. It can't be the wind; the surrounding branches are dead still. I squint, trying to see if there's a creature hiding in the branch's foliage. And indeed, something glows red from within the dark mass of greenery—like a smoldering ember.

This is obviously the point where I should be readying Magic Mortar. Instead, I'm counting the period of the swinging branch like it's a pendulum: it's exactly three seconds. With each oscillation, the path of the arc it sweeps increases. The effect is like a child pumping on a swing. And just like a kid would, at the apex of the next arc the branch releases, flying through the intervening distance and crashing into the ground practically at our feet. We all jump back.

"It's just a branch, right?" asks Oscar, uncertainly.

Closer to a bough. Now that it's out of the shadow of the tree it detached from, I can see it's a good five feet long with mostly bare branches sticking out. The only leaves are in a bunch at one end that reminds me of a giant growth of mistletoe.

There's a series of taps, like raindrops hitting a metal roof, and the bough's six largest branches bend—but don't break—to reach down to the ground. When their tips touch the ground, the bough raises itself up on them until it stands at waist level.

My brain is attempting to remap this new configuration, moving it from the plant to the animal kingdom. There's a large clap and out from the bough's clump of leaves pops a triangular mass of bark (it's a head) with two red orbs (eyes, obviously). Two narrow twigs sprout from the top and grow almost three feet (these could be tendrils or hair or…). While I'm still sorting it out, the creature shudders and somehow pulls itself together, transforming from an oversized elementary school craft project into something frightfully alive.

"It's a giant walking stick," observes Tristan. "A giant, giant walking stick, with leaves."

Something's wrong with my adrenaline pathway because my fight-or-flight reflexes aren't properly kicking in. My brain is processing the scene like it's out of a nature documentary and I'm waiting for a British-accented voiceover to start delving into this creature's mating habits. Maybe this dream-like lack of urgency is due to the creature; it's moving like it's stuck in molasses.

But not all of it. Something flicks out and shoots itself into my shoulder. I look down to see a green twig sticking out of my coat, like an arrow. But unlike an arrow, it doesn't end. I follow its snaking length back to the clump of leaves on the shoulders of the creature—no, monster. It's definitely time to upgrade whatever this is to a monster.

I'm just standing there like an idiot when Tristan shouts something and tackles me to the ground. I'm not entirely sure of the order of events past this point, but the twig in my arm snaps, my hat flies off, I hit the ground, and Tris knees over me with his shield up. Tiny plonking noises are coming from the shield, evidently more pokey twig attacks.

"Thanks," I say on autopilot. My brain is trying to work out why my arm isn't hurting. But then my nerve receptors catch up and I feel the pain of a hundred papercuts in my shoulder. I can't see the monster—the shield is blocking the view—I can see Tristan. He's swinging his sword, and wood chips are flying everywhere as he hacks away at the walking stick monster's attack. I flinch with every blow he delivers, knowing that while I'm lying here uselessly, the next assault could be directed at Tris's unprotected face.

I use the distraction Tristan provides to army-crawl forward on my elbows. The monster's moving fast now, twitching, stomping its feet, kicking up dust. It's too close for me to cast Magic Mortar on it, but maybe I can at least hold it back with Frostbite? Before I can even start thinking icy thoughts, a melodious baritone cuts through the air:

"Take that!" Oscar charges in, his metal-tipped boots flashing across my field of vision. Above them I catch another flash as he swings his mace down on the creature, full force, while his pristine cape billows out behind him. He overshoots, so it's the shaft of his weapon that connects with the monster's head. Still, Oscar has channeled his energy into the blow and the force of it drives the beast's bark face into the ground, its front "legs" buckling underneath it. As it goes down, I see the tendril shoots poised to slice Tristan's face collapse stiffly to the ground. The monster's legs flail like a child throwing a tantrum. Oscar leans in, his weight holding the monster down. The leaf mass growing out of the creature's shoulders is vibrating violently, inches away from Oscar's head.

"Get back!" shouts Cole, coming up from behind the monster. He must have been positioning himself while the rest of us were still just standing around. Oscar obliges, leaping backwards with a grace that should be impossible given the weight of his armor.

The walking stick monster rears up; its glowing red eyes snap to focus on Oscar. Meanwhile Cole slides a dagger into the thing's neck joint and from there into the head cavity where I'm guessing its brain, or at least the central nervous system, should reside. The monster lets loose a high-pitched wail that reaches frequencies only dogs hear. Like a total badass, Cole twists the knife, er, dagger. There's a click-pop. The uncanny scream ceases and the monster's head flies off. A goopy white sap bubbles out of the gaping neck hole, accompanied by a truly noxious smell—like industrial cleaning products mixed with cough syrup. Cole yanks out his blade, flicking some of the goop (there's got to be a better fantasy term for it) back in his direction. Boy band instinct kicks in and Cole's hands fly up to protect his face, hopefully in time.

You'd think the beheading would mean it's game over for the giant walking stick, but the rest of the monster is still thrashing like it's in a mosh pit. Its white ichor (that's the word I was looking for) splatters everywhere. The body rears up once again and several legs kick out towards Tristan. He drops his shield to grasp his sword with both hands and slices off one leg at the knee. But the kicks are coming too quick, too close for him to get in a full swing. He misjudges his next angle of attack, and one of the flailing limbs sends his sword flying.

"*Frigus Digitorum!*" Finally, I contribute something to the fight. My skeleton hand dives into the leafy growth on the monster's back and I envision it grabbing on as hard as possible. The effect is both shocking and instantaneous: the leaves that my remote hand touches all shrivel and flake off, exposing a tangle of sticks that begin to crack and splinter. The creature stills and I see its legs trembling.

Tristan recovers, stands up, and delivers a roundhouse kick into its midsection. "Timber!" he shouts as he sends it crashing to the ground.

Tristan's acting abilities are passable at best, but he does have a genuine talent for delivering cheesy lines with conviction.

We hold our collective breath; for now the thing stays down. I keep one eye on it as I stand and retrieve my hat. The monster doesn't so much as twitch. By the time the others show up, I'm about ninety percent sure it's dead.

Souffy and Micah's horrified expressions quickly change to relief and approval as they catch sight of the downed monster. That's only because they didn't come back in time to witness the amateur-hour fight we put on trying to kill this thing. Except for Cole, Cole was like the love child of John Wick and Lisbeth Salander. And I guess Tristan held his own. Even Oscar took the initiative at the right time. It was just the hapless wizard who stood there waiting to be used as monster target practice. I look down at the broken bit of twig still poking out of my arm and try to pull it out in one swift motion, like I'm a tough guy. My gasp and pained grimace spoil the effect.

Oscar steps forward and examines me. "It didn't go in deep, but we should clean the wound out, disinfect it too. Whatever that creature was—"

"It's a blight," whispers Havelin.

"What's a blight?" asks Souffy, looking more carefully at the tangled mass of plant matter that comprised the monster.

"It's the worst thing that can happen to a forest. They're unnatural, a perversion, an infestation."

I never fought any blights in *Heroes Summoning*, but I know perfectly well what infestation means.

"There are more of these things," I say slowly.

Havelin gives a slight nod. The moon goes behind a cloud, leaving us in darkness—Souffy's cheerful glow balls had blinked out of existence when she arrived; the horrifying scene probably erased the music earworm from her brain. And in the darkness, every deep shadow hides potential danger.

CHAPTER 33

Souffy

They leave the monster's corpse and hike at least a mile, up and down two hills, to put some distance between themselves and the infected grove. There's a brief debate about what to call the creature that attacked them. Cole wins with "walking-blight"; he says Oscar's suggestion of "stick-blight" sounds like something you'd call an arborist about. With that settled, they all fall silent. Souffy's anxious thoughts alternate between worrying about the bushes that might jump out at them and a general unease that they're lost. After wading a stream—there hadn't been any stream crossing on the map—and arriving in a clearing, Havelin declares it's time to stop and ask for directions.

In the moonlight, Souffy watches as the ranger clasps his hands and intones, *"Baagn carrey gioot cleaysh."*

A moment later, a great horned owl silently flutters down to perch on a low branch. It cocks its head and focuses on Havelin. Havelin takes a deep breath, puffs out his cheeks, and cups his hands to his mouth. "Hoo hoo hoot?"

In response, the owl launches into a complicated series of hoots, warbles, and screeches. Souffy knows Havelin is gaining valuable information through his Talk To The Animals spell. But it looks like a pantomime performance.

"How come no one told me rangers got to do magic?" asks Micah.

"Did you ask?" Cole counters. Micah glares at him.

Souffy scans the branches above them for suspicious clumps of leaves. She's always found nature to be pleasant, if a bit boring. Not tonight, not here. Her skin prickles, and she feels a constant pressure behind her eyes. She keeps flashing to the dead monster. Souffy's accustomed to seeing dead monsters; the shadowed hallways in her school had been lined with stuffed and mounted beasts—most immortalized in terrifying predatory poses. But the walking-blight was only dead because the heroes killed it, which could have gone either way. Could still go either way. It can't be the only walking-blight in this forest.

According to Havelin, blights can take many forms. They infect and corrupt plants and trees (for unknown reasons, they ignore mushrooms) and the monsters that emerge take on twisted aspects of the host. The underlying cause of the blight is a demon, or perhaps an evil fey, Havelin wasn't sure.

"Blights were a campfire story I heard when I was training to be a ranger," he'd said. "I thought it was an allegory for how groups like the Laska Trading Company broke the circle of life with their destructive forestry practices and fouled the land with their magic infusion workshops."

Havelin's avian conversation now includes head bobbing, both his and the owl's. Souffy, her mind still buzzing with images of dead and living walking-blights, has to turn around lest she break out in nervous giggles. Instead, she wanders over toward where Oscar and Kyle are in deep conversation.

"I'm just saying we both need to get better at casting spells, Oscar. Next time, use Dead Ringer instead of your mace."

"But I don't want to waste mana in case I need to cast Heal Wounds."

"Healing spells won't do much good once someone gets killed," Kyle snaps. Oscar blanches.

Souffy considers mentioning that Dead Ringer is a cantrip and doesn't use up mana, but they don't need her lecturing them about magic. She's just an uncertified wizard who messes up spells. Even if her spells did work, what good would charms or enchantments be against blights? There's the fireball spell Kyle suggested—strongly encouraged—her to prepare. He's even helped her mix the components by embedding brimstone and iron filings into balls of wax. She reaches into her belt pouch to rub one of the resulting globs. It feels both soft and gritty against the pads of her fingertips.

Her thoughts are interrupted by a soft creak behind her. Souffy turns to see the owl silently flap its wings and rise up. The bird hovers for a moment and then swoops away into the darkness.

"Did you get anything, Havelin?" asks Oscar.

"Yes," Havelin says softly. Souffy can tell from his eyes that something bad is coming. "Last night she flew over Rozny Las, she called it the human nesting grounds. She said it had burned to the ground."

There are gasps, followed by silence. No one wants to hear the worst, but Souffy knows she has to ask. "Did she see any people?"

Havelin shakes his head. "She confirmed that there are more green-things, the blight monsters, in the forest. Some of the trees aren't safe to perch in, and she hasn't seen her mate recently." Realizing he hasn't answered the question, he adds, "It can be hard to get animals to focus on human stuff."

"Anything else?" asks Oscar.

"Apparently, there is a road nearby. But it's to the north of us, not west."

"Did we get turned around?" Kyle asks Micah.

"I think I know how to use a compass, Kyle. More likely the map was wrong. Or maybe we shouldn't have put our faith in that egg guy. You know, the one who wouldn't give us his name and mistook Kyle for a middle-aged black man?" Micah turns to Cole when he says this last part.

"But hey, good news, there's a road!" says Tristan. He steps into the center of the group with an easy grace and turns around to face them. He makes eye contact with Souffy just long enough for her heart to flutter. "We just need to head north, right?"

As they trudge north, Souffy calls up Will-O-Wisp. It's so simple to do with this new melody. Cole promised to teach her the whole song once they're someplace safe; she hopes that will be soon.

Traveling north leads them through a marshy patch of the woods. Souffy tries her best to keep to dry spots and fallen logs, but after the second time she sinks in mud up to her ankle, she gives up and just starts slogging. She allows Kyle and Tristan to pass her and falls back to where Oscar and Cole are bringing up the rear.

"You keep rubbing your eyes," Oscar says to Cole. "Did you get some of that blight goop on you?"

"I'm fine," Cole dismisses him.

"Just let me look. I'm trying to be the responsible healer here."

"Yeah, we know. You're the big brother. Do you want an award?" Even when he's being sarcastic, Cole's deep voice resonates with soulfulness.

"What I want is for you to think before doing something rash and st—" Oscar stops and takes a breath. "Short-sighted."

Souffy braces for Cole's response, but at that moment, Tristan gives a whoop of joy. "Civilization! We found the road."

"Can you keep your voice down?" Kyle says as Souffy catches up.

It is indeed a road, in a manner of speaking. Two distinct wagon ruts, along with a smattering of horseshoe tracks, run down the middle of an otherwise overgrown dirt trail. More encouraging is the white-painted fence on the opposite side, beyond which lies a cultivated field with a scarecrow visible in the distance.

"Souffy, does this look familiar?" asks Havelin.

She's about to say no, but then she notices that the scarecrow is wearing beat-up armor. "Uh, yeah. This was the road that that crazy druid chased us down."

"You were attacked by a druid, Souffy?" asks Oscar.

"No. Well okay, yes, but there were reasons."

Havelin is pointing. "See, down that way is that huge white oak. You remember, Souffy?"

She doesn't. But she does recall there being a farm further on, where a very nice family had taken them in, fed them lunch, and then driven them by cart back to Rozny Las.

Oscar perks up. "We need to stop at that farmhouse. I want to check out Kyle's injury again, and yours too, Cole." His tone is clipped. This time Cole doesn't argue.

They follow the winding, up-and-down road. With signs of civilization around them, Souffy can finally turn her thoughts away from the dead blight. They eventually crest a hill and catch an unhindered view of Havelin's tree. Its boughs stretch over the road and its branches catch the moonlight. Souffy can see how someone like Havelin would remember such a tree. It's the type of tree that Arek likes to write poems about. Thinking of Arek, she sends a quick prayer to any deity that may be eavesdropping asking for his safety.

As they descend the hill, Souffy catches a whiff of something acrid and harsh. By the time they reach the tree, the smell burns in her nostrils.

"Oh, no!" cries Havelin.

The giant tree is obviously infected. Sap bleeds from angry black gashes in the bark, and it glistens red in the light from Souffy's spell. The feather moss that hangs from its branches sways menacingly, like tendrils reaching out to find and grasp prey.

"It must have been infected recently," Havelin reasons. "See, it still has all its leaves."

Souffy looks up. Indeed, the tree's canopy is replete with green foliage. There isn't a touch of autumnal brown. As she stares upward, one of the leaves detaches and floats languidly down, gently twisting and turning in the still, night air. Just a few feet from the ground, it catches a breeze and alights on Micah's cheek.

Micah screams. His hands spasm and he bats the leaf away. The bit of green sticks to his hand as he desperately shakes it off.

"Jesus! It's just a leaf," snaps Cole.

"It bit me!" cries Micah, finally flicking it off. "It's alive!" The attacking leaf flutters just above the ground. Micah doesn't wait for it to start rising again; his foot comes down, and everyone hears a distinctly squishy crunch.

"Some sort of bug? Or blight?" Oscar answers his own question.

"More incoming!" shouts Kyle. The tree vibrates and sends a gentle shower of leaf-blights down upon them. He swings his hands in elegant circles while chanting "*Protectorate!*" Above Kyle, Oscar, and Cole, the air shimmers and arrests the fall of several dozen leaf-blights. Micah and Havelin throw their cloaks over their heads and dash under the cover of Kyle's Shield spell.

Souffy tries to follow, only to find a swarm of leaf-blights blocking her path.

"I got this," Oscar calls out, then clasps his hands, and Souffy sees his lips move. She knows the cantrip is working because time itself slows, and she hears the chime of a tiny bell. A single leaf-blight drops to the ground like a stone.

"We need a spell that targets the whole area, not a single monster," Kyle says.

Souffy is looking at the tiny creature that has fallen by her feet. It's a normal leaf on top. But a brown bulge, like a wasp gall or a nightcrawler's rainwater-bloated corpse, grows down the middle of the leaf's underside. White spots cluster at the end near the stem and the usually round lobes of the leaf narrow down to protruding needle tips.

"Souffy, there's one on you!" Havelin shouts at the same moment that she feels something light settle on her head.

Instinctively, she raises her hand, but stops herself just in time. Then, to her dawning horror, she feels a tug on her hair. It's moving. "Get off!" she squeals as she desperately shakes her head to no avail. It's crawling in through her thick curls, making its way down to her scalp.

"Hold still, Souffy," she hears Tristan say in an unnaturally calm voice. She does her best to, despite the certainty that something is pricking the skin above the nape of her neck. She squeezes her eyes shut and feels a sudden whoosh of air. The tugging sensation is suddenly gone, replaced by the chill of the night air on the back of her head. She forces herself to open her eyes. At her feet lies a fist-sized chunk of snarled black hair with half a leaf-blight sticking out.

"Here." She hears Tristan at her side, covering them both with his shield like it's a parasol. His hand brushes past her cheek and reaches behind her head to pluck the other half of the nasty blight from her hair. The sight of it as he tosses it away causes Souffy to shudder in revulsion. "It's okay now," he says, and pulls her close.

No. This is way better than okay.

Her cheek presses against Tristan's chest armor, and his chin rests on her forehead. Somewhere, someone is screaming, "There's too many of them!" But Souffy isn't paying attention; she's focusing instead on inhaling Tristan's clove and jasmine smell.

"Souffy!" Kyle's voice cuts through the pleasant fog overtaking her brain. "Cast your fire spell!"

"You got this," Tristan whispers in her ear.

Souffy gulps; they're counting on her. She takes one of the wax blobs out of her pouch and rubs it between her palms until it softens enough for the embedded iron bits to prick her skin and the smell of rotten eggs to reach her nostrils. "You got this," Tristan had said. Souffy steps out from under the shield and throws her hands up in the air as she yells out the spell.

"Great Ball of Fire!" A warmth rises from her feet to her hands. It gathers in her fingers, as if she were indeed holding fire. She tosses the pent-up magic up into the air.

Souffy's spells never flow like this. They're always slippery, or clumsy, or give her instant headaches. This spell feels… good. She has the urge to cackle. Well, why not?

Laughing, she looks up. Six feet above their heads, a ball of red and orange fire is blooming, replete with yellow sparks for each incinerated leaf-blight. It even catches the remaining blights still clinging to the tree, and as they fry, their noxious stench is transmuted into a disturbingly pleasant smell of pork rinds.

"Way to go, Souffy!" she hears from one of the heroes as everyone runs to her.

"How many more of those can you cast?" asks Kyle.

In the fading light of the Fire Orb, several tree branches sway back and forth. It's the same rocking motion Kyle had described seeing before the walking-blight attacked.

Souffy takes a deep breath, performing a quick mana check-in on herself. "Two more times, maybe." She counts six moving limbs—each a potential walking-blight—before rounding up to 'too many.' "Not enough to take them all out."

"Good thing they're slow at first," says Tristan. "In our world, we have a saying: 'Any fight you can run away from is a good fight.'"

It makes logical (if not linguistic) sense. They only have to make it to the farmhouse, Souffy tells herself as they take off running down the road.

Souffy Ravenus

Class: Wizard
Level: 3

Race: Human
Background:
 Wizard School dropout
Alignment: Chaotic Neutral
Height: 5' 9"
Eyes: Amber
Hair: Black
Age: 20

Str: 11
Char: 14
Dex: 12 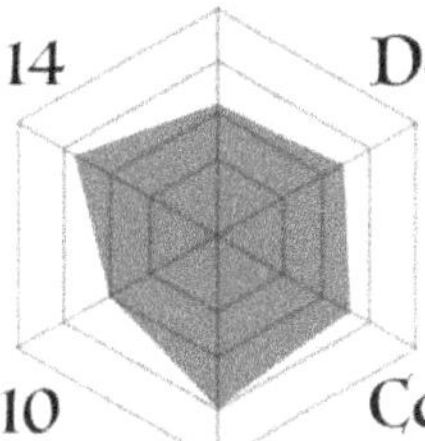
Wis: 10
Con: 13
Int: 15

Skills:
 Arcana
 Deception
 History (Mythreal)
 Lore (Otherworld)

Inventory:
 Spellbook
 Elfin outfit
 Copper earrings

CHAPTER 34

We're on the run from carnivorous leaves and possessed piles of kindling. First quest out, we barely defeated a brood of giant mutant chickens; now we've had our asses handed to us by the magical equivalent of Dutch elm disease. It would be funny if it wasn't so sad. I'm enlightened enough to have nothing but supportive admiration for Souffy's newly tapped fire-bending abilities. But if Mythreal can produce local heroes like her and Havelin, what exactly are we doing here?

Not for the first time, I'm questioning the Divine Wisdom's omniscience.

We're stuck in Mythreal until we do something worthy enough to earn our return ticket home. Or die here. Those, I remind myself, are our options. Just keep running, Kyle.

We've put at least a mile between us and the bloodthirsty tree, and I'm lagging near the back of the pack, along with Micah—unsurprisingly—and Cole—which I wouldn't have expected. He's breathing hard. Oscar was worried about his injuries. And mine. The branch that impaled me had penetrated my coat, vest and shirt, but didn't bury deep under my skin. The bleeding stopped quickly, and now when I touch the wound, I can't feel any pain. Or really, anything at all. I press down on the spot. I press down hard. Nothing. Probably not a good thing. I add it to my list of things to worry about if we're still alive in the morning.

"Guys!" Tristan shouts. I tense, mentally readying Magic Mortar because I'm not making that mistake again. "I see a farmhouse and a barn."

We catch up to him at the lip of a hill and look down into the valley beyond. I can just make out an arrangement of small buildings, behind which lies more forest. I would have preferred something surrounded by wide open fields. But it's clearly a human dwelling and our best chance to get some help.

"There aren't any lights," observes Cole.

"It's past midnight," says Micah. "People are asleep now."

"Yeah, you're probably right," Cole agrees.

Cole never agrees with Micah. As we proceed to the farm, I attempt to read his face, but it's hidden beneath his cowl. Souffy's Will-O-Wisp cantrip winked out back when it started raining leaf-blights, and she never turned it back on. Given the circumstances, the less attention we draw to ourselves the better.

I badly need a distraction, so I have a go at hypothesizing. If Havelin is correct and blights aren't naturally occurring, it means that someone is behind them. Turning the forest against humans would make for a good weapon for either the Trädskydd Druids or the Laska Bay Trading Company in their current conflict. So, who's most likely to have started it? The Druids with their nature magic mojo would possess the ability, but it would be at odds with their tree-hugging ethos. The residents of the logging town obviously aren't prioritizing the sanctity of nature, but they wouldn't be so shortsighted as to ignore the economic downsides of turning the forest into monster ground-zero. All those hours binge-streaming seasons of random shows during the pandemic means I'm prepared for an OMG, never-saw-that-coming reveal. Which in this case would be… Uncle Ferimus?

We turn off from the road and pass through a gate with a cute welcome sign decorated with a drawing of ducklings. Another ten steps and I can clearly discern the shapes of the buildings, but not much else.

"Dadadada daaa daaa da, dadadada daaa daaa daaaaaa," Souffy whisper-sings to herself as she strikes a match. The four glowing balls that form over her head illuminate a sea of green. Thick vines blanket everything: the one-story farmhouse under a peaked roof, the large square barn with open doors and an attached stable, a smaller building that might be a hen house or pigsty, and almost all the ground between them. Only a small patch of turf surrounding a covered well is vine-free, which in my book makes it the most suspicious spot.

I almost wish a monster would charge out of the darkness. Then I could react. Instead, I'm stuck in my brain, tired and injured and certain that whatever choice I make will be the wrong one. We all stand dumbstruck, each of us hoping somebody else delivers some insight or clever quip to make the situation somehow less horrible. No one speaks up. At last, Oscar gives voice to what we're all fearing.

"Do you think everyone got out before…" He gulps. "Before this happened?" He's staring at the cottage. I'm scanning the ground for any disturbing human-sized lumps under the vines.

The jarring sound of metal scraping on metal snaps me back into the now. Tristan, sword drawn, stalks over to the nearest vine. He has the good sense to poke it first and give it a good stomping. When it doesn't react, he swings his sword like a golf club and a divot of green flies up to land by Micah's feet, who jumps back. The cut mess of vine just lies there. Micah leans over and gingerly picks it up.

"Looks like"—everyone, or at least me, tenses—"kudzu. Careful, the stems are covered in tiny thorns."

"Any chance this might be something other than blight?" I ask Havelin.

He leans over to examine the sample in Micah's hand. "I've seen this plant in the forest, but never growing like this."

So, it's almost certainly related to the blight. But it hasn't tried to kill us yet. As a group, we start to move cautiously over the vine-covered ground. I've got Frostbite ready to deploy if I see any vines as much as rustle in the wind. Souffy's holding one of her Fire Orb wax starters. The others clutch their weapons.

We spend twenty minutes collectively holding our breaths and digging through the vines. We find zero human bodies—which is good—and seven chewed-up chicken carcasses. Havelin thinks they were done in by foxes. After the cockatrices, no one's too hung up on dead poultry. The random messiness of things left behind points to a hasty, unplanned exit by the inhabitants. Judging from the spoiled food we find, they probably fled sometime in the past week. I think the vigor potion is wearing off because no one objects when Oscar pulls a rug and some blankets out of the house and lays them out in the small clearing by the well.

"Okay, let's take a short break and then we head out," says Tristan. Somehow, he's still chipper.

"No, we need a longer rest," insists Oscar. "Micah, get over here, your face looks awful."

It must be from the leaf-blight bite. Micah's left cheek is chipmunk-puffy, but with none of the cuteness. He's shocked when I lend him my hand mirror.

"You don't feel this at all?" Oscar pokes him.

"No, it's gone numb. Use your healing spell."

"Sorry." Oscar ignores Micah's indignation. "I'm saving those spells for emergencies. I've got a salve I think is an antihistamine."

"Or you could cast the spell now and go to sleep." Micah keeps tilting the mirror like he's evaluating angles for a selfie. "Your mana levels will be back to full strength in the morning."

"We're not sleeping out here." Cole's using his growly voice, but fails in his attempt at intimidation when he suddenly sneezes. Oscar turns from Micah and pushes back Cole's hood, to reveal watering, bloodshot eyes.

"You did get walking-stick goop in your eyes," he accuses.

"No! It was those vapors that came out at the same time." It's hard to pull off the tough guy act when your nose is running. Cole tries anyway. "It just looks bad, I don't feel anything."

Havelin mumbles something. Souffy's eyes go wide.

"Say that again," she tells Havelin. "Louder."

"I said…" We need to lean in close to hear him. "Some of the worst monster toxins cloak their presence, so you don't feel the poison until"—he gulps—"it's too late."

"You're casting that healing spell, right now." Micah glares at Oscar.

I'm trying to discreetly feel the area around my injury, seeing how far out I have to extend to get any sensation. I'm halfway to my elbow when Tristan's voice cuts through the hissy fit Micah's throwing. "Kyle, have Oscar check out your shoulder."

I don't argue. Unlike Cole, I wasn't trying to hide anything (just waiting my turn). Getting the coat off proves to be challenging. Oscar helps undress me. I relax and let him—countless fast costume changes in too-small dressing rooms means we've seen each other naked, a lot. So when he pulls off my shirt and the others gasp, I know it must be bad. I crank my neck to try to see what all the fuss is about. There's no swelling or oozing pus, but in the light of Souffy's glowing orbs, I see thin green lines forking and snaking around under my skin. They originate from the puncture wound and radiate down my arm, up to my collar bone, and across my chest reaching straight towards my heart. Oh shit.

"On your back," commands Oscar as he pushes me down and lays his hands on me. "I'm pulling out all the stops." He closes his eyes and in a reverent voice says, "*Verhalty, your beauty is the first light of dawn, surpassing the most cherished dreams. Please look benevolently on your humble servant and grant this request. Be whole.*" I'm not sure if that's praise or sweet nothings, but the spell kicks in and I feel like I've been shot up with opioids (not that I ever have, but this is how I imagine it must feel like). And I'm not complaining; it's both buzzy and comforting. I close my eyes, take a deep breath, and bliss out.

"Will this take care of the poison too?" I hear Tristan asking. "Because last time you cast that spell, I still ended up turned to stone."

"That was a curse," says Oscar. "This spell should work on poisons, though." He's trying to project certainty. The obvious anxiety in his voice pulls me down from my healing spell high.

"We need to get out of here," says Tristan. "There has got to be a doctor along with Arek's group."

"Hold on," says Oscar. "We don't even know where they are, and god, or gods, only know what we might stumble onto in the dark." He removes his hands from my chest, and I'm back to feeling myself, half-naked in the cold. Not dying though, so that's something.

"I'm with Oscar." That's Micah.

"I'm with Tristan." And that's Cole.

Great, now we're taking sides. I open my eyes and slide myself into a sitting position and grab for my shirt.

"I think we should go." Of course, Souffy's all-in on Tristan's idea.

"I think"—Havelin's looking back and forth between us—"I think we should stay, for just a few hours, long enough to recover some of our mana."

Oscar sighs. "You're the deciding vote, Kyle."

Neither option is terribly appealing. I use my time getting dressed as a stalling tactic. The probability of us getting attacked if we spend the night here? High. If we head out however, it's guaranteed, but in that scenario, we'll be awake with weapons drawn. Oscar's suggestion is marginally statistically safer; Tristan's plan offers a tiny chance for a bigger payoff. Only what if staying here gives the monsters a chance to regroup? We're going to have to move out eventually. What would the Triad of Valor do?

"I think we should keep going," I finally say. And then everyone starts talking over each other. Which is why we don't immediately notice when Havelin starts screaming.

CHAPTER 35

"Help!" cries Havelin.

By the time we turn around, he's already several yards away from the rest of us. He's on his back, feet first, sliding away from us towards the forest.

"A vine's got him!" Souffy cries. It's twisted around his feet, extending creepers up his legs. Havelin struggles with a knife that a tendril knocks from his hand before it wraps itself around his torso, pinning his arms to his sides. Another creeper snakes up his neck and covers his mouth, cutting off his next scream.

It's all happening too fast. The kudzu has dragged Havelin to the edge of the woods and we've barely gotten to our feet. Except Tristan. He's already halfway across the yard with his sword in front of him, positioned to skewer anything that gets in his way. I see Havelin get yanked into the underbrush, and Tristan leap in after him. By the time we reach the tree line, I can only catch glimpses of Tristan by the flash of his sword. He's bounding over tree roots, dashing between boulders. We try to catch up, but he keeps pulling further ahead.

"Stop!" Micah's pointing at a bush ten feet in front of us. A moving bush. This particular variety of walking-blight must have come off a conifer because the clump behind its head is all spiky needles. I raise my hands to fire off Magic Mortar, but Souffy beats me to the punch.

"*Great Ball of Fire!*" she shrieks. An orb of fire slams into the creature and I jump back to keep from becoming collateral damage. I don't mind watching the creature's bark blacken and crack while the needles spark like firecrackers. It feels good. Burning blight gives off a cheery campfire smell.

"Blight reinforcements, behind us!" Cole warns.

I see two more walking-blights, or—more accurately—running-blights. The smaller one is scurrying towards us, fast. Micah's drawing his bow but before he can even take aim, the monster's already closed the remaining distance and rams him in the solar plexus, sending him sailing backward into a tree. I hear a sickening thump and see Micah collapse like a marionette with its strings cut.

The walking-blight doesn't slow its charge. It's almost on top of Micah's sprawled form when its legs seem to give out and it crumples to the ground. I hear a bell ringing. Oscar has his arms raised, and eyes are black and glossy. Impressive. Except that his back is turned to the other walking-blight. The clump of needles on that one's shoulders starts to tremble. I know what's coming next.

"Not this time," I cry out—I know, it's cheesy—and I raise my hands.

Only to have Cole dash past me. He's wielding a torch that I'm guessing is a limb torn from the walking-blight that Souffy incinerated. Before this blight can turn to respond, Cole's buried the burning end in its ball of needles. The fire doesn't catch right away, but the heat is enough to shock the creature and send it into convulsions.

"How do you like that?" Cole pushes his giant matchstick deeper into the monster, and the tuft of branches and needles starts to smoke as its core catches fire. The creature jerks away, rolling on the ground. But it's too late. As the sticks on its back spark like kindling, the life force leaves its body.

Oscar's Dead Ringer seems to have run its course. The remaining walking-blight is getting back on its feet and still looks ready for a fight. That was only a cantrip after all. Finally, it's my turn.

I clap my hands. "*Sagitta-inspira,*" I say while I snap my fingers. Three magic projectiles later and it's game over for the blights.

Oscar and Souffy rush to Micah's side. "He's going to be okay," Oscar calls out to us.

"I guess someone finally earned his healing spell," says Cole, then coughs. "Smoke," he chokes out by way of explanation. Yeah right.

"You sit down and rest," I say.

For once, Cole doesn't argue.

While Oscar administers a healing spell on Micah, Souffy and I kick some dirt over the burning walking-blight carcasses, putting out the remaining flames in the process.

"Boy Band Law Number Seven? The one about campfires or… campsites?" she asks.

"Yeah." It's good to have a fangirl, even here. "Plus, burning down a magical forest just isn't good heroing."

Post-fight analysis, we're alive and the blights are dead. We came out ahead. Except Souffy's down to a single Fire Orb, Oscar and I can only cast cantrips, and Cole hasn't moved since I told him to sit down. And I have no idea where Tris went. Okay, maybe we broke even.

Oscar pulls me aside and directs a worried nod toward Cole. "Kyle, we need to hole up someplace safe so I can rest up and cast a healing spell on him."

"We need to find Tris first," I answer. Oscar looks like he's going to protest so I call on a higher power. "*We're stronger together.* Twelfth Law." None of us can argue with Marjorie Banks and her Laws of Boy Bands.

"All right, but how do we find him?"

"We do have a ranger." I get up and walk over to talk to Micah. He's sprawled, leaning against a tree, a happy-dopey look plastered on his face.

"Hey Kyle." He gives me a very un-Micah-like toothy smile. The only times I've seen it are when he's on his second drink—by the third one he falls asleep; Micah's a lightweight when it comes to partying.

"Healing spell that good?" I ask, squatting down to talk.

"Yeah." He sighs contentedly. "I've got to get injured more often."

"So, feel up to using your tracking abilities to find Tristan?" I'm not letting him say no, but the only one of us who can outright tell Micah to do anything is Oscar.

"Okay." He gazes upwards and nods.

"Sooner would be better."

"Hush, I'm working on it. I'm listening to the pinecones and the needles sing to me about the state of the forest. In the starlight, they sound like a cello concerto."

I'm afraid Oscar may have overdone it on the healing spell this time, but then I remember Micah's stupid human trick. "You're talking about your synesthesia, right?"

"Oh of course, I'm not crazy. Move your hat, it's squeaking like a rusty door." I oblige. Back in our world, Micah mostly just heard colors and tastes. I'm wondering if he's tapping into the mystic side of his ranger abilities, or if he's just high. Could be both.

"It's in a minor chord, very sad." I think/hope Micah is talking about the pinecones and not my hat. "They sing that the Lady of the Forest is in danger. She's locked in a life-or-death struggle and if no one helps her, she's going to lose."

"Yeah, listen Micah—"

"I think Tristan is with her."

"How do you know?"

He runs his fingers along the bark of the tree he's leaning against. "Because this tree is singing an aria about how beautiful she is. Tristan's always drawn to beautiful women."

"More like they're drawn to him, same difference though." Trying to be as non-judgmental as I can, I say, "You don't usually talk to trees, Micah."

"I'm not talking to the tree, just listening. And it's fading, so if you want me to find the Lady of the Forest, we'd better get going. Now." With that, he stands up.

He's turning bossy; the spell must be wearing off.

"Micah thinks he can find Tristan," I call to the others, because what other options do we have?

The rest of us quickly down the remaining doses of vigor potion. Cole takes two but I don't think Oscar notices. And just like that we head out.

We'll take it carefully from now on, I promise myself. My feet want to go faster, but there's no point running off if we have no clue where to run to. It's been nearly an hour since we lost sight of Tristan. Whatever was going to happen to him, has already happened. He's either rescued Havelin and is now chilling out, flirting with this forest chick, or else he's… nope, not going there. To distract myself I harness my practiced mix of exasperation and annoyance at Tris. This is the guy who once went AWOL with a gangsta-rapper (not a poser, he was later convicted for manslaughter) and they spent the afternoon playing minigolf and bowling. And let's not forget that he managed to score a kiss out of being turned to stone.

I'm walking at the front of the group with Micah. He no longer seems to be suffering from any side effects of the healing spell. He's steady on his feet, and he's lost the stoned, beatific look. Every few moments his eyes go steely, like he's seeing things on a different wavelength than the rest of us. But he's also bopping his head and tapping out a rhythm with his fingers. Occasionally he starts humming.

"We're being stealthy," I remind him.

"I don't want to forget this melody. Or we could stop, so I can write it down?" He furrows his eyebrows at me.

"We need to find Tristan and Havelin as soon as possible."

"Well then, we do it my way. Besides, blights can't hear us, no ears."

It's not worth the argument.

"There." Micah points at the sky. It's lightened to an early dawn gray. I've never been so eager for sunrise. "She's there." Up in the air?

Oh, he's pointing at a tree. It rises far above the other trees, and even at this distance it's imbued with an otherworldly grace, like those African savannah trees with leaves that cluster at the ends of elegantly branching limbs. Only those trees always read as one-dimensional shadows with flat, paper-thin canopies. Not this tree. Its canopy is round and expansive, like it could hold a whole world, and there's a depth and complexity to the branching patterns that fills my mind with wonder. I'm usually not this woo-woo.

On a hunch, I perform a magic check. It's a trick Souffy taught me for sensing naturally occurring magic or BAMS—Big-Ass Mana Spells— phenomena that shift enough mana to warp their surrounding reality. Kind of like gravity wells, except more vibe-y. Souffy can feel this kind of thing through her hair follicles, along with a vague sense of intent; I only get a yes/no tingly sensation in my fingers. I barely reach my hand out before I'm certain that this tree is big-time magic.

"Hey Souffy," I call back. "Is that the sacred tree you once trespassed to see?"

She runs her fingers through her hair, brushing past the bald spot where Tristan sliced away the clinging leaf-blight. Any other guy who almost beheads a girl with a sword would get slapped, or at least treated to a what-the-hell glare, whereas Tristan got hugged. "I think it is. Do you think Tristan's there?"

Imperiled Lady of the Forest, sacred tree encircled by an infestation of blight? I'm going to call it a match.

"There's a good chance. Micah?"

"Damnit." He's frowning. "It's gone."

"Don't worry. You got us close enough. Thanks."

"I'm talking about the melody. It cut out halfway through the chorus, before the bridge."

Traversing the last bit of ground proves to be easy. The sky is definitely turning gray. I can finally see exactly where I'm putting down my feet. The vigor potion has mellowed in me to the point where the buzzing sensation is oddly pleasant. And every time I glance up at the canopy of the tree that is our destination, I get zapped with a sense of awe. I could almost be relieved, if I wasn't bracing for the next bad thing to happen.

In case we hadn't already figured out that we were heading for one of Drevo's sacred trees, the billboard-sized informational placard would have given it away. The tree's got a name, by the way, Saitanna. We pause to examine the sign—and to take a short rest; it's been a long night. Half of the sign is crammed with what looks like the verbatim text of the original treaty between the Trädskydd Druids and the residents of Fort Bydlo. The writing is so small I don't even bother scanning it. The other half, boldly carved in a highly legible font, is a clear warning to any non-Trädskydders to not even to think of going beyond this point without explicit permission in writing from High Priestess Cena, or face consequences, enumerated thereafter, that are far more dire than a fine and community service.

"This sign wasn't here the last time we came," Souffy insists.

At the bottom is a sketch of three figures. It's amateurish but sincere, in a Tumblr-fan-art kind of way. Out front in the center is the figure of a woman wielding a sword. To one side is a cleric (he's holding up the symbol for the blacksmithing god Orthorus) and to the other side, a wizard (he has a staff). I'm not sure if it's intentional or due to the artist's limited skill, but all three are drawn as having the same face.

Below the drawing, a final inscription reads, "Our Eternal Gratitude to the Triad of Valor for Bringing Us to this Land and Restoring its Magic." Then it lists their names.

Cole reads them aloud. "Cleric Isaac Bernstein, Fighter Hannah Bernstein, and Wizard Daniel Bernstein. So, they were Jewish, and... related?"

"Siblings," explains Souffy.

"Their cleric's sporting a mullet," Micah observes.

"Don't be judgy," says Oscar.

After the sign—we blithely disregard the warning—there's an actual trail to follow. The further along it we go, the faster I walk. We're approaching the moment of truth. Either my instincts are right and we're going to find Tristan, or we won't, in which case I have no idea what to do next. I take the lead with Souffy right behind me. If we find Tris, I'll let her throw herself into his arms, but only after I chew him out for running off like that.

It's been one of the longest nights of my life, but the sun is finally rising. Dawn light filters through leaves and lights up dew drops like

Swarovski crystals. The crisp air has lost that biting frosty edge; it's dangling hope for a sweater-free afternoon. It smells like California did when I left a January New York winter and stepped out of the airport: potting soil and fresh green shoots and the heady fragrance of blooming flowers—wait a sec.

"Souffy, is it just me, or does this place feel like spring?"

"I was just thinking that." She chews her lower lip, a sign that she's in pursuit of some useful truth she's misplaced in her mind. Souffy's brain is like a master bedroom walk-in closet, nearly unlimited storage capacity but good luck finding the thing you're looking for right away. "Arek said that the sacred trees are actually much older than three centuries. The Triad's wizard manipulated time when they planted the seeds, sped it up to help the trees establish themselves. That's advanced magic. When you operate it over a big differential, like having decades pass in a single afternoon, it can be tricky slowing it back down to normal time. And he had to do that for nine different trees. I'm guessing he had a hard time synching seasons and figured a half year mismatch wasn't a big deal."

I can't deny that it's nice hearing that Wizard Daniel might have cut some corners on his casting, it's evidence that he may have been less than an all-powerful archmage. And Micah's correct, their hairstyles were 1980's cringe.

After fifteen minutes of walking, we encounter a steep incline followed by a sharp left turn, and the path opens out onto a meadow with Saitanna taking center stage. But my eyes are drawn to the tableau of three figures halfway between us and the tree: a sword-wielding Tristan protecting a crouching Havelin from what I can only describe as the Swamp Thing.

CHAPTER 36

Kyle

By Swamp Thing, I mean the creature from that half-remembered comic book cover depicting a dripping green slime monster looming ominously over a huddle of much smaller humans. On second look, I see that this thing isn't wet or slimy, just very leafy. The kudzu draping off its back, roping around its limbs, isn't just attached to its body: it is its body.

Swamp thing looms two heads taller than Tristan, with big fat threatening fists and the shoulders of a suited-up linebacker. There's not much in the way of a neck, and its head is only identifiable by a pair of eyes, nose and mouth carved into it, like an unlit jack-o-lantern.

I watch Tristan slice his sword through swamp thing's shoulder, severing one arm but getting the sword stuck partway through the chest cavity. While he yanks at it, the monster lets out a forest-shaking guttural roar that sends my heart racing and my muscles into ready-to-flee mode. Its mouth stretches wide enough to swallow Tris's head, flowing locks and all, and it leans down like that's its intent. At the last moment, Tristan manages to slide his sword out and up, braced against the gaping maw, holding it back. Meanwhile, fresh green tendrils are already growing out from the thing's amputated shoulder, re-forming into a new arm.

"I can't use Flame Orb without hitting Tristan," wails Souffy.

"Use for your Flame Bolt cantrip, aim for the regenerating arm."

"*Ignatious!*" she shouts as she claps.

"*Frigus Digitorum!*" I add.

Her flame streaks out ahead of my ghost hand, charring the newly forming appendage and combusting upwards. Meanwhile I clench my non-corporeal digits into a fist and ram it right between swamp thing's eye holes, with enough force to knock the beast backwards, giving Tris space to arc his sword upwards before he brings it down and batter-swings it through the monster's elbow and waist. Killing blow. Micah and the others catch up just in time to see the monster's form collapse into a pile of inert kudzu.

"Hey! You guys made it!" Tristan calls out like he'd invited us to a party.

"Tristan, you're safe!" Souffy squeals with delight. She takes a moment to remember to add, "And Havelin too." To her credit, she runs directly to her old friend. Oscar follows.

Havelin looks awful. He's covered in angry red welts, and his hands are puffy and bulbous, like sausages. His face is so swollen, I can barely see his eyes. Oscar gets to work loosening his armor and asking first-responder-style questions like "Are you able to breathe freely?" Havelin manages pained nods and shakes of the head in response.

"Oh, poor Havelin," cries Souffy.

"I'm all out of healing spells, sorry." Oscar digs in his knapsack for the salve he mentioned earlier. I'm really hoping he's right about it being an antihistamine.

"The swelling just started recently," says Tristan. "He didn't look so bad when I cut him out of the… what are we calling the attacking kudzu?"

"Blights-krieg." Cole's response is so quick, I know he must have worked it out previously. "And that monster-form you just took down, Kudzilla, Kudzthulu?"

"I was going with swamp thing," I offer.

"Yeah, that works. Guessing we'll have plenty more monsters to name." Cole's usually rich bass is stripped, his bloodshot eyes are more red than white. I can't be the only one who's noticing this.

"What happened to you guys?" asks Tristan.

I catch him up on the walking-blight fight, highlighting Souffy's single-handed takedown of one with her Flame Orb and explaining how a side effect of Oscar's healing spell allowed Micah to find this spot. "And you?" I ask.

"Oh, you know." *No I don't, Tris, that's why I'm asking!* He must have detected my exasperation because he adds, "Havelin's been pretty out of it since I freed him, so we went looking for you and…" His voice trails off and he looks chagrined.

"You got lost and ended up here," I supply.

"Yep, I got totally lost. What is this place, anyway?"

He looks up at the tree like it's the first time he's seeing it—could be, Tristan's environmental-awareness stops at caring for his split ends. Still, he had to notice the expansive root system if only to avoid tripping over the aboveground bits that stretch and snake across the meadow—they range in diameter from python up to anaconda. Closer to the tree the roots form a dense mat that extends several feet in every direction, like a giant tree skirt. And not only is the tree itself wider than Tristan is tall, its white-barked trunk is wrapped with rainbow-dyed ropes tied with intricate knots. I mean, how could he *not* notice it? It's the only tree in the clearing.

I've got a great insult ready to deploy, but when I follow his eyes up to the canopy, it dies in my throat. Saitanna. I feel like I could spend a whole afternoon forest-bathing in the mottled light trickling through her leaves, tracing the fractal patterns formed by the branches, watching the delicate vine tresses looping down and speckled with delicate butter-yellow flowers gently swaying in the breeze.

"Like a dream I never wanna wake up from," Tristan whispers.

"That's one of our lyrics."

"Doesn't make it less true. This is a magic tree, right?"

"Yes. It's Saitanna, one of the nine sacred trees planted by the Triad of Valor," says Souffy. "The druids worship them as gods, or demi-gods."

"The Lady of the Forest?" I look at Micah. "The song you heard from the trees about a beautiful woman locked in a life-or-death struggle, could it have been about this tree?" Saitanna doesn't look corrupted. Perhaps the danger is still to come?

Micah shrugs. "You know I'm more about musical arrangements than lyrics." Great, we're back to diva Micah.

I don't want to bother Havelin; he looks like he's doing his best not to faint. Keeping any trace of snark out of my voice, I try again. "Micah, you're our ranger. Can you tap into any of your… special senses to tell us if the blight is trying to infect this tree?"

What if protecting Saitanna, protecting this forest is our real quest? This feels like a gig worthy of otherworld heroes—more than taking arbitrary sides in some local military skirmish. Especially since these trees owe their very existence to the actions of previous otherworld heroes. I've pretty much convinced myself. Now to get my bandmates on board with this new quest.

Micah gives me an eyeroll and loudly sighs (to make it clear that he's the one doing me a solid) before sauntering over to one of the tree's enormous roots. He removes his glove and bends over to lay his hand on it.

"It feels like a tree," he pronounces. "Also, it's not trying to kill me, so probably not controlled by an evil blight."

"For the love of… Verhalty!" Cole explodes. His hands form fists. "Could you be any more useless?"

"Oh please"—Micah actually tosses back his hair—"I think I was pretty useful when I led you guys to this place."

"When it suits your purposes, when it's convenient," Cole snarls. Micah takes a step back and then tries to pretend it was intentional. Cole continues, "I've been engaging with the people in this world, I've been sticking my neck out."

"Maybe too far," Oscar says under his breath.

Cole still hears it. He turns his anger on Oscar. "And what do you want me to do? Huh?"

Oscar doesn't back down. "Maybe not hang out with thieves and assassins? What did you do to earn that magic-storing Vantacoyte?" That Cole doesn't respond to this speaks volumes. "You're running from one reckless act to the next, Cole. You're out of control. What would your sponsor say?"

That was a low blow. I don't think Cole's eyes are watering exclusively from the blight toxin by this point.

"The Divine Wisdom made Cole a rogue for a reason," I say.

"And we're just supposed to put our faith in this Divine Wisdom?" says Oscar.

"In a world where gods are an indisputable fact, yes." I can't believe I need to explain this to our cleric, of all people. Oscar was the religious one back in our world. "Heroes are real here. We need to start acting like ones."

"Easy to say for the person who was handed a book full of superpowers." Micah jumps back into the fray. "Would you be so gung-ho if all you could do was shoot arrows and follow animal tracks?"

Wow. We haven't had a row like this since, since…

"Hey, Kyle didn't ask to be a wizard." Not helping, Tris.

…December 31st, 2022. Worst. New Year's Party. Ever.

"What if we find you some magic arrows, how about that?" Tristan tried to play peacemaker that time too.

It hadn't worked then either.

The details come pouring back in: canceled performance at a posh fundraiser concert—Covid finally caught up with us and we all tested positive—self-isolating in a soulless Airbnb, plenty of alcohol—and whatever else Cole had taken—plus way too much honesty about where our careers were going, or not going. We were (unofficially) broken up eight minutes before the ball dropped in New York City.

"Or maybe an invisibility cloak, a fashionable one?" Tristan turns to the one person not scowling. "What do you think, Souffy?"

"I think that something is coming," she says.

CHAPTER 37

Kyle

Souffy points to the grass at one end of the meadow. It's rippling ominously. I see darker lines of green streak through it. Either we're looking at an oncoming swarm of snakes, or—

"Blights-krieg!" Cole fails to shout; his voice is so shot.

Tendrils of kudzu are cutting rivulets through the grass. Behind them, more creepers are amassing, piling up, spilling over. It's no longer individual vines: they've congealed into a wave cresting towards us. Out of the wake, rise two, no, three swamp things and I see another lurking just within the tree line. Blights are always slowest when they're first forming. If we want to take them out, we need to move first.

"I got this." Souffy steps in front of us and flings out her hands. *"Great Ball of Fire!"* she shouts loud enough to wake the dead—points for presentation. Out flies that glorious orange ball, expanding to encompass the heads and shoulders of the two emerging swamp things. But something's not right. There's no heat to it this time. The orange orb fades even as it grows, until all that's left are bits of ash and a faint whiff of natural gas. Unscathed, the swamp things use their freshly grown arms to push themselves further out of the approaching wave of kudzu.

"Niau's watergate! I'm out of mana." I file Souffy's goddess of war curse away for later, although as a guy, it would probably be crude and misogynistic for me to use.

"It's okay, Souffy." Tristan gives her an encouraging smile. "You just look after Havelin."

Micah's notching his arrow when Cole says, "Wait." He takes the arrow from Micah, wraps the tip in a swatch of fabric, and pulls out a BIC lighter. Something in the fabric sparks upon catching the flame. He hands it back to Micah. "No need to say thanks." It's not a friendly jibe.

"Then I won't. Swamp thing on the right is mine."

"I thought you quit," says Oscar, eying the lighter.

Cole ignores him, wrapping one of his bolts with the same fabric before lighting it.

Micah's arrow hits its target right between the eyes; Cole's bolt goes through the knee of the one on the left. Micah's smirk falters when Cole's swamp thing stumbles and falls forward, even as Micah's keeps lumbering towards us—all the more unnerving now that its head is on fire. Meanwhile, the third swamp thing, now fully formed, is picking up steam, thundering towards us. I see Tristan run to engage it, sword at the ready.

Leaving that one to him, I prep Magic Mortar. This time I dole out one missile per monster: the two on fire and the one hiding out in the shadows. Cole's struggling swamp thing goes all the way down and doesn't get up. The one with the flaming head seems to shake it off. The one in the woods staggers and grabs a tree to stay upright. Interesting.

The blight battling Tristan takes a swing. I see Tristan try, and fail, to dodge it. Swamp thing's uppercut sends him flying backwards almost to the trunk of Saitanna. Tristan's sword thuds dully as it bounces off the ground, at the same time as his head snaps against a knot of tree roots.

I'm turning to run to him when my leg is yanked out from under me. My foot's been swallowed by kudzu. I follow the vines to their source, the elbow of the swamp thing with the flaming—by now, smoldering—head. It's transformed its arms into tentacles, one for me, one for Souffy. It's wrapping around her wrists, preventing her from casting her Flame Bolt cantrip.

Oscar steps forward and I'm hoping he can get Dead Ringer started before I'm dragged to the monster. Only he keeps his hands at his side, his head held high.

"*Show time*," he says.

I hear a woosh and the embers of my captor's head re-ignite with a vengeance. The flames start wicking down its shoulders and chest and the bonds around my leg go slack.

"What was that?" I ask.

"Thaumaturgy cantrip," says Oscar. "It's mostly for showing off. But these plants are so flammable, that if I can make a fire flare, the rest of the monster will burn up. I got the idea from Cole."

I turn back to where Tristan went down. Cole's already by his side, helping him to stand. Tristan has a glassy look to his eyes, like when he's been mobbed by fangirls. My view is blocked by the swamp thing; it's got its arms raised like Frankenstein's monster as it advances towards them. And then it stops. Or rather, it's still shuffling its feet back and forth, zombie-style, but it's no longer moving forward.

Souffy sees it too. "Is it afraid to get any closer to Saitanna?" It's stuck just outside of the ring of thick tree roots.

"I think you're right. It can't step on the tree itself." says Oscar. "Micah, help Souffy move Havelin closer to Saitanna. I'll fight with…" he looks down at his mace.

"Oscar, wait." Now I have an idea. I summon Phantom Hand, grab some of the still burning kudzu vines and throw them over towards the swamp thing. Oscar sees what I'm up to and uses Thaumaturgy to boost the flames. It works—it works beautifully. The vines crackle and twist, and fire licks down the monster's extremities.

"Think we can do some more of that?" asks Oscar, pointing at the advancing kudzu.

It's taken over half the meadow, adding inches like a rising tide. I see at least five growing mounds portending more swamp things on their way, plus the original one, still watching from the edge of the forest. The ringleader? It's less formed than the others, with a blanket of vines falling to the ground instead of forming legs like the others. Something to puzzle over after our current crisis. Right now, we do what we can with our cantrips.

I send my Phantom Hand to scoop up flaming vines and re-distribute them. Oscar encourages them to burn better. Micah wasn't wrong, magic does make things easier. I'm making the mistake of entertaining some optimism when I hear Souffy's, or maybe Micah's, high-pitched scream.

It takes a moment for my brain to parse what I'm seeing. They've leaned Havelin up against Saitanna's massive trunk, and at first, I think they're using the decorative ropes to help support him. But then why would they have wrapped the fibers around his neck? It's not just Havelin. Micah's bow is caught in a snarl of those knotted ropes and Souffy has one coiled around her wrist.

"*Ignatious, ignatious, ignatious!*" she repeats while trying to cast a burst of flame at the rope. It sputters ineffectively. "Just burn already!"

Could this be some protective spell left behind by the druids?

"Saitanna, we're on your side!" I shout into the canopy. Not sure what response I'm expecting from the sacred tree. Despite the imminent danger, my breath still hitches at the sight of all those splitting, twisting branches, bringing home my smallness and insignificance and even if we do make it out of here and I live until I'm a hundred, I still won't outlive this tree. It will still be adding tree rings long after my dead body is reduced to dust.

Hold on: I'm not the emo member of our group.

I don't need magically tingling fingers to know that someone's trying to mess with my head.

Someone… or something. We only assumed that the sacred tree was healthy because of Micah's bare minimum ranger check.

Saitanna must have been blight-corrupted after all. Or—an even worse scenario starts unfurling in my brain, of the oh-shit variety. Havelin said that only a powerfully evil entity, like a demon, could be the cause of the blight. A demon is just a fallen angel, right? Okay, maybe that's technically a devil. But magic trees would be a pagan—*Focus, Kyle.* I'm not sure if it's evil tree mind control or just panic causing my thoughts to keep spinning out like this. I reach up and yank down the rim of my hat, hoping to block out the tree's… influence. Instantly, my thoughts clear. Evil tree— that's the critical idea.

"Saitanna *IS* the corruption!" I shout as loud as I can. "She's the source of the blight!"

"Lyr's flame, you're right!" says Souffy. My bandmates drop several variations of F-bombs. Except for Tristan who starts blathering about flowers. I can't spare the brain-runtime to parse what he's saying because at that moment the ground collapses beneath me, swallowing me up to my waist. A tree root whips out and slams down on my hands hard, then wraps around my shoulders in what could be considered an embrace if it only wasn't pressing down so hard on my collarbone.

Immobilized, I watch helplessly as the ropes tangle around Micah's feet, and Souffy gets dragged closer and closer to the tree where the ropes already bulge over a Havelin-shaped figure. In the other direction, Oscar is trying to lift his legs—he's probably rooted like me. Cole has his knife out, attempting to cut the roots, but is struck by a coughing fit and doubles over. Tristan's gazing blissfully upwards, oblivious to how bad things are going. Saitanna must have gotten into his head.

This is really bad—no, it's worse than bad. We're not going to be able to win this one. We're going to die.

CHAPTER 38

Kyle

Weirdly, the inevitability of our fast-approaching demise bestows on me a moment of relief. Perhaps because there's no more pressure to find that one vanishing path that could lead us—or even just me—back to safety. It doesn't exist.

It doesn't exist.

Oh… this is really happening. We're going to die.

My stomach crashes like I'm on the first drop of a rollercoaster, and the rest of me caves into the now empty space. I'm a mess of hopelessness and grief for every good thing we're losing or that we'll never get to experience. I start listing them out (because that's apparently my coping strategy), and that in turn leads me to replay every bad decision that brought us to this place, this ending:

Tris wandering right into blight ground zero. Micah finally displaying some ranger aptitude only to lead the rest of us here. Oscar's heart-in-the-right-place insistence to take a short rest at a farmhouse overrun with blight kudzu. Cole's impulsive activation of the hearthstone. My wanting to show off my cleverness at finding the secret room, and thus setting this doomed expedition in motion. Or how about all the times I assured my bandmates that we could handle this hero gig because the Divine Wisdom had brought us here for a good reason?

The Divine Wisdom! That's what got us into this mess. We wouldn't be here if It hadn't zapped us to Mythreal, hadn't chosen us from a probably infinite number of better-qualified heroes in the multiverse. Hell, It could have brought back the Triad of Valor for a reunion quest, everyone would have loved that. But for whatever twisted omniscient reason, It picked a boy band—a has-been boy band at that—to fumble through the scenery and screw everything up. And in the process, sacrifice Souffy and Havelin and the townsfolk of Rozny Las and who knows how many more innocent people. *I hope we were at least entertaining to You.*

Something yellow floats lazily down in front of me and I glare at it. I recognize it as one of the tree's flowers. *Wasn't Tristan saying something about them?* Another flower lands by the first. They're fragrant like overly perfumed soap, and burn my nasal passages. My hat's brim prevents me from looking straight up, but from what I can see, there's now a gentle rain of these flowers blanketing the ground.

I see them in Souffy's hair. She's pressed tight to the tree, the rope whipping around her and Micah like a tetherball. They're polka-dotting Cole's black cloak while Oscar struggles to hold him up. Pinned by the root system, I can only watch helplessly.

"Kyle," Oscar calls out to me, "the flowers, they're—" He staggers backwards and Cole's body falls on top of him. Neither gets up.

He was trying to say the flowers are drugging us. That makes sense. I feel—rather fail to feel—my body going numb. I can still sense the pressure of the roots around my legs and on my shoulders, but the pain is gone. The world is turning gray, save for the flowers. They're doubling in their intensity; their neon glow burning into my retinas.

"Kyle!" Miraculously, Tristan is still standing. He attempts to walk towards me and manages three steps before he trips, or maybe faints.

"Tris!" I shout back, or think I do. My voice seems very far away. Far louder are the sounds of rustling and crunching behind me.

I manage to twist my body to see beyond Saitanna. Filling the meadow are all the different kinds of blights we've seen, plus some others, like hopping stumps and moss-covered logs that move like alligators. They're keeping a respectable distance from us, save for one. A single swamp thing—the one I saw at the forest's edge—is now venturing nearer, making its way over the tree roots. I hear the fall of footsteps beneath its gown of kudzu. It walks past me, to where Tristan has collapsed, and bends over him. The kudzu head falls back like the hood of a cloak. There's someone inside, but I can't make out any more. My vision is clouding over, things are going dark.

And then I hear, clear as a bell, a female voice shout out:

"Moyllagh, Kalimos. Screeu mie nyn enim!"

It's followed by a smothered silence that I feel as much as I hear. And then the air fills with the roar of wind. It jostles my trapped body and tears off my hat. The flowers blow away in a cloud of yellow, and loose sticks clatter against each other and the tree. The swamp thing by Tristan has vanished, replaced by a dozen or more blights jumping and thrashing about.

"Fire at will!" cries a male voice, and on that command, streaks of burning arrows fly overhead. Some hit blight creatures, but most strike Saitanna. Battle screams and the thunder of boots reverberate as armored humans swarm the area. There are too many to track, although with the flowers gone, my head is beginning to clear.

What's important is that they're attacking Saitanna, hurling fire at her, both the magical and good-old-fashioned kerosene-fueled kinds. Her trunk is proving resistant, but some of her branches are catching. Flames dance on the wood. There's a rumbling in the forest like every blight in the region is being summoned here. Maybe they are.

A walking—running—blight clatters towards me, not at me, I think I'm just in its path. Lack of intent doesn't mean that I'm not going to get crushed under its fast-approaching hooves. But the creature slows at the last minute because a plate mail-clad figure with a Laska Trading Company logo on their cloak charges it with a flaming sword. The sword rips through the monster, sending its now-burning body straight at my head. A bark-covered hand stops it just before it collides with me and volleys it away. The hand belongs to a woman, I think it's a woman, a brown, woody woman, who's leaning beside me. She's not made of tree bark, I realize, it's more like armor. There are human eyes looking through the eye holes cut in the bark. I'm guessing she's a druid. But since she just saved my life, I'm assuming we're on the same side now. She lays her hand on the roots encasing me.

"*Wither*," she intones. The roots become squishy and bend underneath me.

I'm about to thank her when she lets out an anguished cry, tears welling up in her eyes. I blink to clear my own watering eyes. It's smoke, rich and heady, like a clove cigarette. Saitanna is burning. The whole canopy is ablaze, a second sun in the sky.

I think of how impressive the sacred tree was to me in this short time and imagine what it would mean to someone who'd known it their entire life. And now they're killing it. Like putting down your dog, but worse. The druid pulls me out of the dirt and I try to stand, or at least kneel, but my limbs have turned to gelatin. A night of battling for my life has caught up with me—maybe it's the post-vigor potion crash that Souffy had warned us about. Either way, I'm splayed out on the ground, barely able to keep my eyes open.

I watch the soldier with the flaming sword run to the tree and begin slashing at the ropes binding the others.

"Lyr's flame," I hear him say in an oddly familiar voice, "it's Souffy, and Havelin, and… an incredibly attractive stranger!"

"Get them to safety." The druid next to me speaks with one of those sexy, vaguely European accents. She's holding me by my arms and dragging me backwards, away from the tree. So, I'm looking up when the giant fireball, easily twice the size of anything Souffy's produced thus far, hits Saitanna. It splatters on the trunk, wrapping the tree in a fiery embrace of destruction. The druid who's hauling me away has streaks of tears running down her bark armor cowl.

"It had to be done," I try to say, but my lips aren't working. I hope I'm managing a sympathetic smile as I fall unconscious.

CHAPTER 39

Souffy

Someone cuts away the ropes and drags Souffy across the roots, but gently, cradling her head and supporting her shoulders. They rub salve on the burns in spots where the fibers had twisted into her flesh. Souffy thinks she hears her rescuers offering assurances of her safety, that her friends will likewise be alright and that they're administering something to counter the toxins from the flowers, but the voices are coming from so far away. She feels as if she's sinking into a deep, dark hole.

The emptiness is inside her, metaphorically (or maybe physically). There's a lively debate ongoing within the magic community concerning how mana is accessed and stored, but real-world experience proves that you can only hold on to so much of it at once. And Souffy has completely bottomed hers out.

Such utter depletion of mana hasn't happened to Souffy since her first year in magic school when students were required to cast cantrip after cantrip to "build up those magic muscles." That was how Professor Potts had phrased it. Souffy had lasted longer than anyone else in her class, but it wasn't much of an accomplishment considering that the stupid lily illusion she was attempting to cast kept coming out looking like a mushroom. Potts instructed her to imagine the lily's delicate petals and floral fragrance while the class snickered behind her back. And just when Souffy had resigned herself to casting fungus, the illusion cantrip inexplicably warped itself into a baby gelatinous cube. It was a relief when she had finally passed out.

This time she's burned through her mana on spells that worked as intended, even better: spells that felt good to cast. It's left her body aching all over, and even moving her fingers takes more energy than she can summon. But on the inside, Souffy somehow feels bigger. It's like the empty space inside her has grown, ready to be filled with more mana, more spells, more potential. As the world around her turns hazy, her final lucid thoughts are that this is a very pleasant way to lose consciousness.

She's reawakened by a faint breeze carrying an earthy, wormy smell, infused with the now-familiar mix of jasmine and spice cake that brings a blissful smile to her face. She opens her eyes and (as she'd hoped) Tristan is indeed sitting by her side.

Her first thought is relief—*he's okay*. The next is admonishment—*of course he is, why wouldn't he be?* He's the otherworld hero who single-handedly rescued Havelin and the only one of them who didn't panic or freeze up at any point during that long night of running and fighting.

"Hey, Souffy, you're awake." She wonders if he knows how long she's been gazing at him. "How are you feeling?"

"Good, well-rested." She allows him to help her into a sitting position.

There's a damp chill to the air, and a gray quality to the light that makes her think the day is either just past dawn or just before dusk. She closes her eyes to sense the location of the sun. It's dawn. Souffy's attunement to elemental forces has always been a curious magical quirk, but now that she seems destined to be an evocation wizard, it makes perfect sense.

"You were asleep for over twenty-four hours, Souffy. The rest of us were out of it for most of yesterday while we were being healed," says Tristan.

"I was? How are the others?"

"Doing well. Havelin was in pretty bad shape, but there was a cleric who gave him magical CPR. They say he should be good as new after a couple of days of bed rest. Lucky break for us, getting rescued like that when we did!"

Yes, rescued. And their rescuers must have brought them here, to what appears to Souffy to be the inside of a tent. The rough canvas fabric that makes up the walls and roof is draped over a framework of bark-covered logs, and she suspects there's nothing but dirt under the rush flooring. Other than the rustic materials, the interior of the tent makes for a properly furnished bedroom outfitted with a large bed and a carved wardrobe. As Souffy is taking all this in, the tent flap is pushed back, and a woman enters.

"Minstay's Blessing, you are awake!" The woman is wearing a plain, practical green dress that contrasts with her elaborate tattoos, the many amulets around her neck, and the diminutive antlers embedded in her decorative headpiece. A strong sense of magic hits Souffy. It's wild magick, like that of a warlock or a…

"You're a druid." Souffy's words come out bluntly, but the woman just nods. She has a pixie smile, rosy cheeks, and dimples.

"It's okay," Tristan says. "The druids are good guys. This is Cena, she's their leader."

Souffy recalls that name from the war council meeting back in Bydlo, and had imagined its owner to be someone much older and more crone-like. High-level druids are extremely long-lived, but Cena looks to be only a few years older than her. Even as Souffy's processing this, a tall man wearing banged-up militia armor steps into the tent behind Cena. Souffy can't conceal her shock as she recognizes him.

"Arek? You're here too? But your messenger bird said that you were barricaded in Rozny Las defending it against the… Trädskydders."

Rather than respond, Arek gives Cena a meaningful look to which the latter responds with a pinched smile. It's like they're Magic Missiving each other, only Souffy isn't sensing any magic.

"A lot of things have changed since I sent that messenger bird." As Arek speaks, Souffy sees Cena's smile dimples re-emerge.

"They rescued us together," Tristan explains. "The Trädskydders and the people of Rozny Las have teamed up to clear the forest of the blight. Turns out the war thing was just a big misunderstanding."

"No, it was our fault," says Arek. A pained expression crosses his face. "We were too quick to blame the Trädskydd Druids for something that was obviously not their doing. It should have aroused our suspicions that a society dedicated to protecting the forest would stoop so low as to pervert nature to attack a logging camp. Instead, we acted on our worst instincts and sent soldiers to attack your homes." This last bit is directed at Cena.

"We were also blinded by our prejudices," Cena responds in a more gentle and forgiving tone than Souffy would have expected under the circumstances. "For so long my people have vilified the Laska Bay Trading Company and all those associated with it. We were willing to stand aside and do nothing so long as the blight directed its attacks against your people. That was a mistake; we should have heeded Wizard Ferimus's warnings."

This exchange makes no sense to Souffy, and the bashful look that Arek is giving Cena is equally confusing. Souffy grasps at the one detail of the story that she can parse.

"Wait, Ferimus? My uncle was here?"

"He came to our sacred grotto eleven days ago." Cena reluctantly tears her eyes away from Arek to explain. "Ferimus told us he'd had a vision that a sacred tree would destroy the Drevo Woods, but we couldn't bring ourselves to believe such a thing was possible. It was the Triad of Valor's final request before they departed that we druids protect the sacred trees above all else. If only we'd acted sooner; so much death and destruction might have been averted." She sighs deeply.

Arek places a supportive hand on her hunched shoulder. "There is much to regret. But what's important is that you risked your life to come to me. You snuck through a camp filled with angry soldiers to tell me the truth to my face." He moves his hand to her cheek.

"Well, my original plan was to assassinate you." She giggles. "But then our eyes met, and everything changed."

"I'm so glad you decided to have a go at me with a knife instead of a blow dart." There's a twinkle to Arek's eyes that Souffy has only ever seen before when he talks about trees.

Cena puts a finger on Arek's lips. "Our eyes met, and I knew in my heart of hearts that you were not my enemy."

They stare silently at each other. The moment stretches and becomes uncomfortable, at least for Souffy; Arek and Cena are oblivious to everything except each other. Tristan gently nudges Souffy's shoulder and motions in the direction of the door flap. Souffy scrambles out of the bed and follows him out. A woman in armor is striding towards them, towards the tent, a stack of important-looking papers in her hands. She gives them a questioning look. Tristan emphatically shakes his head. The soldier makes a sharp u-turn and walks away.

Souffy replays the conversation between Cena and Arek in her head. From the stories that Arek has told Souffy over the years, the Trädskydd Druids had objected strongly to the Laska Trading Company building Rozny Las, and the townsfolk didn't think much of the druids (Arek had used the word dirt-worshiper and worse). How could such bitter foes turn into allies in a few days? Then Souffy considers what she had seen in the tent: the looks, the blushes, the touches. And suddenly it makes sense.

"The Rozny Las soldiers and the Trädskydd Druids joined forces to defeat the blight tree because their leaders fell in love?"

"At first sight," Tristan confirms. His lips curl into an easy grin. "Kyle says it's tropey, but I think it's sweet."

Souffy would rather have used the word 'inconceivable.' But Arek had been looking at Cena like she was the first snowfall of the year. And Cena had returned that look with one suffused with the same delighted happiness. It's more than infatuation or lust, Souffy realizes. It's all those emotions that even the best mage couldn't artificially instill with a love potion: exuberance and awe, trust and understanding, gratitude and joy. Souffy sternly reminds herself that she's completely over Arek. Still, she can't help but be a tad envious of what he and Cena have.

"I suppose Arek's found the one woman out there who's as much into trees as he is." She tries not to sound catty about it.

"Yeah, I know what you mean," Tristan replies. "When they're not being all lovey-dovey, they're working on this plan to make the Laska lumber operation sustainable."

Souffy imagines Arek and Cena snuggled up together, engrossed in talk about forestry practices—pure torture as far as Souffy is concerned. But she has to admit that staying up late into the night, deep in conversation on a topic she's passionate about with someone who shares her enthusiasm, would be (as Tristan said) sweet.

She looks at Tristan, trying to imagine the two of them in such a relationship. What would Souffy and Tristan talk about late into the night? What are their shared interests?

You both like how he looks. That's what Kyle would say—in exactly that voice.

"Can we see Havelin and the others?" she asks. She's worried about her friend. She also doesn't want to dwell any longer on Cena and Arek's epic love story.

"Sure. I think it's this way. This place is a maze."

Souffy can see that. They've emerged into a forest, dense with other tents. But it's a strange forest, full of thin, anemic trees that don't seem to reach up to the sky as much as droop to the ground. The canopy above consists of massive horizontal branches that crisscross to form almost a ceiling over the camp. On closer inspection, she notices that what she initially thought of as tree trunks aren't growing up; they're growing down. As Tristan leads Souffy to the edge of the camp, it finally dawns on her that she's not in a forest after all.

"They built this whole village under one of the sacred trees," she marvels. Not only that, it's the tree's live branches that support all the tents.

"Our label shot us in a music video under a tree like this one, but smaller," says Tristan. "It was in Hawaii—that's in our world."

The Neverboylanders were shot? But before Souffy can question Tristan about it, he says:

"Hey Souffy, we are going back to our world eventually, right?" They're walking single file between two tents with Tristan leading the way— she can't see his expression, but he sounds more pensive than usual. "Like, the deal is that we complete a quest, and the Divine Wisdom sends us back?"

"Yes…" This isn't something Souffy likes to think about. "Usually. You get a choice. Most heroes, like the Triad, choose to go home together. But not always. Paladin Wu stayed behind in Mythreal after the other Heroes of the Realm departed."

"How come he stayed?" Tristan turns to Souffy, the better for her to appreciate the small vertical wrinkle that's formed between his scrunched-up eyebrows (it's so adorable). Souffy can understand his confusion. Kyle has described so many wonderful things from his world: smartphones, 3D printers, awards shows, streaming services, influencers, fusion food. There are bad things too, Kyle said, like the pandemic and climate change. And they don't have flying cars, but it still sounds like a fascinating place to live.

"Paladin Wu has said that Mythreal is a better fit for him. He's traveled all over the realm completing quests, both solo and alongside local heroes," says Souffy. Tristan nods slowly and has such a serious look on his face that she adds, "Grandmama likes to tease him and says that there was a girl involved, but I'm not sure."

Souffy would love to see Martin Wu's reaction to Tristan. Even better, what will Zorianna say when Souffy shows up with five otherworld heroes of her very own? She still hasn't asked the Neverboylanders if she can join them, but she's certainly proved her usefulness in battle. Surely they'd say yes if she asked. All she has to do is ask. Now might be a good time.

"Tris—"

"Hey, I think that's our tent," Tristan cuts her off.

It's a large tent with clean canvas sides; it looks as if it has only recently been assembled. On entering the tent, Souffy sees six cots arranged three to a side. She recognizes Havelin's compact form lying on one of them and immediately runs over to him. He's asleep but already looks so much better than before. His skin is no longer puffy or flushed, and with the exception of some scabs on his face and arms, he appears like his normal self.

"He's under some heavy healing spells," says Oscar. In her rush to Havelin's bedside, Souffy hadn't noticed him sitting up one bed over. "But they say he'll be as good as new by the time the Seolia arrives to take us back to Bydlo."

The other heroes gather to stand in a semicircle surrounding Souffy and Havelin. She takes a moment to appreciate that they've all survived the blight onslaught. Their clothing is torn and stained, even Oscar's, and Micah has a small cut under his eye, however, to Souffy's eyes, the Neverboylanders are even more alluring than when they arrived through the portal. Perhaps it was the night spent fighting for their lives, but there's a warrior's gravitas, almost an aura, to their expressions.

"When the Seolia arrives, that's going to be an awkward homecoming," says Cole. "Soldiers coming out thinking it's D-Day, and Arek will be like, naw, we already took down the big bad and we're all friends now. Hey, want to meet my new girlfriend?"

"At least they'll show up ready for a fight, instead of needing to be rescued," says Micah. "I could've died, that was so embarrassing."

"I'd rather be rescued than dead." Oscar tries to keep his tone light, but Souffy detects an undercurrent of irritation. Maybe he's just tired.

In contrast, Tristan is his usual cheerful self. "Guys, guys, this is just a temporary setback. Like Marjorie says, you're not going to sell out every concert. Right, Kyle?"

"I'd have gone with 'c'est la vie,' but Tristan is right." The agreeableness of Kyle's words doesn't mask what Souffy senses is resignation. His shoulders slump and there's something else off about him. "We learn from our mistakes, we come back stronger. And we're going to receive some real training once we make it to the capital." His head jerks—*that's it, he's missing his hat.* "No offense, Souffy."

"About that." All their eyes turn to Souffy. It's now or never. "I was thinking… hoping… I mean"—*big breath*—"I want to join your band!"

She doesn't know exactly what she's expecting. In her happiest imagined scenario, the Neverboylanders not only agree that this is a splendid idea but follow up by saying they'd been secretly hoping all along that she would be with them for all their adventures in Mythreal. More realistically, she supposed that perhaps they'd raise some concerns about her family or

Lenora's wishes, but nothing that couldn't—shouldn't—be overcome. What she isn't anticipating is their blank, uncomprehending stares.

"You… want to join the band?" Micah speaks first, slowly, "Like… a roadie?"

"Or… as our manager?" adds Cole, looking utterly confused.

"No." Souffy tries to gather her thoughts. Kyle mentioned that back in their world, they had a woman who managed all the mundane aspects of their lives so they could focus on performing. The day before yesterday, Souffy would have been quite happy to play that role. But after their battle with the blight, something new in her has awoken. Lobbing balls of fire really is the best. "No, I want to adventure alongside you. To be one of the… Neverboylanders." Or whatever name they'd end up being called by future generations. *Just please,* Souffy sends a request to the Divine Wisdom, *don't let it be "the Heroes of Bydlo."*

"Souffy." Oscar's voice is pitched so kindly that Souffy's heart sinks. It's going to be a "no." "We appreciate all the help you've given us. I mean, really, time and time again. And, of course, we want you to come to the capital with us, but the thing is…"

"We're a *boy* band," says Micah, taking over from Oscar. "Emphasis on '*boy.*'"

"It's an unspoken boy band law, the Yoko Ono edict," says Cole. "No girls in the band."

"Oh. Okay, I see." Even though she really doesn't. She must have committed some terrible cultural faux pas, but she doesn't want to compound her mistake by demanding an explanation.

"Guys!" says Kyle sharply, breaking the increasingly awkward silence. "We're not a boy band over here, we're heroes. Souffy doesn't want to sing with us, she wants to fight alongside us! And given her Fire Orb spell, we'd be idiots not to take her."

Souffy looks at Kyle anew and feels a warm glow ignite deep inside her. It isn't just that Kyle is supportive, he believes she'd be good for the team. It drives away the doubt and brings a smile to her face. And in response, is that a blush she sees spreading across Kyle's cheeks?

"Kyle's right," says Tristan. He steps towards Souffy, reasserting himself as the center of her attention. And then he takes her hand.

He. Takes. Her. Hand.

"Souffy, come with us." Around her, there are now murmurs of assent. She's in! She's going to join them. They like her. Tristan likes her, and maybe… more.

Her mouth moves, and a sound comes out.

"Is that a yes?" She hears Cole say. And some semblance of conscious thought returns.

"Yes," Souffy manages to reply, and yanks her eyes away from Tristan.

Oscar is now wearing a big welcoming smile on his face. Cole's expression is stern, but approving. Micah is grinning wickedly and raises a conspiratorial eyebrow at her. And Kyle… Kyle isn't in the tent anymore.

CHAPTER 40

Okay, it's a chicken move—not even cockatrice level—slipping away from the group to sulk. But having to watch Souffy in the throes of Tristan Ives-inspired fangirl ecstasy while he's giving her his best bedroom eyes—yeah, that didn't escape my attention—that's the straw breaking my back. I mean, we were outsmarted by something with cellulose for brain cells, rescued by the people we were intending to save and/or defeat in battle, and, to top it all off, I lost my hat. I just need some time to properly feel sorry for myself.

My brooding doesn't need to be lengthy, just a circuit around the camp to regain my equilibrium. Then I'll go back and be genuinely happy that Souffy's coming along with us on the next, hopefully more successful, chapter of our hero's journey.

I walk past soldiers and druids and Laska Company folks, and no one spares me more than a passing glance. It's like I'm back on campus. Blessed anonymity.

I miss my hat.

A wizard's hat turns heads (if only as a defense mechanism). I asked Arek and Cena after it, but no one had seen it as they were retreating. It's not a big deal, I'll just buy a replacement when we get to the capital. Except, that was the hat Souffy had given me, back when I thought I might have a chance with her.

The friend zone and me go way back. Tristan metamorphosed from ugly duckling to swan in the second half of sixth grade, at about the same time that everyone else with a Y chromosome was turning greasy, smelly, and zit-faced, i.e. everything middle school girls steer clear of. Except not me: I was surrounded by girls, the smart and savvy ones who recognized that hanging out with me was a gateway to hanging out with Tristan. It was an effective strategy. In middle school Tristan wasn't capable of maintaining a relationship that lasted more than two weeks. With that kind of turnaround, the smart money was on getting as close to him as possible, social circle wise. Tristan got better at girlfriend-care-and-feeding as he grew older, but the longest his relationships ever lasted (according to some scarily well-researched fan sites) is five months and eleven days. I'm not sure how he screws it up—maybe he's just so good-looking and charismatic that it plays on a girl's insecurities and she gives up on him before he gets tired of her, or maybe he's just a lousy boyfriend.

Mental note: I need to point out to him that he's now courting a girl who can literally set him on fire if he messes things up with her.

I've wandered into a part of the camp that wasn't featured on the tour Arek gave us earlier. There are fewer tents here, and they look more settled, with a buildup of old leaves against the canvas where they meet the ground. I pass one with an open flap and spot a flash of familiar red.

It can't be. I step back and poke my head in. It is.

My hat!

It's not breaking and entering, I tell myself—the flap is open, and besides, it's my hat. I dust it off, in case there might be blight cooties on it, set it on my head, and sigh with contentment. There's no logical reason why, but wearing my hat makes things better.

"Ferimus?" creaks a voice from deeper inside the tent.

My eyes adjust to the gloom inside to see a form wriggling out of a hammock. It's an old man, and not just senior-citizen-discount old, but ancient. I walk over to lend him a hand getting down. He weighs nothing, and once standing, only comes up to my chest. There's something familiar to his raisin-y visage.

"Is that you, Ferimus?" he asks.

It's so dark, my brain adds. It's the guy from the bird egg.

"No, I'm Kyle."

"Ehhh? I knew you'd be back, Ferimus. I found your hat." He points a shaky finger to a spot just above my head.

Oh? Oh! Souffy gave me her uncle's hat. Suddenly the deal with the messenger bird using it as a nest makes sense.

"No, my name is Kyle." I remove the hat and step out of the tent, back into the sun, so that he can see my lack of melanin. His eyes go wide with realization. But that only lasts a moment. Then the foggy expression settles again on him, and he shuffles past me.

I catch up with him a dozen steps out of the tent. "Excuse me. But you sent a message to the Wizard Ferimus via bird egg over a week ago."

He looks up at the name of Ferimus, but when he sees it's only me, he shakes his head sadly and keeps on walking. I'm beginning to think that it wasn't just the age of the bird egg that was obfuscating the message. Could this guy, like Tristan, have accidentally fed the messenger bird at the wrong time? The magical equivalent of a butt dial? Maybe. But just to be sure, I don my hat and step in front of him.

"Ferimus"—his face lights up—"you're back."

"Yes, I am Ferimus," I lie, only belatedly realizing I should have gotten Cole to do this. "And your name is?"

His face crinkles as he laughs. "Raskin. Honestly, Ferimus, I know you're absentminded, but we've been friends since you arrived in Bydlo. You're barely past your first half-century. I was sharp as a diamond well into my second."

"You're over two hundred years old?" I remember someone saying that druids were long lived, but, damn, that's impressive. My response elicits another laugh that devolves into a hacking cough. I lend Raskin my arm to lean on.

"Oh, to be so young again," he manages once the coughing subsides. "This year will be my 333rd birthday. I'm sure Cena sent you an invitation. She's a good grandchild."

"Cena's your granddaughter?" She didn't look much older than me.

"Great, great, great-granddaughter." While I'm processing this information, he adds, "So, did you find her?"

Her? I don't think he's still talking about Cena. I wonder how far I can push the absentminded wizard routine. Messenger bird egg-Raskin had mentioned a name. "You mean Janassy?"

He nods. "She's going to break your heart, you know. They all do."

Well, that one hit a bit too close to home. "'Tis better to have loved and lost, than never to have loved at all," I counter.

Can't there be at least one geeky, misunderstood wizard with good taste in hats who gets the girl? Speaking of wizards and hats, Ferimus (who we've clearly established is not in fact out gathering herbs) is still missing. Since we're stuck here until the Seolia shows up, I could try to locate the guy. Souffy would like that.

"You young people are such romantic fools." Raskin delivers this pronouncement with a mix of peevishness and resignation.

I'm remembering more of the message. "She went looking for the sky rock." That has got to be the meteorite. Which we've established does weird stuff to light, magic spells, and livestock. "You said she hadn't returned."

"Yes."

"And?"

"Yes?"

It's like pulling teeth, which is another thing Raskin doesn't have. What I wouldn't give for one—just one—overly verbose and helpful NPC.

"How do we find her? How do we find Janassy?" I press.

"Last time, you went to see Ashenfal."

Great, more people to keep track of. But at least it feels like progress. "Okay, let's talk to Ashenfal."

Raskin chuckles. "Ferimus, you wish to summon Ashenfal twice in less than a fortnight? Not to insult your looks, but I fear you aren't attractive enough to entice her to make a second appearance."

Not attractive enough, really? I'm not on Tristan or Micah's level, but I'm a seasoned boy-bander; I know how to turn heads. I sweep off my hat, cock my head just so, and give Raskin a sultry half-smile while raising a rakish eyebrow.

Raskin blinks once, twice, then clears his throat. "Impressive illusion. She should be by the tree."

"Lead the way," I say as I put my hat back on.

CHAPTER 41

Kyle

Raskin takes me along a trail with few tents and no people. The aerial roots grow denser here, occasionally forming thickets across the path crowded enough that I need to take my hat off to squeeze through. We eventually reach an open space and there before us is the true trunk. Colored ropes like the ones on Saitanna are wrapped around the bark, and even though I know this sacred tree is blight-free, my heart pounds faster. Raskin shuffles right up to the trunk.

"Did I ever show you this?" He bends down—I swear I hear his knees creak—and pushes aside the dense grasses at the tree's base. I get down on my knees beside him, but can't make out what he's pointing at.

"*A Little Light,*" Raskin whispers. At first, I think he's asking me. But then he twists his wrist and suddenly there's a small flame burning in his hand. Now I can see faint markings; it's a series of letters, each carved in a different style, and numbers.

HB **IB** *DB* 4/10

I recognize those initials. "The Triad of Valor," I say.

"Yes," says Raskin, "they engraved these marks on each of the sacred trees they planted. As a child I used to sneak off to watch them work."

"So, the number is what, a date?" But if the Triad mucked with the flow of time to speed up the growth of the trees, would it matter when they were planted? Raskin doesn't answer. There's something else carved below the initials.

TOV 4VR

"Classy." I wonder which of the Bernstein siblings snagged that vanity license plate when they returned home. Probably the one with the mullet.

"The impudence of some people." A woman who definitely wasn't there a moment ago stands casually with her hand resting on the tree. Or, maybe I should say a feminine being: it's obvious that she's not human. Her skin is a canvas of brown, green, and purple swirls, and her spiky hair is bleach white. The overall effect comes across as more cool-punk-girlfriend than creepy-monster-chick. She's "wearing" a few strategically placed leaves—emphasis on "few"—but in a casual way like it's not a big deal just how much of her well-proportioned breasts are exposed. I stand up, consciously fixing my eyes firmly on her face.

"Ashenfal, my loveliest." Raskin pops up from his squat rather spryly. He straightens his spine and flashes her a gummy smile. "That you should show yourself today is indeed an honor."

Ashenfal ignores him and addresses me instead. "I assume that a hero like you would never stoop to such"—she shudders delicately—"base vandalism."

"Never." Marjorie Banks' 7th Law of Boy Bands, also known as the campsite rule: *Always leave the hotel room, or any public space, in better shape than you found it.* "I'm Kyle Moretti, otherworld hero at your service." I hold out my hand; she regards it like a dead mouse in a cat's mouth. I adjust quickly, sweeping my arm to my chest and executing a gentlemanly bow, doffing my hat as I do so. This wins me an approving nod.

"You may address me as Ashenfal." She says this as if she's granting me a boon. "I'm a dryad," she adds. Yep, dryad would have been my guess.

"And this is your tree?" I ask, making small talk.

"Dryads don't own trees. That's a human myth." Although she looks thirty-something, I'm picking up the vibe that she's much older. I make a mental note to be extra-polite. I need to impress her to find out what she knows about Janassy and Ferimus's whereabouts. "But it is true that I, with the help of my sisters, have tended and nurtured the sacred tree Nortrellis since it was planted by the Triad of Valor."

"You've done a great job." As a rule, I try to compliment women on what they've actually accomplished, otherwise it's just shallow pandering. "She's magnificent."

"It," she corrects me. "Humans like to impose their concept of gender on all living things. Trees lie beyond your simplistic binary notions, or your perception of time. To a tree, or an immortal being such as myself, a season passes like a single day, a century like a year. How can humans, whose lives flicker so briefly, understand time on its true scale? No sooner do they bloom than they begin to wilt." She glances at Raskin before dismissing him. "Whereas the trees just grow ever more glorious. What do you think, Wizard Kyle?"

I think that somebody likes to overuse sweeping poetic phrases and ends up sounding pretentious.

But I've charmed both studio execs and professors emeritus; I've got this. Employing my most convincing "aw shucks" voice, I say, "Guess I need to make the most of the fleeting moments I have. Like now, I'm appreciating a magnificent tree diligently cared for by a beautiful dryad." Did I lay it on too thick?

Ashenfal laughs, delighted.

Dryad charmed. Achievement unlocked.

"Why did you seek me out, hero?"

"I'm looking for the Wizard Ferimus, I believe he might be with someone named… Janassy." There's a hunch I want to confirm. "I think she might be a dryad?"

"Yes, that is so. Ferimus begged that I lend him my gift to read the forest. I'm not certain if he was able to make proper use of it. Wild magick is better suited to druids; it confounds wizards who trap their narrow, desiccated spells in animal-skin books." She glances at the courier bag at my side that I keep my spellbook in. Well, that's a straight-out challenge. I may only have been a wizard for a week, but I know which team I'm batting for.

"I'm always open to new experiences," I say, meaning: *I'm totally going to use this dryad forest magic-with-a-"k" to find Ferimus, or at least Janassy.*

Ashenfal nods at what she perceives is my submission and proceeds to repeat the word *"Reveal"* over and over in a random sing-songy way. I get a strong whiff of ripe greenhouse fragrance as she steps right into my personal space and takes my hand in hers, placing it palm-down on the bark of the sacred tree. Finally, she leans in and plants a scratchy kiss—dryads' lips are rough like cat tongues—on my forehead.

The magick kicks in.

I was bracing for a physical shock, but the experience is more akin to falling into a bathtub filled with lukewarm water. A strange pressure envelops me and there's a tingling, like a weak electric current applied to my skin. I recognize this feeling, this energy: it's pure mana.

I've been aware of the mana within me since I started casting spells, but in an abstract, am-I-hungry way. This mana has mouthfeel, like a just-picked strawberry, soft and bright and fresh. Brand-new mana, I realize. The sacred tree is synthesizing it, probably in its leaves.

"How can it be producing so much mana?"

Ashenfal smirks. "Didn't I say that a tree experiences time differently? This is the now, but also what has come before, a memory of past mana, a year back at least. Is it too much for you, Wizard Kyle?"

"Nope, I'm good." And I mean it. I have a ways to go to develop my combat reflexes, but my problem-solving skills—finely honed over years of boy-banding and college classes—are primed for a challenge like this. Hacking a magic system is just what my ego needs.

First, I need to figure out how to control what I'm experiencing. Until now, my hand has been pressing into the sacred tree Nortrellis; I pull it back slightly, experimenting. The intense sensations against my skin recede, and I can now perceive the quanta of mana individually as sparkly particles, or if I squint another way, as a flowing silver-white liquid between me and the bark of the tree. I look at other parts of the tree; it's like I'm viewing the world with an overlay of magical energies on top: I can see the mana trickling through the finer branches, gathering in the boughs, overflowing into the main and secondary trunks, fanning out through the roots, leaching into the soil. It's being pulled down—drawn like a current—into what feels like an underground cable. Still maintaining contact with the tree, I turn to follow its snaking course through the forest.

"What… is that?"

Ashenfal rests her head against the bark, her eyes closed. I can feel her presence just outside of me, piggybacking on my perceptions, skimming my thoughts in a manner similar to how Magic Missive operates.

"Humans call them ley lines. They're the remains of the roots of the Worldtree planted by Minstay, Goddess of Nature. It almost caused a second war between the gods before Kalimos smote it with a lightning bolt."

A war over a tree? Mythreal's mythology is weird.

But, back to the problem at hand: How did Ferimus think that this would help him find Janassy?

I'm still too close to see the big picture. Gingerly I pull my hand back until the pads of my fingers are ghosting the bark. I close my eyes and, in the darkness behind my eyelids, I can still see the bright mana, streaming from the canopy down to the trunk. I tilt my hands just so and the perspective tilts in response until I've got a bird's-eye view looking down on the root system and its ley lines. Better, but what I see in my magic vision is still limited to what's in front of me. What if… I bring my second hand up to the tree and the image stabilizes, like a touch screen.

I push my hands together and zoom out so I'm looking over the whole forest, then turn my hands counterclockwise and the view rotates in response. It's even better than a touch screen; I'm operating an interactive map. I'm navigating this wild magick with my own familiar conceptual overlay. Cool. I take a few moments just to play around with it, feeling nostalgic for my smartphone as I do so.

I quickly find the magick's limits. The portion of the realm I can see this way isn't all that big, with impenetrable barriers to the east and south where the magical map meets the ocean, and fading to black in the west and north. I'm guessing it only covers the Drevo Woods in detail, but I can't be sure because I don't recognize any underlying features for reference. It's just… concentrations of mana, distributed like clouds. There's an empty space to the north and a particularly blurry spot to the west. Interesting, but I can't do much with the data in this state. I need another hand.

"*Dexterarious*," I whisper and bring out my Phantom Hand.

"What are you up to, Ferimus?" Raskin asks.

"Interdisciplinary magic." I half open my eyes so I can see both the magic map and my hands at the same time. It's kind of like wearing bifocals.

Another appendage means that I can manipulate time in my visualization of mana, pausing the flow, reversing it, isolating discrete time periods. But Phantom Hand can do even more. In the physical world, when I command it to pick up a book, it handles the particulars of balancing the tome's weight and shape. Here, in this weird magickal space, I can mentally request it to, say, hide any mana outside the ley lines, and Phantom Hand does something to turn the diffuse fuzziness into a map of defined streams. I'm not sure how it's doing this; the hand appears to be typing, or maybe playing a keyboard instrument? Best not to go there—thinking about how exactly magic works is the easiest way to flub a spell.

Instead, I focus on this newer, cleaner version of the map. I can see clear channels, like the veins and arteries of the forest's circulatory system. The places where the ley lines cluster are probably where the sacred trees were planted. But why guess? I took ten credits of data science in my junior year, and now I'm going to put those hard-won A's to practical use.

I zoom in and out of the map, calling to mind various statistical algorithms to divide and group the flowing mana. I work out a basic sorting script to further classify the results, subvocalizing the code like an incantation. Most importantly, I make myself believe that it's going to work. And it does: previously indistinguishable particles of mana are transformed into curated and tagged data points. Neat!

Now for the fun stuff.

I lay out my new and improved—not to mention color-coded—data visualization, and the map view turns from a pretty picture to an information-dense dashboard. The locations of the sacred trees are now obvious from the energy spikes along the ley lines. I drop pins to mark them: N for Nortrellis, ST1 to ST8 for the rest. They're staggered throughout the forest with each positioned so that it is connected to at least two ley lines. The Triad of Valor chose good locations to optimize mana to ley line transfer, although they missed connecting a tree directly to the largest ley line. That empty space in the north that I noticed earlier would have been ideal. *Must have run out of seeds.*

I limit the display to just the mana created since yesterday morning. The ley lines adjacent to ST3 in the east go dark. So that is, or was, Saitanna. I further isolate the mana into quarter-hour segments and display them sequentially, to show the changes over the past day. It looks a bit like a weather radar animation as it loops.

"I've never seen a wizard spell the forest-vision like this," says Ashenfal, sounding dubious. "It's very colorful, but what does it mean?"

"See how the mana flows into the ley lines? It moves a certain distance, and then leaks out. That's how the mana produced by the sacred trees is distributed out to the rest of the forest. This is a representation of the network that turns the Drevo Woods into a magical ecosystem."

"Yes, the sacred trees create the magic that feeds the forest. It took you all this work to figure out something obvious?" Ashenfal says dismissively. "Most wizards discover that with a simple Sense Magic spell." But she's inched closer to me to peer at the colorful vision suspended above my hands.

I'm prepared to counter her skepticism. "Does Sense Magic tell them which trees feed into which ley lines, or how the loss of a specific sacred tree might affect different areas of the forest?"

A command to my phantom hand causes my model to jump back in time to before Saitanna was corrupted.

"This area"—I use the forefinger of my Phantom Hand like a laser pointer—"was being actively sustained by Saitanna." I run the visualization forward to the present. "Now it will draw from these other two sacred trees primarily, and, to a lesser extent, Nortrellis. And that will put more strain on all three trees, possibly affecting other areas of the forest that they supply mana to." Perhaps just a tad peevishly I add, "Something to keep in mind as you care for and nurture the forest."

Some of Ashenfal's easy air of superiority slips. "This… could be useful."

Spurred on by her reaction, I decide to show off some more. "You can perform more specific diagnostics. I can probably pinpoint exactly when Saitanna became the source of the blight." I jump back by the hour and the glowing stream of mana slowly returns to the ley lines. "It seems like blight-Saitanna wasn't just not contributing mana to the network, but actively pulling mana out from nearby ley lines and the surrounding trees. If Arek and Cena hadn't stopped it, it could have choked off a huge area of the forest." I keep going back in time until everything looks normal. I glance at the time counter I'd conjured at the corner of the magickal display. "Five days ago, Saitanna was uncorrupted. See? Back then, it had no effect on the surrounding flow of mana."

"That recently?" Ashenfal purses her lips. "Are you sure?"

I re-check. "Yep, five days." And then it hits me. Five days ago was when Rozny Las was attacked.

CHAPTER 42

Kyle

The information sinks in. Five days ago, the sacred tree Saitanna was (at least according to the ley line network) a happy sacred tree contributing to the forest's mana stores. And yet, five days ago the blight was strong enough to destroy Rozny Las, and the attack started the day before.

For confirmation, I swipe my map to the right to the coastline at the northern tip of the bay, the location of the town. There, I see the same massive drop in mana levels as my algorithm detected around Saitanna when it was fully blight-compromised.

"But this means…" Ashenfal's voice trails off.

"That Saitanna wasn't the original source of the blight. She, I mean it, was just another victim."

It. Ashenfal says trees don't have genders. Which doesn't square with the trees telling Micah that a Lady of the Forest was in peril. Assuming Micah wasn't just high off of the healing spell, then there was an actual (female) Forest Lady. It's not a hard logical leap to think dryad, and from there to think Janassy. But none of that is a priority right now, so I shove those speculations to the back of my consciousness and focus on the relevant data at hand, literally.

"When the blight takes over, it pulls measurable amounts of mana out of the nearest ley lines," I say. "Just like normal plants do, but on a completely different scale. Hmm, let me try something." I set about comparing the mana fluctuations around Saitanna to those near Rozny Las just before the nearby ley lines were hijacked. Sure enough, there are enough similarities between the two for me to create a profile, a pattern of mana flow that portends the arrival of the blight. I assign this pattern a dangerous-looking purple-black color to make it obvious that—when this shows up elsewhere—it's a bad thing.

Armed with this new diagnostic, I scroll backwards through time, only to see streaks of that angry purple-black spark throughout the forest. The pattern of streaks is not completely random, they seem to form lines through time. And there's an exceptionally strong gathering of them ten days ago, to the north of Rozny Las.

"That's where the logging camp was," says Ashenfal, following my train of thought. "The one that was attacked."

Before the logging camp attack, the streaks become smaller, just little occasional outbursts of bruised darkness. They angle north and seem to stop at that empty space in the map, the one where there's no sacred tree to feed the ley lines (whatever vegetation is present there doesn't seem interested in pulling mana). So, the blight might have been doing something up there, but my system can't see it. The traces vanished around thirteen days ago.

"What's up there?" I ask.

"It's a dead spot," says Ashenfal offhandedly. "It's in the Belclav mountain range, partway up a mountain the humans call Haramus. That area has poor soil and very few trees grow there. But that's in the past," she says to dismiss the topic. "What matters is the blight infestation in the now. Can your magic show that?"

"Real-time? Sure." I fast-forward the system through the past week and a half—partly because the animation looks cool. Except that it shows black blight spot after black blight spot breaking out all over like acne on a teenager's face. The Trädskydd–Rozny Las alliance seems to have taken out many of them but others are still festering. They're scattered across the map, several of them uncomfortably close to sacred trees.

"The druids must be informed of this," says Ashenfal. She waves her hands and what looks like glitter (pixie dust?) sprinkles down on my interface which momentarily glows. Was that a magical screen capture I just witnessed?

"You'll help them?" Incorporating a legion of dryads would probably help the fight.

"I will inform them about the blight and about these specific areas." Ashenfal notices my judgmentally raised eyebrows. "Dryads nurture the forest, we are not warriors."

"If the blight manages to get to just one more sacred tree, there might not be any more magic forest to nurture." I scan back to just before the Saitanna was taken out to emphasize what's at stake. Ashenfal purses her lips as she regards the expanding darkness, draining the connecting ley lines.

"If we dryads were to be required to destroy a sacred tree, then we absolutely could not join the fight. A dryad's immortal life is tied to the lives of the trees she tends, and if any one of us acted against a sacred tree, even a corrupted one, she would forfeit that immortality. You're mortal so you can't possibly comprehend what it would mean for one of us to lose that gift."

By that logic, you don't understand mortal things, like death, I think to myself, but that's not a conversation where we can meet in the middle. Besides, my grim silence speaks volume.

Ashenfal looks almost chastened.

"You are an exceedingly clever and astute wizard," she compliments me, either as atonement or to change the topic. "I've only met one wizard more impressive, the otherworld Wizard Daniel."

"You're saying I'm as good as the Triad of Valor's wizard?" I take a moment to preen.

"Hardly." She laughs, and not in a friendly way. "Wizard Daniel rained down a cloud of poison to stop an army of giants, and he summoned monstrous tentacles to hold the ice giant king so his sister could cut off the king's head. He was, irrefutably, the more extraordinary wizard in all ways, except…" She looks me over going from head down to feet and back up again. "You are far more pleasing to rest my eyes on." Ashenfal leans in with a hungry expression, one that I've seen before. "Our magics mesh so well together, perhaps we should explore other… compatibilities?"

Still forcing my eyes not to stray below her neckline, I remember those rough lips, her arrogance, not to mention that there's still a lot of blights out there endangering the forest. I take a decisive step back. "I think the druids need this information as soon as possible."

Ashenfal pauses, takes the hint. "Of course." She turns to leave. "Perhaps later, I shall call upon the other heroes in your party."

That would be entertaining. I should probably give the guys a heads up. As I contemplate this, Raskin wanders over besides me, watching Ashenfal saunter away.

"Ah, to be young and blessed by the attentions of the dryads. I envy you, Ferimus."

"I'm not—"

"Yes, yes, I know. You've given your heart to Janassy. And for that I pity you. When you're young and pretty, they'll pledge their undying love to you. Such happy times." His voice catches and his eyes go watery. "Then, one day you wake up old and no longer comely, and just like that they forget all their promises."

Ashenfal has by now slipped behind an aerial root and disappeared. Raskin is staring at the spot where she vanished. Or maybe he's lost in his memories.

I take a guess: "You and Ashenfal used to be a couple?"

"Long ago, back when I was a fit new initiate. She was quite enamored of my tattoos." He raises a frail arm; the once-intricate ink pattern on it is crumpled and runny, like water-soaked newsprint. "She told me I was different from the ones who came before, that what we had was different."

Different doesn't guarantee permanent, I don't say. I'm trying for something comforting, but all that comes to mind are snarky comments concerning Ashenfal. Raskin's absentminded ease has been replaced by something more pained, more raw. I feel scummy about putting him in this situation, for tricking him.

I try for a distraction. "But there are other people who love you. A wife, or partner, right?" Great-great-great-granddaughters don't get delivered by the stork, even in Mythreal.

"My wife…" Raskin falls into breathy gasps, like hiccups. "She's been gone for so long. I can't even remember her face." Way to go, Kyle. "I can't remember any of them." He's full-on crying now. "Only Ashenfal has… has remained the same. It's so hard getting old, Ferimus."

Although it feels way too intimate for someone I just met, I put one arm over his shoulder and pull him close. I imagine he's a twelve-year-old girl (he's not much bigger than one). After a while the wheezing stops, and his breathing slows to normal. He's chewing his gums, and his eyes have cleared.

"It hurts to see her, but that doesn't stop me from seeking her out. Just to get a sliver of the memory of who I was when she loved me. Young Raskin, so powerful and respected and full of life. It's ridiculous the lengths I'd go to for that. I probably seem the biggest old fool to you."

I think back to last month, when I finagled the registrar's office to let me graduate early, sublet my apartment, dumped all my possessions into storage, and flew cross-country for a chance to sing chorus and dance in the background for a band whose fans had outgrown them and whose tour would be running on nostalgia fumes. All for a miniscule chance of recapturing that time when I was shiny and special, to share even one moment of pure joy with an audience who loved me, loved me and my four best friends.

"No, no you don't seem like a fool to me at all."

Raskin cough-laughs and favors me with a gummy smile. "But still old, right? Older even than this tree, if you don't count the time magic." More cough-laughs. "You know, Wizard Daniel was extraordinary when smiting enemies, but not so adept at manipulating space and time. The first few times he tried the time acceleration spell, oh my, those were exciting. But he eventually got it down. I was just a wee thing back then, used to sneak out to watch them when they weren't looking. Nortrellis grew a hundred years in an afternoon. So wondrous, that's a memory that stayed." He puts his hand to the trunk of the tree and startles. "Is this your work Ferimus?"

I'd kept my Phantom Hand on the tree all this time so that the visualization spell was still running. Raskin, being a druid, must be tapping into it.

"Yes, it shows what happened when Saitanna was corrupted by the blight and—"

"This, this spot." He taps—pokes his finger through—the blank spot up north. I zoom out and re-center. Raskin nods solemnly and declares, "that's where you thought you'd find Janassy."

I did? I mean, *Ferimus did?* I wonder what made him think that?

I scroll back to nine days ago, when Ashenfal said Ferimus showed up and she granted him use of her forest magick. There's a thick patch of angry black where the blight has overrun the loggers' camp but nothing noticeable around the blank spot. I layer on older data, everything Ferimus would have been shown, but I still don't see anything happening in the dead spots.

No, wait. I spot the faintest smear of mana. Probably just noise? I zoom in to a tiny spot within the dead zone, showing just the occasional pinprick dots of mana. Still telling myself this is just a data artifact, I scroll through time, trying to pinpoint when this mana showed up. Nothing, nothing, and then…

Two weeks ago, for less than ten minutes starting at 9:25 p.m., the mana shows up, then disappears. Like someone hurled a mana-filled baseball.

Or a rock.

"The meteorite!" My exclamation causes Raskin to startle. In a more controlled voice I say, "You called it a sky rock. A part of it must have fallen in the Drevo Woods, just like it crashed through Malza's barn." My heart is now beating triple speed. Random events are coming together into an explanation. "Ferimus sends his messenger bird to Janassy to ask her to go looking for the sky rock. She doesn't return so you send the messenger bird back saying she's missing. And Ferimus is so concerned he takes off through the hearthstone, leaving a note for Souffy." Raskin is nodding. I'm not sure if he's confirming my hunch or just humoring me.

It doesn't matter. The timeline fits. I know I'm right.

"So Ferimus shows up here at the Druid's camp, uses Ashenfal's magick to somehow figure out where the sky rock fell, and goes after that on the assumption that Janassy must be nearby." I'm monologuing, but I need to get it out of my head to make it real. "One piece of that meteorite caused the sheep, the blink dog and those cockatrices to become enormous. Maybe it's radioactive, or the mana equivalent? It could have mutated a plant into the blight." I pause, then ask, "Do you know what grows up there, Raskin?"

"Nothing!" Raskin barks clear as day. "There's nothing up there!" He seems as surprised by his outburst as me.

"How do you know?" I ask. "Have you been up there?"

Raskin shakes his head empathically. He looks unhappy again, but not in that melancholy regretful way. His eyes are darting around, his breathing's heavy.

"Are you not supposed to talk about that part of the forest?" I guess.

"Ye—" he gets out before his gums snap shut. His face strains as he tries to open his mouth. Frustration gives way to resignation. When he finally speaks, he just repeats:

"There's nothing up there."

There's obviously something up there. Raskin wants to tell me, but he can't.

"Are you under a spell that keeps you from talking about this? Answer me truthfully."

A spell preventing a person from talking about something should also be designed to keep the person from admitting to being spelled. So it's unlikely he is going to say yes, and he might be forced to say no. Or… Raskin stays silent and gives me a measured look. I'm not sure if it was Ashenfal's influence, or him connecting to the tree, but he looks almost clear headed.

And his silence speaks volumes.

"It's okay, you don't need to tell me anything. Just let it go." I say as gently as possible. I pretend that I'm Oscar and actually good at this comforting stuff. "It's okay, you're fine." And then, because I feel lousy for saying all this while still pretending to be Ferimus, I remove my hat. "Raskin, you've been a big help. I think I'll be able to find Ferimus and Janassy, and maybe the source of the blight thanks to you."

This time his eyes don't go glassy. "You're a hero."

"Yeah."

"Oh, dear." He doesn't look happy. "I told Ferimus it was dangerous going there. He just laughed, said if he got into something he couldn't handle, he'd petition the Divine Wisdom for some heroes." Raskin shakes his head. "And now he's gone, and you're here, and that means…"

Another detail clicks into place. The reason the Divine Wisdom called us here. There was a request. There is a quest. We're here to rescue Ferimus. And to find the source of the blight. And to stop it.

CHAPTER 43

Kyle

After his big reveal, Raskin becomes fuzzy again. I'm forced to put the hat back on to cajole him to leave the sacred tree. Instead of leading me back to his tent, he takes me to a spot where the aerial trunks have ribbons woven between them, giving the place a maypole feel.

Closer in, I see a crater dug into the earth. It's about ten feet deep with dirt-packed steps leading down. I follow Raskin into it. With each step, small lights magically flare up. At the bottom there's a simple log bench facing three cylindrical columns of polished obsidian, or maybe onyx, ranging in height from just above my eye level to over six feet tall. Not too hard to guess who these monuments are honoring. At this point, I could lead a Triad of Valor nostalgia tour.

"This was one of my projects, when I led the Trädskydd Druids, nearly two centuries ago," says Raskin as he takes a seat. "No one comes here anymore, but it's a good place to sit and think. Or nap."

He motions me to join him, but as I come closer, I notice the photograph placards at the bases of the columns. They're more than photographs; these are ID cards. I lean in to read the details.

The first ID belongs to Isaac Bernstein. It's both a driver's license and an emergency responder card for Jersey City and surrounding areas; it states that Isaac is authorized to operate a paramedic vehicle up to a ceiling of 30,000 feet—of course, the Bernstein siblings came from a world with flying cars. Further inspection reveals that Isaac was twenty-two years old, an organ donor, and undeniably sporting a mullet.

Next, at the base of the tallest column, is Hannah's ID. It states she's twenty-four, a Staff Sergeant in something called the National Protectorate. This one gives a year: 1982. If a parallel version of her lives in my world, she'd be almost seventy.

So, a military enlisted fighter and an EMT cleric. The Divine Wisdom was evidently in a pragmatic mood when It chose these heroes.

I'm dreading checking Daniel's ID. I have enough imposter syndrome as is, I really don't need to find out that he was a Talmudic scholar or, worse, that his world had magic and he was already adept at it. But no, Daniel Bernstein, age nineteen, was a freshman in the Computer Science department at Bronx Community College—bit of a letdown. According to one CS major I met playing *Heroes Summoning*, a programming background provides the best real-world skills for building a wizard character. But Daniel doesn't look like a budding proto-wizard in his photo. He looks young and baby-faced, and not in that dreamy-prom-date-Micah way, more the pasty-with-acne-scars variety.

I remind myself that these IDs reflected who the Triad were when they first arrived. By the time the youngest Bernstein was taking down ice giants he probably had acquired a wizard's gravitas, although apparently he wasn't handsome enough to charm Ashenfal. But on those initial quests, with his soldier sister and medically-trained brother, Daniel must have felt as much out of his depth as I do now. He was still a teenager, and the little brother to boot.

Okay, I'm warming up to Wizard Daniel, this pimple-faced, community-college computer nerd that the Divine Wisdom saw potential in. And the Divine Wisdom was right. Judging by how they're honored by both the citizens of Bydlo and the Trädskydders, Daniel and his siblings became proper heroes.

And it wasn't just them. Time and again, the Divine Wisdom has selected individuals from a multitude of worlds to alter—for the better—Mythreal's history and society. And now It's chosen the five of us, Never Boy Land. Maybe I should put some trust in Its judgment.

It doesn't mean we can't fail. It doesn't mean we can't die. But it does mean that we can kick ass given half a chance. And we do have a chance. It's up to us to take it.

Okay, that was inspirational. Now for the hard part, persuading my bandmates.

Raskin is snoring. This seems a safe enough place to leave him be.

I'm humming the melody from our first chart-topping hit on my way back to the tent, my steps keeping pace with the up-tempo beat. Everyone jumps to their feet when I burst in. Cole's already got a knife out.

"Good reflexes," I say.

"Hey Kyle, we were—" Tristan starts.

"Glad you're back," Oscar interrupts, but his smile is on the plastic side.

Tris's expression turns from confused to dawning realization and I'd bet a bottle of top-shelf healing potion on his interrupted sentence ending with "just talking about you." Which is hardly surprising; I ran out on them after all. And starting with my discovery of the hearthstone, I've been instrumental in taking several steps along this adventure that have almost gotten us killed. So, I've earned a certain amount of behind-the-back kvetching. But if they're still sore over our recent thrashing by the limbs of the forest, it's going to make it difficult to convince them that this quest I'm proposing will be any different.

I perform a quick scan of the room. Tristan, Oscar, and Souffy are clustered by the bed where Havelin lies in his magically-induced coma. Cole and Micah are standing on the other side of the tent as far apart as possible from each other while still within sniping distance. Probably best to just go for it.

"I have good news and bad news," I announce.

Souffy scrunches her forehead. "Does that mean it's the same news but can appear good or bad depending upon how you look at it?"

"No, it's one of each," says Cole. "Give us the bad news first." He always chooses bad news first.

"The sacred tree wasn't the cause of the blight, and killing it didn't stop the spread. The blight's still out there." Over gasps of dismay, I barrel on, "But we have a tool to identify where the blight is currently active. And also where Souffy's uncle is… probably." For clarity I add, "That part is the good news."

I'm keeping the story short and simple because replaying the last couple of hours to my four bandmates—and dealing with their random questions—would take forever. Plus, I don't want to be sidetracked defending my untested, cobbled-together magic kludge.

"They located Ferimus? Is he alright?" asks Souffy. I have her full attention; maybe I should have talked up my specific contribution to this outcome.

"He's in the north, a place called Mt. Haramus. It's the same area where the blight originated from. As for how he's doing"—answering her second question is proving more awkward—"it looks like he might be the one who petitioned the Divine Wisdom to send us here in the first place, so he probably got himself into some trouble."

"And that's good news?" asks Cole, droll and bristly.

"It's good news that we finally know why we were called here." I try to not sound defensive. Cole appears unmoved and I'm sensing disbelieving vibes from Micah. I shift my pitch to the more sympathetic side of the tent. "This is our quest."

"That's great, Kyle," says Oscar, his body language practically shouting the exact opposite. "But…"

"You do remember how we fared against the blight the last time, right?" says Micah.

"We didn't do that badly," I argue. Well, ok, not strictly true—but we rallied. "It was the sacred tree in the end that got us."

"If you can't win the boss battle, you still lose," says Cole.

"This isn't a video game," Micah snaps back, not sure at who. The tension in the room is palpable. Oscar steps in.

"We agreed that we won't rush into danger until we've worked on our fighting skills," he says in his most reasonable voice. "Even if there's more blight out there, it seems like Cena and Arek's forces have it under control. I'm not sure if they need otherworld saviors inserting themselves at this point. We need to respect their culture and beliefs."

Yeah, and what if Chosen Ones are an integral component of their culture and beliefs? But I decide to change tack.

"How about we focus on finding Ferimus? Then all the trained soldiers and druids would be free to go after the major blight incursion. There's hardly any blight activity in the area where Ferimus went missing." Or at least none that my magic app could pick up.

"But didn't you say that's where the blight started?" Tristan inconveniently asks. Bet that was the one detail of the conversation he picked up on. I can tell that "It's the right thing to do" is losing the argument. Time to go for self-interest.

"Listen, if helping Ferimus is the quest we were called here for, then accomplishing it might be enough to earn us our ticket home." I see Souffy flinch. Us leaving this soon would break her heart.

Mine too. We're in a world where magic is freaking real, where literally everything is possible. And all we've experienced of it so far is one town, one forest, and—let's face it—some pretty lame monsters. I don't want to leave yet.

But that's just me being a geek. What Micah and Cole and Oscar and Tristan really want is to get on with the comeback tour and relaunch their careers. And that means returning to our world. A quick glance around confirms that I'm reaching them; only Oscar is still frowning.

"Going home would be awesome," he says. "But we do have to be realistic. Excepting Souffy and her Fire Orb, we've needed to tag-team to take down even a single monster. Meaning that if we were to face off against more than four blights, we'd go to multiple rounds, and each round increases our chance of getting seriously injured. I've the capacity for two healing spells. After that, we're carrying any damage we incur into our next battle."

He's laying it out slowly, logically, living up to his self-appointed role as the responsible older brother. "It's not that I think we can't complete the quest, Kyle, but there's a big risk that somewhere along the way someone's going to get hurt badly enough to... not make it." I think back to all the sessions of *Heroes Summoning* where I or a teammate died. They blur together. Oscar continues, "If it's a choice between only some of us going home now, or waiting until we're strong enough to all go back together later, I'd pick the latter, no question."

"But what if we..." I draw a blank when faced with the prospect of one of us dying.

"We don't all have access to gobs of magic, Kyle," says Micah.

"We're still just musicians cosplaying as heroes," adds Cole, unhelpful but true.

That's three against, meaning it's over, vote-wise. I'm less upset with losing, more frustrated with myself for believing I could have swayed their opinions in the first place. Why should they listen to me? I'm just their backup singer. I turn to Tris. He'll probably try sitting on the fence just so I won't feel like everyone's against me.

"We all go home together," he pronounces, looking right at me with steely eyes.

Well.

That's that.

I can't even get Tristan on board. And I've already spent my one allotted drama-queen exit for the day. Nothing to do but nod and put on my best team-player smile.

"Um, do I get a say?" It's Souffy. I'm mortified to have forgotten all about her.

"Yeah, of course," Oscar says too quickly. Apparently I'm not the only one.

Souffy says, "I know we shouldn't run off unprepared like last time. However, if it's the Divine Wisdom that summoned you for this, then it must be a quest that only you can accomplish. You have to have faith."

She gives each of my bandmates a hopeful smile, saving the last for Tristan. She might not be my fangirl, but she is on my side. That works for my ego. Since she just invoked faith, I turn to check our cleric's reaction.

"Honestly, Souffy." He sighs. It's never a good sign when Oscar sighs. "I think the Divine Wisdom might have made a mistake this time."

"No." Souffy half laughs as if he were joking. "The Divine Wisdom doesn't make mistakes."

The First Law of Mythreal: *The Divine Wisdom never makes mistakes.* And the Second Law of Mythreal: *The Divine Wisdom NEVER makes mistakes.*

Souffy continues, "You were specifically chosen because you are the heroes capable of bringing balance to this world." She pauses, looks around at all of us. "You do believe that, don't you?"

"I do," I say. My earlier epiphany is still ringing in my head. But there's silence from everyone else. Souffy flashes me a grateful smile and turns to the others.

"It's alright if you don't." Her voice catches but she soldiers through. "My grandmama said that a couple of the Heroes of the Realm didn't initially believe in the Divine Wisdom's omniscience, that it took time to fully embrace their calling."

"Yeah, maybe we just need time," says Tristan. "Or, you know, evidence." And then he throws in a thousand-watt smile.

Souffy blinks several times before nodding vigorously. "You're right. I'll go find some evidence." She pivots to the tent door.

"I'll come with you," Tristan offers.

Souffy stops mid-stride. Her eyes flicker briefly to Tristan before sliding around to meet mine. "Actually, I think Kyle would be best for helping me."

Tristan's smile falls, more confused than disappointed, I'd wager. I'm looking at Souffy's expectant eyes. "Kyle?" she says.

I don't make her ask twice.

CHAPTER 44

Souffy

Souffy strides out of the tent with her chin held high and no outward sign that her heart is sinking like a stone. She'd said it was fine that the heroes didn't believe in the Divine Wisdom's will, but it doesn't feel fine. It feels like failure, her failure.

Behind her, Kyle quickens his pace until they're walking side by side. He pushes his hat back so she can see his face.

"Thanks, Souffy, for what you did back there." But she didn't do anything. If she had, they'd still be in the tent with the other Neverboylanders, planning an expedition to rescue Uncle Ferimus. Perhaps reading her confusion, Kyle adds, "For choosing me over Tristan. To help you, I mean."

"Oh?" She had been so agitated back in the tent—so in the moment—that she now needs to pause to remember precisely what transpired.

Tristan offered to come with her. Souffy turned him down. She said she'd rather have Kyle with her. Why had she been so sure of that decision?

"You're better at magic and quests," she says, answering her own question.

Even now, Tristan's offer to help sends Souffy's stomach cartwheeling and her pulse racing. But more than wanting to get closer to Tristan, what Souffy really wants is to prove that he, and also Oscar and Cole and Micah, are wrong. For that, she wants Kyle. Needs Kyle, she amends. "And you are the only one who believes in the Divine Wisdom."

"Of course that's why. I mean, it makes sense." Kyle shrugs and smiles with just his mouth. His eyes hold the same resignation she saw when his friends rejected his plan to continue on their quest.

Maybe, Souffy realizes, she isn't the only person who needs support right now.

She touches Kyle's shoulder. He stops walking.

"The Divine Wisdom chose you to be the group's wizard, Kyle. That's a big deal, and I'm not saying this just because I'm a snob about magic. My grandfather says that just as fibers are woven into a tapestry, magic is woven into the reality of Mythreal. Drawing power and manipulating mana is like following a thread. Different magic users will be able to follow different threads, to manipulate and draw power from their particular magics. But only we wizards, through our study and dedication, can begin to see the greater pattern. It is this knowledge, this perspective, more than the mastery of any particular spells, that distinguishes a wizard from other magic users." The words flow easily; she's reciting the preamble to the lecture she's been subjected to many times, wheeled out to convince her to apply herself more diligently to her studies. But what she says next is all her. "From what I've seen, Kyle, you're on your way to becoming a great wizard." For some reason, she adds a wink.

Kyle's cheeks turn pink, making a contrast with the sky-blue of his eyes. "That… that means a lot, Souffy. Thank you." He smiles, and this time his eyes join in.

"Of course," she says quickly and turns away, her own face growing uncomfortably warm. "I'm counting on you to help me find evidence to convince the others. What do you think would work? Maybe finding a sacred text or a testimonial?"

Kyle's forehead furrows in thought. "Honestly, rational arguments don't work with my bandmates." He gives a half-laugh, half-snort. "What we really need is a *deus ex machina.*"

Souffy claps her hands. "What a brilliant idea. Now, where do we find one?"

"I meant that as—" Kyle starts, but he's interrupted by the sudden appearance of a druid so old he looks like a gnarled tree. Despite his age, he hobbles quite vigorously up to Kyle.

"Ferimus," he calls out, grasping Kyle's hand. "I was just coming to find you. Cena and her new beau have taken their forces out to fight the blight. It's all thanks to your magic map."

"This is Raskin," Kyle says by way of introduction. "He thinks I'm your uncle because you gave me his hat."

"Oh, right." Souffy had been wondering when that would come out. She hopes Kyle won't be upset or, worse, give the hat up. He looks so dashing in it.

"And this must be your niece," Raskin says. He turns to Souffy. "Your uncle has told me so much about you. Very amusing stories, reminds me of the trouble I used to get into when I was young. I especially liked hearing how you freed the dancing bear in the marketplace."

Souffy turns to Kyle to explain, but he's giving the old druid a measured look. He turns to Souffy, eyebrows raised, and taps his ear.

"What is it?" Souffy Magic Missives him.

"I think Raskin knows something about the area where the blight came from, where your uncle might be. But—here, I'll show you what happens."

He turns to the old druid. "Raskin, tell me about the spot in the forest where Janassy went to look for the meteorite. What's up there?"

"There's nothing, nothing at all." The words come as if forced out, and afterwards, Raskin's lips snap closed like a trap.

"He's obviously under some sort of secret-keeping spell," Souffy sends back to Kyle.

"That's what I thought. Do you think you can break it?"

Souffy's initial assumption is no. Spells that hide or alter memories are tricky to cast and even more devilish to undo. However, there's a simpler way to keep people from speaking, and judging from the way Raskin's jaw has clenched, Souffy wonders if it might instead be a physical suggestion spell. "Let me try something."

She twirls her copper earring and speaks directly into Raskin's mind.

"Tell me about the thing you're not supposed to talk about."

Raskin looks plaintively at her, his lips trembling.

"It's alright; your mouth is closed, so this isn't talking." For once, Souffy's talents to convolute logic to her desires are an asset. "You can just think it. How's that?"

Raskin's eyes go wide with sudden relief. "Even better," he Magic Missives back, "I can show you."

His face breaks into a wrinkly smile. He grasps her shoulders, bringing their faces close enough for Souffy to catch a solid whiff of old-person smell. Raskin probably only meant to touch foreheads, but he misjudges the distance (or maybe he's just that desperate to reveal his long-kept secret) and keeps going until his skull smashes into hers.

Souffy momentarily sees stars. And then the stars become memories.

CHAPTER 45

Souffy

Souffy's Magic Missive cantrip is supposedly only good for relaying short messages. But combining spells, especially those involving more animalistic branches of magic, can lead to unpredictable results. Such as reliving one of Raskin's own memories as he himself experienced it.

From within Raskin's memory, Souffy feels smaller, lighter, and grubbier. She's a child—maybe six or seven—crouching under a bush. Narrow branches poke her arms and moist dirt pushes through her fingers. Souffy's nostrils sting from the chilly air while child-Raskin's druid-trained senses parse out the smells: the musty decay rising from the earth mixes with the heavy sweetness of spring sap. His heightened awareness also allows her to pick out details in the moonless night, to distinguish, by degrees of shadows, the figures he… she… is spying on.

It's hard to separate where Souffy's perception ends and Raskin's memory begins. She feels his emotions—excitement, anticipation, and just a smidgen of guilt. It's a mix that she can easily relate to. Raskin is doing something he knows will get him into trouble, but he can't resist, because, because these are the otherworld heroes!

Not Souffy's heroes, she realizes as she watches the three from Raskin's hiding spot. This is the Triad of Valor. They stand about ten feet away. A tall woman in bulky armor, Fighter Hannah, watches as the two men walk a wide arc around her. The shorter one with the staff, Wizard Daniel, is holding a small bag from which a stream of sand is pouring out to form a line. The larger man, Cleric Isaac, follows him and speaks urgently.

"We gotta speed things up." Isaac's words come out muffled, like he has a cold. "Time moves faster here, but not that fast. Back in our world it's been almost six months. I need to be home. Now."

"I'm casting as fast as I can." Daniel's odd articulation stretches the words in the same way his brother does. Souffy thinks this might be their otherworld accent.

The wizard moves towards the bush Raskin is hiding under. Souffy feels the sensation of holding her breath while her heart pounds unbearably loud in her ears. Yet somehow Daniel doesn't hear it. Rather than pour the sand into the bush, he swerves and instead runs the line of sand around it.

"Time magic is exhausting. Just restoring my mana isn't enough, I need a real break to mentally recuperate," he says as he walks away.

"You rested all afternoon and evening. And don't think I didn't see you hitting on that dryad for much of that time." Isaac is following behind Daniel on the inside of the ring of sand, his hand raised as if he's running it along a wall.

"I'm out here now, ain't I? Would it kill you to show a bit of gratitude?" Daniel says as he returns to the starting point and closes the sand circle. It's larger than a standard magic circle, over two carts in diameter.

"Ugh, it's like you two are in junior high again." Hannah speaks in the most nasal voice of all of them. "Any breaks in the barrier, Ike?"

Isaac shakes his head. "Nope, it's good."

"One time." Daniel throws up his hands. "It was just the one time. And I caught it right away. We only aged a month—less than a month— probably."

"Well, excuse me if I don't want to go back to Krystal as an old man," says Isaac.

"You already are an old man," says Daniel.

"Enough!" shouts Hannah, and even Raskin-Souffy jumps. "Knock it off, or so help me." She glares at both of them. "Let's just get this stupid sacred tree planted, and we can get the hell out of here."

Whether responding to Hannah's orders or out of habit, the other two heroes spring into action. Hannah digs a hole in the center of the circle with a shovel. Isaac produces a seed and, after blessing it, drops it in the hole. Then Hannah covers it up. They take care not to disturb the sand line as they all retreat outside of the barrier. Daniel stands at the edge, waving his staff and chanting.

A film of iridescent purple and green rises up from the sand, firming up to create a barrier that stretches high into the sky. Time magic is usually invisible, so Souffy suspects Daniel has layered on some simple light spells to fancy it up. She isn't judging; it's standard wizard practice—Souffy has plans to add some sparkles to her own Fire Orb castings as well. The primary spell is evidently working too. Behind the barrier, the air changes; darkness lightens to gray, which, in turn, erupts into bright colors. Lumps become visible red-orange rocks sprinkled with light green lichen and the brown stumps of trees. The colors then deepen before muddling back into shadows, and as the sped-up day ends, blackness once more encroaches. The cycle repeats, faster this time. And again. And again. Until the patch of ground behind the translucent barrier flickers between night and day as if Souffy were rapidly blinking her eyes.

In the space just beyond Souffy-Raskin's bush, tiny green tendrils free themselves from the dirt, opening two leaves apiece to the heavens. A few more light pulses, and the ground is blanketed in green. Moments later, broadleaf plants unfurl and produce flowers; a whole lawn spreads out. And just as quickly as it bloomed, the magically accelerated patch of meadow begins to brown and wilt. Time speeds up to a point where days blur into weeks, to months. A blaze of autumn colors erupts only to be covered in white. Souffy watches winter snows build up and recede.

Spring returns to the world behind the barrier. The first seedling to punch up through the soil comes from the mound of dirt in the center of the ensorcelled space. It's already thick as her finger, and a green so intense it radiates a kind of light from inside itself. When its first leaves appear, Souffy sees that they're needles. The new sacred tree reaches higher, rising a foot, then two, above the other rapidly sprouting plants. It branches and fills in the space with more needles. Autumn comes, followed by winter. Amongst the white of the snow, the sacred tree stands out, a triangle of green like a miniature version of the spruce trees Paladin Wu insists on decorating each winter solstice.

Spring returns, and the sacred tree resumes its miraculous growth, this time emitting a palpable hum as it pulls vast quantities of mana from the air. Souffy-Raskin is enthralled, but the part of Souffy that's still herself detects a dissonant note that starts to feel like a toothache. By this point, summer is in full bloom behind the barrier, but the closest plants around the sapling turn brown, shrivel up, and fall away to dust. This wilting spreads haphazardly outward, seemingly along paths, like branches... or roots.

Souffy hears Isaac's voice. "Well that hasn't happened before." As he speaks, a prominent line of withered brown approaches the spot where Daniel is spellcasting. It reaches the barrier and Daniel startles; it's like he's been punched from below. He staggers to keep his balance.

"Daniel!" shouts Hannah as she draws her sword.

Daniel stops himself from falling into the barrier by throwing out his staff, slicing it through the film wall. Black smoke seeps out through the tear. Hannah charges towards her brother, but the wizard holds up his hand.

"Stop! The time barrier's been pierced," he manages to say before the smoke engulfs him and he collapses in a violent coughing fit.

"Isaac, do something!" Hannah says as she inches forward, her sword ready to slice.

Isaac folds his hands and bows his head. *"Hear me, O great Orthorus,"* he begins his incantation. Rays of golden light emanate from him, extending towards the torn barrier and pushing back the foul smoke. As Hannah lifts Daniel to his feet, he's already casting a new spell. This time he doesn't bother with a light show.

In front of their hiding place, Souffy sees individual grains that mark the edge of the barrier rise languidly as if straining against something more than just gravity. It isn't just the sand being affected. Souffy-Raskin's breath and movements feel slowed and turgid, like she's underwater.

"What are you doing?" asks Isaac, his voice gone deep, the syllables stretched out.

"When I say the word"—Daniel's voice is pitched low—"run." Souffy-Raskin's sense of self-preservation kicks in, and she pushes up to stand. It takes forever to get her limbs to respond.

"Shit, there's that druid kid!" says Hannah, turning to Souffy-Raskin. "I told you to stop following us!"

"I'll get him," says Isaac. Souffy-Raskin stretches up her hands, desperate for Isaac to save her. Each of his steps towards her takes longer, and Souffy fears time will stop altogether before Isaac can reach her. But reach her, he does. Like a dance, he picks her up and swings her over his shoulder.

"Now!" shouts Daniel, and they all pivot away from the barrier.

At first, it feels like they aren't moving at all. But then Isaac's foot comes down, and the pressure constraining Souffy-Raskin's breath lessens slightly. Isaac's next step comes quicker; it feels like the rope that's been holding them back is slackening. By the following step, Souffy-Raskin can raise her head to see what they're running from.

The grains of sand are no longer floating lazily—they're vibrating. She sees Daniel raise his hand and snap his fingers. The sand, along with the Slowdown spell Souffy knows he's cast on them, shoots back through the barrier. The first grains to enter the time-accelerated space explode into dust. More sand follows, clouding the air. It grows thick and still, like a dull fog, and Souffy can't see past it to what's happening inside.

Her world goes fuzzy, then black. It could be all that time-distortion magic, or perhaps young Raskin himself had passed out from overstimulation. Either way, the memory shifts to young Raskin awakening to the sound of the heroes bickering. Their voices are normal-nasally, so they must have outrun the spell after all.

"But why would the elves give us an evil sacred tree seed?" Hannah is saying. "They wanted us to restore the magic of this forest."

Someone has propped Souffy-Raskin's body up against a large rock. The Triad are sitting, or in Daniel's case, lying among a scattering of various-sized boulders. Raskin's memory tells her that they're in a different place than the earlier events, in the midst of some sort of talus slope.

"Maybe it was a test?" suggests Daniel.

"Or a mistake?" says Isaac. He's drinking from a flask that he hands off to his sister.

"If it was a mistake, they'd just pretend they'd meant it as a test all along. Bunch of stuck-up goyim." Hannah takes a swig from the flask.

"Even that archer you said was hot?" asks Isaac.

Hannah coughs, and the others laugh. "Maybe not Lanfaren," she admits.

Daniel sits up. "When we get back to our world, I'm never roleplaying as an elf ever again."

"I'll hold you to that," says Hannah. She playfully punches Daniel's shoulder. "Good thinking, reversing the time spell."

Daniel rubs his shoulder. "Couldn't have done it without Isaac."

"We're in this together," Isaac says, giving his brother a fist bump. The sun is rising, casting long shadows over the rocky landscape. Isaac looks to the north. "So, what are we going to do about the—what do we call it?"

"Doomsday Tree," says Daniel.

"Did you just make that up?"

"Yeah, sounds cool, right? My spell slowed down time, but it didn't stop it. At this rate, it's going to take the Doomsday Tree at least a thousand years to make it past the sapling stage, maybe five thousand before it matures enough to do any serious damage."

"Five thousand years should be plenty of time for the Divine Wisdom to rope in some otherworld schmucks into saving the world," says Isaac.

"But will it count as completing our quest?" asks Hannah. She looks at Daniel.

"Technically, we're just supposed to plant the trees and have them send mana back into the ley line system. Nine trees should be able to do that, right?"

"I hope so," says Isaac. "I really don't want to be sent on yet another Final Quest. I'm running out of time."

Hannah pats her brother on the back. "Don't worry. We'll get home before Krystal's due date. Don't want the kid coming into the world without their favorite aunt present."

"Or favorite uncle," Daniel chimes in. They all chuckle. Daniel turns to look north and says, "Do you think we should warn anybody about that tree?"

"You know how these things go. If we tell anyone, then a bad guy will somehow find out about it and try to use it as part of their evil plot," says Hannah. "Best not to say anything. Although I feel like we should do something to help the heroes who will eventually be sent to deal with the tree."

"I'll pray to Orthorus," says Isaac, "have him make a holy weapon we can leave here. Then I'll make a prophecy before we leave, to give enough clues for the future heroes to figure it out."

"We're good then, except for little Dennis the Menace over there," says Hannah.

"On it," says Daniel. He approaches Souffy-Raskin and raises his hand in front of her head. "*You must speak of this night to no one, and should anyone ask you about this part of the forest, you tell them there's nothing here.*" Then he flicks a finger at Souffy-Raskin's forehead.

A bout of pain breaks the spell. Souffy tumbles out of the memory and backwards into Kyle's arms. Or maybe it's just momentum from the headbutt Raskin had delivered to establish the initial connection. Either way, Kyle catches her easily. His arms are surprisingly muscular.

"You okay there, Souffy?" After she nods, he asks, "What did you find out?" It's as if he just assumes whatever she'd tried has worked. That, even more than his physical support, makes her feel warm inside.

She looks up at Kyle. "I have news that is good, and news that is bad. Which do you want to hear first?"

CHAPTER 46

Souffy

"Let's start with the good news," Kyle says as he helps Souffy regain her balance.

"Mayor Galam was right, the Triad of Valor did leave behind a magic weapon. It's for defeating the Doomsday Tree," says Souffy.

"What is the Doomsday Tree?"

"That's the bad news."

"Perhaps this conversation should continue somewhere more private?" Raskin stage-whispers. "The forest has ears, you know." His eyes seem clearer after having shared the memory. Or maybe reliving the reckless adventure of his youth has given Souffy a better understanding of the man.

Raskin leads them to his tent where someone has laid the table with a bowl of mashed apples, a pot of honey, and a loaf of bread still warm from the oven. Souffy's stomach growls at the sight, evidently having perceived the time spent in the memory as real. Raskin chuckles and offers the food to share. In between bites, Souffy narrates what she learned to Kyle.

When she finishes, he says, "So the Triad left a ticking time bomb in the forest, covered it up, and the Divine Wisdom still sent them home?"

"It appears so." When Souffy had experienced the events as young Raskin, the Triad's actions—even when they were chastising him—had been exciting and marvelous. Now back in her own mind, Souffy is less impressed, if also a bit pleased.

The Triad's missteps confirm the superiority of her own otherworld heroes. Kyle, Souffy is certain, would never have locked away a child's memories like that to hide his own mistake. Not that he would have had to; Oscar wouldn't have planted a magic seed without checking it first. And Tristan is too much of a hero not to have turned back to destroy the evil tree. Souffy returns to Kyle's question. "I suppose, if every quest were resolved completely, there'd be a lot less quests for everyone else."

"Quests like an ancient evil that no one even knew about being unleashed upon the world and—conveniently enough—there happens to be a holy weapon that can destroy it?" There isn't a hint of a smile on his face. But Souffy sees past the facade. He's just as excited at the prospect as she is. Now they're the ones Magic Missiving without words.

"Sometimes, the Divine Wisdom works in obvious ways." Souffy tries and fails to keep a serious face. "We still need to find the weapon, though."

"I know where it is." Raskin has been so quiet through this exchange that Souffy's forgotten all about him until he speaks again. "Wizard Daniel didn't spell me so I couldn't speak about the weapon. I never saw it, but I remember the location."

It's all coming together, thinks Souffy. Although she really hopes Raskin will simply show them the location on the map. Even Souffy recognizes the problem with taking an ancient and somewhat senile druid on a quest like this. It would be far less awkward (and more fun) if it were just the two of them—Kyle and her.

And the other Neverboylanders, of course. The Divine Wisdom wouldn't have summoned them all if each one of them didn't have some critical role to play in the quest.

"Do you think discovering the history of the Doomsday Tree and the existence of a holy weapon are enough," Souffy asks Kyle, "to convince the others?"

At the mention of his bandmates, Kyle's face goes blank. But just for a moment; then he's back to his normal, thoughtful self. "Probably. They'll believe you about unlocking Raskin's memory. When Cena and Arek come back, we could ask for some reinforcements, that will assuage Oscar's concerns. We'll have you do the proposing this time; Tristan can't say no to a cute girl. Not that your arguments aren't enough, just that, you know…" His voice trails off. Kyle is presenting the responsible course of action and he looks about as happy as Souffy feels whenever she has to be responsible about something.

"Or, we could get the weapon by ourselves." The words tumble out of her lips before she can rein them back. Now that she made the proposal, Souffy keeps talking, "And when we show it to the others, they'll understand—like you and I do—that rescuing my uncle and stopping the Doomsday Tree is what we're meant to do."

The words hang in the air, sounding silly to her. Kyle is certain to say no.

Instead, he turns to Raskin. "How far away is this weapon?"

"A day's travel." Well, that seals it, Souffy's impulsive plan won't work. "Or, just over an hour by druid deer," Raskin adds.

"Druid deer?" Souffy can't hold back a squeal. She's ridden one once, at a traveling carnival back when she was six years old. They only led her around a circle three times. But for those precious few moments, she'd felt herself a proud warrior princess.

"What's a druid deer?" asks Kyle.

Raskin chortles at this. He hobbles over to a chest, grabs a handful of leather straps, and motions for them to follow him out of the tent. He leads them away from the main camp, to the edge of the sacred tree's canopy.

Kyle starts to look a tad nervous. "Just so you know, I've never even ridden a horse."

"Riding a druid deer is nothing like riding a horse," Souffy assures him. "It's… magical."

They walk past the last of the sacred tree's supporting trunks and into a grove of white birches and bushy ferns. Raskin chooses this spot to stop and claps his hands three times. "*Nobre corcel, ven a min*," he says. Then he puts his fingers to his mouth and issues a wheezy, sputtering whistle. Moments later, there's a rustle in the ferns; two creatures emerge. They're the size of elk but with the oversized ears and sensitive eyes of deer. They have elegant antlers and thick ruffs of fur around their necks. The combined effect is one of grace and strength. Souffy knows heroes are supposed to act stoic and collected in these moments, but she can't stop herself from bouncing with delight. Druid deer!

The deer don't appear fazed by Souffy's enthusiasm. They wander over to where Raskin stands, lower their heads to his outstretched hand, and allow him to harness them with the leather straps he's been holding.

"That doesn't look very secure," Kyle says as Raskin cinches the straps. "And shouldn't there be a saddle?"

"You'll never fall off a druid deer," Raskin tells him. "Unless they want you to. In which case, a saddle would be of no help."

Souffy runs her hands through the thick mane on the deer's neck before vaulting up and throwing one leg over to straddle her steed. Even without stirrups, she feels secure and grounded. Her hair roots tingle as some of the deer's energy and mana flows through her. Druid deer aren't telepathic, but they bond with their rider, blurring the distinction between animal and human. Souffy instinctively knows her deer is male and named Vaclet.

"Do you have a map?" Kyle asks Raskin.

"The deer know where to go." He offers Kyle a frail hand. Kyle wisely demurs and clambers (perhaps not as gracefully as Souffy) onto his deer.

"This is seriously weird," he says once he's fully seated. "Souffy, is it supposed—" The rest of his sentence is lost to the wind as the two deer launch themselves into the woods.

Souffy's deer takes the lead. She thinks she can hear Kyle screaming behind her, but the whoosh of air past her ears drowns him out. Vaclet springs upward and then dives down, his hooves thrumming on the ground. He ricochets off rocks and trees. It would have been excruciating, but the magic that guides the deer and keeps her from careening into trees also keeps Souffy pasted to his back. She becomes an extension of Vaclet's body, and they move in unison, not opposition.

Kyle's deer catches up, and the two creatures dart between trees, drawing close and then scattering apart in a joyful race. As she grows accustomed to her steed's movements, Souffy steals a glance at Kyle. He has one hand on his hat, the other wrapped around his deer's neck, and he's looking at her with pleading eyes. They're going too fast to talk so Souffy twirls her earring to Magic Missive.

"Are you getting the knack for it?" she asks.

"Does this look like me getting the knack?" he shoots back.

"Maybe try asking your deer to slow down. Not with words, just… think slow thoughts."

Kyle's eyes don't lose their wild look, but he manages a short nod. Over the next few minutes, Souffy notices both their deer's frantic paces lessen. They're still leaping gracefully, but in a straighter line. Tentatively, Kyle loosens his vise grip on his hat and sits more upright, both hands now on the harness.

"Better?" Souffy Magic Missives. They're still traveling at a speed that on a horse would be an all-out gallop.

"I've been through worse, like the time we had to ride jet skis for a soda commercial, but that still doesn't mean I'm liking it. Thanks for the suggestion, though."

Souffy wonders what a jet ski is. But there's something she's even more curious about. "When Raskin first found us, he mentioned a magic map that could identify blight locations. He said it was thanks to you. Why did he say that?"

"Oh, yeah, that." Over several Magic Missives, Kyle relates the story of how he combined wizard and forest magic along with techniques that sound suspiciously mathematical, while also matching wits with a dryad. Kyle keeps trying to trivialize his accomplishments, but Souffy can see enjoys answering her question.

When she has a clear picture of what transpired, she says, "If you'd explained all that to Tristan and the others, I bet they would have been more receptive when you suggested finding my uncle."

"I think me geeking out on wizard stuff would have had the opposite effect."

"No, they really respect how smart you are." While Kyle was away, the Neverboylanders had told her several Kyle stories, most of which called out his intelligence. Perhaps Cole and Micah had poked fun at Kyle, but it was good-natured (mostly).

"Smart, but not in a useful way. The stuff I learned when I went off to school isn't applicable for a music act. As far as Never Boy Land is concerned, I'm kind of extra."

Souffy starts to protest.

Kyle cuts in, "It's not that they don't care about me, or want me to be a part of the band. It's just… like you and your family, they expect you to be a certain sort of person, right?"

Souffy nods. As a child, it was expected that she'd become an accomplished wizard. As each of her magical failures proved that course less likely, she'd been relegated to smaller and smaller roles in the family until they finally washed their hands of her altogether and sent her packing to Bydlo. Proving to them that she has become a competent adventuring evocation wizard was going to be difficult, if not impossible.

"Same for me. NBL's like a family, and I'm the sibling who doesn't quite fit in. I'm not emotionally supportive enough for Oscar, not musical enough for Micah, way too much of a nerd for Cole, and Tristan…" Kyle shakes his head. "I'm not sure what's going on with him these days. He's a celebrity; they're different than regular people. But that's just how it is. It's okay." As he relates these things through Magic Missive, the deer draw close enough for Souffy to hear Kyle sigh and say aloud, "I'm okay with that."

All this while, their druid steeds had been following a twisting brook upstream. As the ground slope steepens, the deer slow their pace. Their hooves beat out a staccato pattern as they spring from rock to rock between rapids. The stream narrows, bringing them to a picturesque waterfall cascading down a rocky ledge a bit taller than Souffy.

"Should we get off or—" Kyle swallow-gasps as his deer leaps vertically to the ledge above. Vaclet follows. The glorious moment of weightlessness before his hooves connect with the ledge convinces Souffy to learn the Fly spell once she levels up enough.

The source of the waterfall turns out to be a large, shallow pool, its surface shimmering silver in the afternoon sun. Souffy is about to comment on the delightfulness of the scene but the words turn to ash in her mouth when she spies two unnatural creatures on the far bank. *Blights*, her brain supplies. A walking-blight with a serpentine neck scans the forest behind the pond as a swamp thing oozes vines over the scraggly bushes that hug the water's edge.

We haven't yet been seen, she thinks to herself. She and Kyle could just sneak past. Even if they were spotted, the blights are on the opposite bank, and the deer could easily outrun them. They are already on a quest; no reason to engage in unnecessary combat. Yes, sneaking past is the sensible approach—responsible. Souffy catches Kyle's eye and sees his smirk.

"Which one do you want to take?" he whispers.

"Swamp thing." She grins back and reaches into her pouch for her firestarters.

"*Sagitta-inspira*," Kyle intones, and with a snap, he fires his first magic bolts through the walking-blight's neck, sending its head flying.

"*Great Ball of Fire!*" Souffy shouts ecstatically and watches the resulting cheery-orange orb burn through the swamp thing even as Kyle's remaining projectiles topple the walking-blight. It doesn't get up.

"High five!" Kyle nudges his deer closer to hers. He raises his hand, facing the palm to her. Souffy mimics his actions and looks expectantly. Kyle leans out over his mount to lightly slap her hand. "Otherworld custom," he explains sheepishly as he hops to the ground.

"Oh, like a fist bump." She slips off her deer and looks appreciatively at the mayhem their magical attack has wrought: scattered bits of broken tree limbs and smoldering heaps of leaves cover the far bank. The battle was over no sooner than it began.

"Nice smiting, Kyle."

"This looks more like the work of a disgruntled gardener than a pair of wizards," says Kyle as he surveys the remains of the corpses, but he appears pleased with himself.

What's left of the swamp thing begins to vibrate and shudder, but it isn't the monster; it's the scrubby plants beneath it. Souffy recognizes them. "Rolling thistle bush," she says, pointing. And now that she's spotted one, Souffy realizes that there are at least twenty around the edge of the pond.

"Why are they called—" Kyle begins as the dead swamp thing's vines fall away, and the bushes begin rotating like wagon wheels across the water's surface. "Never mind. Looks like they're headed our way."

"I can cast two more Fire Orbs, for certain this time," says Souffy.

"Can you redirect the fire once you send it out?"

"I think so."

"Then we might get by with just one," says Kyle. "Come this way."

Souffy follows him along the water's edge to where a shallow but rapid stream feeds into the pool. The rolling thistle bush blights (*we really need a shorter name*, Souffy thinks) seem to sense their movement and clump together before changing direction towards the wizards' new position.

"Wait till they hit the current in the center of the pool." Kyle points to the spot. "Then Fire Orb the first blight and I'll line the rest of them up so you can shift the flame to them all before the spell runs out."

Souffy does so. Since the blight's outer branches are already wet, it doesn't flare up as readily as the swamp thing did. Soon enough though, her flame penetrates to the plant's center, and she hears the distinctive woosh as the magical fire catches properly. Kyle has summoned his Phantom Hand and positions it to shove other blights into the already burning one. Between the hand, Souffy's control of her fire, and the stream's current, there's soon a sizable and quite merry bonfire floating in the pond. Eventually, the blights are reduced to charred skeletons, which are then carried away by the current over the falls.

"High five!" Souffy shouts. Kyle fumbles to get his hand up as Souffy whips hers towards him. The resounding clap echoes off the rocks.

"Ouch," squawks Kyle. But he smiles as he shakes out his hand. "We make a good team."

"We do," agrees Souffy. They're standing next to each other. *We're the same height*, thinks Souffy as she looks straight into Kyle's eyes. Gentle blue eyes, the color of a summer sky, but with a shimmer, so maybe like a perfectly calm lake reflecting that sky—Souffy doesn't usually think in metaphors. The real Kyle isn't placid like that lake, though. He has worries, regrets, and doubts, just like Souffy; but he also has the patience, quick thinking, and confidence to overcome those insecurities.

When they're together—like now—it feels like those good qualities of his flow over into her, and Souffy feels grounded in a way that she never did around Havelin, Arek, or Tristan. With Tristan, it's like her feet don't touch the ground, which is also fantastic, but not like this. And Tristan doesn't have such pretty blue eyes.

It's because she's considering Kyle's eyes (and also because of the wide brim of his hat) that Souffy doesn't notice the rolling thistle brush blight hurtling through the air behind Kyle. It isn't until the creature is less than a few feet away that she catches sight of the thorns glistening with their unnaturally fluorescent orange sap. Too late to do anything but gasp in horror.

Kyle turns into the attacking monster; its nearest thorns almost raking his perfect face. Souffy gasps as she recalls law number six: *Never damage the face!*

But before this iron-clad law of boy bands can be transgressed, there's a flash of metal, and the blight separates cleanly into two halves that fall harmlessly to either side of the stunned wizard. Kyle jumps back, practically into Souffy's arms. In the place where the blight had launched itself at Kyle, there's now a sword. And holding that sword is Tristan. His cheeks are flushed, and he's breathing heavily, but otherwise he's as fresh as the morning dew.

Kyle looks between Tristan and Souffy, his expression a mix of relief, confusion, and frustration. Souffy knows exactly how he feels.

CHAPTER 47

Kyle

Okay, credit given where credit is due. Tristan knows how to make an entrance. We're… how many miles away from the druid camp? A lot, I'm guessing (I don't think druid deer travel normally through space-time). And all of a sudden, completely and unexpectedly, there's Tris, swinging his sword and taking out the monster. It reminds me of several scenes from his action movie. All that's missing is the facile quip to top it off.

"Glad I caught up with you guys." Aaaaand, there it is.

Souffy's just standing there, speechless. Before we get to the inevitable tearful reunion bit complete with rapturous gushing, I ask, "How exactly did you get here, Tristan?"

"Ashely sent me." Seeing my confusion, he adds, "You know, the green and purple lady?"

"Ashenfal, the tree dryad," I correct him. I look around to see if she's followed us too. No one's obviously lurking in the tree shadows, which have stretched out in the late afternoon sun. I'm suddenly aware of just how much time has passed since we left Raskin.

"Right, Ashen Gal." Great, so now he thinks she's a superhero. "She showed us that blight map you made."

"You need to start learning people's names," I snap. I know I shouldn't be chewing out the guy who just saved me, but Souffy and I were having a moment back there. At least, I think we were.

"And you need to keep us in the loop about what you're up to," Tristan snaps back. He leans in, his sword still raised. Awkward. Tristan re-sheaths the weapon, his eyes never leaving mine, and says, "We couldn't find you anywhere in the camp, you just disappeared."

"We were collecting evidence," says Souffy. "Like you asked us to."

What I wouldn't give for Souffy's total absence of guilt when justifying her impulsive actions. It's a superpower even Tristan knows not to mess with. I guess that's why he keeps his focus on me.

"How come you didn't tell us that you were the one to come up with the magic map spell that finds blights, Kyle?"

"Because…" Maybe Souffy was right about them respecting my abilities, but post-fight endorphins are still coursing through my veins, so I snark, "It doesn't find blights. It detects fluctuations in the flow of mana through the forest and the absence of mana correlates with—I see your eyes glazing over, Tris." They aren't really, but Tristan's scrunched up forehead means he's failing to grasp the basic principle. "That's why I didn't bother trying to explain it."

"You didn't need to explain anything, just tell us about it. We'd have believed you."

He's angry. That's fine, I'm angry right back at him.

"Would me taking credit for the map have convinced you guys to go on a quest to find Ferimus?"

Tris looks like he wants to say yes, but we both know he'd be lying. I realize I don't actually want to stay mad at him. I'm not ready to admit it yet, but I'm glad he's here.

"So, you just decided to run off on the quest on your own?" he asks.

Given where we are, the druid-deer peacefully munching on a patch of grass nearby, and the dead blights scattered all around us, his question is purely rhetorical.

"We're going to find evidence," Souffy insists. "We discovered there's an evil sacred tree called the Doomsday Tree. It's in the same location where the blight infestation started. There has to be a connection. And the Triad of Valor left a magic weapon that can defeat the tree. We're going to collect the weapon and bring it back so we can all go on the quest together, right Kyle?"

"That was the plan." Not that I ever really believed it would stay that simple. I should at least have left a note for the rest of the crew. "Sorry, we thought we'd be back sooner."

Tristan glances between us, frowning. "Oh… okay." Either Souffy's explanation or my apology has mollified him. He seems relieved for an excuse not to be angry anymore too, and his expression brightens with resolve. "In that case, let's go together and find this weapon!" He looks expectantly at the water's edge.

"We haven't reached the spot yet," Souffy explains. "The deer were taking us there." And herein lies the fundamental problem with Tristan being here, now, like this: two deer, three heroes. "I suppose," she adds weakly, "we could walk the rest of the way? Surely, we're almost there."

Famous last words. The deer seem agreeable to this new arrangement, becoming our guides rather than steeds, but their choice of route: random stream crossings, clinging to narrow rock ledges, gaily jumping over thickets of prickly bushes, leaves a lot to be desired. Along the way we fill Tristan in on the details. Since I've already been through my part with Souffy, I let her do the talking. She makes me sound good.

"Does anything here look familiar?" I ask Souffy. The sun has by now sunk behind the mountains and the sky is turning a dusky gray.

"No, there were plenty more rocks in the memory. It was a field of boulders on a slope." That sounds like it's on the side of a mountain, and we're still very much in the forest. I'm suspecting that Raskin might have been optimistic about the distance involved.

Someone has to say it, and it looks like it's me. "I don't think we're going to get there tonight. Should we make camp here?"

"I guess we'll have to," says Souffy.

"Cool," says Tristan. "I've never been camping in a magical forest before." He says this like it's a good thing. "Oh, and I brought supplies."

I had noticed he was hauling a knapsack. He now opens it up to reveal a bed roll, a pot with table settings for one, a bundle of dried rations, an ax, a length of rope, and a flint for starting a fire (not that we'd need the last with Souffy around).

"I'll go find some firewood," she offers. "You boys can make camp."

In our world, one "makes camp" by setting up tents, inflating air mattresses, and unrolling sleeping bags. Here we just pick a flattish space alongside a fallen tree, because shelter or something.

My attempts to tie up the deer for the night fail; a bob of their heads and the rope I've tied around their necks magically slips off. I feed them some of the dry oats from Tristan's stash, and they settle themselves down. Hopefully they'll stay around until the morning. I still have no idea how Raskin called them to him in the first place. I should have asked him before we left. I should have asked him for a map.

While I'm wrangling the deer, Tristan gathers rocks to make a fire pit. He grunts as he heaves a flat one with a little too much energy, and I turn just in time to see it slip out of his hands.

"*Dexterarious*." Out shoots my Phantom Hand, catching the stone before it slams into Tristan's foot.

"Wow," says Tristan as the hand whisks the stone around the pit. "You're pretty amazing with that magic hand spell."

My impulse is to correct him: it's a cantrip, not a spell. *Oh, just take the compliment*, I tell myself. "Thanks." Since I've materialized the hand, I send it to roll a few larger stones closer to the fire pit to serve as seats. Now would be a good time to apologize for blowing up at Tristan for the messenger bird thing. But when I glance at him, he's got that stretched, pained expression from earlier when we were arguing and my words fly from my mind.

"Kyle"—I brace myself for whatever is coming next—"you're really good at magic." He takes a deep breath while I hold mine. "And at figuring out how this world works, you've gotten solid at slaying monsters, too." All that praise makes me feel guilty.

"I still shouldn't have gone off without telling you guys."

"No, it's okay, I get it. You're trying to save the forest and fulfill our mission. While me and the others, we just want to go home and do our world tour."

It's not that I don't think Tristan is being genuine. His admiration is real. But it comes down to that same line—chasm really. It's me with my geeky heroing on one side and Tristan and NBL on the other.

"Nothing wrong with a world tour," I say, trying to bridge the distance.

"Yeah, for someone like me." A celebrity, a performer, a star. "But you hated touring."

"No, I didn't." Well, actually… "Okay, maybe I wasn't exactly thrilled by the constant travel or the grueling show schedules." Or how our handlers kept a spreadsheet to plan and track all the clothing we wore, or that we had to come up with at least three PR-approved social media posts each day. That part was awful. "But Marjorie said it wasn't going to be like that this time."

Tristan doesn't look convinced.

"I signed up for the comeback tour, didn't I?"

"Only because I asked you to! You ghosted Marjorie after she emailed you about getting the band back together and you were ignoring my texts. I had to call you up and beg you to say yes."

"You didn't beg, Tris. You convinced me." The way I remember it was Tristan excitedly telling me how he and the others had signed on. That it wasn't just going to be a nostalgia tour, that Never Boy Land was going to be even bigger this time. It would be Tristan's fan base, along with Oscar's voice and Micah's musical genius and Cole's stage presence. And me, if I wanted a spot. "How could I say no to the adrenaline rush of performing while basking in the adoration of our fans?"

"You said no before. You left show business and went to college on the other side of the country."

Harsh, but true, to an extent. I realize I've never explained my decision to him—to anyone besides Marjorie. My excuse was I just said I needed some time out of the spotlight. I take a deep breath and Tristan looks at me even more intensely.

"When the band formed, we were fourteen, just out of middle school. For seven years, a frighteningly large percentage of the Earth's population knew me as Kyle Moretti of Never Boy Land. And then the band broke up and I realized that if I didn't do something, I was going to be Kyle Moretti, former member of Never Boy Land, for the rest of my life. I don't have the musical abilities the rest of you have to accomplish anything significant by myself in the showbiz world. I was twenty-one; I wanted to prove, to myself as much as everyone else, that I could do something on my own. I figured getting a degree from an Ivy League school could be that something, for my Wikipedia page if nothing else."

Tristan doesn't look so sure. "I thought you might have regretted being in the band. Not having a normal life."

"What? No. Never. Never!" I repeat myself. "Normal lives are boring. Being with the band, being with you guys, it was the best time of my life." I'm trying to convince Tristan, but the sincerity behind the words surprises me. "College was good, but honestly it was rather predictable, being in the same place for months on end, wearing the same clothes. College parties aren't how they're portrayed in the movies. In reality, they're incredibly lame, and"—I'm wading into some scary-honest territory—"most of the time, I was lonely. I missed hanging out with you guys."

"For reals?"

"Yes, Tris, for reals. Why do you think I spent so much time playing *Heroes Summoning*?"

He doesn't laugh, but he sounds more like himself when he says, "I missed the band too. The solo albums, the tours, the acting, it was just work.

Never Boy Land was family, for me at least. You guys became like brothers to me."

Being an only child, Tris was pretty much my brother since we met. The others took some getting used to. But after the first six months of living together, Micah was definitely the bratty younger sibling, Cole was the prankster, and Oscar's band role literally made him the responsible older brother. And, thinking over the past week, none of that has changed.

"Mythreal might not be a world tour, but we're having some quality bonding time, right?" I finally elicit a smile from Tristan.

He laughs. "When we're not at each other's throats."

"That's what bonding looks like with us."

We become quiet for a moment. Then I ask. "We good now?" I definitely had my cathartic moment for the day.

Tristan's still chewing on his lip. There's something else on his mind. "I don't feel obligated to include you in all the opportunities I'm offered, Kyle."

Whoa, that came out of nowhere.

"I never said—" Except that I did, to Souffy. "You were eavesdropping when you were turned to stone!"

His sheepish grin says it all. "Listen, Kyle, I was grateful to you for being my first friend in elementary school. And I guess I did make a bunch of friends later on, but you were my best friend. Always. You were the smartest and coolest and bravest, I'd never have left Portland to sign on with Marjorie if you weren't coming too." He takes a big breath. "I know we're not close like that anymore—"

"We are," I cut him off. There's something fragile in the way he's looking at me, a bit of the dorky first-grade Tristan peeking out from under the handsome hero. "We are close. We've been literally saving each other's lives this past week. That's the most acceptable form of deep heterosexual male friendship there is. And before that, we were in a boy band together." And because all that's more than true, I reach out and hug him. Not an easy feat given the plate mail he's wearing. "We're best friends. We're BFFs."

"BFFFs," says Tristan, hugging me back. The hard edges of his armor dig painfully into my cheek, which reminds me how this conversation started.

I pull back and ask, "Tris, when you were turned to stone, did you have access to any other senses?" Did he see me wrangling that stupid rooster?

"Well, I couldn't see because my eyes were closed." Phew. "I don't remember if I could smell. But touch," his cocky grin is back, "I totally felt Souffy's kiss."

There's a clatter of dropped sticks behind us. "Aaaahhh!" Souffy's voice wavers between a scream and a wail. Her hands are shaking erratically—not something you want to see in your fireball-wielding wizard. Luckily for Tristan, Souffy's embarrassment wins out over her outrage and she dashes back into the woods.

"Better run after her and apologize," I say.

"You're the smart one," he says as he takes my advice and starts after her.

CHAPTER 48

Kyle

Tristan comes back in one piece: not even a single hair out of place, let alone singed, and with a bounce to his step. I shouldn't be surprised. If he wasn't so good at soothing women's hurt feelings, he'd have accumulated a lot more angry exes. Souffy's back as well, but she's harder to read. She informs me that Tristan's punishment for not properly thanking her for breaking the petrification curse is to chop firewood. So either Souffy's finally over her schoolgirl crush on Tristan, or they're dating. I've never understood his love life.

Tristan drags a midsize tree back to the campsite and goes full lumberjack on it. Souffy's in charge of the fire. Because we don't have a fire grate, I'm using my Phantom Hand to hold up the pot with soup for our dinner. The ingredients are dried noodles and something wrapped in wax paper that smells like peat moss—Souffy assures me it's a bouillon cube. I'm not convinced, but the longer the broth simmers, the better it smells.

Tristan's ax neatly splits a slab trunk in two. "Showoff," I say. I'm not referring to the flying bark chips, rather that Tristan's stripped down to his lightweight undershirt, now open at the front. Every time he lifts the ax over his head, Souffy sneaks a peek.

"Not really." Tristan throws back his head, shakes his hair out. Maybe this performance is his real peace offering to Souffy. "I just got stronger."

"You definitely have been working out." He's almost as ripped now as he appeared in his movie (I know for a fact that they used CGI to give him that six pack).

"No, I mean like since yesterday. This morning I woke up feeling faster, more fluid. Like I have something extra I could bring to a fight."

"Do you think you leveled up?" asks Souffy. She uses the opportunity to give Tristan an appraising look as he finishes splitting the last piece of kindling.

"Did you seriously just say 'leveled up?'" I ask. I should be acclimated by this point to Mythreal's gleeful embrace of anachronisms picked up from otherworld heroes, but game mechanics terms are just too on the nose.

Souffy fails to pick up on my snark, and explains, "It's a well-documented phenomenon that many ascribe to intercession from the Divine Wisdom." She's in full textbook regurgitation mode. "When an adventurer or magic user has accrued enough experiences, they may rapidly develop new skills or affinities. The specifics depend on one's class. For instance, when a wizard levels up, they master one or two new major arcana spells with almost no effort."

New spells? I now wonder if that's why I was able to create my mana distribution detection spell.

"You mean Kyle could get a new spell, like your Fire Orb?" Tristan joins us by the fire and Souffy scoots over to make room for him.

"Or some other spell," says Souffy, sounding less than thrilled by that suggestion. I'm guessing she likes being our exclusive fire mage. "I think the soup's ready."

I command the Phantom Hand to pour. We don't have much in the way of containers, or silverware for that matter. Tristan gives Souffy the bowl and spoon, I get the mug and fork, which leaves Tris with the pot and knife.

"Actually, there was one spell you had in your book that looked intriguing: Find Familiar," I say. The soup has somehow acquired chunks of potatoes and carrots, confirming my suspicion that the bouillon cube was indeed magic.

"You should absolutely find a familiar, Kyle. All proper wizards have one," says Souffy.

"What's a familiar?" asks Tristan, skewering with his knife a piece of what looks like meat.

Souffy turns to Tristan. "It's a helper spirit that takes the physical form of an animal. It communicates with its master telepathically and can even aid with spells."

"Do you have one?" asks Tristan just as Souffy takes a sip of the soup.

She squeezes her eyes and shudders like she's tasted something vile. "I prefer not to think about mine. Every time I've summoned him, no matter what my desired animal—I've tried cat, fish, sparrow, and rat—he always shows up as a spider. I don't usually hate spiders, but Mordred's hairy and"—she spreads her hands—"this big." I hope she's indicating Mordred's leg span, not the girth of its carapace. "I refuse to call him unless I'm being tested, and even then…" Another shudder.

"A creature that flies would be useful," I say.

Souffy nods with approval. "Like a hawk, or an eagle."

"Or a great white snowy owl, you could name it Hedwig." Tristan grins at Souffy but she doesn't catch the reference.

"How about a raven? They're a common enough bird, so it wouldn't raise suspicions. And, in our world at least, they're fairly intelligent," I say.

As we finish dinner, Souffy and Tristan offer up more avian suggestions and the conversation devolves into a game of which Earth birds are also present in Mythreal. Souffy's never heard of ostriches, but penguins and passenger pigeons are both known. I only half listen to the conversation; I've already decided on a raven.

While Tristan cleans up, Souffy pulls out her spellbook. Dusk is long gone and it's now full-on dark out, so she casts her Will-O-Wisps by humming the chorus to "Never Gonna Give You Up." *Curse you, Cole, you've Rickrolled fantasyland.* Souffy's notes for Find Familiar are exceptionally disorganized. She's crossed out and written over large portions of the spell multiple times, probably in vain attempts to de-arachnify it. Despite the resulting mess, the words and critical details jump out at me and I have no problem copying the spell into my own book. Less than an hour later, I have it down.

"You're going to cast it now?" Souffy asks.

It's getting late. We should really turn in. But Souffy's grinning at me with anticipation and excitement. "Sure, why not."

"Cool, magic!" Tristan comes over like he's expecting a stage show. No pressure.

Souffy unpacks a small travel brazier and some incense that smells of sandalwood and patchouli. For herbs she hands me dried thyme and oregano from our food rations.

"Beginner level spells are a lot more forgiving about the particulars, it just needs to smell good to attract the spirit," says the woman who keeps unintentionally summoning spiders.

"Now what?" asks Tristan.

"I meditate." Technically the spell calls for choosing a repetitive chant in order to make one's mind receptive to the presence of the spirit realm, but I think I can achieve the same effect with the techniques I picked up from a mindfulness rec class I took sophomore year. I remind myself of the details: settle into a comfortable position, sit up straight, relax my shoulders, focus on my breath, and slip into a state of open awareness. Or try to. After five minutes of attempting to ignore an obvious distraction, I give up.

"Tristan," I say, eyes still closed.

"Yes Kyle?"

"I can hear your breathing. Go check the camp perimeter or something."

"Okay." He chuckles as he gets up, like he's won a contest.

"I'll come with, and cast an Alarm spell," I hear Souffy volunteer. I guess he has.

Back to meditation. After a minute I catch myself debating whether I've properly quieted my thoughts and whether thinking about quieting my thoughts counts as a thought. That's when I feel something bump into my upper arm and the nerve to my elbow momentarily goes numb. My eyes fly open, but there's nothing there. A spirit!

I return to the practice. This time when something grazes my wrist, I only flinch a bit. Soon more spirits join in: a pushing against my stomach, a tapping on my cheek, and what feels like a small animal walking over my leg. There's a kind of over-the-blanket feel to their touches, like they're pushing through another plane of existence. I get the uncomfortable feeling that I'm being examined, judged. Which is all but confirmed as several of the stronger presences lose interest and leave. But there's one bit of energy, something light and not-evil feeling, circling me.

It's curious.

Eyes still closed, I raise my hands over the brazier and sense an energy gathering between my palms. It's like touching a Van de Graaff generator. My skin tingles and I feel the hairs on my arms rise up.

What am I to be? the spirit asks.

In my mind, I picture a large black bird, making sure the beak is hooked like a raven's and not straight like a crow's. I open my eyes and see the smoke from the burned incense forming a bird. The plumes gain substance and thicken into tangible detail—individual feathers, talons, beady eyes. When everything looks right, I seal the connection.

"*Welcome Friend.*" There are more authoritative greetings, but I don't want that kind of relationship with my familiar.

The spell turns sparkly and the now perfectly formed raven flaps its wings, rising phoenix-style above the embers. It circles the fire, lands by my side, and cocks its head at me expectantly. I have some bread ready and hold it out. The spirit-raven snatches at the crust and scarfs it down. I get a distinct impression that it would have preferred meat. But for now, we're both content to sit and bask in the spell's afterglow.

Footsteps approach. "Is that your familiar?" Tristan's back with Souffy in tow.

"Great job, Kyle," says Souffy. "Now you need to name her, or, is it a him?"

"Her." Familiar telepathy isn't like the voice in my head when Souffy sends Magic Missive. Instead, there's an abstract idea that my brain converts into images and words.

"A girl? You've totally got to name her Tinkerbell," says Tristan. "Our fans will go wild!" He sits down and my familiar regards him with beady raven eyes.

"We are not naming her—"

"Tinkerbell, Tinkerbell!" my familiar squawks happily.

"She talks!" Souffy claps her hands. "That's fantastic. I thought only parrot familiars were capable of human speech. And what a pretty name, Tinkerbell."

I'm outvoted. "Fine. But she goes by Bell, okay?"

Bell hops towards Tristan and flutter-jumps onto his knee. "Ahh, she likes me," he coos.

"All females like you, Tris."

Tristan flashes a big smile at this. I catch a glimpse of it through Bell's eyes. I'm not sure if it's bird or spirit vision, but there are more colors in it than my brain is used to dealing with. Tristan's smile somehow appears extra brilliant as rendered in those additional colors.

His image keeps popping into my head as I try to fall asleep. And leads to me replay our earlier heart-to-heart. Tris didn't say it outright, but he thinks I won't be returning home with them. I can't say I haven't thought about it. But every time the idea of staying behind came to mind, I pushed it down, unexamined. Maybe it's high time to examine it properly.

"There's no place like home" is the primary motivation for fictional characters who find themselves in another world to return. Fictional, meaning the creators have never left their own world. Or, maybe they did. But in that case they also came back to their own world, so there's some selection bias going on.

Practically speaking, I'm an only child, so not coming back would be a shitty thing to pull on my moms. Also, I'm under contract to Marjorie's agency, not that I think the entertainment lawyers could enforce anything in this case. Then there's the band itself, and Tris.

But does any decision I make now even matter? I could die fighting the Doomsday Tree, or the Divine Wisdom could line up more quests for us before letting us leave. A few more months here and maybe I'll be as ready to return home as the Bernstein siblings had been.

There are too many unknowns to lose sleep over. So, I don't.

I wake up the next morning to find that my druid deer has indeed wandered off (can't say I'm heartbroken to see him gone). Fortunately, Souffy's deer, who deigned to stay behind, seems agreeable to helping us. It doesn't really change our plans: we only need a single deer to lead us, and, once the weapon is in our hands, to ride back with it, then we convince Ashenfal to use her magic to retrieve the rest of us for the ensuing showdown.

We pack up what little there is of our camp, make sure the fire is completely put out, and set out to follow our solitary guide deer who leads us up a slope and out of the deep forest. Deer, at least druid deer, don't seem to understand the concept of switchbacks, and the next hour of uphill makes me grateful, for once, that wizards aren't saddled with armor. It's drier up here, the leafy trees giving way to hardier firs and cedars, their dark green needles contrasting with the relatively barren ground underneath. We're still proceeding uphill, but gradually and at a slant.

Above us, Bell hops from tree to tree. Our magical connection allows me to reach out, to experience her flying. It's more awkward than I'd have imagined. It seems to involve constant trimming of wing angles, interspersed with frantic flapping as Bell adjusts to the air currents. Perhaps her awkwardness is because she's new to her physical form, or because she's staying low in the trees, not soaring in the open sky.

I have to be careful not to focus too much on Bell or I forget my own feet and trip myself up. So I just check in briefly and receive snatches of what she's seeing. In the distance ahead of us the mountains loom and the trees give way to stretches of bare rock. Bell's also checking out the forest and wildlife below—I had no idea there were so many squirrels around. It's easy to identify our party; my red hat makes for an excellent target. I'm debating taking it off when I catch a glimpse of something that's definitely not a squirrel.

Either Bell picks up on my interest or she's just naturally curious, because her eyes immediately lock on the spot. The thing moves. There's a hunched, lurking quality to the creature that makes me think of Cornelius. But it's not a raccoon.

Bigger, not so furry, Bell sends. Apparently, she can read my thoughts as well. I stop walking and close my eyes to give her my full attention.

The creature is downhill from us, at least one hundred yards to the west. And it's some kind of animal, not a mutated plant monster. Perhaps a wild pig? I tell Bell to check it out and she obliges, keeping just below the canopy. The image she sends back is definitely not that of a pig.

My first impression is a trashed doll, like one that's been abandoned in the park all winter long. Its joints are outsized and knobby, the skin between them stretched and flabby, green with brown highlights, or perhaps it's just filthy. It's wearing some sort of pelt wrapped around its pot belly and an animal skull hat that hides its face. Bell drops from her branch, swooping low over the creature, causing it to jerk its head up to look at her. I finally get a clear view of a beaky nose, sharp teeth, black button eyes, and pointy ears.

"It's a goblin," I say aloud.

CHAPTER 49

Kyle

"Goblin?" squeaks Souffy. "Where?"

I jump out of Bell's viewpoint and back into my own, just in time to see Tristan spin around to look back at us. His foot catches, he topples backwards. Something snaps and I see a rope snake up a tree at the same time as a collection of objects clatters noisily down.

I give us all props for our reactions. Both Souffy and I are readying spells, while Tristan literally bounces back to his feet by executing a kick up, in full armor no less—I don't think that's physically possible in our world. We strike an eye-catching movie-poster tableau, not that the items that fell (some rusted armor, a wagon wheel, and half a cauldron) need taking down. Tristan, shield at the ready, walks over and gives the armor a poke with the business end of his sword, just in case.

When nothing happens, he asks, "What was this junk doing up in a tree?"

"It's a warning system," Souffy explains. "If there are other goblins around—" Further elaboration isn't necessary as I hear a woosh and I suddenly find myself hatless. I throw up a magic shield in front of Souffy and me just in time to intercept the next arrow. Tristan takes cover behind a tree.

"Where are they coming from?" he asks.

Souffy points in a slightly different direction from Bell's location. Of course, it's never just one goblin. There's an incline nearby housing several boulders, a fallen tree, and a bush, any one of which could be hiding our attackers. I check in with Bell, but the goblin she'd been tracking has vanished. I mentally call her back to fly over the potential positions of our ambushers. She alights on a nearby tree, giving me a clear view.

"Two goblins behind the bush," I report. "Maybe another coming this way, I'm not sure."

"I've got this." Souffy jumps up and shouts, *"Great Ball of Fire!"* The resulting sphere is at least a half a foot larger than yesterday's; it instantly engulfs the bush, the dried leaves going up in crackly sparkles. The goblins spring out from behind it like popcorn. One, charred to a brisket, staggers to the ground and stays there. The other, just a bit singed, bounces and rolls down the hill. Tristan's running after them, and takes a good slice out of the goblin's side even as they attempt to get up.

"Curse you, Lyr's spawn!" the goblin spits out as Tristan readies his next swing.

Tristan freezes. "Wait, they can talk?"

The goblin doesn't wait for Tristan to recover before turning and scampering up the hill. "They're getting away!" shouts Souffy.

"Frigus Digitorum." My spooky hand flies out to grab the goblin by the shoulder and applies a Vulcan death grip. Through the spell, I can feel the creature's last bit of life force draining away. Between the burns and bleeding, they're close enough to death's door that my Frostbite can push them through. As happened with the cockatrice when I used this cantrip, I experience a building nausea and a metallic tang in my mouth. Only this time, maybe because the goblin is self-aware, or because just a bit more of the cantrip could kill them, there's also an itchy burning sensation on the back of my neck and around my temples, pushing itself into me. And I don't want it there. I cancel my Frostbite, causing the goblin to fall to the ground, unconscious, but still alive. Guess I won't be pledging myself to the necromancy arcana when it comes to magic specialization.

"I didn't realize they could talk," says Tristan. He's staring blankly at the downed goblin. "Does this mean they're people?"

"No, they're goblins," says Souffy. She seems oblivious to the moral implications of killing a sapient creature. Guess that particular cultural issue wasn't covered in her otherworlder studies.

"But, they… he…" Given the facial hair, I think Tristan is correct to go with male. "He could have a family, maybe a wife, and kids," says Tristan. I'm not sure if goblin society works that way, but he's right about goblins being intelligent and self-aware. "Is this what heroes do?"

"Yes," says Souffy with far more conviction than I feel. "How else are you going to protect people if you don't stop the people trying to kill them?"

"But to stop them by killing them? Isn't that a bit much?"

Souffy shrugs. "Grandmama used to say that killing is the most effective way of stopping your enemy, unless, of course, they're undead."

"Kyle?" Tristan turns to me, as if I'm going to have the right words to resolve this fundamental problem. His troubled eyes go wide. "Kyle! Behind you!"

The warning gives me just enough time to turn and see a goblin—the one that Bell spied earlier—leaping at me, the dagger in their hand aimed right for my face. "*Dexterarious!*" My Phantom Hand catches the blade, but the goblin still lands on my chest, knocking me to the ground. I'm looking right into their jagged brown teeth and inhaling their fetid breath when a flash of silver sends their head flying. I push the body away as snot-green blood starts burbling out. Tristan, breathing heavy, lifts me to my feet.

Technically, I'm the one who almost died. But that's practically a daily occurrence in Mythreal. I'm more concerned with Tristan. I study his face for signs of shock or moral panic. "You okay?"

"They were trying to kill you." We stare at the headless body, each resolving our cognitive dissonance. Tristan processes his first. "So, are we supposed to check the bodies for treasure or something?"

In the video game, that was indeed the standard protocol. There was usually a coin or two, and you could carry an infinite number of captured scimitars and short bows to sell to the village weapons shop. But in the game, searching the corpses for loot happened with just a mouse click. Here, we'd actually have to touch them.

"Oh by the Twelve, please no," says Souffy. "Living goblins are nasty enough—they believe that bathing is a mortal sin. Dead ones, covered with that horrible smelling blood and the inside bits…" She scrunches up her nose and shudders. "I can't even."

I'm relieved to see that the native is also wigged out by the thought of picking over a corpse.

"Works for me. I suppose we should get going, before more of these guys show up. Right?" says Tristan.

I nod in agreement. "You're getting good at this adventuring stuff, Tris." I wonder why I'd never asked him to join me for a *Heroes Summoning* session. We used to play card and board games all the time as kids. I guess I figured that superstar Tristan wouldn't have the time or interest. Now I'm thinking I was wrong.

"Uh…" Souffy's worried voice cuts through my thoughts. "Where's our druid deer?"

I remember seeing it just before the arrows started flying. I call on Bell to give me the bird's-eye view. My hopes go up when she sees something reddish nearby, but on closer inspection it's only my hat, which I send her to retrieve. Souffy looks at me hopefully but I shake my head, signaling no.

Bell drops my hat next to me, and I pull out the rusty arrow stuck through its peak, then ease it back on. Without the deer to guide us, we have no chance of finding the magical weapon. Even worse, we've lost our ride home. And we haven't a clue where we are relative to where we started. As a bonus, we've already eaten half of the food supplies Tristan brought.

Souffy turns to Tristan. "Maybe the dryad who sent you to us will come and retrieve us?"

I'd forgotten all about Ashenfal. "And Oscar and the others know we're out here, they'll make sure someone comes for us."

"Hah, hah," rings out a rusty-oil-can laugh. It's emanating from the goblin I Frostbited to unconsciousness. He's awake now, although it looks like he's using up his last breath to taunt us. "The rescuers need rescuing."

Souffy walks up to him. "What do you mean by rescuers?" she asks.

"Not talking." He tries to spit at her but his spittle barely flies an inch. "You're going to have to torture it out of me."

Well, that's not going to happen. But we need information from this creature and neither Souffy nor I have any kind of truth telling spell. I consider the goblin. He's not doing so hot, and it's not just recent damage. He's sporting some wicked scars and he's missing several teeth. I'm guessing he's had a hard life. Although it's not our musical genre, I've listened to—and covered—enough country-western songs to guess what might tempt him.

"Or we could bribe you," I say. "Care for a drink?"

He looks at me, looks at my wizard hat. "Whadda you got?"

I pull out my water canteen and consider. "Tris, do you think goblins are more the Jack Daniels or straight vodka type?"

Tristan bends down closer to the goblin than I'd risk, and says, "I'd go with tequila."

I wave my hand and close my eyes. I imagine a pretty, slightly weathered bartender with a wry smile pouring out a shot, the smooth, smoky taste on my tongue that turns to fire in my throat and the alcohol smell that works its way up my nostrils. "*Alakazam, drink of the worm. Inebriate.*" Not taking chances, Tristan levels his sword against the goblin's throat as I dribble some of my transubstantiated spirits into his mouth.

A bit of life returns to his eyes. "That's the stuff."

"And if you want more," says Souffy, "you'll tell us who you think we've come to rescue."

He gives Souffy a skeezy smile but his eyes stray right back to my flask.

"Ah, fuck 'um," he says and turns back to Souffy. "Guy's dark, like you. Big burly fellow with fancy braids. 'E's a wizard."

"Is his name Ferimus Ravenus?" asks Souffy. Although at this point, I can't see it being anyone else.

"You want more, give me more of that liquor."

I oblige, figuring it will loosen his tongue. He smacks his lips appreciatively.

"Don't know, never bothered learning 'is name. You got to be as dumb as a froggywog not to gag a wizard. The dark lady gave him to us a week ago. Maybe more, can't remember. She threatened us if we didn't keep him prisoner."

"Where are you keeping him?"

"At that piss-poor excuse for a base. East of here, by the big rock, maybe an hour walk, for a goblin."

Tristan has a big silly grin plastered on his face. "How crazy is this, we fight some random goblins and they just happen to be the ones holding your uncle prisoner." He looks to Souffy. "Is this how the Divine Wisdom stuff works?"

"Yes." She giggles. "Didn't I tell you?"

I'm somewhat gratified to see our goblin prisoner roll his eyes.

"Or it could be because we've been wandering north into the wilderness, the same direction Ferimus was originally headed," I offer. We need to be careful not to conflate the Divine Wisdom's will with magical thinking.

CHAPTER 50

Kyle

"Goblins should live in caves!" slurs Ullurg. He's told us that his name in Goblinese means "Unending Headache." Which—given how he's downing the water-turned-tequila—he will probably experience tomorrow. Provided he doesn't die before then from the blood loss, third-degree burns, or what looks like skin rot from where I held him down with my Frostbite. We moved our prisoner out of sight of the sprung trap and dead goblins and secured him to a tree, although it looks more like the rope is holding him up. And by "we," I mean Souffy's Invisible Servant spell because none of us wanted to actually touch him.

"It ain't right, building a fort," Ullurg continues. "Outdoors! Nature!" He spits derisively, or tries to; he lacks the strength, and the green-tinged saliva dribbles down his chin. "Cregyolk was thinking out ov 'is arse when 'e ordered us to leave a Perfectly. Good. Cavern!" He practically shouts this last bit.

"Didn't you say the kobolds kicked you out of the mountain cave?" Tristan asks. Personally, I stopped trying to follow our drunken prisoner's incoherent ramblings three tequila shots in. It basically amounts to: everything was perfect before they were chased out of their digs in the Bydlo forest and now the new, younger management is making a mess of things. I'm hoping he's right about their leadership being incompetent, because we're planning on infiltrating their fort to rescue Ferimus.

"You said they have about a dozen goblins out on patrol during the day," says Souffy. Unlike Tristan she's taking her role as interrogator seriously. "How many goblins stay in the fort?"

"Those shirkers!" Ullurg tries to pound his fist against the ground, it's more of a flop. We left one of his hands free so we don't have to help him drink. I'm less worried about his teeth now, but his breath smells like something's died in his mouth. "Always some lame-ass excuse. Gotta guard the prisoner. Gotta repair the stockade. Gotta make more arrows to replace the ones you lost, Ullurg."

"That can be frustrating," Tristan commiserates. "It's like you're not appreciated or valued. Have you ever tried talking to them about how their behavior makes you feel?" I give Tris a nudge, we're pumping Ullurg for information, not giving him career advice.

"How many of those no-good shirkers are lazing around the camp right now?" asks Souffy.

Ullurg's eyes travel down to Souffy's breasts, and stay there. "Pour me a drink, missy. Helps my memory."

Tristan fills the cup instead and Ullurg takes a long draught. Initially we limited him to small sips for fear that he'd pass out. But either the ethanol reverts to water when it's drunk, or goblins have superpowered livers, because this is the second canteen I've Prestidigitated and Ullurg is still going strong.

"The number of goblins in the fort," I prompt him.

"There's that moron, Cregyolk, his bootlicker, Gerernorst, and his sister, Milborg, Perzog, piece of work, that one is." Ullurg counts off names, and insults, on his fingers—Perzog is mentioned twice. When he gets to the end of the list he regards his hand, he's missing a pinky. "A lot."

I'm rounding up to twenty goblins. That is indeed a lot. The plan is to have Souffy set off one of her Alarm spells to draw the goblins out of the camp while Tristan and I sneak in and free Ferimus. It's an extremely bad plan.

"And another thing!" Ullurg non-sequiturs. "After patrol, Cregyolk sends me out hunting 'cause your human stomachs can't handle perfectly fine day-old rats. That's how they develop proper flavor. 'E's more trouble than he's worth."

He's talking about Ferimus. "Why are you keeping him then?" I ask.

"When you live in the forest, you don't go pissing off the trees. 'Specially when they start moving on their own."

"You mean the blights?" asks Souffy. "This woman you mentioned, she was with the blights? What did she look like?"

Something resembling sobriety returns to Ullurg and his eyes nervously scan the surrounding forest. He'd been quite happy to spill secrets about his compatriots, but the mention of blights has him spooked. I suspect we won't get any more information about this dark lady.

Personally, I'm worried about more goblins. I sent Bell to locate the goblin camp, so I've lost my aerial surveillance. We only have Ullurg's disgruntled opinion that no one's going to notice his patrol's absence.

I had spent many hours of gameplay battling goblins in *Heroes Summoning*, often just grinding for experience points. This is the first time I've gotten to know one. It hasn't sparked any empathy or guilt for our role in his imminent demise, either from his injuries or at the hands of his fellow goblins when they find out that he snitched. Ullurg is nasty, petty, and downright disgusting—Souffy isn't the only one he's been mentally undressing. There's nothing in his stories to indicate that the other goblins in his colony are any better. But even if the forest would be a far better place without them, does that make it okay for me to kill them?

I'm saved from this moral conundrum by the return of my familiar.

"Tinkerbell!" she croaks as she lands in front of us, startling Ullurg. Tristan hands him the canteen to distract him.

"Did she find the goblin's base?" asks Souffy.

I open my mind to Bell's thoughts and perceive flashes of hills and lakes and the world spread out below. The hills drop down to a river valley that ends in a towering granite dome (that's probably Ullurg's big rock) which looms over a man-made—goblin-made—enclosure. Bell must have ridden a wind current down because the images suddenly spiral closer. I pull a loose sheet of parchment from my spellbook and sketch it out. "We're here, the valley they're in is over there," I explain to the others as I draw.

I see through Bell's eyes that the fort itself is in even worse shape than Ullurg implied. The structures inside, huts I suppose, look like they were built by inattentive beavers and the walls of the stockade lean out dangerously. In one spot, the wall has fallen over completely, and the opening has been patched with horizontal boards to make a barrier three feet lower than the rest. The repairs are on the other side of the camp from the main gates. I mark both spots on my map.

"So"—I indicate a point beyond the gates—"Souffy sets up her Alarm spell somewhere around here, and then gets herself to safety, here." I move my finger towards the base of the dome. "Then Bell will fly through the detection barrier, setting off the spell. Meanwhile Tristan and I will be hiding here, under the cover of the river's banks." I tap the squiggly line where it snakes close to the broken section of the walls. "The Alarm goes off. The goblins run out to investigate, or at least focus their attention outside the gate. That's when we move in."

"And my uncle?" asks Souffy.

The only view of Ferimus is from thirty feet up. Ullurg had started salivating when he saw Bell and I was worried another goblin might shoot her for a snack, so I only had her do one flyover of the camp. But it's obvious from the subject's size as well as his full beard and long hair that there's a non-goblin in the camp.

"He's tied to a post here." I point to the center of camp. "It doesn't look like he's heavily guarded."

"Maybe the guards will leave their posts to see what the Alarm is about," says Tristan. "And he's a wizard, so he can cast some magic spells as we fight our way out."

"And I'll be ready with a Fire Orb when Bell leads you to my location," Souffy adds.

Their completely unwarranted confidence helps to calm my nerves. It's not like we have many options. It comes down to distracting as many of the goblins as possible and hoping we can deal with the rest.

It's nearing noon. Because goblins are nocturnal and have night vision, we want to execute the plan in the afternoon. Also that's when, according to Ullurg, his entitled bosses start drinking from their secret stash before settling down for long siestas. Here's hoping.

Souffy casts Mystic Armor on both of us, so due diligence. We leave my canteen next to a snoring Ullurg—it's covered in goblin cooties by now—and head out. From there, we proceed in a silent, stealthy manner through the woods. I'm constantly checking in with Bell in case there are more goblin patrols, but either Ullurg was telling the truth about lax security, or we're lucky. Either way it gives me plenty of time to think.

I resolve not to go down the "things that could go wrong" rabbit hole, which leaves my mind flashing on the image from earlier: Tristan slicing through the neck of the goblin holding me down. Effectively, as Souffy might say, stopping someone from killing me. As the person about to be killed, I have no problem with it. Come to think about it, if I'd used a spell like Magic Mortar that wasn't directly sucking out life essence, I'd have been fine with ending Ullurg's life.

I wonder if all that *Heroes Summoning* gameplay has desensitized me to killing, or killing goblins at least. I'll find out soon enough. It's not physically ending a life that's worrying me, it's the thought of the person I could become afterwards. Guess I'll burn that bridge when I get to it.

Two hours later, Tristan and I are hiding in the shadow of the river embankment. Through Bell's eyes, I see Souffy casting her spell.

"Be ready," I tell Tristan. From this vantage point we can see the occasional helmeted goblin head bob along the parapet of the fort. The newly patched section didn't get a connection, so the patrolling goblins turn around at that point. This is really happening.

Tristan's hand comes down on my shoulder. "We got this," he tells me.

"We SO don't got this. This plan is going to fall apart, and we'll be ad-libbing most of the way."

"We're great at ad-libs, remember our first AMA performance when the background music went out?"

"As traumatic as that was, we didn't have to dodge murderous goblins on stage."

He shrugs in a you-got-me way. "It could work. Some of our crazy plans have, you know. Like becoming famous YouTubers."

"That only happened because of your lip-synching."

"It also only happened because you set up the channel, figured out how to record with proper sound and lighting, and did all that research on what the algorithm was looking for. See? Teamwork. Those goblins won't know what hit them."

I could argue more with Tristan—I can always argue more Tristan. But there's a comfort in his certainty, no matter how misplaced. He is right. Probably anything is possible in Mythreal.

Before rationality reasserts itself, Souffy's air raid siren Alarm goes off and echoes across the valley. A goblin guard's head pops up on the ramparts and scans around wildly before dashing away from us.

"Let's go," says Tristan.

The next part comes easy, second nature easy. We spring out of our hiding spot and dash to the lower replacement wall. Tris is a few steps ahead of me and when he arrives, he pivots, his hand cupped halfway to his bent knees. The moment I step into his interlaced fingers, he's heaving me upwards. Just like we practiced in countless rehearsals and performed at our shows—me paired with Tris, Micah with Cole. Those synchronized assisted backflips drove the crowd wild. This time it's dead silent and I keep my body straight as I launch up. My arms catch over the wall's edge; my chest slams into the side facing me. I hang like this from the wall and look down. No startled goblins look up, that's good. It appears that this area of the fort is blessedly deserted. I swing my body over and drop five feet to the ground inside, staggering backwards on impact, but I manage to stay upright. I've been holding my breath and now let it out with relief.

And when I inhale again, I realize the reason why no one's hanging around this part of the complex. All the discarded chunks of offal that even goblins won't eat are piled next to a hovel that reeks worse than a line of porta-potties at an outdoor music festival.

Forcing down a gag reflex, I turn back to the wall and throw my rope over. With an assist from my Phantom Hand I brace the line as Tristan walks himself up. He sticks the landing, throwing out his hands for balance—also for style.

There's an excited squeak that for a moment I confusedly think is a fangirl, but is in fact a startled goblin. I suspect my brain was waiting for this moment because I send three Magic Mortar shots directly at the goblin's chest while they're still just standing there, staring. The goblin sinks to the ground soundlessly. Tristan's staring too.

I don't make eye contact as we move the body behind the midden. The goblin's skin is warm but it's obvious they're not breathing. A bit of tension goes out of my chest, knowing that I didn't freeze, didn't let them shout out to the camp, that I was capable of acting without feeling. Or maybe it's just the fight winning out over the flight response. It was over before the goblin felt any pain, not that it changes that they're dead by my magic. I decide I've expended all my available moral quandary for the time being. We still have half the compound to cross and if I don't kill or maim any more goblins, it will because I've been killed or maimed myself.

Tristan pulls out his sword and we dash to a structure next to the wall. It appears to be a storeroom full of unappetizing root vegetables. I tilt my head far back to see the ramparts over the brim of my hat. I'm hyper aware of just how perfectly target-shaped and colored my wizard hat is. By all logical arguments, I should have left it with Souffy. But when I'm wearing this hat, I feel like a wizard. And when I'm a wizard, I can do this shit.

Anyway, there's no guards, up above or on the ground. Souffy's distraction may just possibly have worked. We continue dashing and crouching until our luck runs out. In an open space, facing away from us are two goblins, armed with nasty-looking spears. They're about twenty feet away, and between them is a post the size of a midsize tree with a man slumped against it.

He's gagged, with his hands bound behind his back to the post and one ankle shackled to the ground. If I wasn't already convinced that this was Souffy's uncle, I'd have a hard time identifying him as the wizard whose portrait hangs in the classroom back at the tower. The Ferimus in the painting, while a little stiff, was rocking the elder-statesman-rapper look: chest-length box braids studded with pearls and silver rings, scholarly glasses, pointy ducktail beard, and deep creases lining his face that implied an earned arrogance. The man before us has the same braids, but they're dirty, unadorned and unraveling at the ends; his facial hair is crazy-mountain-man wild and the lines on his face make him look broken.

"How else are you going to protect people if you don't stop the people trying to kill them?" Souffy's words bring with them a moral clarity. To save Ferimus, we need to stop those goblins. And if that results in their deaths, it's something I'm willing to live with.

Now, about saving Ferimus. In an ideal world, I'd employ Souffy's Magic Missive, which just goes to show: you always need the cantrip you didn't take. I make do with a small mirror to reflect the sun through Ferimus's cracked glasses. His eyelids flutter and then go wide as he sees me. I put my finger to my lips and, in the quietest of whispers, say *"Dexterarious."* I hand a knife off to my Phantom Hand before sending it ever so slowly over to Ferimus.

I can't do much about the rusty iron chain around his leg. But if I can work his hands free, he might help us out with some magic. Careful of Ferimus's hands and wrists, I cause the knife to start sawing on the rope.

With the first creak of the fraying rope, one of the goblins' ears twitch. Even as the goblin starts to turn, Tristan charges, sword out and bellowing just like he did in that one scene from his movie. The goblins jump up, but Tristan's already swinging his sword at the first's neck as the second readies their spear while taking a step back. The first guard must be wearing some sort of neck armor, because Tris doesn't quite manage to cleave their head clean off. He's still disentangling his weapon from the mostly severed neck when goblin number two decides the odds are now in their favor. They charge Tristan, spear angled at Tristan's neck.

I don't have time to cast a spell; instead I make a twisting and stabbing motion with my own hand and my Phantom Hand flies out and drives the knife into the back of the goblin's ankle. It's where I think the Achilles tendon is. I choose the attack based on mythology, not physiology, and while the goblin screams, they don't collapse into a heap. It does slow them down, however, just enough for Tris to shake his sword free of goblin number one and slide it into the approaching goblin's throat, or that's what I'm guessing. There's a lot of blood in the way—not sure if it makes the scene more or less gruesome.

An arrow whistles through the air. From above, on the ramparts, I see several more goblins, in various stages of notching their arrows. We'll need to hide behind something to avoid being skewered. I feel their eyes on my hat as I run over to Ferimus who, hands still bound, has fallen to his knees. I stare uselessly at the ropes. Where did my knife go? Oh yeah, goblin. Maybe I can Prestigiditate the rope fibers into—

Thwok! A goblin arrow embeds itself an inch into the post next to my head, and my mind goes blank.

"Here." Tristan runs up and shoves his shield into my hands.

I do my best to block myself and Ferimus from the goblins' view, while Tris wedges his sword against the rope, freeing Ferimus's hands with one slice. Then he turns to the chain, and positions the tip of his sword to slam through it.

My brain finally starts working. "Hang on," I say before Tristan messes up his sword. I reposition the shield so that I can reach one hand over to the chain. *This is Alchemy 101*, I tell myself, *a simple reaction to oxidize an element. "Alakazam, water and air bring death to this iron."* Beneath my fingers, the gray of the metal chain link turns a warm brown, its smooth surface becoming rough and flaky. "Now try breaking it." Tristan brings down his sword and the magically rusted metal crumbles obligingly.

More arrows are flying now. One strafes Tristan's neck. I could throw up a magic shield, but then I'd be out of spells. Ferimus has by now removed his gag and I'm sincerely hoping that he's got a spell ready to go. Instead, he looks intently at me and says, "Is that my hat?"

"Souffy said I could have it."

"Give it here, quick." His stare is so intense, I just hand it over. "All right then," he says as he places it on his head, flicks the brim, and begins to hum a tuneless spell.

The hat shudders and wobbles as it starts to turn, then picks up speed to a gentle spin, not unlike a baby crib mobile. The buckle even begins to glow.

I glance at Tristan. "Are you seeing this?"

"Yep," he confirms. "Hat still looks better on you."

For some reason, that makes me feel better.

CHAPTER 51

Kyle

While staring at Ferimus and whatever this is—Cole would call it hashtag whatever-this-is—something zooms over my head and into the rotating hat. It's an arrow.

Ferimus grabs both Tristan's and my hands. "We should get going before any of them find the courage to come down and fight us," he says calmly. "The infusion isn't strong enough to affect melee weapons." He steps out of the nominal protection of the shield, pulling us along with surprising strength for a man who's been chained to a post for over a week. As we follow him out of the site of his former imprisonment, I witness two more arrows embed themselves into the hat. These guys either really hate the hat, or—

I hear another thrum of a bowstring, and turn to see the single point of the projectile coming straight at my face, only for it to swerve at the last moment and angle upward, once again embedding itself into the wizard hat.

"You're magically attracting all the arrows to my, er, your hat!" I exclaim. We're picking up speed, almost running as we head in the direction of the compound's gates. It's not the original exit plan, but then, neither was any of this.

"I've infused the essence of lodestone into it," he explains even as another arrow skewers the hat. "So it attracts the arrowheads. My initial intention was for it to repel metal, but I must have reversed the polarities."

Two thoughts—neither which I say aloud because we are in fact running for our lives: magnetism doesn't work that way, even in this world, and yeah, this guy is definitely Souffy's uncle. Also, does this mean he's keeping the hat? (Okay, that's three thoughts).

"Oh, it's like a magnet! I think I can feel it tugging on my sword," says Tristan. "That's so cool!"

"No, not really." Ferimus shakes his head, even as the hat spins on, unaffected. "When it's attuned, the artifice generates heat, making the hat uncomfortable to wear in warm weather."

Beyond a row of barracks, I can see the gates. They're closed, but not barricaded. Meaning that we can push our way through, provided we make it that far. There now appear to be fewer arrows in the air. Maybe they all ended up in the hat—it's starting to resemble a pin cushion. Something heavy flies over our heads and lands in front of me. Looks like they've switched to spears. I push myself to run faster.

Ferimus glances at Tristan. "I'm sure we've met, but I'm so bad with names. Are you with the garrison, or the Laska Trading Company?"

"We're from California," Tristan says unhelpfully.

"We're otherworld heroes," I manage to get out between pants.

"Otherworld heroes?"

I don't have time for this; we're almost to the gate.

"Get your sorry green arses out there and stop them!" a hoarse voice shouts and three not-so-burly goblins stumble out of the gatehouse. Their breastplates are partially strapped on and only one is wearing a helmet. They growl at us—but I can tell they don't want to be here either.

"We just need a show of force," I say, dropping Ferimus's hand. "*Frigus Digitorum.*" My Frostbite skeleton hand shoots straight into the face of the foremost goblin, tumbling them backwards. Tristan roars from his diaphragm while swinging his sword high enough to knock the helmeted one to the ground. The third goblin takes a step back, glances at their two downed colleagues and falls to the ground—soccer-player style—clutching their ankle and conveniently out of our way. We're at the gates now, and Tristan pushes them open just enough to squeeze through. I glance back at the fortress to see a few bows aimed at us from the stockades, but the shots go wide, and the arrows don't even fly close enough to swerve towards the hat.

"Which way is Souffy?" asks Tristan. We're still running full-out. The troops sent out to investigate the Alarm spell could return at any moment, at which point I fear the goblins' fighting spirit might re-emerge.

"This way," I say. Bell's above us, showing me a route to our rendezvous spot clear of goblins. "Follow the raven." We take off through a denser patch of woods. Tristan takes the lead, and we form a single line. We're still running, but by now it's more of a morning jog than an all-out sprint for our lives.

Ferimus glances back at me. "I'm sorry," he says. He's breathing hard so the phrases come out in spurts. "But did you say you were heroes from another world? And also, are you referring to my niece, Souffy Ravenus?"

"Yes, and yes," I say.

"Oh, my." Ferimus taps the hat; it stops spinning. "Souffy, you say?"

"Souffy's awesome," says Tristan.

"It was her Alarm spell that lured away most of the goblins so we could rescue you," I add.

"It was very… loud."

"You did petition the Divine Wisdom for us to come?" I take two quick steps to catch up to him. His voice is so uncertain; I feel like I need to see his expression. "Right?"

We've slowed to a quick walk. Our destination, the rock wall, looms tall behind the pines ahead of us.

"I…" Ferimus tugs at his beard. "Yes, yes I did. Now I remember. It was when Janassy was handing me over to the goblins and threatening them with these monstrous creatures made of vines. And it occurred to me that things had gotten quite out of hand, that it was more than the druids or the militia could handle, so I made a direct request to the Divine Wisdom."

"How does that work?" asks Tristan. Good question.

"It's nothing too complicated. You must embrace the totality of the problem in your mind, including any of your own culpability in the matter, acknowledge that it is more than you or the people around you are capable of dealing with, and turn the whole thing over to the will of the Divine Wisdom, accepting whatever It deems is the best approach. People think you need to fill out paperwork, and it does improve your chances to formalize the request with a ceremony. But when things are truly desperate, the people of Mythreal know to turn to the Divine Wisdom. It's instinct."

"It must be nice, having a direct line to a god," I say.

"We are blessed. Now, mind you, I thought the Divine Wisdom would send local heroes. Not that I'm complaining, I'm quite grateful for the two of you showing up when you did."

"And Souffy," adds Tristan.

"And…" His befuddled expression makes me suspect that he finds Souffy's involvement in his rescue more extraordinary than the presence of otherworlders. It wasn't like I had doubted Souffy's stories about her family—but wow, just wow.

Tinkerbell interrupts my thoughts with a happy caw. We've arrived at the rendezvous point, as evidenced by our fire-evocating wizard bounding towards us.

"Souffy," says Ferimus.

"Uncle!" Souffy throws herself into Ferimus's arms and I throw out a steadying hand to keep him from being bowled over. "You look awful. Come over here and sit down."

I send Bell out to keep watch and Souffy takes us over to the edge of the granite monolith where there are several large scattered rocks. She helps Ferimus sit on one and hands him some water. He sighs contentedly after taking a deep draught. But only for a moment, then his worry lines return.

He looks back and forth between Tristan and me. "Where are my manners? You know my name, but I never inquired about yours."

"I'm Tristan Ives." He says this with a theatrical bow. "And this is Kyle Moretti. The others are back at the druids' camp."

"Others?"

Souffy jumps in. "The Divine Wisdom sent five heroes, Uncle. There's no mention in our history of so many heroes ever being sent at once. It must be a truly Epic quest."

Ferimus slowly shakes his head. "Five otherworld heroes for… plant monsters?"

"And cockatrices," adds Tristan. "Giant ones."

"It's more than the blights." I sit on a flattish rock and motion for Souffy and Tristan to do the same. It looks like we're getting to the exposition part of this rescue mission. "It appears the Triad of Valor left some unfinished business."

I explain about the Doomsday Tree, how the Triad contained it by slowing down time and left a magical weapon to defeat it should it rise again. I try not to sound judgy, but my disapproval creeps into my tone. When I get to the part about Wizard Daniel putting a silencing spell on Raskin, Ferimus snaps his fingers.

"I knew it, I knew it! Every so often Raskin would say something about the north, about the Triad, that implied sinister goings-on. But he'd always clam up right after. A demonic tree would explain why the Drevo Woods treaty requires a wizard to be installed in the fortress."

"We think something disrupted the spell, freeing the tree," says Souffy.

"Something, or someone. Oh Janassy." Ferimus sighs and shakes his head dejectedly. "This is worse than I thought."

I'm not quite following. "You think Janassy freed the Doomsday Tree?"

"It's all very complicated," says Ferimus. "Almost a fortnight ago, a strange object was seen hurtling across the night sky, dislodging small pieces of itself. One of those pieces crashed through the barn of a local farmer. I'm a naturally curious person, often to my own detriment, and when I went to investigate, I discovered…" Ferimus taps at his head, as if to dislodge the thought.

"That it made the livestock bigger?" I offer.

"Yes, that." The sharpness returns to the wizard's eyes. "But not only that: the tomcat was shrunk to the size of a mouse—very cute—the milk collected the previous night had frozen, the feed grain had all sprouted, and the red paint on the barn had changed to a lovely shade of blue." None of the rest of which Malza ever mentioned, but of course she wouldn't (that might have been, you know, helpful). "I'd never heard of such spellcraft, and when I probed the rock that had caused the damage, it yielded strange results."

"It canceled Souffy's Sense Magic spell," says Tristan.

"Oh, you found the rock?" Ferimus is back to his usual muddled expression. "Did I leave it in my workshop?"

"We found it in the tree stump lodgings in the Drevo Woods," says Souffy. "After we found the hearthstone portal in your hidden room. How many secrets have you been keeping from me, Uncle?"

Ferimus leans over and gently pats Souffy's hand. "Quite a few, I'm afraid. We are Ravenus wizards, after all."

Redirecting the conversation, I say, "But back to the meteorite, the rock that fell from the sky?"

"Meteorite," Ferimus repeats. "Well, more than one of them fell that night, so I sent my messenger bird to Janassy. Oh, she's a dryad—" We all nod. "To see if she could locate it. And then a few days later, my bird returned, only I cracked the egg and there was Raskin saying that Janassy wasn't back yet. And at that moment, I experienced such a horrible premonition, headache, nausea, rainbow auras around everything. And the image of a tree swallowing the forest. I assumed that part was a metaphor; I was always rubbish at interpreting visions. But I did gather that something dreadful had happened to Janassy, so I headed out at once to investigate."

"Without telling me," says Souffy, pointedly.

"I left a note."

"Saying you were gathering herbs. That's lying, Uncle."

"I thought it best not to involve you." Ferimus again reaches for Souffy's hand. This time she pulls it away. "It's just that you're still so inexperienced, Souffy, and your spells…" He sighs. And this, I remind myself, is one of Souffy's supportive relatives.

I continue with the story that we know. "So Ferimus, you traveled to the druid camp. There, you relayed your vision to Cena and convinced Ashenfal to lend you some forest magick that allowed you to find where the meteorite landed. How did you do that by the way?" My inner geek needs to know.

"Oh, I didn't. Unfortunately, dryad magick, while impressively powerful, isn't appropriate for that sort of thing. No, what happened was I remembered that I'd given Janassy one of my rings once, as a token of my affection, and, as Souffy knows, I had gotten into the habit of putting location spells on my various possessions because I'm always misplacing them. The ring's spell was still active, so I just followed its signal. I have seven-league enchanted boots." Ferimus looks down at his stockinged feet. "Or, rather, used to."

"What happened when you found Janassy?"

"Nothing good." Ferimus lets out a truly mournful sigh. He removes his (my) hat and begins wistfully plucking out the goblin arrows. "She told me she no longer cared for me. That she'd outgrown me and had a new, more fulfilling purpose in her life. I remember thinking that if I were better at divination magic, I would have recognized that my premonition meant a dissolution of our relationship, and I could just have stayed home. But then she knocked me unconscious. When I woke up, I was bound and gagged in a goblin camp and Janassy was controlling these plant monsters. I can only assume she used the power of the 'meteorite' to create these, I believe you called them blights, in order to resurrect this Doomsday Tree."

That's not the assumption I would have reached. While I'm mentally sorting out all this new information, Tristan jumps in.

"Wait, did she say why she was leaving you? That whole 'it's me not you' deal, that's never what's really going on."

Tristan has been through more breakups than even his fans can keep track of, so I let him work this angle. There are other parts of Ferimus's theory that aren't making sense to me either. Originally, I supposed the meteorite had mutagenic properties, but the effects Ferimus described at Malza's farm seem less biological, and more physical.

"I imagine it's because I've gotten old," Ferimus says. "I'm no longer the handsome wizard who first arrived here twenty years ago."

"Wow, you've been together for twenty years? That's amazing. You think she'd end all that just because you've picked up some wrinkles?"

"She's a dryad"—Ferimus shrugs—"eternally young and beautiful. They like their lads to match."

"Girls are into more than just looks, it's what's inside that counts," Tristan insists. "At least, that's what they tell me."

Ferimus turns his attention from his hat to look Tristan up and down. "Do they now?"

"All the time. Back me up on this, Kyle."

Thankfully Souffy jumps in. "But why would a dryad want to free an evil tree that would destroy the forest?" We're all silent as we contemplate that one.

Before Tristan can ask why dryads are into trees in the first place (that's totally what he's thinking) I say, "What if the Doomsday Tree was already free when Janassy went looking for the meteorite? It could be the one controlling both the blights and Janassy."

"But you said the Doomsday Tree was trapped in a slow-time spell," says Ferimus.

I'm ready for that objection. "And you said the meteorite at the Stannish farm caused the grains to germinate, manipulating time similarly to how it altered the sizes of the animals. The meteorite could have disrupted Daniel's time spell, or even sped time up."

"And if the tree was free, it could totally have turned your girlfriend evil," says Tristan.

"And it could have sent her out to infect other parts of the forest," I add. "That would explain the blight's weird distribution. It literally followed lines. And two days ago, Micah—he's our ranger—received a message from the trees that there was a Lady of the Forest who was in danger. It all fits!"

"Very impressive," says Ferimus. "You're quite clever, Kyle, even by wizard standards."

"Yes, he is," says Souffy. She beams at me. "I think you should give him his hat back, Uncle."

Ferimus considers the now de-arrowfied hat like an old friend. He smiles softly and hands it to me. When I put it on, he says, "It does suit you."

CHAPTER 52

Kyle

Things are so much better with my hat back. I close my eyes to savor the feeling, only for Bell to interrupt my thoughts with a mental image of several goblins making their way towards us.

"Time to go," I tell the others. If the goblins were to trap us against the rock wall, things would be over in a bad way. Fortunately, they're still a ways off, and I know from Bell's scouting that less than a mile from here the valley opens up along the river. It's out in the open, which sounds bad, but given that goblins prefer cover for their sneak-up-and-shoot-them-in-the-back tactics, they might decide we're not worth the effort. Not the best strategy—we've been out of those since Souffy and I set off on druid deer, or before when we jumped through the hearthstone. Come to think of it, since the sheep. And look, we're still standing, or running.

As we make our way north along the edge of the granite dome, I ask Ferimus to turn on the hat spell. I don't like the idea of being an arrow magnet (and it's going to make a mess of my hair) but I'm down to one spell, meaning I don't have the option to cast Shield if we're attacked. So, arrow magnet it is.

Mood-wise, I'm strangely ambivalent. Perhaps it's because, by rescuing Ferimus and committing ourselves to taking on the Doomsday Tree, we're proceeding down the Divine Wisdom's intended path. Or maybe after so much facing down death and running for my life, I've accepted this as the new normal. Like back in the early days, when the band was hitting three malls a weekend for shows and meet-and-greets, and I started associating Panda Express with real Chinese food.

We're traveling in single file. Tristan leads with his sword and shield, then me, followed by Ferimus, with Souffy taking point with her literal fire power. We veer away from the granite rock face, down an embankment, and through a marshy meadow. I'm trying to keep the water out of my boots, so I'm only occasionally checking in with Bell. There are at least five goblins tracking us, but I can see they're wearing sullen expressions, no bloodlust. I'm just rounding a boulder when I hear the distinctive plonk, like someone plucking the E-string on a bass guitar. I look to the right where I think the sound came from and see the point of an arrow coming at me. Tristan sees it too and yanks me forward, only for the arrow to take a hard turn into my hat.

"Oh, yeah, magic hat. Sorry, Kyle."

"I'm not complaining."

"It came from behind that fallen tree," says Souffy, who's now caught up to us. *Great Ball of Fire!*

I'm not sure how many archers she gets, but three goblins manage to hop out from behind it. Two still have bows. I ready my Magic Mortar, but Ferimus grasps my arm.

"Wizard Kyle, if I may." He reaches up under my hat's brim—like he's a stage magician—and pulls out a long white feather with a pointy, blackened tip. How many enchantments has he hidden in this hat?

Ferimus holds the quill out and, with exaggerated wrist movements, writes an incantation in the air. Sparkly letters spell out *BOO!* He blows this word towards the monsters; it becomes bits of glitter floating on a breeze. The goblins start to blink like they got dust in their eyes, and then break out in screams worthy of a horror movie, running in different directions, all away from us.

"Fear spell," Ferimus explains. "It sends visions of being attacked by one's most terrifying foe. Given the goblins' pragmatic approach towards fighting, I doubt they'll be coming back."

But that was only the opening salvo of the ambush. While we're watching the goblins flee in terror, another arrow skewers the back of my hat. I pivot and dash into the open space behind us to draw the hidden archers' projectiles away from everyone else. I really hope they don't switch to using stone arrowheads. From behind trees, bushes and rocks, goblins pop out to shoot and duck back down, whack-a-mole style. There are five— no, more. They keep shifting about. They must have noticed I'm unarmed because three of them decide to charge me at once. Just the number I was hoping for.

"*Sagitta-inspira!*" One magic projectile for each. The leading goblin goes down hard and their teammate, also wounded, stumbles over him.

Neither of them gets up again. The third attacker stays on their feet but staggers behind a tree, probably hiding there in case I have more magic.

I make the mistake of looking back to see how the others are doing. Yet another goblin darts out at me. I dodge but not far enough; their wickedly curved sword grazes my side. Looking down, I see blood trickling down my pants. Okay, maybe that was more than a graze.

"Kyle!" Tristan leaps between us and hacks off the offending goblin's arm. The detached limb arcs upward, trailing a thick stream of snot-blood while the remainder of the goblin topples back.

Behind me I hear Souffy say, "Mu's teeth, stand still so I can Flame Bolt you!"

Tristan and my attackers are taking us in a pincer maneuver, their natural cowardice encouraging sensible tactics.

"*Protectionate!*" shouts Ferimus and I hear the telltale sound of metal clanging against a magic shield.

By this point, goblins are springing out from every available inch of cover and then ducking back again whenever they risk facing Tristan's sword or Souffy's Flame Bolt. I'm down to my Frostbite cantrip, which I deploy on a charging goblin that's managed to slip past Tristan. I aim for the goblin's sword hand so my spell is both draining and holding them back. My stomach churns as the necromancy of the cantrip affects me as well, but the cut on my side hurts more.

"Kyle, behind you!" shouts Tristan.

I glance back while maintaining the cantrip on the goblin in front of me. Which gives me a brief view of two incoming goblins before the closest one's sword rams under my left shoulder blade. The Mystic Armor Souffy cast on me earlier seems to work like a non-Newtonian fluid, firming up under pressure but turning to liquid under less direct forces. So, the initial hit is pure impact, knocking the wind out of me and throwing me forward. But—whether by technique or randomness—the goblin pushes the blade just so and it gently slips through the magical barrier. My nerves scream out as the ragged blade tears through fabric and flesh. Maybe I scream out loud as well.

I fall to my knees practically on top of the severed goblin arm. Spurred on by adrenaline, or maybe testosterone, I seize the limb by its elbow and swing it, along with the short sword still held in a death-grip by the hand, at my attacker. I'm thinking defense—not offense—but the extra reach of the forearm means the tip of the scimitar gashes the goblin's face.

Their eyes go wide and they drop their own weapon while springing backwards. I bare my teeth and rattle the goblin arm. Technically, wizards don't have a berserker mode, but I don't think the goblin knows that.

As I'm concentrating on making a scary face, I feel the Frostbite cantrip blip out. Meaning there's an unhindered goblin with a sword getting ready to run at me. And I've lost track of the direction they're coming from.

"Got them!" I hear Tristan yell, followed by the swoosh of his sword and a short-lived goblin scream.

The next moment, Tristan is by my side, and the goblin in front of me takes another step back. The brief respite gives me a moment to reorient myself. When the fight started, we were back-to-back with Souffy and Ferimus. Now, a chaotic minute or two later, they're over ten feet away, and dealing with their own goblin hordelet. Souffy's facing two singed goblins; one's cloak is on fire but they haven't noticed yet. She's holding both of them off with the threat of a pointed finger. It's working for now, but eventually it's going to occur to them that they should charge her together. She's also trying to threaten the goblins coming at Ferimus. I count four against one; even if Ferimus wasn't exhausted from multiple days as a captive, those are bad odds.

I motion to Tristan. "Go help Ferimus." He gives me an are-you-sure look. "I got this," I lie.

Now there are two goblins, one with a knife, the other with a club, and me clutching the severed arm of their fallen comrade. Not taking my eyes off them, I lean over to grab the short sword the first goblin dropped. I have two swords—that also means I don't have any hands free for spellcasting. I think the goblin who's holding the club realizes this and advances, waving their weapon menacingly before them.

Because things can always get worse, I hear a racket from above, and Bell starts having a fit in my mind. *Something with feathers is coming*, she projects into my overloaded brain, *several somethings*. I can now hear the high-pitched shrieks of the new arrivals with my own ears.

"Bird! Bird!" Bell's screeches cut through the clamor of the fighting and everyone, goblins included, pauses to stare at the sky. "Biiiiiig bird!"

CHAPTER 53

Shadows sweep the ground. I look up to see three dark objects circling. They're the shape of birds; the size of small aircraft. Silhouetted against the sun, their wing feathers flare out like fingers, their beaks end in sharp hooks, and their talons… something weird is going on with their talons. It's like they're clutching something. The monster-birds' harsh screams reach us as they ride the air currents down.

But that's a distant danger compared to what's facing me here. Club-wielding goblin takes advantage of my momentary distraction and springs six feet in the air; they come down with their (non-magnetic) weapon swinging. They're close enough for my brain to recognize that they're female and I hyper-fixate on her painfully bad bowl haircut, half-inch-thick monobrow, scarred cheekbones, and a piece of gristle stuck between her chipped front teeth. Survival instinct (or years spent religiously following the 6th Law of Boy Bands) has me raising my sword to prevent her from smashing my face in.

But before it comes to that, a black mass crashes down on the goblin's back, driving her into the ground with a crunchy squelch. Whatever just saved me rolls gracefully out of the fall. My brain processes it as a dark clump in a pool of shadow. Then it rises in a smooth motion. The shadow resolves itself into a cloak rippling around a human form: a tall, wiry form that is both familiar and welcome to me.

"Cole!" I scream—total fangirl style. But come on, not only did he just save my life, but he looked cool doing it. His hood obscures everything but his chin and the tip of his nose. He turns to the remaining goblin.

"I'm Batman," he growls in his lowest octave. The goblin squeaks—actually squeaks—as they dive into the bushes. Cole turns back to me, pushing back his cowl to reveal a stupid-big grin on his face. "I've been wanting to say that ever since I got this costume."

"Where did you come from?"

He points upwards, to one of those giant birds now ponderously flapping away. I recognize the thing in its claws as some sort of hammock. As soon as it clears the space above us, the next giant bird—an osprey with crazy eyes—swoops low. The human that leaps down from its grip gleams silver in the sunlight.

"*Holy Shield!*" intones Oscar. From what I can see of the magic shimmering in the air, he's directed the barrier at his feet. He lands and the shield instantly crushes two of the four goblins advancing on Ferimus and Tristan. That Oscar next tumbles over and needs to be helped up by Tristan does not make his appearance any less beatific.

The final bird—your classic majestic bald eagle—almost scrapes the ground as it glides in. Micah, replete in his green ranger cloak, leaps off. Before his feet touch ground, he pivots, draws his bowstring, and fires on the goblins advancing on Souffy. "*Dreen-chruinn!*" he chants. The loosed arrow shimmers, and when it impales the goblin, tiny green thorns erupt from its fletching, which take out the second goblin as well.

"Kyle, rangers get their magic once they level up! And they've got cool spells, not just for talking to animals!" He's using that cute sing-song voice. Annoying, but it means he's in a good mood.

A moment ago, there were eight goblins ready to kill the four of us. Now there are seven of us. The remaining two goblins do the math and take off at a sprint. Micah notches a bow and aims for one of their backs. Cole—not to be outdone—grabs the sword I forgot I was holding, and throws it at the other. Neither weapon finds its mark; Cole and Micah had gotten careless in their overconfidence. The goblins vanish behind some rocks.

"Guys!" says Tristan. "Great to see you! How did you find us?"

"When you didn't show up this morning, the druids asked the King of Eagles for help. We've been circling the area all afternoon looking for you," says Oscar.

"You flew here? That's amazing!" says Tristan.

Micah snorts. "Hardly. I'd sooner fly coach, middle seat with babies on both sides, than do that again."

Cole points to Ferimus. "Is this guy a good guy or a bad guy?"

"Good guy. He's my Uncle Ferimus," says Souffy. "And Uncle, these are the rest of the Neverboyland heroes. Oscar Jones, Micah Cardigan, and Cole Silva."

Ferimus bows with each introduction. "I once briefly met the otherworld hero Paladin Martin Wu at my sister's wedding. I was barely older than Souffy at the time and I recall the frustration of feeling I'd been born too late for the age of heroes. And now here you are, so it appears I was also born too early."

"Nonsense, you're never too old to be a hero," says Oscar. He looks over Ferimus and his goblin-induced injuries: bruises on his arms, rope burns on his wrist, caked blood on his socks. "But you might benefit from a healing spell. You too, Kyle."

"No, allow me," says Micah. He takes a leaf from what I thought was an elegant boutonniere and crushes it between his hands. *"Feelgood Berries!"* He sings it like it's a commercial jingle. Eight small red berries appear in his palm. "Eat them and you'll feel better."

I take three. I feel like I've just consumed a hearty but low carb meal. Even better, the pain recedes and my wounds improbably start to close up. "This is great, Micah." I'm still going to request a proper healing spell from Oscar once Micah's out of earshot. "How many magic spells can you cast before you need a rest?"

"Ashenfal said two. So, I guess I'm out. But it doesn't matter, Oscar's brought magic re-up potions." He hands out the rest of his magic berries to the rest of our sorry crew.

Cole takes a step towards me. "Hey Kyle, why is your hat spinning?"

Sparing me from having to explain, two new arrows sail into my hat. Cole jumps back. At this point I don't even flinch.

"More goblins?" asks Souffy with exasperation rather than fear. "You cretins have lost! Give up and go home!" In response, another arrow flies at her, but that one too angles over to my hat.

"It came from somewhere over there." Micah points to a bush-covered slope. There are way too many goblin hiding spots in this area.

"I have an idea," I say to the others. "Just don't hit the raven, okay?"

I ping Bell and she sails over the spot where we saw the arrows come from. It's not hard from my familiar's vantage point to spot the goblins; there's nearly a dozen of them spread around there. Bell dive-bombs a cluster of four, grabbing a lock of hair from one and tugging hard. I think the show put on by the King of Eagles has her wanting to prove herself. An angry goblin springs after her and might have succeeded in catching her if Micah didn't shoot him through the arm first. Souffy follows up with a Fire Orb to the bush. A solitary goblin makes it out.

"Gracious Verhalty, show them the light!" Oscar intones. What looks like lightning shoots out of his hands, and knocks the last goblin to the ground. The surrounding bushes rustle as the rest of the goblins cut their losses and run. That's hopefully the last of them—knock on wood.

"What's with that bird?" asks Micah.

"Kyle summoned a familiar," explains Tristan. I preen a bit, glad to have evidence that I too have upped my magic game. "Her name is Tinkerbell." Never mind.

"Tinkerbell?" Micah asks incredulously while Cole snickers.

"It's a good name, Kyle," says Oscar.

"Tristan named her. And she goes by Bell." I'm smiling despite myself. I'm just grateful they showed up, and not only because we'd all be dead by now if they hadn't.

Cole wanders over to check out the goblin corpses. "What did you do to piss these guys off?" He bends over one of the twisted and charred bodies.

"They're evil." I shrug. Apparently, I don't have any moral qualms when it's a life-or-death situation. "I suppose it was because we invaded their fort and rescued Ferimus."

"Don't worry," says Tristan. "We're not required to search the bodies or anything."

"This one's got nice boots, though," says Cole.

"My boots!" cries Ferimus.

Cole takes a hold of the sole of one of the boots while bracing his own foot on the dead goblin's knee and pulls it off without getting any goblin blood on himself. He repeats the maneuver, then hands the boots off to Ferimus. "Where are we going next?"

"How about somewhere that goblins can't jump out at us?" suggests Oscar. He's always the best at practical stuff like that.

We leave the goblin corpses behind and trek over to that open basin we were originally aiming for. There, we arrive at a shallow river, running with clear water and patches of foam as the rivulets pass through rapids. The basin is surrounded by snow-capped mountains that are downright Instagrammable. Also, no one's shooting at us, so I'm (conditionally) calling it peaceful. Best of all, we stop to wash away the dirt and various goblin bodily fluids still clinging to us. And Oscar's even packed a lunch! It's not Thai takeout, but bread, cured meat, and apples are delicious when you're hungry. Someone applies a Restore cantrip to my clothing, and Oscar slips me a healing spell while Micah isn't watching, so I'm feeling slightly buzzed on top of it all. But even if I wasn't, I think this is the most content I've felt since we've arrived in Mythreal.

Oscar and the others fill us in on their experiences with Ashenfal. Unsurprisingly, Micah was a hit and has been invited to come to a dryad gathering. They had heard from Raskin that we were going after a weapon, but (what with his enchantment) he still couldn't tell them why we needed it.

"Inquiring minds want to know. What's really going on here?" asks Cole.

Everyone turns their attention to me, including Tristan and Souffy who could just as well have told the tale. I take a deep breath and start with the Triad of Valor and the replanting of the forest (along with a bit of scientific exposition on the ecology of magic forests) before laying out just how the Bernstein siblings flubbed the final tree-planting ritual, and the danger thereby posed by the Doomsday Tree. Then I speed us forward to the present, looping in the meteorite and the effect we think it had on the time-containment spell, and also what the Doomsday Tree probably did to Janassy. I give them chances to ask questions, and they do, but we stay surprisingly on topic. I get to the end, and to the tricky part—agreeing what to do next.

"So, now that Ferimus has his seven-league shoes back, we could send him, or someone else, to the druid camp for reinforcements." It's the safest approach.

"Or, we go ahead with your original plan of finding this weapon," suggests Oscar. I was not expecting him to say that.

"And then we go after the Doomsday Tree. Bet you it's not fire resistant," says Souffy. That, I was expecting.

"And rescue Ferimus's girlfriend," adds Tristan.

"Right," I say. "The problem is we don't know where the weapon is. Raskin's druid deer were the ones who knew the way, and they're gone now."

Cole smiles. "Good thing we asked him for a map before we left. We even got him to mark where he thought you'd be going."

He unfurls the map in question. There's the druid camp in one corner, and an *X* marked next to a mountain in the other that could be any of the several peaks that I currently see around us.

"Did the birds happen to tell you where they were dropping you off?" I ask.

"Nope," says Cole, "but let me try something." He pulls out his sobriety medallion and holds it over the map, swinging it in a counterclockwise circle. Two thirds of the way around its circuit the pendant stops as if caught by a magnet and holds itself improbably over a river with a granite dome drawn to the west. Ferimus uses his magic fear quill to mark a You-Are-Here spot. It's not that far away from the *X*.

"Did it always do that?" asks Souffy.

"Magical upgrade. It's surprising where you can find active branches of the Thieves' Guild. I called in a favor."

I turn to Oscar. "And you're okay with this? With all of this?"

"When in Mythreal." He gives an easy smile followed by a laugh. Oscar has the best laugh of the group, warm and melodic. "Seriously though, yeah, we're in."

"Great!" Tristan stands up. "The band's back together. Oh, and Souffy too."

"Excuse me." It's Micah. "I haven't said my piece yet." He stands dramatically (it involves bracing himself on his bow and giving the cloak a swish). We wait. "Marjorie's Third Law: *A Boy Band with dedication, devotion, a bit of luck, and great hair can save the world.*" He beams at us. "I updated it."

There's still at least five hours of sunlight left. We set off at a brisk pace with Bell circling overhead to keep watch. As we climb higher, the trees thin out and the going gets easier.

There's a bounce to my step, and that giddiness you feel the day after you've pulled an all-nighter. We're back together, in a way we haven't been since… since the start of the pandemic when we went into lockdown.

I flash back to that March seven years ago: the internet was filled with stories of there not being enough room in morgues, of old people trapped in nursing homes unable to see their children, of mobs the size of fangirl posses going rabid over toilet paper. And I felt, we all felt, so (unironically) hashtag blessed that we were bubbled up together. We've always been at our best when we're looking out for each other.

Ahead of me, Souffy is explaining her take on divine callings and destiny. "It's not as if you can't die while following the Divine Wisdom's will. But then, you might fall asleep and wake up dead." Heaven forbid one should die such a boring death. "I'm so glad you've put your faith in the Divine Wisdom and decided to come on the quest!" She practically squeals out this last bit.

"Yeah, that. But also, Kyle thought it was a good idea." I snap to attention when I hear Oscar mention my name. "He's usually right about these things."

"Annoyingly so," says Micah.

"Is that a compliment?" I ask—he makes it sound like an insult. "Are you complimenting me?"

"More like stating the obvious," says Cole. "You're not our designated 'smart one' for nothing."

"Actually, I am, all the better cliches were taken."

"What? No." Oscar looks surprised. "You're our secret weapon. All the other music acts were jealous."

"Secret weapon?" asks Souffy.

"Like in an interview when a reporter would sneak in a gotcha question or find a way to slip in one of the verboten subjects," says Tristan as if Souffy would understand any of that. But I don't interrupt, this is about me. "And before one of us can say something that would land us all in trouble, Kyle sails in with a joke, or a diversion, and the interview keeps going without a hitch."

"He always knows who everyone is and their connections in the industry, and he'll figure out a way to casually drop the information during a conversation, so we don't look like idiots," says Micah. They're right. I did do all those things. I just didn't think they noticed.

"And the way he intimidates alpha males is fantastic," says Cole.

"Tristan's the one that intimidates alpha males," I say.

"Tristan's the one that charms them." Cole smirks. "You take them down."

"Alpha males?" asks Souffy, eyes wide with wonder. "You have werewolves in your world?"

"That's just a phrase we use for powerful, dominant men in our world," explains Oscar. "Studio execs, producers, headliners. They're usually older, white, and rich."

"And asshats," interjects Micah.

"They think boy bands are just a pre-packaged set of pretty faces in fit bodies to be marketed for a couple of years to naïve adolescent girls. They'll insult you, manipulate you, make you feel guilty for things that aren't your fault." It's not often that Oscar gets this bitter, but I've heard stories about previous bands he's been with. "And they like to talk, a lot. Kyle has the knack for saying just the thing to cut through their condescension and make them reconsider us, to get them to take us seriously."

"Like that Swedish producer who refused to even listen to Micah's arrangements," says Tristan.

"Tris, Souffy has no idea what you're talking about," I say, and then realize I might be the one making assumptions, so I ask her, "Do you?"

She shakes her head. "But I'd love to hear more."

We let Oscar try to tell the story. "So, there was this bigwig music… composer, and our first time with him in the recording… place that we're going to re… hearse, Micah suggests a change to the song he's given us to sing. And Karl's words were, 'This song is going to hit number one,' um, that means to be the most popular song in our world, 'either for you, or for the next boy band on my list, the one that's not stupid enough to try to fuck with my art.' And when Micah tries again to get Karl to just listen to his version, Karl goes off on a ten-minute rant about, well, about the history of another famous music group and one of their songs. And when he's done, Kyle corrects him on three different factual points."

Tristan jumps in. "Karl didn't believe Kyle so he calls in his secretary and makes him check the Wikipedia page, and when Wikipedia doesn't support him, he makes the secretary go through the Rolling Stones archive and then Kyle shows him a clip from a documentary on YouTube that proves Karl was wrong. And it was a documentary that Karl was interviewed for."

"The guy was so schooled, he dropped the ego act and started actually listening to our suggestions. And that's how Micah got songwriter credit on our first album," adds Cole.

That and the fact that I let slip to Karl's secretary just which social media giant Micah's mom was a head honcho at. But the anecdote is already confusing enough as it is.

"Anyway, that's why we listen to you, Kyle," says Oscar. "You're the brains of this outfit."

"And why Marjorie said I needed to make you say yes to the reunion tour," adds Tristan.

We've stopped walking and they're all looking at me—big smiles all around. I feel my cheeks going hot and am tempted to hide under my hat.

Instead, I let myself grin and push the brim back. "Thanks guys. It feels good to hear that." I feel a group hug coming on, when Souffy gasps.

"This is it. This is the place from Raskin's memories!" She points at a pile of rocks stacked into a pyramid with a thin slab resting against the base.

"Are you going to check it out?" I ask Micah.

"It's man-made. That makes checking for traps the rogue's job."

"I like how he knows how useless his class is," I hear Cole mutter under his breath. He walks up to examine the structure before attempting to move the slab.

"Need help?" asks Oscar.

"I got it." The rock topples over with a sharp clatter. Cole reaches into the shallow cavern now exposed to the air and pulls a sizable object out. "It looks like a treasure chest."

"Treasure?" Micah bounds over. "Pick the lock."

Cole walks back to me. "Kyle, do you still have that magic key ring?"

"Good idea." I dig in my bag for it. "You're pretty clever at these nerd games." I hand him the keys. "We should have played *Heroes Summoning* together."

"You should have asked me." But he's smiling, so I know we're good.

"Do you think we'll be able to use this magic weapon?" asks Oscar. "What if they didn't leave any instructions about what to do with it?"

"I don't think that will be a problem." The chest now opened, Cole holds the weapon up for all of us to see. It makes me glad for the Triad being down-to-earth siblings from New Jersey.

"What is that?" asks Souffy.

"It's a chainsaw," says Tristan. "That tree's not going to know what hit… um… sawed it."

"We'll first need to get past Janassy," says Ferimus.

Not to mention all the blights she controls. If we were overpowered like the Triad of Valor, this wouldn't be a problem. But we're not, we're a boy band.

We're a boy band. According to Micah's new version of law number three, we can save the world. I've been thinking, ever since we were zapped to Mythreal, that our chosen profession was our liability, but what if I was wrong? The Divine Wisdom chose the members of Never Boy Land over countless otherworld choices, so there has to be a reason. An idea's been forming in my mind that's more hairbrained than any in Tristan's movie, but it has potential. The hard part will be convincing my bandmates—

No. I stop myself: what they said this afternoon about me being their secret weapon, what Souffy said on that hellish deer ride about them respecting my intelligence, what Tris said last night about he and the others believing in me—it's time for me to trust my bandmates the way they apparently trust me. I take a deep breath, and go for it:

"So, about getting past Janassy." Everyone turns towards me. "I think I might have a plan."

CHAPTER 54

Janassy

Kakosylium, the sacred tree, is calling her again. Some days it feels like there's never a moment when it isn't calling her. This is what it means to be part of something greater, Janassy reminds herself: *this is what you wanted.*

Once again (how many times this day, she's lost track) she scrambles along the granite dome and down to the nearly dry fen. As her bare feet dig into the cold dirt, she reaches out with her dryad magick and does some calling of her own.

She doesn't begrudge the sacred tree for needing her to perform this task. At this critical stage of its development, the tree is still struggling to survive, to gather the substance it needs to thrive. It won't have to for much longer; the time spell is racing through decades in a day. Perhaps even this very hour, its magnificent roots will pierce the ley line, and then it will have unlimited access to all the mana it needs. But until that glorious moment, it's up to Janassy to hand-feed her charge, her master.

A plant-creature timidly approaches. Janassy reaches out and gently strokes the bark cheeks of the bush-deer. It's her own name for this wondrous, galloping, trotting collection of branches and foliage. When the Kakosylium had gifted her with its supernatural resin, the dryad's heart had soared. Now she could bring new life to the forest—finally give the flora a literal leg up in the battle against the humans who so ruthlessly cut their lives short.

"Come along now," she says. Janassy uses her magical connection to the creature's mana to lead it back to the mountain's rocky face and along the granite ledge. Its wooden hooves clack against stone; it's the only sound in this unnaturally quiet place.

The world of the high mountains is beautiful in a stark, unforgiving way. Summers bring an intensity of wildflowers as the vegetation makes the most of the short growing season, but now in fall, their energies have been spent in the production of seeds. The grasses and low shrubs have shriveled to a gray mass. At a distance it's indistinguishable from the granite ground. The dwarf trees root in small patches of hardened dirt, barely eking out an existence due to the harsh winters and depleted soil. What vibrant life there is now takes the form of lichens that paint the rocks in extravagant red, yellow, and orange streaks.

It strains Janassy's comprehension as to why the Triad of Valor thought it a good idea to plant a sacred tree in this unforgiving environment. She understands that they wanted the sacred trees to have access to the Taproot ley line, the one that in antiquity had anchored the World Tree and now reaches deep into the foundations of Mythreal. The other sacred trees in the Drevo Woods are indirectly connected to it. A sacred tree in this location would be able to directly feed its own mana-energy, and any excess from the other sacred trees, directly into mana-stores across the realm. Or drain it dry, as is Kakosylium's intent.

But this was hardly the only place that such a connection could be made. Had the Triad consulted with any of the dryads, her sisters would have directed the Triad to other, more hospitable locations where the tree could just as easily have linked with the Taproot ley line.

Janassy, followed by the bush-deer, squeezes through the gap created by a split in a massive boulder. She half-jumps, half-inches her way down the rocky ledge to the ravine the Wizard Daniel had selected for the planting. It opens out to the north and is cut through with a vein of green, toxic serpentine rock. Janassy shakes her head; they really couldn't have chosen a worse spot to plant a tree.

She should have said something. Only (thinking back) she recalls how headstrong and in-a-hurry the heroes had been. Also, they just weren't terribly attractive; it was easier to look the other way and judge silently. Humans disparage dryads as superficial for choosing to keep company with only those who are pleasing to behold, but Janassy has noticed that the humans never make their bouquets with wilting greens, or flowers with missing petals.

Why should she settle for someone whose black hair has dulled with unsightly streaks of gray, who has grown a paunch around his waist, whose visage is marred by creases every time he smiles—even if imagining that smile still warms her heart? Janassy has learned that these imperfections portend more changes still, until the handsome wizard lad she'd spied in the woods so many years ago is no more than a memory. Janassy has accumulated more than enough of these memories. She doesn't need any new ones.

She's living in the now. She's serving Kakosylium and making her small contribution to the greater plan. Perhaps her efforts won't be immortalized in an epic poem, but (as the sacred tree constantly assures her) to be consumed by something greater than oneself is its own reward.

Janassy and the bush-deer have reached the time barrier, beyond which there is only gray soil because every last bit of green life has been drained from it long ago. The light inside flickers as weeks speed by in minutes. The bush deer startles and digs in its hooves. Janassy isn't sure if it's the time dilation or some survival instinct that spooks it. She slaps its hindquarters, and it leaps through. Once inside, it becomes calm again. The hum of Kakosylium calls, promising it that its brief life will be gifted to something greater.

Janassy follows the plant-creature. As she crosses the barrier, the tree's presence flows into her, and her mind shifts to experience time as it does. The past—from the moment the tree sprouted and was welcomed by the sun until it had fallen dormant the previous autumn—is compressed into a single moment. Even the cruel curse Wizard Daniel had laid upon it is wrapped tightly away, deprived of the power to hurt or cause regret. The tree's attention is bound in the present and entirely focused on sending its mana down into its roots to make them grow, inch by inch, towards the Taproot. It's almost there. And then a glorious future will unfold, one where Kakosylium will have unlimited access to mana which it will use to subjugate the Drevo Woods—no, the whole world—and all those parasitic creatures: humans, elves, dwarves, even the gods, will kneel before its might. Making that future a reality is Janassy's new purpose, her true purpose.

Janassy and the bush-deer turn the corner, and there it is: Kakosylium. While short and stunted—Janassy blames the poor soil conditions—it's like no other tree she has ever known, closer to a sculpture in shape and design. Its white branches spiral and arc, like a waterfall trapped in ice in the dead of winter. The only color is to be found at the very tips of its gnarled branches: a sprinkling of dense, green needles. Janassy has to coax even that sparse foliage to bud; the tree prefers to focus its energies exclusively on reaching the Taproot ley line. Once it connects and has access to unlimited mana, Janassy is sure it will sprout a canopy comparable to—exceeding even—any of the other sacred trees.

The tree calls to the bush-deer, which in response, trots haltingly to the trunk to place its head against the bark. Janassy watches as the creature's body shudders violently and springs two feet into the air. When it lands, its legs clatter and fall to pieces like so much kindling. The mana that it had collected and used to animate its limbs has been subsumed into Kakosylium. Any scraps of mana that remain in the corpse of the bush-deer will soon be pulled deep into the earth, decaying into nutrients that will also feed the tree.

Janassy turns around; she doesn't need to stay for this process. The first time she'd led a plant-creature to the tree, she forced herself to watch, to witness and shed tears for its sacrifice. But over time, she's grown strong and risen above such maudlin sentiments. She is, as the dryad saying goes, finally growing some bark.

It's a quality she's always admired in Ashenfal and the other dryads. She used to wonder how they manage to be so self-confident and righteous, so impermeable to doubt. Now she knows.

It's simple really. The trick is not to care.

It also has the perverse side effect of making others do more to try to please you. Initially, she had to beg and coax the plant-creatures to follow her to their doom. Now, she commands them. She has driven the humans out from their encampment. She has leveled Rozney Las. She had converted the great Saitanna and when those so-called heroes had defiled its sacred grounds, she had urged it to attack and strangle them. She has accomplished so much. She should be happy.

She is happy. But also tired and empty.

It's so much work, being part of the great plan.

Janassy slogs back up the rocky path, retracing her steps to where other plant-creatures—three vine-golems, another bush-deer, and a lizard-log with an enormous mouth—mill about while they await their turn. Maybe these will be the last of the sacrifices, and their donated energy will be enough to allow Kakosylium to reach the Taproot. It's as she's motioning to the largest vine creature that she hears a sound that resolves into a melody.

Babe, when it's just you and me
Hanging out, feelin' free
Ain't no other way I want it to be
Just you and me

It's a song, or at least, it's being sung. The melody is unlike any of the druid chants and lacks that fragile, haunting quality of Elven arias. It reminds Janassy of a song she'd heard sung by a party of troubadours who'd once spent a week in the forest when their wagon broke down. But the pitch is lower, the tempo faster. The vocals dip in time to a relentless implied beat and the music somehow fills the forest and the valley. More startling, it starts to fill something inside her.

> *Dancing all night, sleeping all day*
> *With you in my arms*
> *I ain't never going let you go*
> *Oooh-oh-oh-oh baaybeee*

The singer is male. No, wait, there's more than one singer! They seamlessly trade verses, until the nonsense words blend together in a strange harmony. The volume increases; Janassy's knees wobble. Such power! The music flows into her, pulsing under her skin, squeezing her heart. It hurts, like when the feeling returns to one's feet after a long swim in a freezing mountain lake. The pain stabs with each step, but you have to keep walking. Janassy, followed by the plant-creatures, turns away from the rocky slope and wanders down into an open meadow with a stream running through it.

> *Cause I won't let you go*
> *Oh no no no no*
> *You're all I want, my everything*
> *Girl, you don't know how great you are*
> *There ain't anyone better, better than you*
> *How you do it, I don't know, but don't stop*

Janassy spots the singers, five young men. From their fine features she assumes they must be elves, but their ears don't appear to be outsized, or pointed. And she's never seen an elf who could sway their hips like that. Recognition dawns. These are the same heroes who Janassy fought and almost defeated at the roots of Saitanna.

She should order the plant-creatures to attack. But this time their weapons hang forgotten at their sides, and they use their hands to gesticulate to the music. Janassy watches—entranced—as the heroes snap into identical poses and then gyrate joyfully. She notes that the one in green is a ranger, a friend of the forest. And another bears the symbol of Verhalty, the goddess who created the fairies, on his armor. But it's the one in the middle, with hair like sunlight, who draws her in. The heroes slide past each other, taking on a V formation, like a flight of geese. Then the golden-haired one steps forward, and his voice alone sings the words. Although he's still several yards away, their eyes meet.

> *It's the way you smile, the way you laugh*
> *Fills my life with meaning*
> *Makes me know what it is to be alive*
> *Girl, light up my life*

There had been a time when Janassy was new—not young, dryads are never children, they burst into being fully formed—when she'd experienced the world and its seasons for the first time. Unlike humans, dryads' memories don't fade. Janassy can remember every detail. She had exclaimed with delight when she caught sight of the first crocuses, green against white snow, her voice echoing through the still-sleeping forest. Later, she ran, leaped, and tumbled in fields of wildflowers under a sun that seemed to never set. When her first autumn came, she shook the trees to rain down red and gold leaves, dancing underneath as they fell around her. And during that first winter, when everything was asleep, she watched the shapes her breath made in the air, taking comfort that this was all in preparation for a new spring, a new cycle.

When did she lose that breathless anticipation, that delight in all the wonders around her? Had her innocent exuberance already been fading when she fell for her first elven lad, the one whose hair smelled of honeysuckle and who sighed when she stroked his ears? He wrote poetry comparing her to a willow tree, to the wind, to so many, many flowers. Until then, she'd thought herself happy. But then pleasure blossomed into love, and it was as if her feet didn't touch the ground. Time spent tending trees and plants went by in a blur as she waited for her love and the endless hours spent in his presence. Time passed. The boy became a man and grew cold and contemplative, as elves often do. Still handsome, but no longer warm in the way he had been. It was fine, because there were others: elves, humans, a couple of demigods, and one incredibly charismatic dwarf. To each she gave her heart. And when the fervor of love broke or faded (as always happened) and her heart was returned, it was a little more hardened and battered. It eventually became such a broken mess, she didn't even want it back. She supposes it's still with Ferimus who she left in the care of the goblins.

It doesn't matter. Kakosylium hadn't required her heart, and perhaps that was why it had been so easy to give it the rest of her: mind, body and soul. Around her, the heroes continue their serenade.

Holding you tight, that's how it's got to be
With you in my arms
I ain't never going let you go
Oooh-oh-oh-oh baaybeee

Maybe she'd been wrong. Maybe she still has her heart.

The golden-haired one (he could be a demigod after all) approaches her. She welcomes his presence, like she welcomes showers in early spring. His skin is the color of milkweed, his teeth sparkle like morning dew. Janassy has always been the recipient, never the giver, of poetic comparisons. It's rather fun. The man holds out his hand, and the outside world—the plant-creatures, Kakosylium, the great plan—falls away. The other heroes are still there, their voices casting a spell to shield Janassy from everyone but this one incredible, beautiful, perfect man.

Janassy raises her pale, worn hand with its black, claw-like fingernails. Its appearance dismays her. When was the last time she took the time to bathe in a stream or properly bask in the sun? Kakosylium hasn't cared what she looks like, so she'd stopped expending the time and effort to groom herself. And the more drab her appearance, the less it seemed to matter.

But it matters now. She needs this man to see her in all her dryad splendor. She summons the nature magick always coursing through her body, and it catches her up and spins her around. Layers of accumulated mold slough off revealing glowing skin; a gentle breeze blows the spiderwebs from her hair. The mana energy surges through her, and she stands straighter.

The man gasps—proof that she's gotten it right.

"Wow, girl. That's some kind of magic." And he smiles, clasping her hands in his. His skin is slightly calloused, but not rough. She knows the others are still singing, but the only melody she hears is his voice. "I'm Tristan, from Never Boy Land," he adds.

"I'm Janassy, from the Drevo Woods."

Tristan looks into her eyes, and for the first time in such a long time, someone truly sees her. She could cry. She could dance.

She wants him. Even more than that, she wants this feeling.

And she will have it. Once more, she gathers mana from the earth.

"This is all I ask, that you keep me first in your thoughts, holding me above all others."

She seals the spell with a kiss.

CHAPTER 55

Kyle

Everything's going according to plan, and I know I shouldn't say that, but it's undeniable. Sometimes when you step on stage—it just clicks—the pieces coming together. It's been over a week since we practiced this song, practiced any song, and not a note is out of tune. We're hitting all the beats, and even without a background melody, our dance moves are in perfect sync. We're in the zone. It doesn't hurt that the acoustics are fantastic, maybe something to do with the natural rocky amphitheater created by the surrounding mountains. And the song itself (voted the Song of the Summer for the 2018 MTV VMAs via a social media poll) is one of our best.

We hit the vocal switch, Tristan's clean tenor gives way to Oscar's soulful baritone, and we all join in with the chord progression at the bridge. It's magic. Not real magic, except—I check the sensations in my hands—yes, there's definitely some Mythreal magic getting in on the action as well.

Our audience of one (I'm not counting the blights) is enthralled. Janassy, hands clasped with a beatific expression plastered on her face, is gently swaying in time with the beat. By now, Ferimus has canceled the time acceleration spell, and Janassy hasn't shown any sign of noticing. I close my own eyes to peek through Bell's far sharper ones to confirm that our Ravenus wizards have almost made it to the Doomsday Tree's secret… lair? Grove? We only need to hold Janassy's attention for a moment longer, just enough to take RazorChain—that's the name the Triad had inscribed on the weapon's handle, classy as always—to the tree and start sawing away.

The plan is for them to slice through the bark around the entire trunk, thereby disrupting the mana flow and hopefully damaging the Doomsday Tree enough to sap away some of its power. In an ideal world, a weakened tree would lose its hold over Janassy, she'd order the blights to stop their attacks, and she might even tell Ferimus that she still loves him.

Tristan thinks we can break the Doomsday Tree's hold over Janassy with just our performance. If he's wrong, Micah and I are ready to unleash our magic attacks to take her down. At which point Tristan and Cole will tie her up while Oscar applies a healing spell.

It would have been smarter to have Cena and Arek's forces in reserve; attack plans, like headliners, are better with backup. But if the Doomsday Tree is growing as fast as we fear, we don't have time to wait for reinforcements. If it's causing this much trouble now, I don't want to see what the Doomsday Tree could accomplish once it can draw on unlimited stores of mana.

Maybe it won't come to that. Micah holds the high note while the rest of us crescendo with oo-ah-ahs. Janassy jumps and claps her hands in delight. When she first appeared, she looked bedraggled and waterlogged, as if she'd recently been uncovered after being buried under winter snows. Her lichen cloak and skirt of leaves clung to her body, drowned-rat style. Her green skin was splotchy with fuzzy white spots. Her locks were pulled back in the kind of ponytail women resort to when they haven't washed their hair in far too long. If there ever was a dryad in need of a boy band, she was it.

Grown women needed boy bands just as much as teenagers, that was Marjorie's manifesto (one of Marjorie's manifestos).

According to our manager, teenage and young adulthood is an emotional rollercoaster with the thrills coming largely because everything is brand new and happening for the first time. I can still hear the oft-spoken lecture:

"Do we adults fall in love and get our hearts broken? Obviously yes, and it still feels amazing and shitty in turns, but it's no longer *special.* By now we know that *it* happens: to us, to our friends, to strangers. It's just part of the human condition. Even if you had the narcissism to go all drama queen about your experience, what are you going to do about it? *Post on Facebook?* Fine, whatever. You still need to wake up in the morning, show up for work, get your car's oil changed and all those dismal adult responsibilities. But guess what, under all those layers of womanly experiences, there's still a gawky adolescent girl who has no clue how awesome she is and who still has the ability to *feel,* and *feel deeply.*" Marjorie's polished this particular speech to Ted Talk levels.

Her theory is that boy bands are a conduit to those unadulterated emotions. Through our earnest voices, naïve lyrics, joyous dancing, non-threatening masculinity, and willingness to be ridiculous, we allow our older fans to time travel, if only for the span of a concert or album, back to those girls they had been. The aging jock equivalent of this is attending sporting events.

When I was sixteen, it felt like Marjorie was selling this idea too hard. When I turned twenty-five, I started to get it. And now, watching Janassy pull off a real-life magical girl transformation, I totally buy it. Marjorie was on to something.

A wind picks up out of nowhere and billows in iridescent spirals around Janassy, twirling her leaf skirt, lifting up the shawl, and expanding it into a ground-length, shimmering-black cape. Her skin glows neon green and her silken hair flows free like Spanish moss. But more than her going from a "four" to at least an "eight," Janassy is radiating confidence and her smile is big and open and hungry. I'll admit she's a bit scary like this—I've always found powerful women to be scary.

I see Janassy mouthing some words, and then she reaches out her arms and straight up kisses Tristan.

Oscar turns to me. "Hot dang, it's working."

I feel sorry for Tristan's lips. Janassy's gone in for a full lip-lock. Ashenfal just kissed me on the forehead when she had cast that spell on me.

Oh.

Shit.

She's casting a spell. And I'm pretty certain it's not to impart on Tristan the ability to see the flow of mana in tree bark. I break formation and sprint to Tris's side, which is how I catch the instant his eyes fade to pure white and his whole face turns doughy. I've read about this kind of thing in Souffy's textbook; they're the classic symptoms of a Charm spell.

Charm is a beginner-level spell and can be cast by most types of magic users. It instantly turns a stranger into your best friend, your embarrassingly gullible best friend. That's pretty much its limit—it's not full mind control and it can't turn the victim evil, or at least that's how it works when humans cast it. Janassy's a fairy; her abilities are supercharged with wild nature-magick and pumped up on the high-drama intrigue of *A Midsummer Night's Dream.*

"Tris, get away from her!" I yell, too late. Tristan is already giggling, smiling inanely with his mouth hanging open. It's like that time a fangirl roofied his drink, except this time it was done with magic, and Tristan's in possession of a deadly sword.

337

"It's alright guys. Janassy's our friend," he says, turning to us. "This is all one big misunderstanding."

"He's being mind-controlled," I shout. "Plan B!"

Micah's already pulling back his bowstring. "*Dreen-chruinn*," he intones as he sends an arrow in Janassy's direction. But even as I'm seeing the small green thorns materialize around the arrowhead, there's a flash. Tristan's sword has sliced the arrow in half. It falls harmlessly to the ground.

"Don't hurt her." Tristan doesn't get angry. That vengeance attack scene in his movie took twelve takes before the director gave up and fixed his expression in CG. But Tristan does do hurt, and he's now looking at us as if Micah had just kicked a puppy.

By this point no one's singing anymore. You could hear a pin drop in the ensuing silence. Or, in the distance, the sputter of a magical chainsaw revving up.

"Kakosylium!" screams Janassy in a suddenly harsh and creaking voice. "Treacherous humans. You thought to lull me into submission with your angelic faces and demigodly bodies!"

"Yeah, not cool guys." Tristan shakes his sword at us in disapproval.

I could just Magic Mortar him and Janassy both. You're allowed to attack your best friend if he's being mind-controlled, right? But what if I killed him in the process? I can't risk it.

"We must protect the sacred tree! To my side, my noble knight," Janassy yells and grabs Tristan with one hand while pointing at us with her other. "Plant-creatures, put an end to these defilers!"

Three swamp things, a walking-blight, and a centipede tree log with a two-foot-deep gash for a mouth that's bristling with teeth splinters all charge at once, while Janassy and Tristan run off towards the tree.

Oscar steps out in front of me. "Kyle, go after them, we'll take care of these guys and catch up."

"You sure?"

Instead of responding, he forms his hand into a namaste gesture and intones, "*Gracious Verhalty, show them the light.*" Something between an impossibly bright spotlight and lightning bolt shoots out from his hand and turns the advancing walking-blight into a pile of charcoal on the spot. Micah's already notching his bow, and Cole's vanished into the surrounding landscape in preparation for one of his sneak attacks.

"You guys are the best!" I shout back at them as I run after Tristan and Janassy.

Those two are already halfway across the granite plateau by the time I burst out of the forest.

"Tristan!" I shout.

He turns and waves. "Hey Kyle. I've got to help Janassy, there's some evil wizards attacking a sacred tree!"

"That's Souffy and her uncle. They're our friends!"

Tristan slows down, but Janassy yanks his arm. "Janassy says no. They're just disguised as our friends!" I hear him say before they disappear between two rocks. So much for trying to reason with him. Tristan is highly suggestible under ordinary circumstances and magical mind-control aside, Janassy's giving off that Marjorie woman-in-charge vibe that we're all conditioned to follow without question. So he really might attack Souffy if Janassy orders it. I make myself run faster.

On reaching the rocks, Tristan and Janassy disappear behind a boulder. When I catch up I find a steep incline down. I need to slow down to catch breath so I don't take a tumble and twist my ankle. By the time I scramble down to the bottom, there's no sign of Janassy or Tristan. Which way should I go? I can hear the chainsaw, but it's echoing off the rock walls and seems to come from everywhere. Luckily, Bell went this way with Souffy and Ferimus. I spare a moment to pause, close my eyes, and connect with my familiar. Bell shows me the remainder of the route as well as the ravine where Souffy and Ferimus are currently standing next to the Doomsday Tree. The reception's grown fuzzy-white for some reason, but I catch a glimpse of Ferimus putting down the chainsaw, and turning to somebody. "Janassy, did Tristan cure you?" I hear him say.

Not good. *Warn them*, I tell my familiar. I can't spare any more time.

"Charmed! Charmed!" I hear Bell screech as I bound the last few yards down the slope.

I find a trail of footprints and blight tracks in the dust. I'm hoping all those blights ended up as mana fertilizer; facing off against a cursed sacred tree, its dryad protector, and a possessed swordsman is more than enough for your modern working wizard, thank you. I follow the footsteps past a crater with a beach ball-sized meteorite resting at its center, thereby confirming our theory about how the tree was freed from its barrier. A shiver runs up my spine. Nerves? Or, no, it's physically getting colder. There's suddenly frost on the ground and—I look up—snow. I guess I know what season the time spell stopped on.

"Tristan, what are you doing?" screams Souffy just as I turn at a flat-out sprint into what I'm calling the Doomsday Grove. Granite escarpments crisscrossed by veins of quartz rise on two sides, meeting in a pile of boulders and creating a bowl about the size of a large lecture hall.

"He's being controlled by Janassy," I yell even as I'm taking it all in.

It's like an establishing shot, right before the fighting gets real. But the setting's all Hallmark-holiday-card-pretty thanks to the gently falling snow. Ferimus is on his back, clutching at his wrist, the chainsaw idle at his side. Tristan is standing over him, sword drawn, red along its edge. Not good. Janassy's standing back looking smug. Souffy's about ten feet away, pointing her fingers at Tristan like a gun.

"*Ignatious!*" a spark flies out of her finger-gun and lands on Tristan's foot. He hops away from Ferimus, almost falling but catching himself with his sword.

"See Kyle? It's not the real Souffy. She'd never use a fire spell this close to a sacred tree!"

"She totally would, Tris!" I shout back. At least he still thinks I'm the real me.

I spare a glance towards the Doomsday Tree. At least I think it's the Doomsday Tree—it's the only plant in the vicinity. Given the enormity of the other sacred trees, I was expecting something... bigger? It's at most eight feet tall and barely two feet in diameter. Not that it lacks presence; it's a full-on spooky witch tree. Intricately twisting layers of bone-white bark crawl up the trunk and wrap around the cramped and twisted branches that poke at the sky like a hundred claws. Out of the very tips of the branches sprout dense tufts of scruffy green needles, dusted in white snow. The tree is basically a parasite, so it probably doesn't even need leaves. Instead, it's grown thick, twisted roots that reach out from its trunk in all directions. Remembering how Saitanna trapped me with its roots, I watch where I step. Even at a distance of thirty feet, I sense the oozing of its magic. It's a malaise of dark depression that's clammy on my skin—makes me yearn for a shower and exfoliant.

Meanwhile, Tristan's advancing on Souffy, his sword aimed right at her face. He's probably just trying to scare her, probably. Souffy's trying for another Flame Bolt, I can see the falling snow melting around her fingers, all the while backing away.

"Aim for his sword," I suggest.

Souffy nods and points, but just as she fires, her foot slips and she falls backwards, the Flame Bolt arcing uselessly upward. Her head cracks sickeningly against a rock. She lies in place, looking dazed. When she reaches up to her head, her hand comes back tinted red with blood. Tristan's still advancing.

"Finish her!" screams Janassy.

"Tristan!" He's not listening to me. "Tris!" I start running to them, to do what, I'm not sure.

"It's not Souffy," I hear him muttering. "It's just a girl. It's not Souffy, It's just a girl." Is he trying to fight the spell, or are those just Janassy's words in his head? He reaches Souffy and raises his sword.

"*Dexterarious!*" I shout. My Phantom Hand shoots out, but I'm too far back. Tris is already swinging. I need something, anything, to stop him. WWMBD? "Tris! Boy Band Law Number Eight!" I only hope he notices that she's bleeding.

Tristan's blade stops inches from Souffy's face. Just enough time for my Phantom Hand to swoop in and wrench the blade from his grip. Since I now have control of it, I try swinging the sword at the Doomsday Tree, but it bounces off harmlessly.

"How dare you attack a sacred tree, human!" Janassy is waving her hands in circle patterns. "*Medr Verde e Feroz!*" She completes the spell by throwing a kiss my way.

The earth in front of her erupts in a mass of slithering vines that grow like a fast-forwarded stop-motion animation towards me. Before I can even start to cast Magic Mortar, they've wrapped themselves around my throat and yanked me off my feet. I manage to wedge a hand under some of the vines so they don't cut off all my air. But I can neither chant nor gesture for a spell. Janassy's vines pull me towards her. I still have my Phantom Hand active and command it to do something, anything, to hold me in place. It grabs my foot. Now I not only look ridiculous, I think my hip is going to dislocate, but at least I'm no longer being dragged towards a dryad radiating murderous intent.

I turn to Souffy, but she's still lying prone. What I do see is that Tristan has recovered his sword and is rushing towards me.

"Kill him, slice him to pieces!" Janassy screeches.

Tris draws his sword. I can't do anything but gasp.

I look up pleadingly. He's so close now. The sword is coming down. I can see the soulful brown of his irises. *Wait a sec, his eyes are back to normal.*

The sword slashes through the vines. They go slack and fall away from my neck. I'm too busy sucking in air to say anything. Tris bends down and helps me to sit up.

"You overcame the spell. How?" I finally manage.

"She ordered me to break one of the Laws of Boy Bands, can't have that."

"Number six?" *Never damage the face.*

"Nope, number thirteen."

I think for a second. "That's not on the official list." It's just what Marjorie would holler at us when our roughhousing got out of hand.

"Not a bad rule for Mythreal, though." Tris smiles.

My throat's scratchy, but I manage to recite it. "*No matter how much they deserve it, you're not allowed to kill your bandmates.*"

CHAPTER 56

Souffy

Souffy's heart stops—her whole world stops—as she watches Tristan swing his sword at Kyle.

She's lost them! Lost them both, because there's no way Tristan would ever forgive himself for killing Kyle.

Souffy squeezes her eyes shut and braces for the inevitable screams. Instead, after an unbearable moment, she hears laughter—Kyle's laughter! When she reopens her eyes, Tristan is helping his friend to stand. Souffy's so relieved, the tears that had been welling up in her eyes roll down her cheeks. She should have known that a dryad's Charm spell couldn't overcome the deep bonds of friendship between the Neverboylanders.

Now there's only one enemy, Janassy. Two actually, Souffy amends, but the Doomsday Tree isn't actively attacking them at the moment.

"Wretched humans. Hateful mortals!" Janassy, suddenly no longer regal or enchanting, screeches. She raises her arms in a fashion reminiscent of the Doomsday Tree's painfully twisted branches. Her eyes are black holes.

Souffy knows the signs of a truly evil spell, so she scrambles to her feet, readying her Fire Orb. Out of the corner of her eye, she sees Tristan and Kyle likewise preparing themselves. Ferimus also stands up and approaches the dryad cautiously.

Janassy points a finger at Tristan, but it isn't an incantation that comes out of her mouth. "You! You come to me with your sweet words, your promises of love and devotion! And they're worthless. Worthless! Happily ever after? Happily never after!" That last bit doesn't make sense to Souffy. It doesn't have to. A great rant is more about the delivery than the logic, and Janassy has that part down. The dryad spreads out her hands, better to encompass the metaphorical whole of mankind—emphasis on the *man*.

"You never last! You sag and wither and die, over and over, and over again. Do you have any idea how that feels to an immortal like me? No, because you're already dead by then! That's always your excuse."

"You go, girl," Souffy hears Kyle say, but not too loudly.

"And you!" Janassy turns on the Doomsday Tree. "With your grand plans of world domination and unending demands, day in and day out. You never even brought me flowers! I'd rather spend an eternity by myself than waste another moment tending to you!"

She pulls on her hair and directs the final bit at the sky. "What's the point? Divine Wisdom, what's the point of any of this?" She howls in pure rage. Her scream echoes off the cliffs—who knew dryads had such impressive lungs? Eventually it dwindles to a creaking, strained rasp that sounds to Souffy like a tree falling in the forest.

"There isn't any." Ferimus's voice is soft, but earnest. He takes a step toward the dryad. Souffy isn't sure she's ever seen an act of such bravery. Suicidal bravery, granted, but still.

"What?" Janassy's facing Ferimus, turned away so that Souffy can't see the dryad's expression. Her arms have dropped to her sides, and the tension appears to have drained out of her shoulders.

"There isn't a point. There's just us. Just now." Ferimus shrugs apologetically. "Making the best of it. That's not so bad, is it?"

He holds out his hands to her. Janassy doesn't move. Souffy wonders what the dryad is seeing in her uncle. Ferimus has certainly seen better days. They'd cast the Rosewater Rejuvenation Ritual on the Neverboylanders before their performance for Janassy, but Ferimus hadn't been included. He's still covered with mud and dried goblin ichor. His hair and beard, usually so carefully tended, are now frizzed and dreaded into clumps. His cheeks, sagging after a week of subsisting on nothing but rats, are covered in a dirty stubble. Dehydration has left his lips cracked and bleeding. And he doesn't even have his hat anymore. The whole ensemble is not a good look on a man attempting to approach an angry dryad. *She's going to smite him,* Souffy thinks hopelessly.

Only Janassy doesn't. Instead, she says, "What are you even talking about, Ferimus?"

"Isn't it better, even if it's short, to spend your time with the one you love?"

He smiles. Familiar wrinkles sprout around his eyes and between his thick eyebrows. Ferimus had given Souffy that exact same smile when he'd found her weeping the first time her Grandfather's messenger bird egg informed her she wasn't fit to take her certification exams that semester (and the second time also, after which time she had stopped crying). Back then, when Ferimus had patted Souffy's shoulder, the comfort she got from him wasn't because he could do anything to help her—he couldn't—but from knowing that he genuinely wanted to. It made her feel less alone.

"But you're a mortal!" cries Janassy. Her voice cracks, and Souffy suspects she's holding off sobs.

"I know. I'm sorry. That's not even the worst of my faults." Ferimus takes a step forward. "But I love you. It makes me so happy to love you."

"But not forever." Her righteous indignation is replaced by a tone of resignation.

Ferimus shakes his head. "No, no. But for as long as I possibly can. That, I can, and will promise."

And then Janassy sobs, loudly and wetly. She takes the final step to close the distance between them and buries her face in Ferimus's shoulder.

There's the sound of pounding footsteps, and the rest of the Neverboylanders run into the grove.

"Snow?" Souffy hears Micah ask, and Cole shushes him.

"Awww," says Oscar, catching on to the scene before them.

Everyone watches silently as Janassy's muffled sobbing tapers off into sniffles, and her shoulders cease their shaking. Janassy and Ferimus are going to be okay, of that Souffy is sure.

She turns to Kyle and Tristan to tell them her thoughts. But before she can speak, the ground lurches up and collapses back down, sending them all sprawling. Her scalp itches worse than the time her brother cursed her and Mallynda with a magical lice infestation.

But this isn't a spell. It's just mana, so much mana. It's even more than was in the portal that transported the Neverboylanders to Mythreal.

"It's the tree," says Kyle. "Its roots must have reached—"

The rest is drowned out by a buzzing, as if someone had smashed a hornets' nest. The sound is definitely coming from the Doomsday Tree. Souffy watches as its sun-bleached bark brightens to blinding white, and then beyond, to a searing intensity beyond color. It's absorbing so much mana that it begins to vibrate and its branches clatter against one another like the bones of some giant skeleton. Not just vibrating, they're growing, reaching out three, five, eight feet. There's a thunderous crack and a sizable bough crashes down. It's followed by another, and another.

"Maybe the mana's too powerful for it? By consuming so much at once, it's destroying itself?" Oscar asks.

"I don't think we're getting that lucky," Cole replies.

He's right, Souffy suspects. Especially as she sees the fallen branches gathering together, like the spokes of a wagon wheel. No, the way they're joining up, lengthening, and undulating is more like the oversized limbs of a harvestman. Only there's no body, only legs—way more than eight— tapering to viciously sharp claws. The creature, now assembled, is taller than a draft horse, and fast. One claw-tipped limb shoots out at Tristan, sending his shield flying.

She hears the others casting: "*Sagitta-inspira!*" "*Show them the light!*" "*Dreen-chruinn!*" Each spell takes out a leg or two, but the creature has many more to spare; it doesn't even stagger.

"Boss battle!" cries Cole.

"Worse," Kyle shouts back. "It's a distraction to give the Doomsday Tree time to absorb more mana!"

"Who's got the chainsaw?" Oscar asks.

"I do," Souffy hears her uncle say, followed by an abrupt noise like a stuttering burble that rises to an angry snarl. The leg-blight (that name will have to do until they kill it) rattles in dismay. It rears up on half its appendages while the other half thrash violently.

"Hold it back." Tristan waves his sword. "Keep it away from Ferimus!"

Souffy aims at a nearby limb. "*Ignatious!*" The stick arm bursts into flame, and Souffy spares a glance towards her uncle. The spiky chain that gives the weapon its name is whipping around the blade so fast that the individual teeth have become a glittery blur. And when Ferimus applies the whirring edge to the trunk, it sinks into the wood like a knife into butter.

"It's working!"

She speaks too soon. The Doomsday Tree pulses, and Fermius is thrown bodily backwards. Souffy watches in horror as RazorChain flies in an arc, its deadly spinning chain now sailing towards her uncle's legs. Just before it hits his robe, someone grabs the handle. It's Janassy.

Ferimus recovers, stands up and she hands him the weapon. This time, they approach the tree together, Janassy bracing both Ferimus and the weapon. Four hands guide RazorChain to the trunk as the two of them work towards a common goal. It isn't heady and romantic, thinks Souffy, but there's a solid feel of trust and mutual support in their actions. Something deeper than just fluttery excitement and light-headed euphoria.

Not that Souffy doesn't adore those feelings, but looking at Janassy and Ferimus together, she wants that kind of love too, maybe even more. A love that lasts when one person gets old and loses their dashing looks, or even betrays and abandons the other to a horde of goblins. She also thinks of how Cena and Arek stopped a war because of their love and shared passion for forestry. A shared passion, that shouldn't be so hard to find. Souffy is nothing if not a passionate person.

"Souffy, look out!" Kyle shouts towards her. The leg-blight, still intact and furious, takes a swing at her. "*Frigus Digitorum!*" he yells, and his skeleton hand catches one of the descending limbs. Thus assisted, she has no problem lopping the limb off with a Flame Bolt. He gives her a thumbs-up, and she remembers his words from their last blight fight. The two of them do make a great team.

RazorChain is already halfway through the Doomsday Tree. The leg-blight is attempting to approach closer, but Tristan keeps swinging his sword at its joints, hobbling the monster and buying Janassy and Ferimus more time.

There's no denying how insanely gallant Tristan is. The sight of him merely standing causes Souffy's stomach to flip-flop. When he's like this—heroically battling a monster—she has to stop herself from swooning. But how does she make him feel? He likes her, that much is clear, but evidently not enough to overcome a dryad's Charm spell. If he doesn't feel deeply for her in the heat of battle, how much less would he care when they're going about mundane tasks like eating breakfast together or packing for a quest?

What would they even talk about? Not magic, or the differences between their worlds, or why people act the way they do, or how to go about completing a quest, or any of the many topics she's spent hours discussing with a certain red-hatted wizard.

The pitch of RazorChain's growl rises to a whine as the blade nears the far side of the trunk. And then, with a pop, RazorChain cuts through. The top of the Doomsday Tree rests on the base as if the tree were still whole.

"Timber!" shouts Cole.

Souffy's sure there's no magic behind the command. But at that very moment, the top branches sway, and then the whole tree topples majestically over, sending the ground shaking once again. The leg-blight vibrates even more intensely, and then suddenly shatters. Bits of Doomsday branches rain down all around them. Ferimus does something to calm the weapon. The clearing, a cacophony of battle sounds up until this moment, falls silent.

"Is it over?" asks Oscar.

"Yes," says Ferimus. He isn't looking at the tree, but at Janassy. Now he's the one holding and supporting her. There's something different, more fragile, about her aura now. Kyle had said that Ashenfal had refused to actively fight the blight because destroying one of the sacred trees the dryads had tended would forfeit their immortality. Janassy must have known that taking RazorChain to the Doomsday Tree would make her mortal. But the look on the dryad's face isn't that of loss. She's crying happy tears because she's in Ferimus's arms.

"We need to make sure it's really dead." Kyle turns to Souffy. "This calls for an evocation wizard. Will you do the honors, Souffy?"

She's going to deliver the finishing blow. How absolutely amazing! Just a week ago, she was struggling with enchantments and illusions, never suspecting this talent was hidden within her. It's thanks to Kyle for encouraging her, for believing in her. She feels like she could do anything now, maybe even tell him how she feels.

Souffy readies the spell's components, throws up her hands, and joyfully cries out, *"Great Ball of Fire!"*

CHAPTER 57

Kyle

It's Souffy's most impressive Flame Orb yet. Easily seven feet in diameter, and hot enough to melt all the snow in the clearing and give me an instant sunburn. The tree goes up in a mini-mushroom cloud. I assure Oscar that the explosion's shape is due to the excess mana pulled up by the Doomsday Tree, and that it isn't radioactive. Okay, I don't actually know that last part for sure, but it would be a real dick move by the Divine Wisdom to give us cancer after we'd just saved the realm.

We saved the realm! Not bad for a first campaign.

It's considerably more satisfying than the majority of the quests in *Heroes Summoning,* and not just because it's IRL—IFL, In Fantasy Life? Those video game quests usually relied on MacGuffins: immensely powerful magical items that the final boss inevitably got their hands on that required an epic fight to prevent generic world destruction. Although *Heroes Summoning* climaxes always seem to happen in the vicinity of a castle or town, so that the end credits can feature a Valhalla-style feast for the heroes, and if any post-battle cleanup is needed, it's handled by the liberated townsfolk or reformed minions. None of the above applies here. Instead, we're the only ones around to hack up the remains of the Doomsday Tree's root system and clear out all the scattered branches and seed cones, because it would be a BAD THING if D.T. Jr. germinated from some leftover evil sacred twig. Unlike some other heroes I could name, we finish the job right.

As I lift a large bough, I notice specks of green scattered around the soil. On closer inspection, I see they're tips of tiny sprouting plants. Another side effect of the mana? We throw the wood we've collected in the crater left by Souffy's Flame Orb where bits of Doomsday Tree trunk merrily burn. It makes for a very pleasant bonfire. The sun's already setting behind the mountain ridge, and we've decided to set up camp here tonight. It's a good location, sheltered from the wind and, with the fire, comfortably warm—also, we're all too exhausted to find another spot.

"It's not just the fire," Oscar observes. "When we got here it was winter, but now I'm picking up definite spring vibes." That's when I register that we're surrounded by a field of fresh grass and delicate plants with tiny white flowers.

Ferimus bends down and presses his hand into the now-warm earth. "I may have rushed the canceling of the time spell. There appear to be certain observable accelerated chronometric effects."

"We're not going to leave here and find out thirty years have gone past on the outside, are we?" I ask.

"Oh no." Ferimus makes a thoughtful face, then cocks an eyebrow. "But let me check." One Sense Magic spell later and he assures us that the seasons may be running a tad fast, but the rest of us are on regular time.

By the time Micah comes back with several freshly killed rabbits for dinner, knee-high bushes with shiny green leaves are springing up throughout the grove. Janassy has returned from foraging with wild onions and strawberries. I don't see how those could be native to this biome, but I'm not complaining. Cole fries the onions over the bonfire, and we wolf them down along with the grilled rabbit. For my own contribution, I Prestidigitate some of our water into champagne, making sure to produce a non-alcoholic variant for Cole.

Tristan pours out the drinks. Counting the two crystal wine glasses that Ferimus pulled out of my hat, we have enough containers for everyone. "Toast time," he says.

Janassy stands. "To the Drevo Woods, may its magic continue to flow and renew the plants within, and may all of its inhabitants live in peace and prosperity."

Before we can drink, Ferimus slips in, "And to the Divine Wisdom, which in Its ineffability, chose the finest heroes from all possible worlds to save us!" He then adds sotto-voce, "It's always wise to include the Divine Wisdom in toasts, just in case It's listening."

We raise our various cups and drink.

"It's like bubbly mead," exclaims Souffy, and she takes another gulp. I was aiming for Dom Pérignon, and privately think I nailed it. She giggles as she looks at each of us in turn. Her eyes fall on me last. "To Never Boy Land, the New Heroes of the Realm!"

After we all drink, she's still looking at me. I feel my cheeks heating up. It's the alcohol. Cole snickers, and now all of them, including Oscar, are smirking. To deflect their attention, I say, "And to our fireball-lobbing wizard, Souffy Ravenus. It's good to have you on the team!"

After that it's open season for toasts.

"To Hannah, Isaac, and Daniel Bernstein," says Cole, "wherever you all ended up."

"To healing spells!" Micah offers.

"To the Thieves' Guild," says Oscar.

"Tinkerbell!" my familiar joins in.

We've drained our cups.

"One more," says Tristan.

I refill the glasses. I'm slightly buzzed, so I'm not sure if I've got the Champagne cantrip quite right this time. It doesn't matter. Tristan stands up, his smile even bigger than when he was Charmed.

"To getting the band back together," he says.

We all join in. "To getting the band back together!"

I am completely relaxed, which means that my brain is jumping from one idea to the next. I'm thinking of all the things we're going to need to take care of starting tomorrow: getting back to the Trädskydders base, helping take down the last blights, warning Micah to be careful with the dryads—or maybe warning Ashenfal about Micah, investigating what exactly is up with those weird meteorites, making sure Souffy's allowed to travel with us to the capital. But the one thing I keep coming back to—what I really, really want—is to rebook our Bydlo concert. Like Tristan says, the band is now back together.

We eat, have more to drink, make jokes, show off our singing as well as some silly human tricks, and tell each other repeatedly and earnestly how much we love and appreciate them. Overall, it's a pretty great after-party. One of those with people you like—no gatecrashers or reporters—with no hustling, no live-streaming, everyone just enjoying being with each other, some especially so; I notice Ferimus and Janassy discreetly making out in the shadows.

All that's missing is for the fangirls to start making their moves on us, trying to snag their bias for an unforgettable memory. On cue, Souffy stands and looks around the fire. Her eyes fall on Tristan and pause for a long, lingering moment. But then she turns to me, and motions me to follow her.

"You don't need my help," I tell her when we wander out of earshot. "Just go up to Tristan and tell him what you want to say." Or throw yourself into his arms, I've seen that approach work too. "Trust me, he likes you."

"Tristan? Oh no. I mean, that's not…" She collects her thoughts. "I didn't call you over to talk about Tristan."

Oh.

"Oh? What did you want to discuss?" I ask largely to buy time. There's no mistaking Souffy's intense nervousness. I've lost track of how many times this has happened after a show. Girls, or women, or on a couple of occasions guys, who've talked their way backstage, or snuck into the hotel, propositioning me for a night to remember, for them at least. I could be virtuous and point out that I turned a lot of those offers down, more than half. Or I could be honest and say that sex between two (or more) consenting adults who are attracted to each other can be, if not mind-blowing, at least hella enjoyable. But what's foremost in my mind is that no matter how potentially awesome post-world-saving coitus might be, it would be seriously awkward waking up next to Souffy tomorrow morning, not to mention interacting with her afterwards. Sleeping with one's co-workers never ends well.

"I've been thinking, Kyle, about how supportive you've been about my magic, about my abilities. You've pushed me to try things I never thought about, to change the direction of my life. I wanted to let you know how much it means to me."

And now I'm completely confused. If this is a hookup offer, it's an extremely earnest one. "We make a good team," I say lamely.

"A team, exactly. Like Cena and Arek, or Janassy and my uncle. And I was thinking, if we're so good at being adventure partners, maybe we'd be good at other things, closer things."

I hazard a guess. "You mean, dating?"

"Yes! Or no. I think the otherworld term is 'going steady.'"

Going steady sounds like something a Triad of Valor Bernstein might say. "Being exclusive, you mean."

"Exclusive. That sounds nice."

"It can be." I'm not commitment-phobic or anything, but this is going a bit fast. "It's not something people just jump into."

"Oh?" Confusion spreads over Souffy's face. And a truth occurs to me. Souffy's nature is to jump, usually only bothering to look down after her feet have already left any supporting surface. She comes up with a plan on the way down. It's actually the perfect mind-set for lobbing a fireball. And now she's applying it to her love life. Oh, boy.

My gut instinct is to throw up a Shield spell and retreat—fast. Tristan isn't the only one who's never been in a traditional long-term relationship. Come to think of it, I don't think any of us have. Nothing like spending one's formative teen years as an international pop star to leave you completely unprepared for navigating the normal adult dating scene.

I fall back on Kyle's Rules of Relationships. Souffy's sailed past Rule Number Two. She's easily among the top three amazingly cool girls I've ever known (or hot, given her fire affinity). Which is why I've been so not-so-secretly crushing on her since we arrived.

But on my Rule Number One, she's failing, hard:

Never, never ever, fall for anyone on a rebound from Tristan. Never. Even if she says she's not. ESPECIALLY if she says she's not. Never.

I've added another "never" to that rule for every time I've broken it. I always regretted it (painfully). Still, Souffy and Tristan haven't done more than kiss, and does that even really count if he was a statue at the time? I force myself to remember that look, that long look, Souffy gave Tristan before she turned to me. But afterwards, she did turn to me, that has to count for something.

Despite a voice screaming *No!* in my head, I say, "We could do a trial exclusive, see how that goes?"

"Oh, like your and Tristan's childhood friendship? That was so sweet the way he asked to be your best friend." A giggle and a wistful smile sneak out as Souffy mentions Tristan.

Especially if she says she's not. Never. Still…

"Souffy, how do you feel about me? Not us together, just me."

"You're so nice, Kyle, and very clever, and you always tell such interesting stories, and," she pauses, "you're nice." She said nice, twice. You can't get a flag redder than that.

Souffy wants a relationship, and—good for her—she's recognized she can't have it with Tristan. So she's settled on me. Settled. Kyle's Rules of Relationships Number Three: *She needs to see the real me, and be crazy excited to be with the real me.*

"But you don't love me, Souffy." I think I know the real Souffy. She's fearless and impulsive and honest and she burns bright. Combine the way I feel about her with Rule Number One and she'd break me, possibly permanently.

"Love? I… I'm not sure." Souffy looks back at the campfire, toward where Ferimus and Janassy are cuddling, and then to where Tristan is laughing with Oscar. "It's different than what I feel about Tristan."

"That's the second time you've mentioned Tristan, Souffy."

"Oh?" It takes her a moment to make the connection, but when she does I can see it on her face. The bubbly excitement is replaced with something more contemplative. "Oh." She sighs, not sad-like, more like me when I'm working through a tricky math problem. "I was just so sure I'd gotten it right, back when we were finishing off the Doomsday Tree. But maybe I'm still missing something about relationships."

"Maybe. Some things are better not to rush into." I think I've just happily-ever-aftered myself into the friendzone. *Way to go, Kyle.*

It's confirmed when Souffy gives me an unambiguously platonic hug and says, "You're so clever, Kyle."

Then why do I feel like an idiot? Still, the last person you want to break up with is a fire wizard.

We walk back to the campfire and sit down next to each other—close, but not cuddling close. Tristan's watching me, making assumptions. Because, of course he is. He opens his mouth, to tease me I'm sure, only I'm saved by a sudden blast of cold air enveloping us, putting out the fire like someone turning off a light switch. But it's not dark. An orb, perhaps two feet in diameter, of brilliant yet gentle light is shining out from where the fire was burning just seconds ago.

Souffy stands up tilts her head to the sky while turning in slow circles. "It's the Divine Wisdom. Can't you hear It?"

Nope. I check with Oscar, and he also shakes his head.

"It must mean for you to convey Its will," says Ferimus.

"You're right," says Souffy, and she takes a deep breath. "It's thanking you… us… for the deed we've performed here. It says It had faith in us all along. And…" Souffy gives a small laugh. "That unconventional methods can lead to fortuitous results." Then Souffy's face drops. "It says that your courage and ingenuity and friendship will be justly rewarded. Should you choose, you may return home."

"Like, we could get zapped back right now?" says Oscar. "Without a chance to say our goodbyes?"

"No," Souffy pauses, obviously listening. "You have two weeks, until the next full moon. At that time, you may enter the Hero Shrine in Bydlo and be returned to the precise moment you left your world. You can even bring…"—Souffy sounds out the word—"Soo-ven-ears."

"Does It expect an answer right now?" asks Cole.

Souffy's head whips around and in a loud stage whisper she says, "Yes, right now. This is the Divine Wisdom. You don't tell It to come back later."

"What happens if we say no?" says Micah.

Souffy goes back to listening. "It says you would need to complete more great quests, culminating in a Final Quest, before another opportunity to depart is granted. The coming year will present numerous opportunities for heroism. Malevolent forces, both ancient and new, are assembling to tip the balance of mana and power in Mythreal and threaten widespread chaos. But It says that with so many other worlds to choose heroes from, It could find others to take up the mantle." Having thus delivered the message, Souffy explains, "You really can just go home." She can't help herself from sighing as she says this.

I glance around at my bandmates, trying to judge their reactions. They're all looking decidedly… indecisive. This is the problem of not having a headliner, no designated leader. It's all about building consensus. Although, I start to realize, they're all now looking at me.

"What?" I ask.

"You make the decision," says Oscar.

"What?" I say again.

"Brains of the operation," says Cole, smirking.

"And you get the blame if things go wrong later," says Micah with a smug smile.

Great, no pressure.

I know what I want. I know what Souffy wants. I even know what Marjorie wants, or would want if she were live-streaming this. I know what's best for Never Boy Land, the music act, at least. I think I know what's best for Mythreal. So, basically, between all these conflicting desires, I have no clue what to do.

Tris has his usual big stupid grin on his face.

"You're not helping," I tell him.

He shrugs. "I, we, trust you. Just remember that one thing." And he looks at me expectantly.

"Yeah, I know. Twelfth Law of Boy Bands." *We're stronger together.*

And I know what to do.

CHAPTER 58

The five singers' harmonies cut out simultaneously, and silence descends upon the rustic outdoor amphitheater. The audience holds its breath, just in case there's more to come. But then the performers signal the song is over by raising their arms, and the crowd erupts into wild applause. Farmers, shopkeepers, militia soldiers, druids, and a contingent of dryads who've pressed themselves up against the stage, all of them hooting and screaming in delight.

At first, the Neveboylanders' style of music was confusing, and the audience's appreciation was more in the acknowledgment of the heroes' role in defeating the blights and saving the Drevo Woods. Also, how could they not clap when the five young men cut such fine figures in their strange but magnificent white suits, and gyrated with such enthusiasm. But now—two hours and three costume changes into the show—the people of Bydlo have acclimated to the music: its arrangements, repetitions, strange nonsense words, tributes to perfect girls, and otherworld customs. And they love it.

Mayor Galam leans close to his wife. "What would you say to including an all-night dance party as part of next year's summer harvest festival."

"It wouldn't be your worst idea," says his wife. "You insisted on constructing this ridiculous arena. It only makes sense to make use of it."

But her tone lacks its usual acrid edge. The heroes are now singing a quieter ballad about loving someone forever no matter how many times you disappoint them, during which Galam has taken hold of Lenora's hand. The magistrate glances over at her son who has his arm around his fiancée; she remembers Galam at that age, when they first met. Lenora sighs contentedly and rests her own head on her husband's shoulder.

When the rescheduled Never Boy Land concert was announced, local interest was so great that the town square was deemed wholly inadequate. In order to accommodate the predicted crowds, a new performance space was built just outside the town's northern wall. The Trädskydd Druids contributed their earth-moving magicks to carve out an amphitheater, and the Laska Bay Trading Company financed the stage's construction. Ferimus modified the proclamation announcement system to amplify the singers' voices and the accompanying musicians' instruments, so that the performance could be heard clearly throughout the venue.

On the night of the show, concertgoers brought out blankets, and vendors set up booths. In a large, cleared area in front of the stage, people danced, or at least tried to. After the first few songs, the adults retreated, and now the space is mostly filled with overexcited children jumping around, chasing, and running into each other.

Everyone is having such a grand time that nobody even notices the two thieves steadily working the edges of the crowd. Between songs, when the crowd rises to clap, cheer, and (for a large portion of female viewers) scream their lungs out, a furry, masked bandit and his black-feathered accomplice snatch unattended skewered meats and pastries. They ferry these off to a private spot—away from all the human noise—to enjoy a magnificent feast.

By now, the sun has long since set, and the arena is illuminated by a dizzying array of light spells. The magic school students and various trade mages have invoked spells to create floating balls of lights and bright spotlights, upon which Wizard Kyle has cast an overriding Click Track spell to make them pulse in patterns coordinated with the beats and musical arrangements of the performance.

Souffy, Dryden, Havelin, and Boryk have secured choice center spots on the rise of the hill forming the back of the amphitheater—close enough to see the performers' faces, but not so close as to have to crane their necks to look up at them.

"Hard to believe they're leaving tomorrow," says Dryden. NBL has taken a break from singing to dance energetically to the musicians' instrumental section. "Not that I'm staying around much longer myself," he adds. Dryden has signed up for a military tour that will, over the next few years, send him to the furthest reaches of Ozema.

"Everything changes," says Havelin. He will also be departing Bydlo, to travel north with the Trädskydders. Cena has offered to train him in druid magicks as well as in advanced forest lore.

"Change is good," croaks Boryk, who has been given a special dispensation for that night to use his voice. In anticipation, he memorized the lyrics to all of Never Boy Land's songs, and over the course of the first half of the show, sang along with such abandon that he stripped his voice raw. It's unlikely that Boryk will have problems keeping his vow of silence come morning.

"Change is good," agrees Souffy. The heroes have started synchronized clapping, and now everyone in the audience has joined in.

Tristan kneels on the stage, his hand stretched out over the edge while a dozen girls and dryads strain to touch it, touch him, if only for a fleeting moment. Souffy understands their single-mindedness. This will likely be their only chance ever to physically connect with otherworld heroes, to make a memory they will treasure forever.

A single beam of light lands on Cole, who breaks into an impressive speech (or maybe it's poetry? it does rhyme). Souffy had no idea a person could enunciate while speaking so rapidly, at least without magic. Cole's solo ends and he steps back into line. The band then repeats the chorus and, through welcoming arm motions, gets the audience to shout-sing along. The instruments fade over the course of the chorus, leaving just the singers' voices, chanting their lyrics into the sky.

The final line is sung exclusively by Never Boy Land. They reach the last syllable and—one by one—they cut out until only Tristan's angelic voice carries the note. At last, even he trails off, and as one the five men take a bow, letting the deafening roar of the crowd wash over them. The noise doesn't let up when they stand, so they bow again, and again, and again. Tristan's lips move, but even with the PA system at its loudest, no one can hear him over the roar. The situation seems to amuse both him and his bandmates. It's obvious to everyone present that the Neverboylanders are having the most fun of anybody here.

Tristan motions to Kyle, who does something with his hand, and Tristan's next words boom over the crowd:

"Thank you Bydlo, and Rozny Las, and everyone living in the Drevo Woods! Thank you for coming tonight. This has been an awesome show, one that we'll never forget, ever. We'll never forget you." He waits until the screaming subsides. "You guys were there for us from the start, back when we were heroes only in name. The experiences we've had over the last month have been magical. And not just because there was literal magic involved."

Cole jumps in. "And when we return home, no one's going to believe a word of it."

Micah runs to the edge of the stage and calls out. "But that's future-Never Boy Land's problem… because we aren't going home just yet!" Wild cheering drowns out his next words. After the crowd subsides somewhat, he speaks again. "We're staying here in Mythreal 'cause we're the New Heroes of the Realm! Look out Dark Forces, we're coming for you!"

"And making the world a better place," adds Oscar, a wry smile on his face.

Then Kyle claps his hands, and the floating balls of lights flash in rainbow patterns. The next song starts. The musicians play with abandon, and the Neverboylanders sing their hearts out, the energy building and building until the last line of the final chorus. This time, they all hold the final note for an impossibly long moment. And then the crowd is on their feet, cheering on their hero-idols as they leave the stage. When the screaming subsides, Havelin asks:

"Is that the end?"

"Oh no," says Souffy with a contented smile, "there's always an encore."

Marjorie Banks' Laws of Boy Bands

1. Always have Legal read the contract first

2. Never say no to an opportunity for self-promotion

3. A Boy Band with dedication, devotion, a bit of luck, and great hair can ~~accomplish anything~~ *save the world*

4. There are no headliners in a boy band (but there is a pre-determined order of appearance)

5. It just takes a single offended fan to start a backlash campaign

6. Never damage the face

7. Always leave the hotel room in better shape than you found it (the campsite rule)

8. Thou shalt not leave a girl collapsed or bleeding on the pavement (the Damsel in Distress rule)

9. Just smile at the haters

10. The first thing anyone should recall of you is, "He was so nice"

11. Never speak ill of your bandmates

12. You're stronger together!

We're stronger together!

13. (unofficial) No matter how much they may deserve it, you're not allowed to kill your bandmates

AUTHOR'S NOTE & ACKNOWLEDGEMENTS

Like Souffy said, there's always an encore. There will be four more books in the Boy Bands & Dragons series, each continuing the adventure from the perspective of a different band member. Up next is… Oscar Jones!

In the meantime, check out my Patreon page for artwork, behind-the-scenes author notes, additional NBL and Mythreal short stories, and sneak-peeks of unpublished chapters.

This book wouldn't be possible without so many wonderful individuals who have encouraged and supported me through the writing and publishing process.

First and foremost and always, is my husband and life partner, Maciek. You've been a fan of the stories in my head since our first date, and your belief in me and my abilities, backed up by your unwavering support and thoughtful critical analysis, is why this book exists.

Thank you Eli for introducing me to the isekais that inspired this story, Tomek, for always asking questions, and to my friends and family for their enthusiasm and well-wishes for this crazy project of mine.

A has-been boy band embarking on a D&D adventure is not an easy sell and I am eternally grateful to Weaver and Riverfolk Publishing for taking a chance on me and my book, to my editors, Maxine and Tamsin, whose insights and attention to detail leveled up my manuscript, and to Zaq for overseeing the process that turned a Google doc into a real book.

This book wouldn't be as delightful without its amazing illustrations. Thanks to my wonderful artists: RAIT Visual Works, who were more than up for the challenge of creating characters that embodied both boy band and fantasy archetypes and who also provided the heartwarming illustration for the commemorative plate, Fuyu for his charming book cover, Gahmeur H. who captured Never Boy Land in their boy band youth, and Maciek (again) for the fantasy map, Laws of Boy Bands, cover typography, and the graphic design skills and logo that brought all the pieces together.

Since I will always be a researcher at heart, I want to shout out to the seminal texts that I returned to again and again for guidance and fact checking: Maria Sherman's *Larger than Life: A History of Boy Bands from NKOTB to BTS*, and the *D&D Player's Handbook* (5th edition).

I am deeply indebted to my UCSC Scicom instructors and editors whose guidance transformed me from scientist to writer, and for my cohort, the incomparable Iconoclass, whose support was critical to surviving the process. I also want to thank all my writing and critique partners who have given me feedback on parts, or all, of this story: Elana Gomel, Abby McArthur-Jones, John Robert Fay, the Berkeley Writers Circle, Hannah Nevins, and my beta readers Chris Harget and Jenna B.

Last but not least, thanks to Renee K. Nelson, my podcast-in-crime partner and the best writing soulmate a writer could wish for.

ABOUT THE AUTHOR

Life takes strange turns. Trained as a scientist and journalist, Kim Smuga-Otto somehow ended up writing a story about a boy band who saves fantasyland. In addition to being the author of the *Boy Bands & Dragons* series she writes short science fiction and fantasy and co-hosts a writing advice podcast, *Words to Write by*. She lives with her husband and two children in Santa Cruz, California.

FOLLOW THE AUTHOR

Patreon: www.patreon.com/user?u=62698656

Podcast: https://wordstowritebypodcast.com/

Follow us:

riverfolkbooks.com

Facebook /riverfolkp

Twitter /riverfolkp

Instagram /riverfolkp

If you want to discuss our books with other readers and maybe even the author, join our discord server using the link on our website